The Seeker

Sandy James

Printed in the United States of America
Second Printing: September 2015
ISBN: 978-1-940295-11-4

Chapter One

Of all the things Kara missed, electricity was at the top of the list. When the last remnants of power died almost three months ago, it took with it all the things that had made life easier. Lights. Heat. Coffee.

Throwing sand on the small fire, she inhaled the sweet tendrils of smoke snaking up from the pine pyre and tried for a moment to pretend she was simply out camping as she'd done in the old days.

Before *they* came.

"C'mon, Chance," she called to her Labrador. "We need to get moving."

He bounded out of the pines and stopped at her side to nuzzle her hand, which elicited an affectionate stroke.

God had sent her Chance. That was the only explanation. Kara had a knack for eluding *them*, but that one time she'd ventured back to town for food…

Two of the far-too-tall bastards had found her, and one grabbed her. A big dog had come out of nowhere, seized the Vymaln by the throat until its yellow blood flowed while she was able to pull the knife out of her boot and stab the second in one of its hearts. She'd run a good five miles before she stopped that day, and her new pet had matched her step for step. She'd named him Chance and lavished him with love. Now, they needed each other. Companions forever.

A good long look around told her she was still far enough in the forest that she didn't have to be on her highest level of vigilance.

She was wrong.

Chance crouched and growled low in his throat.

Kara froze.

"No, boy," she whispered, giving him a quick slash of her hand. "Stay."

Listening hard to find where the danger was coming from, she strained to hear the creatures that moved almost silently despite their massive height and weight.

The click of a weapon cocking sent Kara groping for the dagger sheathed against her thigh, but in her heart, she knew it was already too late.

"Run, Chance!"

She hoped he'd listened as she whirled to face the threat.

One of *them*.

Bug-eyed, asshole Vymaln.

This one stood about six-three, and the color of its skin was a brown

3

rather than the more common puke green. Seeing them dressed like people always unnerved her. Their bodies weren't much different, and they'd claimed they wanted to blend in when they'd arrived. They claimed they were just immigrants seeking refuge.

Big fat liars. Every stinking one of 'em.

"Share the world," they'd said.

Share the world, my scrawny ass.

A paralyzing pulse-gun was aimed right at her B-cups. The aliens' hands were shaped almost human, although they had six fingers with an opposable thumb, so they'd learned Earth's weaponry with little difficulty. And they'd brought some toys of their own—stun-sticks that acted like Tasers and more deadly weapons, like those damned pulse-guns.

Had she ever learned to make the ridiculous trilling and clicking sounds they called a language, Kara might have tried to reason with it. Of course, a creature had to be reasonable to respond to reason. She hadn't been any better learning the Vymaln language than she had Spanish.

Tucking her dagger behind her, she slowly stood up to face the alien. "It's okay, buddy. You don't need to stick around. Nothing to see here. Just a stupid human out traipsing around the wilderness. Too skinny to make a good slave."

The high-pitched speech grated on her ears as it spoke to her. Kara had always thought of any of them as an "it" rather than "him" or "her." Just seemed to fit since they didn't have boobs or hips or any other way to determine gender, and she sure as hell didn't want to see one naked. They'd adapted by wearing androgynous human clothing. They could understand English, even if they couldn't speak it well, always sounding like someone talking while breathing excessive amounts of helium. This one didn't seem to want to communicate even though it had to know English since it was wearing a Whispering Lake Police Department uniform.

"Under arrest," it said.

"Fuck you."

Kara threw the dagger, hitting the creature square in the chest.

Unfortunately, that action only pissed the Vymaln off. It jerked the knife out, tossed the weapon aside, and screeched a piercing sound akin to microphone feedback.

It charged at her like an NFL tackle going for a sack on a star quarterback. Long, thick arms slammed into her chest, knocking her to the ground as she gasped to recapture her breath. When it tried to throw itself on top of her, she brought her knees to her chest and kicked it off,

4

sending the thing stumbling backwards.

Gaining her feet, Kara searched around for any kind of weapon, trying to see if she could get to her dagger. The alien grabbed her ankles and tugged, making her slam face-first against hard ground. It started to crawl on top of her as she rolled to her back.

The thing blanketed her from head to toe, and she couldn't catch a breath. If it didn't move, she'd be smothered by its weight. Not that it would care, nor would it listen to any pleas for mercy.

As if she'd ever utter one.

After avoiding capture for so long, to get caught by surprise ate at Kara's pride. She'd been alone for months, keeping to the woods and back roads and staying away from where people were stupid enough to gather. Anything to keep from becoming just another Vymaln slave.

The alien got to its feet as Kara tried to gulp air back into her lungs, although that dirty aquarium smell of the Vymaln almost made her gag. It whipped a pair of handcuffs from a black belt around its tubby waist.

"Oh, hell no." She'd rather die where she lay.

Or better yet, escape.

One beefy hand caught her left wrist, and the first cuff was slapped on as she kicked and rolled around. A quick scramble to her feet, and she got loose. Despite her shortness of breath, she made for the thicker trees, knowing all the while she didn't stand a chance.

The sizzling bolt hit her right between the shoulder blades, stinging like the time she'd accidentally touched a live wire. All Kara could do was gasp as she sank to her knees and did a face plant onto a bed of pine needles, entirely paralyzed. She would have thrown some very profane vocabulary at the bastard if she could've moved her mouth. Since the stuns usually lasted about five minutes, she tried to start a mental count of seconds while simultaneously praying this paralysis ended much quicker.

The Vymaln grabbed her limp arm and rolled her over, letting out an eerie sound akin to a chuckle. If she could have moved her legs, she'd have kicked it in the face and knocked that smug grin right off those green lips. It finished attaching the handcuffs to her wrists, which now rested against her abdomen.

A loud growl came from her right.

No, boy. Run. Please run.

In her peripheral vision, she saw her dog jumping on the alien's back as his teeth tugged and ripped at the police uniform. Before Chance could do much damage, the alien grabbed him with both hands and flung him at one of the tall pines. A cry came from her lab as his back hit the tree with a sickening thud before he sank to the ground, silent as death.

5

A tear leaked out of the corner of Kara's eye. She wanted to scream. She wanted to get up and kick some alien ass. She wanted Chance—her only friend—to be alive.

The bug-eyed creep grabbed her by her wrists, jerked them over her head, and dragged her through the maze of trees.

Her head sagged back, listing from side to side while her butt and legs bounced against the myriad objects lining the forest floor. Roots. Branches. Dead leaves. Thoughts flew through her mind at the speed of popcorn kernels rising to the right temperature, exploding as she scrambled to find a way out of this disaster.

A shadow caught her eye, moving through the trees as though stalking her captor. Could she be so lucky? The silhouette disappeared, perhaps only a figment of her frantic imagination.

The alien stopped in front of a Whispering Lake police car. Since the Vymalns controlled everything now, they could still get gasoline. Why in the hell they even went through the motions of maintaining human establishments like police forces was beyond her. Maybe they thought it would keep the humans they hadn't enslaved or killed in line.

When it dropped her hands, letting her head plop hard against the ground, something huge jumped out of a tree and landed on the alien's back. All Kara could do was listen over the echo of her pounding heartbeat.

The scuffling continued, and about the time she couldn't take not knowing what was happening another second, the alien slammed onto the hood of the car. Yellow blood dripped from wounds to its face and hands.

What in the hell could fight one of those things? Their mass made them twice the weight of humans. Bullets barely pierced their thick alien hide and usually only made them falter for a few steps. Nothing could get through their steely bones. The only weapon that worked was a thin blade like a dagger, and that was only if a person could get close enough to slide it into the breathing slits between their ribs or throw it hard and simply get lucky. Even then, they had a superfluous heart. One stab and a little providence and one heart stopped, slowing a Vymaln considerably. But no one got two shots. *Never* two. Probably because a Vymaln could snap a person's neck with a flick of the wrist.

A head shot? Not with their impenetrable skulls. Take out an eye? They'd grow another in a day. Take out two eyes? Didn't matter. Their hearing was like sonar.

No doubt about it, whoever was trying to rescue her was going to die.

The alien let out a death rattle, and the sound of something heavy crumpling to the ground was followed by the echo of heavy footsteps moving away. Then dead silence.

Two hundred ten. Two hundred eleven...

Her heart beat so hard and fast that her captor, or whatever had just taken out her captor, could surely hear it. She wasn't sure which represented a better choice. A Vymaln or something that could kill one?

Her fingers started to tingle, which meant the paralysis was wearing off early. Giving her lips and tongue a try, she was grateful they had some movement. She couldn't bear the quiet a moment longer.

"What just happened?" She sounded as if she'd come from a dentist who'd shot up her whole mouth with Novocain.

Footsteps approached, and she tried to turn her head. Her muscles didn't cooperate. They didn't have to. Her vision was suddenly filled with a man big enough to make her gasp and promptly lose count.

Was this guy kin to Arnold Schwarzenegger? Shit, he was huge. Nothing but a mass of ripped muscle. No neck. Well, not much. Biceps she was sure she couldn't span with both hands. His outfit was...odd. A tight olive-drab shirt resembling workout clothing. Military-looking pants—camo—with tons of pockets. A Batmanesque utility belt. Since his head was tilted down toward her, his long, black hair shielded his face, yet somehow she knew he was frowning.

"Who are you?" It came out similar to someone mispronouncing Hawaii.

"You walk?" The guy spoke caveman.

At least now she could shake her head.

With a grunt, he took her cuffed hands and pulled her to her feet. Her weak legs buckled, but the raven-haired Neanderthal caught her under the arms and hoisted her up before tossing her over his shoulder like a sack of grain.

"Dog," she managed to rasp out between her stiff lips.

He whirled around in a circle forcing her arms to fly out helplessly. "Dog? Where dog?"

As if she could point. "Left. Tree." Now she was speaking caveman too.

Chance's limp form must have caught the guy's eye because he jogged toward her dog, forcing huffs of air from Kara's lungs as her ribs hit his rock-hard shoulder. When he got to the Labrador, the man flopped her down on her butt, and she fell to the side like a discarded doll.

A big hand ran over Chance's body, and the guy frowned. "Hurt."

A "duh" almost slipped out. "Bad?"

He answered with a curt nod while he fished around in one of the pouches on the leather tool belt strapped around his lean waist. When he withdrew his hand, some dried flakes were pinched between his fingers.

7

He shoved the stuff into Chance's mouth before Kara could even protest.

Waiting was unbearable, the hope inside her almost too cruel to bear. Chance was gone. She'd accepted it already. This man shouldn't be making her expect otherwise. Then she saw the movement. "Chance?"

The lab gingerly stood up, testing each paw. He licked the big hand hovering over him before he worked his way over to Kara. She could swear her dog was smiling. Chance put two paws against her chest and licked away the tears that had spilled over her lashes.

Caveman came to stand over her, hands on his hips and a scowl on his face.

After she pulled herself together, she stared up at him, feeling helpless but refusing to show it in her eyes.

The terror in the thin human female's gaze came as a surprise. Her eyes were brown and almost too big for her oval face. A very pretty face, one Aiodhan shouldn't be taking precious time to notice.

He'd seen her fight the Vymaln male, every bit as brave as a Seeker. For a moment, he'd wondered if one of his breed had ended up stranded, as he now found himself. Her small stature gave her away as human, but her courage impressed him. Humans weren't known for bravery. They'd given the Vymalns little fight after the invasion. So Seekers came to this planet to hunt down and kill their greatest enemies.

Surely this human knew he wouldn't harm her. He'd saved her life. He'd even saved her canine. Not that he gave a damn what happened to her now.

That was a lie, and he knew it. She fascinated him, especially when she'd taken on that Vymaln scum. For a human female, she had *gadnaomes*. Big ones.

So when Aiodhan had gone to the trouble to save her, what gave her the right to glare at him as if he would harm her?

She pushed herself to a sitting position and used her bound hands to brush the head-tail she'd made of her long dark brown hair over her shoulder. He couldn't tell much of her shape from the thick clothing she wore. Pants much like his, except the color of Vymaln skin. Long-sleeved red flannel shirt and a vest of shiny green material. No, he couldn't tell the shape of her body, but from her high cheekbones to her slender neck, he assumed she didn't eat much.

"Who are you?" She gaped at him as she asked her question.

These words, he understood. Especially since the shock she'd received seemed to be wearing off.

"Aiodhan."

"*A-o-dawn?* Is that a name?"

"Name. Yes."

8

"But...who *are* you?"

"Aiodhan." Was this human's brain damaged by the shock?

Her pretty eyes rolled to stare at the stars for a moment. Then she released a deep breath. "Fine. You, Tarzan—me, Jane. Are you from Russia or something? Can't place the accent."

It was hard enough understanding the humans' language without this woman resorting to odd word choices for everything she said. If she would throw a few more common words he knew his way, perhaps he would recognize what she was trying to tell him. "Tarzan? Jane?"

"Never mind." She lifted her bound wrists and glared at the metal. Her animal set itself back on four legs and watched her. "Just a stupid joke."

All these new words. "Joke?"

She looked at him as though *he* was the thought-damaged one. "Yeah. Joke. You know. Funny, ha ha?"

Aiodhan gave up trying to communicate and got down to business. He hauled her to her feet and held her waist while her legs grew steadier. The shock had made her temporarily weak, because he'd seen nothing but strength before. He liked her scent. Clean. Feminine. When he was sure she could stand on her own, he reached into his pack for his cutter.

"Oh, hell no!" the female shouted as she backed away.

He glanced at the compact, silver cutter, not entirely sure why she was afraid again. Perhaps it *did* look like one of the humans' weapons. He pulled the trigger to show her the laser leaping from its barrel, but she threw her hands in front of her face and turned away.

"No harm," he said.

She cautiously turned back. Her eyes widened at the blue light shooting from the cutter. "Is that a blow torch?"

If a torch was a lighted stick, how could it make wind blow?

Such a stupid language.

"Cutter." Aiodhan pointed to her wrists.

"Cutter. Oh. For the handcuffs."

"Handcuffs. Yes."

"Okay, Tarzan. I see what you want. But can't we just get the key off the dumbass back there?"

How was he supposed to communicate with a thought-damaged female who made up words? "Tarzan? Dumbass?"

She nodded at the dead Vymaln he'd thrown a good distance away from the car. "You're Tarzan. Dumbass is back there and should have a key." Whirling around, she started walking toward the Vymaln.

His hand shot out to grab her shoulder. "No."

Her head whipped around as her eyes narrowed. "No?"

"No."

9

"Why the hell not? I don't mind searching a dead bug-eye's pockets."

He'd had enough. A human, especially a thought-damaged one, would never understand how dangerous it was to touch a dead Vymaln. He turned her the rest of the way around and cut the chain between the shackles.

She lifted her hands in front of her and shook them before she reached down to rub them against the fur of her hound. "Nice bracelets."

Snatching one hand back into his, he held the metal while he cut off the shackles.

"Name?" he asked, hoping to keep her occupied so she'd stop squirming.

"Name?"

"Your name."

"Oh. I'm Kara. Kara Michaels."

"Kara." He liked the sound it made rolling off his tongue. A pretty word for a pretty female—a *very* pretty female, who probably looked better without her clothes than with them.

Wayward and lusty thoughts about this human female were going to get him into trouble. It was time to leave Kara behind before she distracted him from his mission.

Aiodhan freed her other wrist. He dropped the handcuffs on the ground, gave her a satisfied grunt and turned to leave.

"Wh-where are you going?"

The wound on his arm needed tending before it grew sour from the planet's micro-organisms. He'd wasted enough time on this woman. "My transport."

He turned and walked away.

Chapter Two

"You're leaving?" Kara had been alone so long the thought of him disappearing turned her stomach.

He nodded and kept moving.

What choice did she have but to follow? Chance trotted along beside her. "Not without me, you're not."

Using two strides for each of Aiodhan's long ones, Kara waited for him to say something.

He didn't.

It wasn't until they'd gone at least a football field's length away that she realized she'd forgotten her stuff. "Fuck."

The caveman ground to a halt. "Fuck? What is fuck?"

She wasn't about to explain. "Never mind. I need to get my backpack."

"Backpack?"

If he kept repeating everything she said, she was going to get a migraine. And there wasn't any aspirin left.

Kara pointed at the pouches on his belt. "You know—like *that*. Only different. The thing that carries my stuff."

"Ah. Stuff. I know much stuff."

The hell he did.

"Come back with me," she said.

Stupid though it was, she didn't want him to leave. The only being she could talk to was Chance, and he wasn't much of a conversationalist. Aiodhan was the closest thing to a friend she'd had in over three months. At least she thought it was three months. The season was just changing from summer to fall, but she'd stopped keeping track of days because she'd been too busy trying to survive.

But, damn, she was lonely. Now it made sense why solitary confinement had always been such a harsh punishment in prisons.

"No," Aiodhan said.

"Aw, c'mon." She reached for that big mitt he called a hand, surprised to find it calloused, warm, and so strong she didn't want to let him go. "Pretty please?"

Dimples creased both cheeks when he smiled, and it suddenly dawned on her how handsome he was. Tall, dark, and handsome.

How cliché.

"Please? You beg now?" Aiodhan's smile grew as her own lips fell to a frown.

He'd found her hot button. Handsome or not, he could take a hike.

"I *never* beg."

Kara stomped away, heading to get her stuff and go back to her lonely lack of a life. She'd planned on foraging for supplies later at a cabin she'd been watching for signs of in habitants, so she'd stay busy. That was the lie she told herself to keep from weeping at the thought of being alone again.

"Fucking aliens," she muttered under her breath. "It's all their fault. Come here, take over my planet and—"

A hand on her bicep dragged her to a halt. "Not go alone."

"Alone."

"Not alone."

She put her hands on her hips and scowled at him, angry he'd refused to help but now thought he could boss her around. "Alone."

He mimicked her actions while also leaning over her, emphasizing that he had a good foot of height on her. His black hair formed a curtain around his face, making his features so dark, he seemed even more intimidating. "Not alone."

Kara didn't budge an inch, somehow knowing she shouldn't fear him. The absurdity of this situation made a laugh bubble out. "Hey. Know what?"

"No. What?"

"This is our first fight, Tarzan."

"First fight? But you fight Vymaln. I kill many Vymalns. Not your first fight. Not my first fight."

This taking everything she said literally was going to drive her insane. "Drop it."

He lifted his empty hands to stare at them. "Drop what?"

Kara heaved a sigh even as she smiled. "Never mind. Look, can I go get my stuff? You can come too, but I need my stuff."

He couldn't possibly know how long it had taken her to scrounge up the few things she carried. Peroxide. Bandages. A bottle of antibiotics she was saving for a dire emergency. Matches. One last can of tuna. A precious king-sized Snickers bar. They were the few things she had remaining from the scary days where everyone turned into scavengers, scrounging for food, supplies, anything. In the week it took the Vymalns to conquer humanity and start turning people into slaves, everyone panicked, looting and destroying. How stupid that seemed. They should have been helping each other, working on ways to fight their enemy, not stealing from each other.

Kara had stuffed her backpack full of things and run to the mountains. She didn't know where else to go, and all she kept thinking of was a Bible verse.

I will lift up mine eyes unto the hills, from whence cometh my help.

How very odd that she'd forgotten it in the first place. This guy had her good and rattled.

"I need my stuff," she insisted.

Aiodhan thought it over a good long while. "Go. We get your stuff."

Chance bounced along beside her, and she figured she'd feed him the last of the beef jerky as a treat. After all, he'd almost died.

When they'd first started hiding in the hills, the dog had reverted to his ancestors' ability to hunt. Not that Kara could watch when he ate some fat rabbit he'd caught, but Chance's instincts kept her from having to hunt down something to feed him. She ruffled the scruffy fur around his neck, grateful she'd had a companion in the months of loneliness.

Now, she had another. And, shit, what was she supposed to do with Aiodhan?

Making a wide arch around the police car, she found her blue backpack close to where her campfire had been. Thank God, her dagger was close too. She wiped the yellow blood off on some thick weeds and sheathed the weapon against her thigh.

Her new friend didn't help her heft the heavy pack onto her back, and when she glared at him for being inconsiderate, she gaped at what he'd revealed by pulling up his sleeve. "Oh, my God."

Aiodhan cradled his bleeding forearm against him and jerked his sleeve back down. She reached for him anyway and pulled the material back so she could see the long gash. "That had to hurt like hell. You need stitches."

"Stitches? Sew?" A quick glance down to the jagged wound on his arm, and he emphatically shook his head. "*No* stitches."

Why was it the biggest guys made the worst patients? When she'd still worked at the hospital, it was always the men who passed out when she showed them the needle she would use to draw their blood samples or give them shots. "Big baby."

"Baby?"

"Infant."

He tilted his head and frowned.

"Child?"

A shake of his head.

"Small, you know, person."

"Ah. Small. Tiny. Little human." He glanced down at his body and frowned again. "I am not little. Do you make joke again? Was it funny, ha ha?"

God help her, Kara laughed. Long and loud. Something she hadn't done in so long, it sounded foreign. Aiodhan's grin only made her laugh harder. "No, you're certainly not tiny. And I wasn't making a joke. I meant you were *acting* like a baby."

"Baby. Bay-bee," he repeated as if saying the word again would help him understand. "Ah. I see. You mean a just-born. Yes?"

"Newborn. Yes."

"But a just-born would not require these…stitches. He would not hunt Vymalns."

"Of course not, but—"

"Then you do not think I am a just-born?"

"I didn't mean it literally."

"You confuse your own words, yes?"

Kara gave up. "Yes. I confused my own words."

He grunted and nodded. Definitely caveman material, and she still hadn't placed the accent. Then she noticed the rest of the scrapes and bruises. On his hands. His arms. His face. This guy had been through hell.

She gently took his good arm and led him away, following the route through the trees he'd taken before when he'd said something about his transport, figuring it was some car that still had gas. Or better yet, maybe an RV. She could barely remember what a bed felt like, and even if it was only for a few minutes, she wanted to lie down on a real mattress instead of a bed of leaves or moss with her backpack as a pillow.

"We'll stop when we get back to your car," she said. "I've still got a needle and thread, so I can stitch up your arm."

"You sew?"

"I'm a nurse."

"Nurse?"

"I help sick people."

"Ah. But I am not sick." He tugged his sleeve over his injury. "No need for sew."

"Big baby. You're getting stitches whether you want them or not."

* * *

His transport was dead.

He'd known that, but seeing the wreckage from the distance made it real. Just a lump of metal parts. How he'd survived the crash landing was beyond explanation. The next time he slept, he would wake up feeling as an elder—sore and very stiff.

Kara was several paces behind him, and he was impressed that she didn't gasp for breath. He'd marched briskly, anxious to get back to the transport to see if he could salvage anything. The only concession he'd made for his new companion was to glance over his shoulder from time to time to be sure she remained close. Not once did she complain, despite his speed and the steep slope of the terrain.

He'd lost communication with the rest of the Seekers when he'd crashed, so he was on his own. That didn't bother him. Seekers were used to acting independently as they stalked their prey. How many of his brethren had made a successful infiltration? As he hoped their landings had been smoother than his own, his thoughts settled on Pashmar Karr.

She'd been sent on a mission as well, and Aiodhan hoped to catch up with her soon to help. He'd been given a covert strike he had to make first. Pashmar could handle herself until he could join her.

Could Kara handle herself?

He turned to stare at her. The two females were night and day. As light as Kara was dark, Pashmar stood only a few hands shorter than he did. She would tower over Kara. Pashmar's blond hair was cropped short, efficient. Many males would envy her muscles. There was nothing soft about her.

Everything about Kara was soft. Her hair. Her eyes. Her skin.

What exactly was he supposed to do with her?

This wasn't a rescue operation to transport humans off their planet. He was to take out the proper targets, join Pashmar to free and train some humans to start the fight against the Vymalns, and then move on to his next mission. He couldn't take Kara with him when he left this planet, and why in the heavens was he even thinking about that? As soon as she repaired his arm, it should be time for them to go their separate ways.

Yet, he knew that he couldn't leave her alone.

Her dog came bounding up the last hill, heading straight for Aiodhan's transport. Kara was right behind.

He took the last few steps toward his destroyed ship. The only thing intact was the cockpit. He grabbed the door and pulled. With a groan, it came off the hinges. Tossing the door aside, he checked the command console.

Sorting through the twisted wires, he searched for his communicator. Smashed almost beyond recognition, it would require more time than he could spare to repair. As he tugged it away from the console, he heard a surprised gasp.

"Did your plane crash?" Kara set the pack she carried on the ground while she gaped at the wrecked transport.

"Plane?"

"Airplane." She nodded at the transport.

Airplane? Did he know that word? *Ah, yes. A primitive flying machine.* "Not an airplane. A transport."

"Excuse me?"

"Trans…port." Like saying it slower and louder would make her understand. What other words would help her comprehend? He could let her think he was just another human, but she'd figure out that he wasn't from her world. Now that the jolt she'd received from the Vymaln had worn off, she seemed too smart for him to even try that type of deception.

"Transport," he said. "Um…ship."

"Ship?"

Aiodhan pointed toward the stars. "Long way to travel."

"Long way to—" Kara's eyes flew wide. "A spaceship? That's a *spaceship?*" Her breath came in pants, and her wild brown eyes filled with anger. "Oh, hell no. You're not human."

"Not say I was."

She moved damned fast for a human female, not even bothering to grab her pack. Before Aiodhan could haul himself out of the transport, she was already down the hill, her animal running at her side.

Why he chased her, he didn't know. It would have been smarter to let her leave. But the thought of another Vymaln finding her, hurting her?

Unbearable.

"Wait!"

His shout seemed to make her run faster, but she was no match for his longer and more powerful legs. Her long head-tail trailed behind her, and if he grabbed it…

No, that would cause her pain. He reached for her shoulder instead. A quick duck and sharp turn, and she evaded him. Her hound nipped at his heels, further throwing him off balance.

She was going to escape.

"Oh, hell no." His words echoed Kara's in what he realized was a curse as he regrouped, sprinted after her, and tackled her with his arms around her waist. Aiodhan twisted so his shoulder and body absorbed the impact then rolled over until he had her pinned to the ground, his body pressing against hers.

"Get off me, you big ox!"

"No. You must listen."

Her fists beat against his shoulders and arms, although he took mental note that she didn't hit his injury, which would have been the first thing he would have attacked.

"I don't wanna listen. Let me go!"

"No."

He let her struggle until she finally gave up and stilled. The tears brimming her eyes caused some odd clenching in his gut. He didn't like to see her cry. Pashmar never cried. No Seeker would allow tears to fall, to show someone that kind of weakness.

But Kara wasn't a Seeker, and the feel of her lying beneath him was beyond distracting. His body responded to her nearness, hardening and throbbing in demand that he join with her. The shock that he wanted to mate with a weakling human almost made him empty his belly. She shouldn't attract him. He should want his own kind, like Pashmar.

He'd only mated with Pashmar a couple of times, although he knew she was always willing. He'd never felt the desire to be more than her friend and sometime lover, despite the fact she'd made it plain she wanted a deeper and more lasting relationship. A lifetime bonding, which was something he couldn't offer anyone, not at this stage in his life. He just wasn't ready. Pashmar would have to remain a friend, a fellow Seeker, and a warm female body when the sexual need grew too strong to ignore.

One of Kara's knees connected with his *gadnaomes*. He groaned, put his hands over his injured groin, and rolled off her.

The woman was quick, scrambling to her feet and running away as her animal bit Aiodhan's pant leg and tugged to keep him from pursuing.

He brushed the hound away, trying not to cause any harm, and leapt to his feet. "Stop!"

A fleeting glance over her shoulder and Kara's speed increased.

He'd wasted far too much time on this troublesome woman, and if he had any sense at all, he would return to his transport and forget her.

But he couldn't.

This time as he drew close, he skidded under her, knocking her off her feet by tripping her with his own. He caught her against his prostrate body, wrapped his arms around her, and rolled to pin her down again, being sure to press his thighs against hers to protect himself.

"I ordered stop."

"I don't care."

"You stop now. I make sure." Aiodhan threw a grin at her, hoping she'd realize he was making one of the jokes she seemed to like. Humor had always seemed such a waste of time and thought. Yet if it helped calm her, he'd make an attempt.

Kara couldn't believe what she'd just heard, and it shocked her so much she stopped struggling and gaped at him.

A joke? From the caveman?

He was so handsome when he smiled, she almost forgot what he was. *An alien.*

Frustrated tears still overflowed her lashes. She thought she'd found a friend, someone to help make this hell a little easier. "I-I thought you were...like me."

17

His gaze went from her to his body then back to her. "We are the same. Same skin. Same hair."

"But you're from another planet. I saw your spaceship. You're an alien. Like *them.*"

He grunted and frowned. "I not Vymaln."

She took heart that he considered her comparison to the bug-eyes an insult, and why she wanted to soothe that hurt, she had no clue. "Of-of course not."

No Vymaln could be that gorgeous. She stared at his face, trying to see if there were differences between whatever he was and a human man she'd missed before. The scrapes and bruises appeared human enough. He had a cleft in his strong chin. The dimples disappeared when his smile changed to a frown, but she remembered how sweet they looked. Dark eyebrows and eyelashes.

Wasn't anything different?

The eyes. Kara finally noticed his eyes. They had no whites, just deep, dark gray with pinpoints of black as pupils. Fear jolted through her, and she thrashed to try to throw him off.

She had to get away. "Get off me!"

"No."

"No?" She could fight him all day and it wouldn't do a damned bit of good. Her muscles relaxed. "Fine. I surrender."

"Surrender?"

"Can you *please* stop repeating every word I say?"

"Perhaps."

The smile returned, and the dimples were enough to make her smile back despite how disgusted she was with the way things were going.

"What is surrender?" he asked.

"Quit. Stop. Give up." Her eyes searched the darkness of his, and the fear receded. Yes, they were dark, but they weren't the unearthly green of a Vymaln. They did, however, leave her no way to judge his moods.

"You will listen?" he asked.

She nodded.

"I am here to help."

"What do you mean?"

"I am Seeker. My job to kill Vymalns."

Chapter Three

"It's been empty for three days."

Kara watched the log cabin from the row of holly bushes. Aiodhan lay at her side, both sprawled on their bellies, his eyes on the same target.

"No one's come near it since I started watching the place."

Such a surprise he followed her there. He must have understood when she'd tried to explain that the cabin might have precious medical supplies. Better yet, nonperishable food.

Winter would be setting in soon. The berries and nuts would be gone or hoarded by other hungry creatures. The waterways would ice over, making fishing more difficult if not impossible. She was damn sick and tired of fish for almost every meal anyway. It wouldn't be long before she would have to force herself to catch a rabbit or squirrel, although her stomach turned at the thought of killing and skinning the poor thing. She hadn't caught anything. Yet. But if she got hungry enough, she would.

At least Kara's dad had taught her and her brother Joey to live off the land.

Pain sliced through her heart just thinking about her family. The three of them had been so close, a bond that formed when Kara's mother had left them and simply disappeared when Kara was eight.

Every night before she could sleep, Kara prayed her family had escaped the Vymalns as she had and that they remained free. It near to killed her thinking of them in the internment camp, slaving away for the bug-eyes, probably starving to death or suffering from some disease.

A sliver of hope remained that she'd see them again one day, but she refused to let that hope swell. Her whole life, she'd played the hand she was dealt, lived in reality, and never dreamt about things that could never be. Seeing her father and brother again probably wasn't in the cards, so she swallowed the wish.

Drawing herself from her morbid thoughts, she looked at the cabin again. If she was careful to come and go from it without any kind of pattern, Kara could spend really cold nights inside. Vymalns probably still had squads sweeping for people who'd evaded capture or death, which meant she couldn't stay all the time. They'd find her. But by coming and going at random, she might enjoy some nights in a real bed away from the cold.

And just maybe there will be... "Batteries."

"Batteries?"

Kara smiled. She was growing accustomed to Aiodhan's echo and finding comfort in his strong presence. Once she knew he was on her side, she'd accepted him despite the fact he was an alien. That, and she was sick and tired of being alone.

"Batteries," she replied. "Little power supplies. For my radio."

"Radio? Ah. Communicator." He pulled a small, silver object out of his belt. The thing resembled a cell phone that had been slammed onto a concrete walk. "My communicator. Perhaps these...*bat-tear-ies* help also?"

One glance at his communicator told her batteries wouldn't do a thing for him. "Doubt it. But who knows?"

Aiodhan shrugged. "I not know who. Perhaps you know?"

When had she become Abbott to his Costello?

She gave a tress of his long hair a tug. "We'll figure it out later." Pointing to the roof, she smiled. "Solar panels. Probably to keep the water pump working. We might have fresh water."

Did he have to reply to everything she said with a grunt?

They stared at the cabin for several silent minutes. Kara waited to see if she got that tightening in her gut that always alerted her to danger. *Nada, thank the Lord.*

She patted Chance, who was sprawled next to her on the cushion of dead leaves. "Okay. I'm going in."

Crawling out of the cover of the bushes toward the cabin, she barely made it a few feet when a hand grabbed her calf and dragged her back.

"I will go," Aiodhan insisted in a tone that suggested there'd be no argument.

Kara almost gave him one anyway. Growing up the younger sister of a stubborn and overly protective older brother had taught her to revolt whenever given a masculine command. In this instance, she acquiesced, grateful for someone as strong and brave as her alien.

Alien.

Shit, but it was hard to think of Aiodhan as an *alien*. The Vymalns were aliens. Aiodhan was one good looking hunk of—

A foot on her ass made her glare up into his face. "I go now," he announced. "You stay in leaf."

"Bushes," she couldn't help but correct, if for no other reason than to put him in his place. Rolling to her side, she plucked a single leaf from the brambles. She held it up high enough to make her point. "*This*...is a leaf." Her hand swept out to the holly bushes. "*These*...are bushes."

"And *you*...cause anger." Hands had settled on his hips, and his scowl was so hot it could have started a forest fire.

Contrition wasn't one of her better abilities, but in this case, she owed him. She deserved his anger since she'd all but insulted him.

Hell, she *had* insulted him. "Sorry."

More of an apology than she usually tendered. She'd learned a long time ago that apologies never made anything better.

The scowl didn't change, but he directed his gaze toward the cabin. "You stay. I go. I come back when I am assumed no Vymaln."

"Assured, not assumed." Correcting him had become second nature.

His growl made her wince.

Aiodhan approached the cabin, but he was neither cautious nor frightened. He walked right up to it. Instead of peeking in the windows as she would have, he marched to the door, pulled it off its hinges, and headed inside.

Subtle, he definitely was not.

After several interminable minutes, he stuck his head out of the cabin. "You enter!" His bellow could have felled a pine tree.

"C'mon, boy." Kara stood up and brushed the dead leaves off her jeans.

Chance trotted beside her to the cabin and went right on through the door as if he'd always lived there.

Aiodhan patted the dog as he passed. "Name?"

"My dog?"

The caveman rolled his eyes. "I am Aiodhan. You are Kara. Who else to name?" His grin hit her like a punch to the gut.

Damned dimples. She'd always been a sucker for dimples.

"Chance. I call him Chance." She forced herself to glance at the door he'd thrown to the side. "Guess I can fix it to keep the snow out."

His gaze moved around the landscape before returning to her face. "No snow."

"There will be. Soon. We're high enough in the mountains, it'll probably snow in only a few more weeks. Nights are already mighty chilly. Chance will get a thicker coat, but I'll freeze my skinny ass off. Maybe there are some blankets. Or thicker socks. Or…something I can use to stay warm."

She sounded like an idiot, having a conversation with someone from another planet who barely spoke Pidgin English. She'd been alone for so long, she wanted to talk to him, even if he didn't catch most of her meaning. Just being around him made her drop all her guards, and to feel relaxed seemed so foreign.

"Sorry," she said. "I'm a chatterbox today."

"Chatterbox?"

"Can't stop talking. Dad used to say I had diarrhea of the mouth sometimes."

The big man took a step back. "Kara sick?"

His confusion must have been contagious, because now she felt it too.

"Why would you think I'm sick?"

Aiodhan grabbed her shoulder and spun her around. "Diarrhea?" He stared intently at her ass.

So that word, he knew. "I was just kidding."

"You joke much." He frowned before stalking into the house, shaking his head.

The place wasn't a wreck. That came as a surprise. Most of the houses she'd encountered up on the mountain had been trashed by looters. Or by bug-eyes. Who really knew? This place was pristine with the exception of a light layer of dust coating the furniture.

Aiodhan's heavy footfalls sounded down the hallway.

Kara's first place to explore was the kitchen.

She knew from experience not to touch the refrigerator. The food inside would have rotted, and the smell would swarm into the house if she opened the door. Instead, she tried the tap. It sputtered for a moment, but then clear water spilled out. The solar panels still ran the pump. *Thank God!* She opened cabinets until she found a real glass, filled it with water and gulped it down.

Filling the glass again, she set it on the counter, planning on drinking it later, while she braved what she hoped was a pantry. Her hand hovered above the handle for a moment while she tried to rein in her hope. Maybe there was some pasta. Or maybe some canned goods. Or maybe she'd find...nothing.

Teeth tugging on her lower lip, she opened the door.

"Jackpot!" Cans lined one wall. Vegetables. Fruits. Soups. Boxes of everything from noodles to cereal were piled on shelves on the other wall.

She grabbed the Apple Jacks and searched around, holding her breath that she'd find the Holy Grail. "Evaporated milk!"

"Milk?" her echo asked.

She whirled around, frightened that she hadn't heard Aiodhan creep up behind her. Her heart pounded a furious cadence. "Don't do that."

"Do what?"

"Sneak up on me like that. You scared the life out of me."

His grin was far too handsome. "Seekers move silent."

"What's a Seeker?"

"Aiodhan a Seeker."

She waited for him to expand on that explanation, but wasn't surprised when he didn't. Having a conversation with him was like visiting a foreign country where she didn't speak the language. "What do Seekers do?"

"Kill Vymalns."

That was succinct. And it sure sounded like what Earth could have used—four months ago. She shrugged in resignation. "Better late than never."

He grunted, which probably meant he understood her and had taken her words as a slur. Before she could protest, he grabbed the Apple Jacks.

"Food?" he asked.

"Yeah—and look." She pointed at the shelves. "There's plenty more."

Aiodhan pried open the box of cereal and pulled out the plastic bag. Before she could warn him, he tugged it open. The thing exploded all over him and the pantry. Chance came padding into the small room and immediately went about consuming anything on the floor.

Kara laughed as she brushed the little Os off Aiodhan's broad shoulders and chest. "You're a mess."

She couldn't understand why she wasn't angry. He had, after all, wasted a perfectly good box of cereal. But there were plenty more boxes in the pantry, and Chance was enjoying quite a feast. The disgruntled expression on his Aiodhan's face made her smile, as did the cloak of Apple Jacks he wore. She gave one last brush of cereal off his arm.

She liked touching him. That revelation came as a shock. When had she stopped thinking about him as an alien?

Duh.

From the moment he'd been lying on top of her and she'd realized how desperately she wanted him. At first she'd lied to herself, thinking she'd simply been lonely for far too long. That was the only reason to even consider Aiodhan.

Then she'd been honest and admitted that the man called to her on so many levels. Not only was he downright gorgeous, but she liked his scent—clean and male. His eyes had seemed distant, but the more time she spent staring into them, the more she understood the color changed with his moods. The angrier he got, the gray darkened until those eyes were almost black. When he seemed happy, as he did now, they lightened to dove gray.

Damn it if she didn't want him to kiss her. Right now. In the pantry. Standing in the middle of a pile of spilled Apple Jacks.

Yep. That proved it. She was desperately lonely.

Aiodhan watched Kara, the emotions playing across her face shifting and changing. First she smiled, then a frown bowed her lips. What was she thinking?

He didn't see anger, so he assumed she wasn't going to scold him for ruining her food. He would have glanced to the shelves to search for a similar container, but those brown eyes held him captive, the color so inviting compared to that of his species. Tirian gray seemed almost plain compared to her warm brown and the ever-changing size of the black center.

For the first time since they'd left his transport, she was quiet. That concerned him. Her constant words were not only helping him pick up her language, but he enjoyed the melodious sound of her voice. Before he could talk himself out of it, he gave in to an urge he'd had since he met her and reached out to touch her hair.

Kara stood her ground, so Aiodhan caressed the soft brown tresses that had been driving him to distraction. Females on his home planet Tirios wore their hair short. Partly from fashion, partly from the fact it took them decades to grow it longer than a few inches. Tirian males, on the other hand, had to cut their hair often. Because of that difference, he'd never considered long hair feminine in the least.

But Kara's hair? The desire to pull the string binding it and watch it spill across her shoulders was almost overwhelming. Instead, he ran his fingertips down her long head-tail before a growl of sexual need rose from his chest. Before he could stop himself, he picked up her hand from where it rested on his arm and pressed his lips to her palm.

What in the universe was he thinking? He should be planning how he could complete his mission, not using mating rituals on this...*human.*

"*Nivelt!*" he shouted. "I not!"

"Not what?" She cocked her head. Her hand pulled back from his, and she cradled it against her chest as if she'd been injured.

"Not-not—" Mate with her? That's what he wanted so badly he could hardly contain his *kull* in his pants. The independent thing was hard as stone and seeking Kara like she was in breeding season.

Thankfully, she turned to grab another box from the shelf. "Tell you what, let's try a bowl this time," she said with a grin as she left the small room. Shuffling through the cabinets, she found a dish, opened the box and the inner lining, and poured some multiple-colored bits out. "Froot Loops." She scooped some into her slender hand and poured them into her mouth.

Aiodhan reached to pinch one between his fingers. He stared at it for a moment, wondering if he'd be better off eating one of his nutrition packs instead. Her earlier word haunted him.

Diarrhea.

That word, he'd learned. What he didn't understand was why she'd mentioned it when she didn't suffer from the affliction, but it was what he feared would happen should he eat any of this planet's foodstuffs.

The small red circle didn't look too harmful. Surely one wouldn't hurt him.

"Go on," Kara mumbled through a full mouth. "They're great. God, I've missed sugar buzzes."

He ate it. Sweetness exploded in his mouth, making him a little dizzy, as though he'd just drank the fermented fruit of the *ferra* tree. Could he get intoxicated from the small colored circles?

He liked the taste, so he grabbed another. The same explosion rocked his mouth.

"Good," he said as he reached for a handful and started dropping the tasty morsels in his mouth, one by one.

"Wait 'til you try 'em with milk."

Kara shuffled through the cabinets until she found a prying tool. Then she took the small red and white can, punctured it with the tool, and poured some of the contents into a glass full of water resting on the counter. Another cabinet yielded a spoon, and she stirred the white mixture before pouring it over the dish full of Froot Loops. She used the spoon to take a big bite as the white liquid dribbled down her chin.

He wanted to lick it off.

"Here." She handed him the spoon and bowl.

Aiodhan scooped some of the food into his mouth. The white liquid was creamy, complementing the sweetness of the Froot Loops.

"Mmm," he purred as he chewed.

"Good, right?"

He nodded.

"Let's look at that arm."

He set the bowl and spoon on the counter and covered his injured arm with his hand. "No."

"Big baby. I'm checking the bathroom for some bandages, then I'll stitch you up."

She obviously wasn't listening. "No sewing."

Kara ignored him, disappeared into another room, and soon he could hear her shuffling around. A few moments later, she came back with supplies that she dropped next to the food. Pulling out a stool, she patted the seat. "Come here and sit down, big boy."

What word would make her understand? "Boss."

"Excuse me?"

"You are boss."

"Damn right, I am. I said sit." She nodded at the stool while she opened up a package of white bandages. Putting them aside, she grabbed a needle, opened a bottle, and spilled some clear liquid over a silver needle.

"No stitches. Stop being boss."

Her laughter sounded like a song. "Now I see what you mean. Not boss, Aiodhan. *Bossy*. You think I'm *bossy*."

"Bossy. Yes. No stitches." So why did he sit on the stool?

Rolling his sleeve up, Kara grinned. "I'm a nurse, you know. I know what I'm doing. And I always get my way. I suppose you're right. I'm bossy."

"Nurse? You are healer?"

She splashed some of the liquid on the white bandage. "Yeah. I help the sick. And big babies who need stitches, although I've only done this once in nursing school and once on myself about a month ago." She shrugged. "Not like I could go to a hospital. Doctors usually stitch. This might sting a little."

With great care and gentle hands, she wiped his wound.

Aiodhan sat as still as a statue as she stitched his skin closed. Her efficiency spoke volumes about her personality and her abilities as a healer. The whole time she worked over his injury, she spoke in a low, soothing tones, mixing in a mention of what she would do right before she did it. Before he realized it, Kara was affixing a bandage to his cleaned and closed wound.

"You need to keep that dry. I'll change the bandage tomorrow. I'm going to make us a nice dinner now. I think I saw a jar of spaghetti sauce. Do you like spaghetti? Sorry I can't make meatballs, too."

Before he could thank her, she disappeared into the food room, shuffled around for a few minutes, and came out with boxes and bottles.

"Think you can start a fire?" She nodded to a hearth along the far wall. "It's gonna get cold now that the sun's going down. We could use a fire, and I can cook over it. You know what?"

"No, what?"

"I'm going to take a shower tonight. God, it's been *forever* since I took a shower. The water'll be damn cold, but I don't care. I hope there's shampoo. I'm tired of bathing in streams."

* * *

The ice-cold water cascading over Kara's skin pricked like needles, probably poetic justice for having stitched up Aiodhan's laceration. She brushed the discomfort aside and scrubbed her hair, working the floral-scented shampoo through her long locks. A shower, albeit a freezing one. But a real shower.

If she hadn't felt as if she'd been dunked naked into a snow bank, she would've savored it and made it last and last. As it was, her fingers and toes were turning blue. Holding her breath, she ducked her head back under the stream of water and rinsed out the shampoo while her scalp spasmed in protest. By the time she heard it squeaking in cleanliness, she was shivering so hard, her teeth chattered. Turning off the faucet, she groped around for the towel with fingers almost too stiff to move.

There had been clean clothes in the bureau of the only bedroom, and she'd scavenged some men's flannel pajamas. They were huge on her, but as she donned them, the soft warmth of the material soothing some of her freezing skin. Her hands still shook as she pulled hard on the drawstring until it was tight enough the pants wouldn't fall around her ankles the moment she let go. She considered her image in the mirror and gasped when she could almost count her ribs, making her breasts look disproportionately large and a little deflated. Sure, she knew she'd lost some weight, but *geesh*. Her shape now bordered on anorexic.

Except for the little swollen belly. That remained from where she'd gorged herself on the spaghetti she'd made. Mushroom sauce wasn't her favorite, but hell…it was hot and it was good. She'd eaten enough to almost make herself barf it all right back up.

Kara tugged on the shirt and buttoned it, pleased her fingers had stopped quivering. A yawn consumed her whole face. She was bone weary. Although she'd wanted to wash the clothes she'd been wearing, she decided to wait until the morning—a luxury to put a chore aside for once. Besides, she'd washed her other clothes in the lake near here a day ago, so she had something semi-clean to change into, plus she might find more things in the cabin. Not sure exactly what the sleeping arrangements would be, she decided no matter what her alien decided, she was sleeping on the damned mattress. And that was that.

After sliding on the fluffy socks, she sighed, feeling the same as she'd used to after a hard day's work. She'd spend twelve-hours in the ER, running around like crazy, not even realizing how tired she was until she finally stopped the moment she got home. She'd take a hot shower, put on some clean flannels and socks and curl up under the blankets to sleep. And right now, that's what she wanted to do, curl up and sleep for hours and hours.

As cold as it was, it would take forever for her hair to dry. She'd have to sit in front of the fire and hold up locks of it, exactly like she did whenever she'd been camping. Knowing she simply wouldn't have the energy to deal with it tonight, she finally brushed her hair back into a ponytail and rubbed the towel over it until it was as dry as she could manage.

Aiodhan was kneeling next to the fire when Kara walked back into the living area. Chance lay curled up on an afghan on the couch, bedded down for the night. The dog had the right idea.

She grabbed her knife from the coffee table. "I'm heading to bed."

Aiodhan grunted and nodded. That sure as hell didn't tell her much.

She pointed to the bedroom. "In there. I'm going to sleep in there."

He fitted the screen around the fire, got to his feet, and strode over to her. "We both sleep now."

The thought of snuggling up next to that warm, firm body banished whatever had been left of the cold. "Um…okay."

She whirled around and marched to the bedroom. Standing on one side of the bed, she slid her knife under the pillow. She pulled back the blanket while he walked around the other side. When he jerked his shirt over his head, her mouth went dry. Were the pants next?

"It's really cold tonight," she murmured. "I think I'll just keep my stuff *on*."

Now she sounded like an idiot. Aiodhan rattled her in a way no other man ever had. Kara had been on plenty of camping trips where she'd huddled up against guy friends to stay warm. Of course, they hadn't been half naked. It was all perfectly platonic. That's all that this was too. Perfectly platonic.

Liar.

"Well, um…good night." Kara crawled between the sheets and dragged the blanket over her body before turning her back to him. She was so tense, she squealed when Aiodhan's weight hit the mattress, causing her to bounce.

The blanket cocooning her was yanked away.

"Hey!" She rolled over to see it now covered him from the waist down as he gave her a good view of his bare back. "If you're that cold, put your stupid shirt back on." Kara tugged at the blanket. It wouldn't budge. "Aw, c'mon. You can at least share."

Aiodhan turned toward her and yawned. "No more talk. Sleep now, Kara."

"I'd like to sleep, but you stole the blanket. I'm freezing."

As she squeaked in protest, he hauled her into his arms, tossed the end of the blanket over her and yawned again. "Not freezing now."

She couldn't argue with that. The guy radiated heat. Not sure what to do with her chilly hands, she tried to hold them against her, but one brushed his chest.

"*Zot!*" he bellowed.

His tone had sounded exactly like when she shouted a curse, so she assumed it was *damn* or *shit*. She was almost too tired to try to drag the meaning out of her caveman, but curiosity got the better of her. "What's *zot*?"

"*Zot.* Like your damn. Cold hands." His hand reached between them and pressed her palms to his chest. "Warm now?"

"Umm…yeah." Warm as a campfire.

Her eyes grew heavy, and Kara snuggled a little closer to his heat, letting sleep claim her.

Chapter Four

"No! Kevin! Please no!"

Kara's terrified cries woke Aiodhan. As always, he sprang to attention, wide awake and ready to do battle. Crouched low on the mattress, he scanned the room.

No Vymaln. No wild animals. Nothing but blessed darkness.

"Kevin! Not Kevin!" The blanket had twisted around her arms, and she whimpered as she fought it like a pair of shackles.

He peeled the covering down to her knees.

Her frightened moans hit his gut like a hard punch, especially since she cried out what sounded like a man's name. If he was going to get concerned every time she was unhappy and jealous every time a male's life touched hers, his own life would become miserable and his mission would be lost. Instead of being a formidable warrior, he would become as soft as dampened bread.

He should pull away. He should drive her from his thoughts. He should leave her to this home and get on with his mission.

"Aiodhan..." Kara's whisper drew him nearer, but she hadn't called to him, only uttered his name in her sleep.

On his knees beside her, Aiodhan smoothed his fingers over her furrowed brow, wondering if he could be gentle enough to lull her from the nightmare. His hands were too large while she seemed so small, so fragile. Her features relaxed as he stroked her skin, the deep frown softening in peaceful sleep. All he could think of was kissing that perfect mouth, sliding his tongue between those plump pink lips, and freeing the desire he'd felt from the moment he'd first spotted her.

One hand reached over her to press against the cool linen on her other side. He covered her frame with his, supporting himself on his elbows and knees so he left the width of a hand between their bodies, not daring to touch her for fear of losing control.

Aiodhan's face hovered above Kara's, so close that the soft bursts of air from her parted lips brushed his face. Each sweet breath made his heart pound harder. Unable to resist, he lowered himself closer until each time she drew air into her lungs, her breasts kissed his bare chest. He closed his eyes, savoring the torture. Desire threatened to pull him into a grasp he could never break.

"Aiodhan..." Warm fingers touched his waist.

His eyes flew open to find hers staring back. Such a warm brown, like the bark of an ancient *demauba* tree.

"I awakened you." An absurd statement. The only way he could get closer would be to rip off their pants and thrust inside her body.

She gave no reply, but soft, trembling fingers stroked his ribs. She did nothing to pull away. Should he be encouraged by that reaction, or did his size overwhelm her? No force in the wide universe could make him move away now.

Except her refusal.

"Kara." His voice was every bit as soft as hers, barely heard, yet as demanding as a shout.

Her eyes widened when his lips touched hers. Aiodhan eased back enough to give her the chance to deny anything further.

She lifted her face as her lips claimed his. A primitive rumble filled his chest, growing to become part of the kiss. He parted her lips with his tongue and swept it inside to mate with hers.

Kara felt his kiss from the roots of her hair to the tips of her toes. Her whole body rose to press hard against his.

The familiar nightmare had awakened her, and for a moment, she feared she was back in the city the day her brother had been lost to her. He'd sacrificed himself, drawing the bug-eyes to chase him while she slipped away. Like some coward.

God, she didn't want to think about that now. With Aiodhan's kiss came sweet forgetting, and the man certainly knew how to kiss. Just the right pressure, such a thorough tongue. She wanted to lose herself in him. She'd been alone for so damned long…

His knee nudged her thighs apart, and he settled himself intimately against her, the hard length of his erection nestled to her core. Feeling safe enough with their pants still on, Kara indulged herself in fantasy. Aiodhan wasn't an alien but a knight in shining armor who'd come to rescue her, the damsel in distress. He'd make passionate love to her with what felt like a rather impressive cock, then he'd marry her and carry her away to his castle, where they would live happily ever after.

He kissed his way across her cheek to her ear. His tongue ran around the curves before he pressed those hot lips against her neck, sending shivers racing over her skin and heat pooling between her thighs. She tilted her head, letting him know how much she liked what he was doing and hoping he'd continue the sweet torture. Her fingertips skittered across his broad back, seeking out the plains and valleys in his sculpted muscles. The man's body was a masterpiece.

"Kara," he whispered before his weight grew heavier as he moved one of his hands to cover her breast. The heat of his palm breached the flannel, branding her like a red-hot iron. She arched into his touch as her nipples hardened.

His fingers tickled across to her arm where he gently took her hand, raised it to his lips and kissed her palm, much as he'd done back in the kitchen. Such a sweet gesture, so gentle from such a rough man. She moved her hand to stroke the back of his cheek with her knuckles as she smiled up at him.

Aiodhan was lost, the need to make Kara his was strong enough to make him forget the rest of the universe existed. Her beautiful face shone in the light of the planet's moonbeams, and her touch was light and airy. Unable to stop, he'd offered himself to her to mate by kissing her palm. He raised his hand to her, hoping she'd complete the ancient ritual so he could claim her with his body.

Those brown eyes stared up at him, and she made no move to kiss his hand.

Didn't she want him as badly as he wanted her?

Deep, threatening barks from her hound shattered the tender moment. Aiodhan reacted on instinct, pulling his weapon from where it was strapped against his leg, rolling off the bed, and dragging Kara to the floor. When she opened her mouth to protest, he held the palm he'd so desperately wanted her to kiss to her mouth.

"Quiet," he whispered.

The hound snarled then barked over and over. A shrill curse, the sound of which could only be made by a Vymaln, came in response.

"Stay," he ordered, jerking the blanket from the bed and covering Kara. "Do not move."

He didn't have time to wait to see if she would obey.

Silently stalking the intruder, Aiodhan made his way toward the room where Chance had slept. He no longer barked, but his rumbling growl still filled the air. Thank the stars, the Vymaln's back was to Aiodhan, its attention on the intimidating animal.

A female. Much easier prey.

She had one arm raised with a jolt gun aimed at the dog. Not a wise move because it left one of her hearts vulnerable to a blade. Readying his weapon, Aiodhan made his move.

Grabbing the Vymaln by her thick neck, he punctured the first heart under her raised arm, twisted that arm behind her back and waited for her reaction. When she swung with her free arm, he slid his blade neatly between her ribs and into her second heart. She collapsed on the ground, dead.

"Oh, my God. Are you okay?"

Kara stood by the door to the room they'd slept in.

"Back!" he bellowed. "Shut the door!"

He had no more than a few moments before the Vymaln released toxic gas from her dead body. He didn't even take time to throw on one of his protective masks because he had to get her away from Kara. Grabbing the dead alien's arm, he lifted her, slung her over his shoulder, and ran through the door of the home.

He sprinted hard and fast for the trees, drawing one more breath and holding it as he ran. With the last of his air, he heaved the Vymaln down a ravine behind the bushes where he and Kara had hidden. The alien tumbled down the steep hill, landing in a heap on a pile of dead leaves and branches at the bottom.

Gulping air into his burning lungs, Aiodhan fought dizziness until his body calmed. At least he'd been able to get the Vymaln away from Kara before she could be damaged by the gas. Walking back to the home, he shook his head in disgust at his earlier behavior.

He'd almost let himself be led away from his mission because of his lust for Kara. She was beneath him, unworthy of a Tirian—his ancient race with pride and honor in their history. He had to get his thoughts back on his job, locate Pashmar, and start the hunt for the Vymaln leader he was sent to kill.

"What happened?" Kara asked as he stepped back inside the house. Crouched next to her hound, she looked up at him, the worry plain in her eyes. "Are you okay?"

He grunted in reply. A Seeker against one Vymaln wasn't a fight—it was a training exercise. An easy one at that.

"Why didn't you let me help?"

"Help? What help could you give?"

She raised the small knife she held in her hand, the one she'd hidden beneath her pillow.

"You think that shall kill a Vymaln? That you—*little* you—shall kill a Vymaln?" Kara might be brave, but she was too small and too thin to do much except get in his way.

What in the universe had he been thinking in trying to mate with her? *A human!*

A species who'd bowed to the Vymalns and let themselves be conquered far too easily. Pashmar would strike his cheek in anger and revulsion.

Humans were weak. They were ignorant. They would be lucky to survive this occupation, and they would never be able to defeat the Vymalns without help.

Aiodhan was Tirian—a Seeker as well. A human was beneath him. *Far* beneath him. To mate with one would bring shame on all the Seekers. It was time to stop playing with this woman and complete his mission. First task, find Pashmar and see if she'd located the rebels.

After stomping to the bedroom to grab his shirt, he jerked it over his head. Sitting down, he pulled his locator node from his belt. Setting the metal disk on the table, he placed his thumb on the blue light at the center. When it recognized him, the image of the mission map beamed from the top to spread in front of him. The first thing he noticed was Pashmar's red locator symbol was much closer to his own blue symbol than he'd anticipated. When he'd crashed, he'd figured it would take him several days to locate her and the city where his target was supposed to be. Judging the length, he counted less than a day's hike from this place to where she might have already found the insurgent group that sent the distress call the Seekers had received.

Kara sat down next to him. Her scent filled his nostrils, reminding him of the beautiful fields of *allani* plants on Tirios. He tried to push aside his desire to reach out for her.

"What's that?" Her fingers touched the map of light. "Looks like a projected map, but I don't see a projector bulb. How can you do that with that small a…thing?" She nodded at the silver disk.

"Better technology than humans."

Her frown was fierce, appearing out of place on her feminine face. "Obviously. I saw that *fantastic* ship that brought you here. Nice job on that. Besides, I've seen projectors that small before."

He snorted at her. "Human pra-jec-tour do this?" He ran two fingers over his own blue symbol and spread them to expand the image. An overhead view of the house they sat in popped up.

Crossing her arms over her breasts, she said, "As a matter of fact, yeah, they can. Try Google maps. I look at satellite images all the time."

Knowing it wasn't a wise move, he had her focus on his image while he retrieved a marker from his pocket. While he lied to himself that he could simply forget her, he needed a locator to keep track of her. Such a paradox, this desire to hold her close while wanting to push her aside. "Can your…gaggle—"

Her giggle interrupted him. "It's Google. A gaggle is a group of geese."

"*Google*… Can it find you? *That* is me."

"That blue thing's you?"

"Look closer."

He'd take her by surprise when she leaned in to try to read the Tirian letters that spelled out his code name. Just as she lifted from the cushion, he jammed the marker into her backside and pulled the trigger.

"What the fuck?" Her hand flew to her behind as she scrambled to move away.

Chance started barking as he rose from where he'd curled up on a rug and ran to her side.

The glare she threw at Aiodhan as she pet her dog to quiet the animal could have melted metal. "What in the hell did you stab me with?"

Aiodhan lifted the marker to show her.

"What is that?"

"Marker."

"Why did you stab me?"

A quick touch of his fingers to the keys of the map and a new locator popped up. Prompted to enter her name, he tried to spell it best he could in the Tirian language.

"Answer me!"

"Look."

Her hand kept rubbing the place he'd injected the locator. "I don't wanna look. Tell me why you hurt me."

"Did not hurt you. Marked you, Kara. Come." He patted the seat where she'd been. "Sit. Look."

Kara didn't want to sit and look. She wanted to smack him upside his arrogant head. Not in her wildest dreams would she have believed he would hurt her, and her mind was spinning a million miles an hour to try to figure out what drug he'd injected into her. No dizziness. No fuzzy feeling. No desire to pass out.

"What was in the syringe?"

"Syringe?"

"Don't play dumb with me, Tarzan. You poked my ass with that-that-needle."

"No needle. No stitches. Marker. Come. Sit." He pointed at the image of light. "Pink. Kara is pink."

"If you don't tell me—"

Aiodhan grabbed her hand and tugged her down on the couch, then he threw his heavy arm around her shoulders. "Look."

"Fine. I'll look." Letting her gaze shift to the map, she saw a pink icon that hadn't been there before. "What am I looking at?"

"Kara."

"How can I be looking at myself?"

"*That* where Kara is." His finger slid over to the blue avatar that seemed to be joined with the pink. "Aiodhan is here also."

"That's why you injected in me? A tracking device?" It took all of her strength to not sarcastically ask him if he thought she was some kind of endangered species. "Why?"

Her alien shrugged, but the dimple was back in his cheek. Kara wasn't sure she'd ever figure him out. His moods ran hot and cold, never in between. One minute he was tenderly kissing her hand and stirring her blood so hot, she thought she'd melt. The next, he was growling at her like a bear interrupted from hibernation.

Were all aliens bipolar?

No. Vymalns only had one emotion—pissed. Even before they'd launched the takeover, their species was short-tempered and known to lash out with no provocation. Perhaps if people hadn't tried to bend over backward to accommodate them, humanity might have noticed sooner that the assholes were taking over the world.

"Why did you decide to track me?" Kara asked. She'd figured they'd be parting ways soon, and shit, but that thought made her chest hurt.

"Can find you." On that pronouncement, he shut his projector down and jammed it in one of his many pockets. He buckled on his utility belt.

"I must leave." He got to his feet and headed toward the door.

"Leave? Are you kidding me?" She hurried after him. "I'm still in my pajamas."

"You will not go."

"I won't?"

"I have mission."

"So do I. We might as well go together."

Skidding to a stop, Aiodhan faced Kara, a bit incredulous that she had the audacity to give him orders. "*You* have no mission. You are not Seeker."

"Seeker? Oh yeah, you told me that before. Is that where you come from? Seek? Is it the name of your planet?"

"I am Tirian. My planet is Tirios. Seeker is my...um...employ." While Kara's constant talk was helping him pick up her language, some words still escaped him.

"Your mean your job." She frowned. "You told me yesterday your job is to kill bug-eyes. Geesh. What a shitty way to earn a living."

He shrugged, not entirely sure what she meant. But it was time to set up a protective field around the home so he could start looking for Pashmar and scouting his target. He'd wasted enough time, although the notion of leaving Kara behind worried him. A lot.

"I'll go with you. I want to kill a few bug-eyes myself. Besides, I'm still looking for my dad and my brother. You can help me search." Kara hurried to the bedroom, stopping at the door. "Wait for me. Promise you'll wait for me."

With an annoyed grunt and a brisk nod, Aiodhan gave up the fight. Perhaps she would be useful helping him negotiate the strange terrain.

"You grab some food and stuff it in my backpack. I'll get ready to go." On that abrupt order, she shut the door.

Although he had more than enough nutrition packs for both of them, Kara wouldn't like the taste much, especially not after the Froot Loops and spaghetti and their marvelous flavor.

Grabbing her backpack, he went back to the food room and started stuffing items inside. Only a few of the metal cans because of their weight. A couple of sealed boxes and bags. Then he stumbled across something odd.

Picking up the box, he stared at the picture of what the product. He'd never seen the like. Round and dark, they looked like *calobeast* dung with white filling.

Who would eat such a thing?

"Oh, my God!" Kara yelled from behind him.

He whirled to face her, feeling his body flush hot when he caught a glimpse of her pale breasts as she buttoned her too large brown shirt.

"They have Ding Dongs! How in the hell did I miss those?" She grabbed the box from his hand and ripped it open.

His ears rang from her shouts. "You damaged my ears."

She pulled one of the pieces from the box and tore at the wrapper. The dark circle fell onto her hand, and she shoved it in her mouth, taking a huge bite. It wasn't until the bits of fluff and icing fell on her clothing that he realized it was some kind of cake.

Kara hummed as she chewed, closing her eyes as she savored what the Ding Dong. The humming sounds of pleasure brought a smile to his lips. She shoved the rest of the treat into her mouth and closed her eyes. Her cheeks were stuffed, but she still moaned as she chewed.

In his lust-addled mind, Aiodhan imagined her purring and sighing because of his touches and his kisses rather than some piece of cake. His *kull* hardened, a state he found it in far too often when Kara was near.

Opening her eyes, she smiled at him. Bits of the Ding Dong clung to her lips. Instead of kissing them away as he desired, he gently brushed them off.

"Have one," she said when his hand dropped away.

She pulled two more from the box, holding one as she extended the other to him. Not entirely sure if this treat would taste like Tirian cake, he hesitated.

"They're wonderful. Try one," she insisted.

Drawing his lips into a thin line, he took the Ding Dong. They both unwrapped the dark cakes, Kara taking more time to eat this one. She bit into it, then tunneled her tongue inside to retrieve the white fluff. As he watched, all he could imagine was the pleasure that tongue could give him. His rock-hard erection twitched in response, making him groan in frustration.

Kara took another big bite. Through a full mouth, she said, "Go on. Try it."

Aiodhan cast the wrapping away and took a hesitant taste. Just as with the Froot Loops, the flavor burst in his mouth. He'd never experienced the like, but he not only *wanted* to taste more, he *needed* to. He shoved the rest of the Ding Dong in his mouth, wanting to shout the joy the flavor gave him.

Her smug smile made him smile in return. She picked up her backpack and pushed the box inside even though the pack was now almost too full to fasten closed. "Sure not leaving the rest of those behind, even if they're a little stale."

"Stale?"

She brushed her fingertips over his mouth, lingering a bit longer than probably necessary to stroke his lips.

He needed every ounce of his self-control to not hold her wrist and kiss her palm to initiate the mating ritual. Instead, he took a deep breath and let it out in a sigh.

"Stale," she said. "Old. Not fresh."

Aiodhan nodded. If Ding Dongs tasted that good when old, they had to be close to perfect when fresh. "We must go."

As he walked to the door, he stopped when he saw Kara standing in the middle of the big room.

"I'll miss this place," she said.

"I protect it."

Her beautiful eyes found his. "Protect it?"

Fetching his locator, he held it up to show her. "Cloaking field. The Vymaln not know it is here."

"Really?"

Did she have to question everything he said? He growled low in his throat to let her know he was displeased.

"Fine. Whatever. It'll be nice to have a place to come back to." With a smile, she patted her thigh, and her animal obediently came to her. "C'mon, Chance. Time to get moving again."

Chapter Five

Kara stopped when they reached the summit of the foothill overlooking Milestone. "There it is." She nodded at the small town now in view, albeit from a great enough distance she could hardly make out individual buildings. "Milestone. The internment camp's on the far side of the city between here and Whispering Lake. Some old federal prison they adapted."

She'd wanted to see her home again, but the melancholy she knew would accompany that event arrived with a force she hadn't expected. Tears welled in her eyes, but she sniffed them back. Crying wouldn't fix a goddamn thing. Besides, anger was easier for her to deal with, and that rage she directed entirely at the bug-eyes.

She straightened her spine. Milestone wasn't her home anymore. She had no home, not since those bastards arrived.

Aiodhan stared into the distance, and she wondered what was tumbling through his mind. Following him had probably been the wrong choice. He had, after all, said she could stay at the cabin and that she'd be safe there. She and Chance could have rested for a while with someplace warm to sleep, decent food to eat—at least for a short while—and running water. So why in the devil had she trailed after this...*Seeker?*

Only one answer came. She liked him.

No. No way.

Her heart couldn't be involved. Not so soon. Aliens couldn't be trusted. She, and the rest of the human race, had learned that lesson the hard way.

She chose to ignore the little voice in her head that screamed she was wallowing in denial.

"I wonder if my father and my brother are close."

The words were out before Kara could stop them. After so long being alone, she'd developed a bad habit of thinking aloud, needing the comfort of a voice—even her own—to banish the crushing loneliness.

"Tell me of your family," Aiodhan said in a soothing voice.

"Not much to tell."

She fought a battle of how much to reveal to him. Part of her wanted to lean on his broad shoulder and let him help her bear some of the grief. Another part didn't want to dredge up all the hurtful memories, not only of how close she'd been to her family, but the recollections of how Kevin and her dad had been captured.

A warm hand cupped her cheek, nudging her face up until she stared into his gray eyes. The sight of them wasn't unnerving any longer. If she

39

was honest with herself, she'd admit how much she liked looking into them. "You do not want to tell me."

She shrugged and tried to turn away.

His thumb and finger gripped her chin. "Tell me."

How easy it would be to let him take away her responsibilities and her burdens, but Kara had no idea if he wanted to help or even how long he planned to stay. Yes, he'd said he was on a mission to kill Vymalns, but that didn't mean he was going to be in Montana for the whole time he was on Earth. Besides, he didn't even know what her father or brother looked like. How could one man, even one as powerful as Aiodhan, go up against an entire squad of the bug-eyes to get into the camp. "I don't want to talk about it. Okay?"

His eyes narrowed before his hand dropped away. "For now."

Needing to put some distance between them, she glanced back at the trees. "We should find someplace to camp tonight."

Aiodhan stared up at the sun for moment. "A few hours before dark."

"Yeah, but once it gets dark, it'll be *really* dark out here. Only a crescent moon tonight, and I didn't find any flashlights in the cabin. If we don't scout out someplace now, we might have trouble finding a place later." Without waiting for him to agree, she hiked back toward the woods. Thankfully, his footfalls sounded behind her.

Far enough to put Milestone out of her sight and mind, Kara found the perfect spot for the night. While there would be no roof over their heads and no soft mattress, the place was isolated and had already been cleared into a makeshift campsite. Judging from the mild growth of flora and fauna, it hadn't been used in a while. There was a small rock pit for a fire, and a felled tree, cleared of all branches, that had been used as a seat close to the pit.

"This'll do," she said.

Aiodhan grunted before picking up several handfuls of twigs and dried leaves. He tossed the kindling in the pit before he scavenged around.

"Looking for firewood?"

His response was another grunt. She took it as a *yes* and left him to that job. He wasn't gone long before he returned with more than enough wood to keep them warm for the night.

She hadn't taken the time to search through her backpack to see what her alien had grabbed that might make a good supper. Taking a seat on the log, she set the pack down, unzipped it, and rummaged around. Chance flopped down at her feet. He'd disappeared when she'd stopped at the campsite, and since his jowls were wet, that meant he'd found a water source close. Good thing because she needed to refill her water bottles.

"I hunt," Aiodhan announced as he stacked the wood he's gathered in the pit. "I find food."

"No need." She jerked out a can of beef stew. "We can have this."

"Save it. Could need later. I hunt now." He pulled the tool he'd used to cut her handcuffs out of his pouch, flicked the trigger, and lit the fire. The kindling caught flame, and the sweet smell of burning leaves filled the air. "I hunt; you cook."

"Sure thing, Tarzan." Not that she had a lot of confidence he'd catch anything. The guy only had his cutting tool and an impressive knife, although he seemed to find all sorts of remarkable things in the pockets of his cargo pants and that utility belt. Did he plan to catch an animal with his bare hands or throw his knife at it? "You find me something to cook, and I'll be happy to cook it." She couldn't hide the laughter in her voice.

"You doubt."

"No, I don't." She hoped he couldn't see through the lie.

"You *do.* You doubt Aiodhan." Fisting his hands against his hips, he stood in front of her and glared down with eyes as gray as thunderstorm clouds.

"Okay. Fine. I don't think you'll catch anything. Look around you. Everything you could catch that we could eat is either small and lightning fast or big and lightning fast. What did you plan to shoot some animal with?"

"No need to shoot. I need no gun for hunt."

"Are you joking?"

"Not being funny ha ha." He reached one of his hands out to her. "Kara come to watch hunt. See what I can do."

Aiodhan expected her to wave him off. Females, even Seekers, didn't enjoy hunting animals. While they could eat his nutrition packs or the food he'd stuffed into her pack, it would be better to save those for times when they had nothing else. Since he'd seen more than a few species of wildlife in the area, he'd capture a couple, skin them, and roast them over the fire. Kara didn't know how fast he could move or how he'd been trained. The amusement in her expression and her voice would disappear when he brought back their meal.

But she didn't wave him off. She got to her feet and swept out her arm in invitation. "Let's go."

"You follow?"

"I follow."

Staring at her in surprise for a moment, Aiodhan nodded. "You must be quiet."

"I'll be quiet."

He seriously doubted that. Although he loved her non-stop talking, the wealth of words would frighten away his prey. "Kara *never* quiet."

Her pouty lip made him smile. She motioned to her dog. "Stay, Chance. Stay."

Leading the way into the thicker trees, he tried to dismiss her from his mind and began the hunt for their meal.

* * *

"Give up?" Kara asked.

After an hour, Aiodhan wasn't ready to surrender, although each time she spoke, he had to resist the urge to put his hand over her mouth. He'd lost count of how many small, furry animals had scurried to safety whenever she asked a question or made a comment. "Never give up."

"We could just have the rest of the Ding Dongs for supper."

She'd already suggested that a dozen times, and while he loved the taste of the things, they wouldn't do much to fuel their bodies. He'd meant to ask her what the ingredients were so he could try to make them himself one day, but as usual, his question went unasked.

No wonder Pashmar called him *Quiet One* all the time. Thousands of thoughts and questions shot through his mind, like stars on their dying trek across the vastness of space. But he seldom voiced any of them, preferring to keep them private and silent to all but his own mind. He'd probably spoken more words to Kara since he'd met her than he'd said to Pashmar in years.

Something about Kara made Aiodhan lower his guards, all the walls that kept him isolated from others. He hadn't decided if that was a good change or a bad one. Seekers were supposed to be independent, expecting and adapting to being downright lonely. He'd been taught to depend on himself and no one else—with the exception of another Seeker when they worked together, which wasn't often. Even then, he'd preferred solo missions above all others.

So why the need to share his thoughts with Kara the way she constantly shared hers with him?

"Give up?" she asked again.

The smirk on her face made him itch to grab her and kiss her simply to remove it. The only thing stopping him was that he feared once he touched her, he'd never be able to stop.

"Hush, Kara."

She folded her arms over her breasts and frowned at him. "Don't blame me that you haven't caught anything."

"You are too full of words."

"Like I haven't heard *that* a bazillion times before."

"Ba-zill-yon? What is ba-zill-yon?"

Heaving a sigh, she shook her head and looked around the trees for a moment before letting her gaze fall on him again. "I'm heading back to camp. I need to fill my water bottles and start cooking something to eat. Something from a can."

Her laughter led him like a leash, and Aiodhan was helpless to resist. She stepped over a fallen log into some thicker branches and overgrowth before she turned around to talk to him. Again.

Focused on her beautiful face as he prepared to scold her again, he saw the trip wire a split-second too late. He leapt for her, catching her arm to try to drag her back from the enormous net rapidly closing as it dragged up from the forest floor. "Kara! No!"

The sound of ropes being whipped echoed through the trees as the thick net rose all around them from the dried leaves. Before he could move them out of the way, they were neatly captured and dangling helplessly in mid-air.

The twine of the net tugged around them, so tightly her body was crushed against his, and he tried to shift so that he wasn't hurting her. She'd cried out, but the sound was more of shock and surprise than pain. The only thing he managed to do as he attempted to move was to set them swinging in their cocoon of a prison. The sway and rotation made his stomach lurch as it often did when he first blasted off in a transport.

"Aiodhan?"

"Yes, Kara?"

"Know what?"

He sighed. "No. What?"

"I think I might've found a trap."

In all the missions he'd been on, he'd never felt like laughing. Not once. But Kara's words, moreover her disgruntled tone, made him want to let out a hearty chuckle.

"I think Kara is correct. Not Vymaln, I think." This kind of rudimentary trap wasn't their style.

"You mean humans sprung this net? You think it might be humans trying to catch bug-eyes?"

He grunted in response since she couldn't see him nod.

The net dug into his face, and one of his arms was held firmly against his chest while the other twisted painfully against his side. Her hands were pressed against his buttocks, and her face rubbed against the back of his thigh. Damn if he didn't want her despite their predicament. How could he possibly be thinking about mating when they might very well be in mortal danger?

"Bet you wished we ate those Ding Dongs for dinner now, don't ya?" The giggle in her voice brought a smile to his lips.

So much of what Aiodhan had heard about humans was wrong. Dead wrong. They were supposed to be inferior, both physically and mentally. But Kara was showing him she was anything but inferior. Her intelligence rivaled his own, and he'd seen her display the kind of courage he'd only found in his own species. They were hanging from a net—perhaps falling into the hands of someone who meant them harm— and she was making one of her jokes to try to hide her fear.

"How are we going to get down?" she asked.

Since he was held too snug to move, he couldn't even shrug. When he opened his mouth to reply, he quickly closed it again as the sound of several people running toward them echoed through the clearing. "Stay quiet, Kara," he whispered.

"Why do I have to stay quiet?"

"Someone coming." How he'd defend her, he had no idea.

But he vowed to protect her with his life.

A human man was the first to make it through the trees. He let out a loud whoop as he put the strap of a rifle over his shoulder. Aiodhan could see him and the weapon clearly until the stupid net rotated.

"Know him?" he whispered to Kara.

Her face brushed against his leg again. "All I can see is your ass."

"We got two of 'em," a deep voice shouted from below them. "Humans, not lizards."

Lizards. An apt term for Vymalns.

Aiodhan waited impatiently as the net kept slowly spinning so he could see his new enemy and figure out the best way to neutralize him. As the man came back into view, Aiodhan got a good look at the impressive weapon before he took the precious time to notice the man holding it.

Probably a few hands shorter than his own height. Thin, but well-muscled. Light brown hair. Dark eyes. He carried a repeating gun. *An assault rifle*, Aiodhan had learned when the Seekers had been briefed on Earth's weaponry.

Trying to count how many others approached, it was hard to keep focus when Kara's hands and face kept touching him so intimately. "Stop."

"Stop what?" she asked.

As if he could order her to stop touching him when they were bound so tightly together.

By the time the net had turned enough for him to be able to see their captor again, he'd been joined by three others, all males. That boded ill for Kara. Thoughts of the horrible ways these men could abuse her

44

blocked out his training as blood lust flowed through him, something he'd never experienced before.

Oh, he'd heard about the blood lust—a problem many Tirian males experienced when they felt someone, especially another male, was threatening their mates. The Tirian could become so enraged, nothing would bring an end to his anger except the utter defeat or even the death of the rival.

Now was definitely not the time to experience it, nor had he ever expected to think of a human as his mate. If he didn't regain some control, he would only make their situation worse by trying to challenge four men at once. He couldn't protect Kara if he was dead.

Taking deep breaths, he reached for some discipline. She helped him find a thread of control without even knowing it as her hands stroked his buttocks before slipping into his back pockets and holding on tight. "Don't leave me."

Her whispered fears calmed him. He'd find a way to protect her. "Never. I will *never* leave you, Kara."

"Cut them down," the voice ordered. "Let's see what we've got."

Someone had crawled up into the trees, and when Aiodhan realized they were about to plummet to the ground, he waited until he felt the netting give. Twisting, he grabbed Kara, pressing her hard against him so his body absorbed the brunt of the fall.

The air was forced from his lungs, exploding in a loud *oof* when they slammed into the forest floor. Kara pushed up, staring down at him, the concern plain in her eyes before hands clutched her arms and jerked her away.

Aiodhan got to his feet and found the barrel of the assault rifle staring him in the face as a man with dark hair glared at him. "Well, well. What have we here?"

A rumbling growl rose from Aiodhan's chest as he tried to follow Kara with his gaze. The man with brown hair held her at arm's length, his eyes wide with surprise and shock. Then he saw that her eyes held the same expression.

"Kara?" The man's voice was strained as if something was choking him.

"Kevin?" A few heartbeats later, tears began to roll down her cheeks. "Kevin!"

Chapter Six

The man slung his gun strap over his shoulder and opened his arms to Kara. She hurried to him, throwing herself into the embrace of *Kevin*— the same name she'd called out in her dreams. That man now held her close as she pressed kisses to his cheek.

Aiodhan reacted on primitive instinct. Ignoring the danger to himself, he knocked the rifle aside and marched to Kara. Snaking one arm around her waist, he pulled his lips back to bare his teeth. He wrenched Kara away from Kevin and shoved her behind his back, despite her grumbling and weakly trying to resist him. A menacing snarl fell from his lips as he faced his rival with no weapon. He'd bring Kevin down with his bare hands since Intel had told the Seekers that human guns were far from reliable and the humans who wielded them were usually poorly trained.

No, this was a fight for Kara—male to male—to see who could claim her. He sure didn't want her to be collateral damage in the process.

This was ridiculous, really. A folly on his part. He barely knew Kara. Yet he'd understood—the instant Kevin had put his hands on her, Aiodhan had *known* she was his mate.

Nothing and no one was going to take her away from him now. Or ever.

"Who the hell are you?" Kevin asked as he grabbed for his gun.

"He's Aiodhan," Kara said. She tried to skirt around him.

He refused to let her, pushing her behind him again.

"Stop doing that!" A hard pinch on his arm was her retaliation, making his lips twitch into a hesitant smile that he banished. With a shake of his head to earn her obedience, he focused on Kevin and forced aside his pleasure at her courage.

"A-o-what?" Kevin pointed the gun at him, easing his finger toward the firing mechanism.

"Put gun down," Aiodhan ordered. "Then we fight for Kara."

Even a human had to understand this was between them alone and wouldn't be stupid enough to risk injuring Kara or the others. Aiodhan kept a wary eye on the other three men. Each now held their weapons ready, which meant not only was he in their line of fire, so was Kara.

"No guns. A fight between us." He pounded his chest with his fist, then he held it out toward Kevin. "Just *us*. Yes?"

Kevin fired Aiodhan a fierce frown. "Fight you for Kara? What's *that* supposed to mean?" He leaned to the side, trying to get her attention. "Kara? What in the hell is going on here?"

When she tried to step around him again, Aiodhan glared over his

46

shoulder at her. "Stay there. Fight over soon."

"No!" She stomped her foot. "No fighting."

Since she didn't understand, not surprising since she was not only a female but a human, he tried to explain. "I fight for you. You are mine." Surely she'd understand that. What was the stupid word he needed? "Mate. Aiodhan's mate."

"Mate?" Kevin bellowed the word. "Your *mate?* Kara, what the hell?"

"Mate?" Kara's voice blended with Kevin's. "What are you— Aiodhan, so help me God, you try to shove me behind you again and I'll—"

"Stay!"

There simply wasn't time to talk to her now. He'd try to explain it after he knocked Kevin down enough times he'd be unable to get back up. He didn't want to kill the man, but he had to make sure Kevin understood Kara was off limits. Forever.

His rival's reddening face meant he grew angrier by the minute, something Aiodhan could exploit in the battle. It was time to fight for the right to claim her, and he had every intention of winning.

"Don't you dare tell me to stay like some stupid animal." Her hands fisted in the back of his shirt as he took a step toward Kevin, and she tried unsuccessfully to drag him back. Her slight weight couldn't even slow him.

Aiodhan focused on his opponent. "Put weapon down. We fight. Kara is mine." He glared at the other three men. "This fight is us only." He thumped this chest again before pointing at Kevin. "A mate's right."

"Aiodhan, *please.*" The fear in Kara's voice made him turn to face her. Her dark, beautiful eyes were wide.

He cupped her cheek in his palm, amazed at how small and delicate she seemed. His hand all but swallowed her face. She didn't rub her cheek against his palm as she did each time he'd touched her before. "Kara?"

"I won't let you hurt my brother."

Brother?

The word cut right through the haze of his fury. Aiodhan took a moment to finally get a good long look at the man he'd been willing to challenge—even kill—to keep Kara at his side. Same brown hair. Same brown eyes.

And the same smug grin.

This time, when she stepped around him, Aiodhan allowed her to return to her brother. Kevin slung his weapon back over his shoulder and hugged Kara tightly again. While Aiodhan still didn't like seeing another man, even a relative, touch her, he tamped down the blood lust and tried to make sense of what had just happened.

He'd declared Kara to be his mate. In that moment when he'd seen her in Kevin's arms, Aiodhan had known with a clarity that amazed him that he would never let her go.

What was wrong with him? She was a human.

Ah, but what a human! Kara was full of life, courage, and compassion. She was smart. She was a survivor. She was a true Seeker's mate.

His mate.

As she talked softly with her brother, Kara couldn't stop turning to glance back at Aiodhan. Her heart was so full of joy to see Kevin again and to know he was safe and not in that horrific work camp—or worse had been killed by a bug-eye. She wanted to hear all he knew about their father. Yet as she tried to absorb what he was saying, her mind kept returning to Aiodhan's words that warmed her with feelings she wasn't ready to deal with.

"You are mine."

He'd only meant to protect her from Kevin and his men. He'd tossed the word "mate" around, but it had to have been a ruse, a way to convince them that he would protect her despite being outnumbered and unarmed. Besides, his English sucked, even if he was picking it up far more rapidly than she'd ever anticipated. No, he didn't know what "mate" truly meant.

And yet…

"Kara?" Until Kevin put his hand on her arm and turned her to face him, she hadn't realized that she'd lost herself in staring at Aiodhan. "What's wrong with you?"

"I'm fine. I thought those bastards got both you and Daddy, but you got away. Thank God." She looked around, so anxious to see her father again she could barely contain her feelings. If Kevin got away, her father had to have been able to get free as well. "Where's Dad? Isn't he with you?"

"That's what I was trying to tell you. He's not here."

Her stomach fell to her feet. "Is he— He's still— Did they…" She couldn't even bring herself to ask the question haunting her. Her father had to be okay. He just had to be.

"He's alive."

"Really?"

"Really. I saw him two days ago. He's still in the IC."

"IC?"

"Internment camp. We're gonna get him out, Kara. We're trying to find a way to save all of them. We just have to wait for the right time."

Wait. Her least favorite word, but it seemed like that was all she'd done since the Vymalns had taken over. *Wait.*

"Why can't we storm the place?" She stared at his assault rifle. "You guys are armed to the teeth. We can blast our way in."

"No go," Kevin replied. "Guns slow 'em down, but they sure don't stop 'em. Even if we could kill enough of them to get inside, there's that wonderful gas they put off—"

"Gas?"

"Found out that right after you kill 'em, their bodies release some kind of toxic gas, kinda like mustard gas."

She shifted her gaze to Aiodhan. "That's why you wouldn't let me get the key for the handcuffs."

"Handcuffs?" her brother said, nearly choking on the word. "What *handcuffs?*"

Ignoring Kevin, she focused on her alien. "And the bug-eye back at the cabin. You ran out of the house with it. You knew?"

"I knew," he replied.

"Thank you."

Aiodhan arched a dark eyebrow.

"For protecting me."

Kevin glared at her. "What in hell are you talking about? What handcuffs? What bug-eye?"

"Long story." She dismissed going into it now with a wave of her hand. "I still think we should go after Dad now."

Kevin nodded at the crowd that had gathered. "Look, Kara, we're all free. Even after all this time, we're still free. A couple of us even got out of the IC. We'll get everyone else outta there too. Soon. We just have to do some more watching and a helluva lot more planning."

All her fear and anger rushed to the fore, forcing her to grab his down vest. She wanted to shake some sense into him. What could he have been thinking? She'd never leave her father to suffer. *Never!* "But-but-how could you leave him there? Why didn't you get him out too?"

"I didn't have time. It was spur of the moment, and Dad wasn't close. Bill, Clay, and I were on crop detail. We tackled and beat one of the lizards and ran for our lives. We couldn't help anyone else. Not then."

She wanted to slap his face. How could he leave their father behind with those bastards? "Then go back and get him now."

"Kara," Aiodhan said. His hands settled on her shoulders. "They cannot."

Anger clouded her vision, but she whirled to face him. "The hell they can't! They have guns. They can kill those fucking bug-eyes and save him."

The arrogant shake of his head made her anger explode into red-hot rage. She clenched her hands into fists and pounded them against his chest.

Aiodhan didn't even flinch. His sympathetic expression only made her lose what tendrils of self-control remained.

Yes, she was being stupid by thinking about charging into the camp, but her father was there. Why couldn't Aiodhan understand? Why couldn't any of them understand? He wouldn't be there if it wasn't for her. It was all her fault.

Kara hadn't realized she was crying until her alien captured her wrists with one hand and reached up with the other to brush tears off her cheek. She choked back the rest of the irate tears and jammed down the desire to weep in earnest, something she hadn't done since the day her father had been taken. Crying wouldn't bring him back or save him from the Vymalns. Only anger could keep her strong so she could do what needed to be done.

"Fine," she said.

The concession was necessary. For now. She'd watch these new men, find out where they kept the weapons, and come up with her own plan to rescue her father. And she'd do it by herself if she had to.

Aiodhan's eyes searched her, and he must have seen her submission because he nodded. "Soon."

His whispered promise wrapped around her heart, and she trusted him to help her when the time was right. Although that still wouldn't stop her from finding a way on her own if need be.

Kevin cleared his throat a little too loudly. "Kara, you still haven't answered my question. Who *is* this guy?"

"His name's Aiodhan. He helped rescue me from a bug-eye that found me when I came down from the mountains to look for food."

"Helped rescue?" Kevin asked. "Either he rescued you or he didn't."

She hated admitting she'd needed Aiodhan's help. But she had. "Fine. He rescued me. Happy now?"

Kevin's grin said he was.

Kara put two fingers to her lips and whistled loud and long, knowing Chance would find her. Since he hadn't come when they were caught in the trap, he was probably out hunting for his own dinner. Her own rumbling stomach was starting to get annoying enough to have to deal with soon. She'd have to find her way back to where she'd left the damn Ding Dongs in her backpack because she needed chocolate desperately.

Her brother looked Aiodhan over. Since the sun had almost set, she hoped he wouldn't be able to focus on Aiodhan's unusual eyes. The difference in them was hard to notice unless a person was close, and she didn't think Kevin intended to get quite as near to him as she had. Plus guys weren't always the most observant. When the sun came back up, she'd pull her RayBans out of her pack and make Aiodhan wear them. Another reason to go back to the campsite.

"C'mon," Kevin said, inclining his head toward the trees. "Let's go back to our camp and get this all figured out."

"I need to get my stuff first."

"Where's that?"

"Not far. Just a few minutes away. We left a fire burning, too. Need to douse it."

"Kara." Aiodhan's hand was on her shoulder. "I cannot go. I must leave now. My mission."

Her heart seized. At that moment, she didn't give a shit about his mission, regardless of how important it might be. He couldn't leave her. She needed him, even though admitting it was tantamount to swallowing a bitter medicine. Somehow, she had to convince him to stay until she could sort through her tumbling emotions.

"I know. I know. Maybe these guys can help you. They've got weapons. They obviously know a lot about fighting bug-eyes." She marched back toward the clearing where she'd left her things, giving Aiodhan and Kevin no choice but to follow.

Aiodhan had never told her explicitly what his mission was, but it had to involve killing more Vymalns, so it seemed silly for them to part ways now. Killing bug-eyes was fine with her. Besides, the more time he spent with her, the better chance she had of convincing him to help her rescue her father. She had no doubt he had the skill, especially after seeing him so easily kill the Vymaln that had stunned her and the one that had come into the cabin.

Just who do you think you're fooling, Kara?

Sure, she might believe Aiodhan could help free her father, but she had another much more personal motive. One she was reluctant to admit to herself, especially after he'd declared her his mate. She'd bury that reason deep for now and focus all her energy on figuring out what her brother was doing with these guys and just how much firepower his group had. And, of course, how to use that to help rescue her father.

When they reached the clearing, Aiodhan helped her put the pack on her back while Kevin and the other men kicked dirt on the fire until they smothered it. Chance came bounding into the clearing, looking fat and sassy. She didn't want to know what he'd eaten. He stood at her side, staring at the new people. Thankfully, he didn't start barking.

"Kara?" Kevin asked. "We need to get back to home base. You two are coming, right?"

Aiodhan stood in front of her, his mouth hard. She searched his gray

51

eyes, watching them turn darker as he stared at her mouth as if he wanted to kiss her. While she wanted him to go right ahead, she didn't figure Kevin or his buddies needed to see any more evidence of the attraction between her and her alien. He'd already had the earlier show. No doubt, he'd be getting her alone later to play twenty questions. She had more than enough of her own to fire back at him. Right now, there was only one that mattered.

"Are you leaving me?" Kara kept her voice a whisper, waiting to see if anything Aiodhan said could reveal whether any true feelings hid behind his ferocious protection of her. Dumb though it was, she wanted that desperately, no matter how odd that was after such a short time together.

"Please stay." The words came out a breathless plea, the closest thing to begging she'd ever done her life.

Time seemed to stand still.

This was one of those moments in her life she knew would be so important that nothing would ever be the same after. Whatever choice Aiodhan made, her life would then be set upon a path she could never turn back from.

Those unusual eyes revealed nothing, nor did the stiff expression on his face and the rigid stance he took. Seconds clicked by at a maddeningly slow pace before he let out a long breath. "We go now."

Her heart slammed in her chest. He wasn't leaving her. She had to be sure. "We?"

With a growl, he grabbed her hand and dragged her toward Kevin.

Her brother stared at their joined hands for a moment, fixed his mouth into a frown, and then turned to march into the shelter of the trees.

* * *

For humans, they'd managed to create a functional military camp, making Aiodhan wonder if this was the group Pashmar was sent to seek.

Tents were covered with proper camouflage so that any of the Vymaln scouts would have difficulty seeing them from the air. He tried to take a head count, estimating how many people were in the tents, and decided the force numbered near thirty. All were men, from what he could see so far. Every single one who saw Kara stopped to stare.

That didn't bode well. She would never understand the danger she faced here, and he'd have his hands full trying to protect her. If this group hadn't included her brother, Aiodhan would have dragged her as far away from them as he could.

About to suggest that he take Kara back to the cabin he'd protected, he stopped when a man came out of a small tent. Tall. Muscular. Alpha, for sure. When the man tossed the returning group a fierce frown and strode toward them, Aiodhan pegged him as the leader of the unit.

When he stopped in front of Kevin, he glared down at him, glanced to Kara, and then drilled Kevin with intense and intelligent blue eyes. "A refugee? Shit, Kevin. What in the fuck were you thinking bringing a woman refugee here?"

Kevin winced at the shouts being bellowed in his face, but he stood his ground—not surprising since Kara had shown the same kind of bravery.

"She's my sister, Bill." Kevin turned to her. "Kara, this is Bill Carson."

Hands on his hips, Bill looked over to her again. Aiodhan waited for him to notice that she wasn't the only one who Kevin had dragged back to the camp. Then he waited some more because this Bill didn't seem to want to take his attention away from Kara. She shifted her weight between her feet as a flush rose from her neck to her face, especially when Bill seemed to stare at her breasts.

She dragged the zipper of her thick vest up, something Aiodhan had considered doing simply to keep other men from seeing her shape. After what seemed like far too long, Aiodhan couldn't stop from growling like an angry animal when the blood lust rose again.

The sound, together with a similar noise coming from Chance, seemed to draw Bill out of whatever had kept him glued to Kara, and he shifted his gaze to Aiodhan. "Who are you?"

"He's Aiodhan." She took a step in front of him.

Aiodhan tried to drag her behind him. Her responding growl was every bit as fierce as his had been. She drew her tiny foot back and kicked him in the shin. Then she held his arm while she rubbed her abused toes. How odd that he'd let himself smile more in the time he'd been with Kara than he had the rest of his adult life. The woman certainly had the ability to not only excite him but amuse him. A rare talent.

"You broke my toes," she grumbled. Gingerly putting her foot on the ground, she scowled at him. Had the other men not been near, he would have been tempted to kiss the frown right off her face.

"*You* broke toes," Aiodhan countered. Then he dismissed her and turned to face Bill, who had been watching them closely through the whole exchange. His hands were still on his hips, but the anger in his face had faded, probably because of watching Kara try to intimidate a man so much larger than herself.

"She can't stay long, Kevin," Bill said. "You know why."

"No," Kevin insisted. "I don't know why. She's my sister. And she's a nurse. We could use her help."

Bill dropped his hands to his sides and took a few steps closer to Kara. "A nurse? You're a nurse?"

53

"Yeah, I'm a—"

Grabbing her hand, he stomped away, dragging Kara behind him despite the insistent barks from Chance. "I need you."

Aiodhan gave the dog a harsh command. "Stay." Then he hurried after them, snarling as he ripped her hand away from Bill's and put his body between them. "Not take Kara."

"Aiodhan..." Her fingers wrapped around his upper arm. "It's okay, I think—"

"Hush, Kara." He stared at Bill, hoping he'd make a move for Kara again so he had an excuse to pound him to a bloody pulp.

"I need her help," Bill insisted.

Folding his arms over his chest, Aiodhan arched an eyebrow and waited for an explanation.

"Someone's sick, right?" Kara said.

Bill nodded but didn't explain.

As Kara tried to move, Aiodhan's arm shot out to hold her back. Damn, but this woman needed to learn to obey him like a good mate should.

"I have to go if someone's sick."

"Who?" he asked, still not convinced Kara was needed. It might be a diversion to get her alone and vulnerable. What was wrong with the males on this planet? He was clearly offering her his protection, and even though this Bill person hadn't been there when Aiodhan claimed her as his mate, he should have recognized the way Aiodhan treated Kara that there was a bond between them.

His own fault for forgetting these humans didn't follow the same customs as Tirians. The men here weren't known for respecting their women. They often created children without any bonding and then abandoned those children. The women had to sacrifice much to raise those offspring on their own. In his eyes, that made them nothing more than savages. There was no way he'd leave Kara to that kind of fate, which was one of the reasons he'd declared for her. She deserved a mate who would honor her and any children they shared. The thought of her being with any other man turned his stomach and made the blood lust flare to an inferno.

"Who?" Aiodhan demanded again when Bill only stood there, throwing that angry stare at him. "Who needs Kara?"

"I didn't know anyone was hurt," Kevin added. "Did the other patrol stumble on some trouble? I thought the lizards had given up their patrols in this area."

Bill shook his head, taking off his brown cap before raking his fingers through his blond hair. Then he set the cap back on his head. "There's someone in my tent."

With knit brows, Kevin took a step closer. "In your tent? Someone's in your tent? But-but-I thought you were alone."

So Bill was hiding something from the men he led.

The three men who'd followed them to the camp now stepped forward as well, confusion and a touch of anger seeming to radiate around them like mist. Their murmurs grew louder.

"My sister!" Bill shouted. "My sister's in my tent!"

Quiet descended on the group as furtive glances flew from man to man. Kevin spoke first. "Your sister? Thought you didn't know where—"

"I found her while you were gone."

"What do you mean, found her?" one of the other men asked. "What in the hell are you talking about, Bill? How could you *find* her while we were on patrol?"

With a weighty sigh, he put his hands back on his hips. "I rescued her from the IC."

Chapter Seven

Kara gasped and popped out from behind Aiodhan. If Bill could rescue his sister, he could help smuggle out her father, too. "You got her from the camp? How?"

Kevin's hands were clenched at his side. "We agreed that no one went in alone. And definitely not yet."

Not only was her brother furious, but angry glares were coming from all the men surrounding them. She couldn't understand why everyone was so pissed that Bill had found a way to breach the Vymalns' security. They should be *thanking* him.

Bill shrugged, seeming cool and calm, which was why she'd assumed he was leading this group. That, and the fact everyone naturally deferred to him, even after he'd done something that angered them all.

"The opportunity presented itself, so I took it," he said in a soft voice that ironically also held a hint of steel. "Someone had to go first. Every one of you would have done the same if you saw your sister that close. Now we know there's a weakness in their perimeter, and we can exploit it. We just have to plan wisely to get out as many as we can before the lizards catch on."

Kevin's frown was fierce. He'd hardened in their time apart. He looked older, too, as lines creased the corners of his eyes. "You could have brought every one of those bastards right to us. You've told us that a thousand times. Jesus, Bill. Did you even take anyone with you? What if they'd grabbed you, too?"

"I had to do this alone." On that last word on the subject, Bill let his gaze settle on Kara again. "She's sick. I need you. C'mon." He dragged her toward a tent.

Figuring Aiodhan would be angry that Bill was pulling her away, she looked over her shoulder to give him a few reassuring words. "I need to help her."

Instead of trying to stop her, he fell in step behind. Since she knew nothing about Bill and was a little unnerved by the men's constant stares, she was grateful for Aiodhan's comforting presence. He was taller and more muscular than anyone else in the camp, and she had no doubt he'd intimidate most of them—guns or not. He'd sure intimidated her dog. The lab hadn't moved a muscle since his clipped command to stay.

Bill opened the flap to the olive-drab tent. "She's in here, on my cot."

A strong hand gripped her arm, holding her back. "Me first." Aiodhan moved past her, entering the tent ahead of them. After only a moment, he shouted, "Come, Kara."

Her eyes were already used to the dark now that the sun had set, so she didn't have to wait for them to adjust, especially since a bit of light glowed from a small lantern resting on a crate next to a military cot. Kara hurried to the person lying there.

The nurse in her kicked into gear as she assessed her new patient. Female. Probably nineteen or twenty years old. Pale and a little malnourished. Her breathing was steady, and a strong pulse beat beneath Kara's fingertips as she pressed them to the young woman's wrist. "How long has she been out?"

The girl stirred. "I'm not out. I was asleep." She jerked her arm back and groaned as she tried to sit up on the cot. Kara helped her, pleased she didn't try to push her away. "Who are you?" She considered Kara with big, blue eyes that seemed almost too large for her thin face.

"I'm Kara Michaels. I'm a nurse." A quick press of the back of her hand to her patient's forehead revealed no fever. The girl's movements were slow, but they were fluid enough that she obviously wasn't injured.

Those pretty eyes narrowed at Bill. "I don't need a nurse. I told you, I'm fine, so you can quit being the overprotective big brother."

"You don't look fine, sis," he replied. "You look like hell."

"Yeah, well, you're not exactly drop dead gorgeous anymore, either. Things are rough all around." She swung her legs over the side of the bed but didn't try to stand.

"You okay?" Kara asked. "Dizzy? Nauseated?"

She shook her head.

"What's your name?"

"Julie." When she tried to stand, Kara grasped her upper arm to help steady her. As soon as she was sure Julie was able to stand, she turned her loose.

"You shouldn't be up." Bill strode over to stare down at his petite sister.

"Stop worrying. I'm fine. If I were back in Lizard Prison, they'd still have me working in the fields."

"Fields? What do you mean fields?" The questions bubbled out of Kara like champagne after the cork was released. "How many people worked there? What were you doing?"

"Easy," Bill said. "Give her some space."

"We were doing what we've always done this time of year," Julie replied. "Being farmers and harvesting. Except we were doing it for *them.*"

"Why?" Kara figured since Julie seemed to be in decent health, there was no reason to coddle her too much, despite Bill's angry glare. So many questions slammed in her brain that she had to ask as many as she could, hoping the answers might lead her closer to rescuing her father. "Did guys work in the fields or just girls?"

"Stop grilling her." Bill came to stand in front of Julie, letting his eyes meet hers. "Are you sure you're okay? I mean the lizards didn't— You weren't—um…"

Julie got the gist of the question he couldn't seem to ask because she dropped her gaze to the dirt floor.

Because he couldn't seem to spit the words out, Kara eased not only his worries but Julie's discomfort. "Bug-eyes don't rape human women."

God, when had she become so damned blunt? Perhaps being alone for so long had left her unable to be polite or to keep her thoughts and comments to herself.

Julie raised her head and nodded, but Bill directed a glare at Kara. "How the hell would you know?"

"When they first came here, we treated some of them at the hospital. Not often, 'cause we didn't know much about them and they didn't trust us worth shit. But we learned a lot about them, and one thing we found out was that they can't fu—" *Engage the filter between your brain and mouth, Kara.* "Um—they can't *mate* with other species."

"True," Aiodhan chimed in. "Vymalns only take Vymalns as mates."

Bill's muttered *Thank God* made her happy. He clearly loved his sister, just as much as Kara loved Kevin.

And now she knew her brother was safe in this man's hands. She muttered her own *Thank God* and hurried out of the tent to hug Kevin again, needing to see him and touch him, needing to assure herself this wasn't all some bizarre dream.

Aiodhan started to follow Kara out of the tent when the new girl, Julie, grabbed his hand. "Wait."

He turned back to her, unsure why she wanted him to remain. Stepping around, she faced him, still holding his hand though he tried to ease it away from her. If she'd tell him what she wanted, he could go back to Kara.

The notion of Kara in the middle of this group of men irritated him like a prickly rash. He had every intention of taking her back to their earlier camp now that they were sure these people who had trapped them weren't their enemies. There was no way he'd leave her so vulnerable among a group of men he knew nothing about who could easily overpower her.

"Must go." He jerked his hand from Julie's grip.

About to walk out of the tent, he stopped when he noticed she was panting for breath. Before he could ask if she was truly ill after all, Julie dropped to her knees, covered her ears with her hands, and let out a shrill

58

scream.

What was wrong with her? Kara had said she wasn't hurt. Aiodhan tried to help her back up, but she just kept screaming as she skittered backward across the floor.

Kara and Bill came rushing back into the tent while several other men stuck their heads inside to watch the spectacle. Both hurried to Julie, crouching next to her.

"Julie, stop," Bill tried to take her hands, but she jerked them away, pressing her back up against the tent wall.

"This isn't real. It's a nightmare!" she shrieked. "I'm still there." Her terrified eyes stayed fixed on Aiodhan. "And it's not just lizards now. These aliens look like us. Why can't they leave us alone?"

She'd seen his eyes, not that he'd made an attempt to hide them. Concealing what he was from these people would have been a mistake, something they were sure to see as the ultimate betrayal considering how humans had suffered at the hands of the Vymalns. Aiodhan had no idea what to say to calm the girl and let her know he was there to help. Julie knew he wasn't human, and her terror at being held captive by the Vymalns. His skill with their language was improving rapidly, but not fast enough to keep this from escalating to violence.

Kara moved first, rising to her feet and hurrying to put herself in front of Aiodhan.

Bill was a little slower catching on. He kept looking between Julie and Aiodhan before fixing his gaze on Aiodhan's face. Kara's protective move probably triggered the realization that slowly spread over his features. With a snarl, he took his gun from the holster strapped to his hip and pointed it at Aiodhan.

While he could have disarmed the man, Aiodhan didn't want to put the women in danger. Kara could be hit, and Julie had suffered enough already. Until he could find a better way to deal with the threat, he'd play the scene out and try to keep the women safe.

"You brought an alien into my camp?" Bill's nostrils flared with each exhale. "A *fucking alien?*"

"You don't understand," Kara replied. She'd pressed her back to Aiodhan's front, reaching behind her to hold tight to his belt. "He's not one of the bug-eyes. He's here to hunt them—to help us."

"Sure he is. Just like the Vymalns were here to *help* us. He's an *alien*, that's all I give a shit about. Just another fucking alien."

Julie had stopped screaming, but she knelt next to her brother, wrapping her arms around his leg and clinging to him while she stared at Aiodhan with sheer hatred in her gaze.

"Stop," Kara said, her voice calm despite the fact she was trembling.

"Just stop for a minute and listen. Okay? He's a Seeker. He fights the bug-eyes—hates 'em as much as we do. He's here to help us."

Bill set his jaw, and Kara feared he'd shoot first and ask questions later. She needed an ally. "Kevin! Kevin, get in here! I need you!"

Her brother pushed his way inside the tent, his eyes growing wide as he stopped and took in the action. "What in the hell is going on?"

"Your sister brought a fucking alien into our camp. Look at his eyes."

"Kara?" Kevin's brown eyes, so much like her own, shifted between her and Aiodhan. Those eyes widened and his jaw dropped. "What *are* you?"

As she reached to grasp Aiodhan's wrist, she tried to will him not to answer with a squeeze.

He ignored her subtle censure. "I am Seeker. I kill Vymalns."

"I've seen him take out two already," Kara added. "Didn't even break a sweat." A few approving murmurs rose from the men, making her believe she'd found the right tack. "We need him. He can help us gain the upper hand."

"He knows how to kill lizards?"

She couldn't discern which of the guys had shouted the questions, so she replied to the whole group in a voice she hoped sounded authoritarian. "Damn straight he does."

Bill still didn't seem convinced. "How?"

"Trained well," Aiodhan replied. "Know how to hurt them most."

"Can you teach us?" another voice called.

Kara resisted breathing a sigh of relief. "Of course he can."

Although Bill didn't seem entirely convinced, he did holster his weapon. "Why are you here? Why now?" He helped his sister back to her feet. She clung to his hand.

Grumbling grunts from the men grew louder until a teenaged boy pushed his way through them and into the tent. Tall and skinny with big hands and feet he hadn't quite grown into, he raked his hands through his shaggy red hair. "He's here 'cause I called for him." Then he turned to smile at a woman who worked her way to his side. "He's gonna help us kill those lizards, and so is she."

Blonde with very short hair, the women so tall she had to duck through the tent flap.

Kara blinked a couple of times when she saw her gray eyes.

Another Seeker had come to the town of tents.

"Aiodhan Riel," the woman said in a breathless whisper as she smiled and rushed toward them.

Aiodhan grew rigid behind Kara, his hands settling on her shoulders before he moved her aside and took a few steps toward the blonde.

"Pashmar Karr."

They met in the middle, reaching out not to shake hands but to clasp wrists. Pashmar started talking in a language that was a beautiful mixture of sing-song words. Aiodhan nodded but said little. When he did speak, his words were as clipped as his English. Evidently he hadn't been avoiding talking to Kara because he hadn't known the proper things to say. He was simply a man of few words.

When Pashmar embraced Aiodhan and whacked him hard on his back and he returned the gesture, Kara drew her hands into tight fists. The truth slammed into her with so much force she got a little dizzy. She didn't like seeing another woman touching him—hugging him—because she'd started to believe she and Aiodhan belonged together.

And if that wasn't the height of insanity, Kara sure didn't know what was.

As he eased the embrace, Aiodhan turned to Kara. His smile made her breath catch. She'd never seen him smile that way before—except when he'd eaten a Ding Dong. Yet Kara couldn't seem to make herself return the smile, and her fingernails were digging into her palms to the point she was amazed she hadn't drawn blood.

She had no right to be jealous. No right at all. This new woman, the one who was a full foot taller than herself with defined yet feminine muscles and boobs that the men couldn't seem to drag their gazes away from, was clearly Tirian. Aiodhan had a bond with her Kara would probably never understand.

So why did resentment wash over her in relentless waves of envy and anger? Hell, she'd only known Aiodhan a few days. He was an alien.

Her heart didn't seem to care.

"This is Kara." Aiodhan laid a hand on Kara's shoulder. Then he nodded to the blonde. "Pashmar. A Seeker."

Kara inclined her head but didn't take her gaze off Pashmar.

Pashmar was not only considering her every bit as hard, she'd drawn her lips such a tight line that they'd all but disappeared. After several suspended moments, she nodded in return.

Striding over, Bill put himself between Kara and Aiodhan before gesturing to the skinny redhead. "Wanna explain to me why there are two aliens standing in the middle of my compound, Jayce?"

Jayce hurried over as he splayed his fingers through his hair again. "I sent out a bunch of messages. Remember?"

Rolling his eyes, Bill sighed. "I *know* you sent out messages. We're supposed to coordinating with other militias. I sure as shit didn't think you were trolling for more *aliens.*"

With a shake of his head, Jayce gave Bill one of those teenage looks—

61

the kind that said adults were too obtuse to ever understand. "I didn't send messages just to find other militias. I bounced several off of satellites using older encrypted codes, you know, trying to bypass the lizards' channels of communication."

"Why?"

"'Cause I figured if we hated the lizards this much, there had to be other people in the universe who hated 'em too. You know—any enemy of my enemy and all that stuff."

Kara tried to follow the conversation but couldn't take her eyes away from Pashmar. This woman, this Seeker, was everything Kara wasn't. Beautiful. Strong. Confident. If she was a typical Tirian female, it was amazing the males ever left home.

She self-consciously smoothed her hands down her dirty and well-worn jeans. Pashmar's outfit reflected Aiodhan's—and the rest of the men. They all looked like commandos. Kara looked like she shopped at the Salvation Army Thrift Shop.

So lost in her own morose thoughts, she hadn't realized Julie and Bill were not only standing right next to her now, but he'd been talking to her. Julie held tight to her brother's arm, sidling away from Aiodhan and Pashmar. "I'm sorry. What did—"

"I was asking about a clinic," Bill said. "I wondered if you'd stay on here and run a clinic for my men."

"Here?"

"This compound. I know it doesn't look like much, but we've got plenty of food, some medical supplies, and we're booby-trapped to keep the lizards from getting too close without us knowing about it."

"Yeah, I know. I got caught in one, remember?"

"At least they work." His smile was warm, and under any other circumstances, she might have thought him handsome. Blond with blue eyes and a dark tan, he reminded her of surfers she'd seen on a visit to Redondo Beach—so in contrast to her alien with his raven hair and ambiguous eyes. "Besides, the Vymalns have stopped their patrols. They don't know we're here."

"I'm just a nurse."

"That means you know a helluva lot more about taking care of wounds than anyone here. We can give you a nice tent, and we've got tons of medical stuff to help you." Bill glared at his men. "And my men will behave themselves. They'll be perfect gentlemen since it's clear you're a lady. Right, guys?"

Several of the men grunted in response.

Kevin laced their fingers. "Stay. Please. You'll be safe here, Kara. I don't want to lose you again."

"What about Dad?"

The offer to stay was tempting, because she'd finally have a place to belong. She'd also be close enough to try to help Kevin rescue her father the same way that Bill had saved Julie. Even as she waited for her brother to answer her question, she glanced back to Aiodhan. Engrossed as he spoke in low tones to Pashmar, he didn't even seem to care that Kara was making long-term plans. She might as well have been invisible.

So much for being his mate.

She'd been right all along. He'd only been trying to protect her. None of his words had been sincere.

Her heart hurt.

"We'll get your dad," Bill replied. "C'mon. Let's go show you your tent. We can grab some of the boxes of bandages and other medical shit and get you all set up. No beds left, and the cots suck. But—" He snapped his fingers and grinned. "We've got one of those air mattresses left, don't we, Kev?"

"Queen sized," Kevin replied.

"Well, then. That should seal the deal." Not even waiting for an answer, Bill led Julie out of the tent as his men dispersed.

Kara let Kevin pull her out of the tent, her heart breaking as she realized her time with Aiodhan had come to an abrupt end.

Chapter Eight

When Bill and Kevin led Kara out of the tent, Aiodhan had to quell the urge to push Pashmar and Jayce aside and follow them.

Follow?

No. Not merely follow.

He wanted to jerk her back to his side and beat the men who would take her from him. The blood lust rose inside him again, and it took all his discipline to force it back down. There was no way he would leave Kara here alone in the company of these men, most of whom were giving her lustful stares.

Pashmar's gaze followed his as she spoke to him in their own language. "Who is she?"

My mate. "A friend."

A blond eyebrow rose. "A friend? You've taken a *human* as a friend?"

He knew what she was asking. Most of the Seekers had the same derogatory view of humans that he'd held before he'd had a chance to interact with Kara and learn that the prejudices they'd all adopted were so very wrong. "Yes, as a friend. I should see where they're taking her."

"Why? We've found the humans who sent for our help. We've begun our mission. Leave her to her own kind. We need to plan our attacks."

He snorted in response.

She frowned in that scolding way of hers. "Have you seen your target?"

"No, but I've found the camp."

"Are you sure he's even there?"

Before Aiodhan could answer, Jayce interrupted. "If you two want a piece of advice…"

Both Seekers turned to stare at him. "Add-vise?" Pashmar asked. "What is add-vise?"

"Advice," Jayce replied. "You know—information that can help you."

"What is this *advice* you give?" Pashmar stood over the boy, using her superior height to intimidate him. "Why should we listen to you? A child?"

For such a skinny boy, he could throw a fierce glare. Heat radiated from his green eyes, all directed at Pashmar. "I'm not a *child*. I'm fifteen. And I got you here, didn't I? I got a message all the way to outer space without those lizards even knowing, didn't I?"

Pashmar didn't back down at all. "This does not make you fully grown. Only intelligent."

The boy must have thought she was complimenting him because he eased his rigid stance. "I'm damn smart. A genius, actually. Look, here's the advice. Up to you if you two wanna take it or not. Don't speak in your own language too much around here."

"Why?" Aiodhan asked. While he'd tried to hone his skills in English so he could communicate with Kara, he saw no need to speak to a fellow Tirian in such an awkward language. They needed to be able to get their meaning across without tripping over words or misunderstanding.

"'Cause none of the guys here trust you," he replied. "You're aliens. Like the lizards."

"We are not Vymalns!" Pashmar put her hands on her hips and roared the words in Jayce's face. "We are here to assist, to help."

"Yeah, well…" Jayce traced the floor with the toe of his athletic shoe. "Even though I called you, we don't know jack shit about you. Those stupid lizards said they were here to help, too. Look where *that* got us."

This conversation wasn't providing him with any new information. He needed to follow Kara and be sure she was safe. "I must go."

"Go?" Pashmar asked. "Where?"

"I must see Kara."

"The woman? Why?"

"I protect her."

"Why?"

Not only did he wish to avoid explaining the new and entirely uncomfortable emotions tumbling through his thoughts, he didn't want to discuss Kara in front of Jayce. Since he couldn't talk to Pashmar in their own tongue without offending Jayce, he wasn't even sure he could find the proper words. "I make a promise. We talk later, yes?"

She nodded, yet her eyes were hard as stone.

"How 'bout I take you to get something to eat?" Jayce offered, giving Pashmar a shy smile. "What's your name, Amazon woman?"

"Amazon woman?" Pashmar's gray eyes darkened even more. "What is this insult?"

"Not an insult," Jayce replied. "A compliment. You're a warrior woman like the Amazons in mythology. A damned pretty one, too." His cheeks flushed red, but he didn't look away. This boy would grow to be a strong, intelligent man one day. A credit to the humans.

"Warrior. *This* I know." A smile crossed her face. "I am hungry. Take me to eat."

"Sure thing, babe." Jayce started to duck out of the tent but turned back to Aiodhan. "Can I take your dog with me? It's been a long time since I got to play with a pet, and he looks a lot like my old dog. I can find him some food."

"Yes. Take dog and feed him. Name is Chance."

Jayce nodded and left the tent.

Pashmar stopped before stepping outside. "We'll talk later," she said in their own language. "We need to make plans, and I want to know what you've been doing all this time."

"You could've found me."

"My locater isn't working, and I haven't had time to tinker with it. All I knew was you landed hard. I've been searching for you ever since."

Aiodhan nodded, knowing he wouldn't tell her the entire truth about the time he'd spent with Kara. Although there had never been secrets between them before, he wasn't sure how Pashmar would feel about how close he'd gotten to Kara.

Kara.

Bill had said something about a *clinic*, but Aiodhan didn't know that word. Since she was a healer, perhaps he'd taken her to see more injured people as he had when he'd dragged her to see his sister. These humans were far too fragile a species. Seekers took care of their own injuries. At least he always had, although the itch from his stitches reminded him that she'd tended his wound well.

He had to tread carefully. It was perfectly acceptable to view her as his mate, the female he was meant to protect and honor. The way she constantly crept into his thoughts meant she could be coming to mean something more to him, that she might have touched his heart.

That, he couldn't allow. Too much affection for her would weaken him. No, he refused to allow tender feelings to take hold.

Lust, yes.

Possessiveness, yes.

Nothing more.

When he stepped outside the tent, Aiodhan was faced with several angry and suspicious men. Their frowns and the way they muttered to each other said it all—they thought he was no better than the Vymalns who'd treated humans so barbarically. While he didn't honestly care whether they liked him or not, they would have to learn to trust him and Pashmar so they'd be able to help them.

Jayce's message had been what called the Seekers here, although the Tirians had already been keeping watch over the Vymalns' conquest of Earth. They were an enemy who needed to be closely watched, and much of the Tirian technology had been developed simply to monitor all that the Vymalns did.

Better to be prepared than caught unawares, as the Tirian proverb said.

Striding up to two of the men, both of whom put their hands on the butts of the weapons in their holsters, Aiodhan asked, "Where is clinic?"

One of the men narrowed his eyes before he answered. "Why d'ya want to know?" His eyes moved from Aiodhan's head to his feet before returning to his face. "You don't look hurt."

"Where is clinic?" he asked again, trying to keep his voice soft despite his irritation. These humans were smart enough to see he was nothing like the Vymalns. He wasn't sure he had the patience to wait to win over their trust, especially when he was so worried about Kara.

The second man pointed toward the largest tent. "That's the mess and assembly hall. We got a tent behind it that we call a clinic. Ain't much to see, though. It's empty, 'cept for a table and some shelves."

He felt the weight of every stare directed his way as he walked past the eating area. The side flaps had been rolled up, so all the men sitting at the long tables could watch him as he moved by to search for the tent behind it.

Small had been the right word to describe the place. Opening the flap, he stepped inside. Pitch blackness greeted him. His eyes quickly adjusted to pick up the minutest light sources. No one was inside. His heart jumped into a higher rhythm as he pictured all the things that could be happening to Kara at the hands of these men he knew nothing about.

Hurrying back out, he almost slammed right into her. She'd been carrying a box, but she dropped it. Aiodhan caught the box before it hit the ground and then set it down.

Putting his hands on his hips, he gave her a swift appraisal, pleased to see she was fine. He wasn't pleased, however, to see Bill following close behind, carrying her things and holding a lantern.

"Where you were?" Aiodhan demanded.

"You mean where were you."

"Kara..." He growled low in his throat.

"Bill and I were getting some supplies. I'm going to make this a real clinic. Oh, I know they call it that now. It's a joke. No one here knows much about medicine." A nod to the box at her feet. "They've got tons of stuff, though. They raided a hospital before the bug-eyes could get there, so they nabbed bandages and meds and all sorts of great stuff. I can do some good here."

So she was staying—with Bill, Kevin, and these men who hated him without even knowing him. That thought made Aiodhan angrier. Hadn't she heard what he'd said when they'd been captured? He'd declared her his mate for all to hear. There was no turning back from that declaration, even if he wanted to take it back. Which he didn't.

The blood lust that rose each time he thought of Bill or any of these men touching her told Aiodhan he'd been right to claim Kara. She belonged to him now.

It was time to make her understand that.

Before he could say anything, Kevin came into the tent, carrying a big bundle under one arm, blankets and pillow under the other and a handheld light in his hand. He smiled at Kara and then scowled at Aiodhan. "I've got an air mattress for you, sis. I can put it in the back room so you can have some privacy."

"There's a back room?" she asked, squinting. Human eyes didn't adjust to low light as quickly or as well as Tiran eyes.

"It's a nice tent." Bill hung the lantern from a hook above his head. He nodded at another flap. "It has another room. We can set up your bedroom there and keep this part for the clinic. We've already even got some book cases you can use to organize the supplies. Maybe I can scare up some lockable cases for the drugs." Another nod to the empty shelves along one wall and then he gestured to a bare, sturdy table setting near the other wall. "Will that work as an exam table?"

"Perfect," she replied as she favored Bill with a smile.

He smiled in return.

Aiodhan had to resist the urge to drag Kara to his side and punch the grin right off Bill's face.

"Aidan here can stay with the other men," Bill announced. "Go get things set up in back, Kevin. Then we can all get out of here so she can get comfortable and get some rest. Unless… Do you want some help putting supplies away, Kara?"

"It's Aiodhan," she corrected. "And no thanks. I need to put everything away so I know where to find it when I need it in a hurry. Aiodhan can stay and help." Then she turned her gaze to him and nibbled on her bottom lip.

The sound of a small motor broke the silence that had settled over the three of them.

"Sounds like Kevin's getting your bed blown up, and I've got work to do," Bill said. "Get some sleep. I'm sure you'll have all sorts of aches and pains to deal with in the morning once everyone knows you're here. They'll probably make up some just to see you." On that prediction and a wink, he left.

Kevin flipped the fabric flap out of his way as he came back to where Aiodhan and Kara stood staring at each other. His eyes shifted from one to the other before he cleared his throat. "I've got a bed set up in there for you. Need anything else?"

"No. Thanks, though," she replied.

"You're not hungry?"

"I've got some stuff in my backpack if I need anything."

Aiodhan desperately wanted Kara's brother to leave. There was much that he needed to do. While he should go and find Pashmar so they could make some plans, he wouldn't leave until he had a chance to talk to Kara privately.

Judging from Kevin's hesitation, he didn't want Aiodhan alone with his sister. "I can stay…"

"I'm fine, Kevin," Kara said. "I have stuff to put away, and Aiodhan and I need to talk."

Striding over, Kevin pulled her into a tight hug that she returned. "I'm so glad to have you back." Then he left the tent.

Now that Aiodhan had her alone, he found that all the words he wanted to say to her crowded together in his mouth, blocking each other. The biggest problem was that he really didn't want to *talk*. What he wanted was to draw her into his arms and make love to her until neither could move. He wanted to taste her on his lips. To touch her soft skin. To caress her beautiful breasts. His *kull* was hard and ready to claim her. Now that he'd declared that she belonged to him, nothing could stop him from being with her, from touching her the way he'd longed to for so long.

Except Kara rejecting him.

"I should put some antibiotic cream on your stitches." She crouched to pull a small bottle, a white packet, and a tube out of one of the boxes and then patted the table's surface. "Jump up here, big boy. Let me see how you're doing."

Since he couldn't seem to make himself speak, Aiodhan obeyed. Sitting on the table, he let his legs hang over the side. He was so tall, his feet would have hit the floor if he pointed his toes.

She came to stand between his knees, grasping his wrist and setting it in his lap as she gently pushed his sleeve up to bare the wound she'd closed with thread. Opening a packet, she pulled out some gauze before unscrewing the lid on the bottle and pressing the gauze to the opening. She tipped the bottle, wetting the gauze, before setting it aside.

Dabbing the wet fabric against his arm, she kept her gaze on the wound. "This is peroxide. It'll clean away anything that could cause an infection." She gingerly touched the threads, dampening them as white foam formed. "It looks good. You must heal fast, 'cause it's already closing. And no signs of infection."

She finished cleaning the wound, her touch so infinitely gentle that he wanted to close his eyes and savor it, picturing her slender hands on his chest, moving lower until she took his stiff *kull* in her grasp. Instead, he focused on the beauty of her face and the sweet smell of her that drifted his way. He leaned closer to brush his face over the top of her head and breathed her in, releasing a heavy sigh of contentment as he breathed back out. While she set the gauze aside and grabbed the tube, he reached for her head-tail, letting his fingers lace through the soft, brown strands of her hair.

Kara put the cap back on the tube and set it aside. "All done." She looked up to let her gaze meet his. The warmth of her brown eyes heated his blood, making his heart pound a rough rhythm.

Tugging on her hair, he tried to bring her closer. He loved how she stood between his spread legs. Her hands settled on his thighs, kneading the muscle with her fingers and forcing his breath to catch in his throat. Her chin lifted as her lips slightly parted in invitation.

Aiodhan dropped his mouth to hers, his kiss one of possession. While he knew he should soothe her and coax her into his arms, he didn't have the patience. From the moment he'd seen her, he'd wanted her with a passion that still made him crazed. Now that he'd claimed her as his mate, that wanting had turned into a craving so strong, he needed steely self-control to keep himself from simply tossing her on the table and taking her right there. But he didn't want to hurt her or scare her. He wanted Kara to feel for him all the things he felt for her, to come to him willingly and let him take her to the height of desire. To see those brown eyes glaze in sensual pleasure as her body bucked beneath his when she found her release—he'd accept no less.

Her mouth opened to his tongue, and he swallowed her soft mewl of surrender. Stroking the roof of her mouth, he coaxed her to respond even more. A rumbling growl rose from his chest when her tongue moved across his. She tasted so sweet, so much like forbidden desire that the fragile tendrils of his control began to snap. One by one.

He raised his hands to cradle her face, stroking her smooth cheeks with his thumbs and wanting the kiss to last forever. His whole life, he'd never felt this kind of connection to a female. The sex he'd indulged in had been nothing more than a way to give his body the release it demanded. But as Aiodhan kissed Kara, something about her reached deep inside him, finding his soul and merging with it in a way he'd never known existed—one that left him both shaken and sure he'd done the right thing in claiming her as his mate.

When he lifted his head, she followed him with her mouth. He brushed another kiss over her lips, unable to deny her silent request for more. Then he gave her a tender smile as he took the last important step. Reaching for her hand, he raised it to his face, kissing the tips of each of her delicate fingers before pressing his lips to the palm of her hand, his way of letting her know he was ready and hoped she was as well.

The time had finally come.

Chapter Nine

Her body caught fire. Everything about Aiodhan appealed to her, from his masculine and earthy scent to how gentle he was whenever he touched her. Each time he'd kissed her palm, it been such a caring gesture, tears stung her eyes in response. If she tried hard, she could imagine that he really cared for her and wasn't simply responding to a woman who'd shown him some sexual interest.

He stared into her eyes, and she relished the change she saw. The gray was now a swirling kaleidoscope of iridescent silver. She leaned in, wanting to kiss him again but was surprised when instead he scooted farther back on the table, turned her in his arms, and lifted her to sit between his spread legs. He pulled her back against his chest. When he started nibbling kisses along the column of her neck, she tilted her head and heard a murmur of pleasure rise from deep inside herself. Heat raced over her skin, settling low between her thighs and bursting in her core. His hands spanned her waist, stroking their way up until he caught her down vest and slid it off her shoulders before casting it aside.

Aiodhan pressed his big hands to her breasts, palming them through her flannel shirt as he gently squeezed. Kara dropped her head back to rest against his shoulder and closed her eyes, letting herself drown in his touch. So infinitely tender from such a strong man. She rubbed her palms over his thighs, wiggling her backside against the hard length of his erection. His responding growl hit her gut like fire, setting off a series of sparks inside her and making her want so much more.

She wanted it *all*.

She'd only had two lovers in her life, both of whom she hadn't truly loved. The first had been her high school boyfriend, and she'd given him her virginity more out of curiosity than affection. The second had been a surgical intern who'd been just as honest with her as she'd been with him when he'd told her he wanted nothing more than a friends-with-benefits arrangement. Although both men had been able to excite her, neither set her body to singing the way Aiodhan did with each touch, each kiss. The passion he inspired made her tremble with desire, and for that moment, she allowed herself to pretend that he'd truly meant it when he'd called her his mate, that the tenderness he showed her came from feelings that ran as deep as her own.

She smiled at him over her shoulder before removing his hand from her right breast. Holding it up by her lips, she decided to return the gesture that seemed to mean so much to him, but only after she had a chance to taunt him a little first. Gently spreading his index finger to isolate it, Kara ran her tongue along its length. Aiodhan gasped, making her smile as she eased his long finger into her mouth and sucked.

"*Zot, serd bon,*" he groaned close to her ear before he retaliated by running his tongue around the ridges. "Good. Feels good, Kara."

Swirling her tongue around his finger, she sucked it again before moving on to the next. Drawing his middle finger deep into her mouth and applying suction, she had a passing and far too naughty thought that if his fingers were so long, so was another part of his anatomy.

Aiodhan took her earlobe between his teeth and tugged, then he nipped his way back to her neck. Kara shivered in pleasure before she released his finger. Holding his palm in front of her lips, she felt him tense behind her before drawing in and holding a deep breath. Just as she'd suspected, this gesture meant a great deal to him.

She flashed back to the times Aiodhan had brushed his lips against her sensitive palm. Both had been when they were kissing and caressing and she'd believed they were ready to move on to deeper intimacies. Perhaps kissing another's palm was a way to tell a partner the time had come to stop playing and start getting serious. At that moment, her body was screaming for this man—this *alien*—she was coming to love far too quickly.

Although making love to him might be a mistake that would leave her with a permanently broken heart, she needed to feel him inside her and to know they were as close as a male and female could ever be. He'd return to his home, wherever it was, soon enough, leaving her behind to Earth's bleak future. The sweet memories of this precious time they'd spent together would always remain, tattooed forever on her soul.

Kara pressed a slow, loving kiss to his palm.

Aiodhan let out a ragged breath. "I will please you, Kara. A promise I make to my mate."

His words sent a wave of desire through her, a longing for his touch, his kiss. A longing for him to feel for her what she felt for him.

A loud gasp sounded from the entrance to the tent. Her lips still touching Aiodhan's palm, Kara glanced up to see Pashmar standing there, her mouth frozen in a surprised O. Her wide, ghostly eyes narrowed and darkened, and her breath came in livid huffs, making Kara think of an enraged bull preparing to charge.

Aiodhan moved Kara to the side and then hopped off the table. As he took long strides to reach Pashmar, strange lyrical words fell from his lips in an angry string. Pashmar just stared at him before her eyes found Kara again. The hatred clearly written on the alien's features made her shiver.

While she'd felt a stab of jealousy earlier when Aiodhan had greeted

Pashmar so enthusiastically, Kara now realized that it wasn't misplaced. Although she had no idea what he felt for Pashmar, the female Seeker clearly had feelings for him. And now, Kara had an enemy—a potentially dangerous enemy if Pashmar's abilities were close to Aiodhan's.

Aiodhan tried to hold tight to his rising temper, but having been interrupted at such an inappropriate moment, he didn't succeed. Not wishing Kara to know all that he wanted to say to Pashmar, he ignored Jayce's advice and spoke in Tirian. "What made you barge in like that?"

Blinking a few times, Pashmar didn't answer him. Instead, she stared at Kara with such fury, he was amazed she didn't act on it. Obviously, she'd assumed more than she should have about what had passed between them, and guilt nagged at him. He shoved it aside. He'd never led Pashmar to believe that their liaisons had been anything but mutual sexual gratification. Feelings were never supposed to be involved. She'd agreed. Judging from the anger radiating from her like an aura, she'd lied.

Leave it to a female to complicate simple things.

He stepped in front of her, blocking her path to Kara. "You had no right to interrupt."

"No right?" Pashmar's voice was a strangled whisper. "I'm your lover."

"Were. You *were* my lover a couple of times. It was a long time ago. We agreed it was nothing—that it meant nothing."

All the anger she'd been directing at Kara shifted and was now centered on him, which came as a relief. He didn't want Kara bearing the brunt of Pashmar's rage. Her temper was normally hard to trigger, but once burning, it rivaled the brightest star.

"You'd choose this...*human* over me?" she demanded.

"There was no choice to make. You and I are friends, Pashmar. We fight together, and yes, we've been lovers. But you're not my mate."

"But you said we'd be together, that—"

"That's a lie and you know it. I wouldn't make you a promise I couldn't keep. You know me better than that, my friend." Aiodhan took a deep breath, trying to steady himself against the hurt he knew coursed through her. But it was of her own doing. In the time they'd known each other, he'd never given her any reason to believe that they'd shared something more than a pleasing interlude or two. "You're my friend, remember? I told you I wouldn't take a mate."

Her eyes had darkened to an angry black. "Then you're the liar. I saw the ritual. You're taking her as a lover. *I* was your lover, so why couldn't *I* be your mate?"

"I didn't lie. I didn't want a mate."

"Good. Then we can still—" When he shook his head, she bit back her words. "Then leave her be. Leave her here. Come with me. I'll make you happy. I've always pleased you. We're good together." She reached for him.

He pulled his hand back and said the words he now knew would hurt her. Yet they had to be said. "I've claimed her as my mate."

"No! No! You said— You promised—"

"Stop it. I made you no promises."

"You hold me at arm's length and tell me you'll take no mate. Then you claim her? *Her?* Why a human and not me?"

Pashmar was his friend. They'd fought side by side. He hated causing her pain. Never expecting this kind of jealousy, he was not only astonished but dismayed. They'd seldom talked about the future and certainly not about a future *together*. When he'd lain with her, he'd been open and honest about what they shared, and she'd always claimed she had no intention of taking a mate, either. Never had she revealed that she held deeper feelings for him, and he'd convinced himself long ago that he couldn't feel affection for anyone.

Until he'd met Kara.

"I can't explain it," Aiodhan replied. "When I saw her, I knew."

"It's just an infatuation. A stupid infatuation." Her hand reached for his, but again, he refused her. "Leave her here. Come back with me to my ship. We can share a meal and talk. We can plan our attacks."

He glanced back at Kara. She'd picked up a box and was putting supplies out on one of the shelves. While she might not understand the angry words he'd exchanged with Pashmar, she wasn't succeeding in ignoring the gist of them because she was furiously working her bottom lip between her teeth.

"I won't leave her. Not yet. Not in this camp with these strange men."

"Why? They're her own kind. One of *them* can be her mate."

How was he supposed to tell her he didn't trust the other men to leave Kara alone? He was responsible for her safety. How could he explain to Pashmar that now that Kara had accepted him and kissed his palm, he wasn't about to leave her without making love to her?

He shrugged. "She needs me."

She hit him without warning, driving her fist into his nose with so much force, he was amazed he didn't hear bone break.

"Fuck you, Aiodhan Riel."

Turning on her heel, she threw the tent flap open and stormed out into the night.

With a heavy sigh, he tried to dismiss Pashmar from his thoughts, but his throbbing nose and the fact that she was his friend and a fellow Seeker made it impossible. There would be much he'd have to do to repair that broken bridge.

His gaze fell on Kara.

She set her now empty box aside, grabbed a small package and gauze, and walked over to him. "Let me see your nose."

"Fine," he insisted even though he still saw flashes of light behind his eyes.

His nose was running, but he wouldn't sniff hard for fear of it starting to bleed, something he was amazed hadn't already happened.

She had to push up on the tips of her toes to reach his face because he wasn't inclined to bend closer. His nose hurt like hell, and his nostrils were swelling. He winced when she ran her fingertips over the shape of the bone and cartilage even though her touch was mild. Kara was an excellent healer, and the way she made the pain quickly recede made Aiodhan wonder if she had the healing touch. She used the gauze to wipe him clean.

"Nothing's broken," she said. Ripping open the package, she pulled out a small bundle, squeezed it until something inside gave a loud pop, and then shook it for a moment. "Hold this on your nose."

"I am fine."

"It's a cold pack." She pressed it into his hand and then lifted his hand to his face. "It'll help the swelling."

He obeyed, grateful to feel the packet cooling as he held it against his injury. He grunted his thanks.

With a curt nod he took as a reply, she returned to the shelves, picked up a box, and unpacked white plastic bottles.

Aiodhan sat himself back down on the table, shifting the cold pack to the bridge of his nose where the throbbing was worse. There were no words he could give Kara—not about the scene she'd witnessed, nor about all the complicated emotions he experienced for her.

Those feelings bothered him. He had nothing to give such a free and giving spirit. He was hard. Battle worn. A warrior. What did he know about tender feelings? Ashamed of showing any weakness, he told himself that all he felt for Kara was a mate's natural desire to honor and protect. Those plus a healthy dose of lust. Nothing more.

He wasn't capable of more.

She broke the silence. "I don't know what you two were saying to each other, but I think I understand."

All he did was wait to see where she was leading.

"I'm not going to come between you and your girlfriend."

"Girlfriend?"

"A woman you are…close to. Or is she your…" She seemed to struggle for the right thing to say. "Your wife, maybe?"

She thought he and Pashmar were mates, even after he'd claimed Kara in front of so many people. Had her statement not been so absurd, he might have laughed. "No wife."

Her eyes found his, and a smile curved her mouth. "That's a relief. I mean, I'd hate to think you were kissing me when you were married. I'm not a home-wrecker type of gal." After setting the empty box aside, she grabbed another. "So she's not your wife. But she's obviously *something* to you." A few moments passed, and he wondered if she'd find the courage to ask what she obviously wanted to ask. "Were you two lovers?"

"Kara…"

"No. Wait. Don't answer that. It's none of my business." The pill bottles rattled as she shoved them onto the shelf with far more force than necessary. "Besides, I'm human. You're…whatever."

"Tirian."

"It would never work, you know. We live in different worlds." She breathed a shuddering sigh.

Her vulnerability made Aiodhan's heart tighten. Somehow, she'd developed a strong attachment to him, stronger than he'd suspected. Damn, if that didn't make him grin like a fool. He couldn't wait another moment to hold her.

Tossing aside the cold pack, he jumped off the table and stepped up behind her. "Kara."

Instead of rising, she set the box aside and stay crouched in front of him. "You should go."

"I cannot."

"Even if I ask you to?"

Even if you ask me to. Nothing would pull him away. *Nothing.*

"You will not tell me to go."

Kara rose to his challenge, standing with a grace he admired before she turned to face him. Her eyes had become darker, her pupils dilating. "You're sure of that?"

"I am sure."

He cupped her face, pleased that this time she turned her cheek to rub against his palm. Her skin was silky soft. Going slowly, giving her a chance to stop him, he leaned in, watching her eyes widen before closing in invitation.

When his lips touched hers, desire raced through his body like a relentless wind. Kara surprised him when she deepened the kiss first, her tongue tickling his lips. He smiled as he opened his mouth to her, grasping her probing tongue with his teeth and giving it a tug.

Kara looped her arms around his neck as Aiodhan settled his hands against her waist. Lifting, he growled his approval when she wrapped her slender legs around his hips. He grabbed the lantern from the ceiling and carried her through the tent to the back room.

A mattress rested on the floor, covered with soft, inviting bedding. Since she didn't seem inclined to let him go, he stooped enough to set the lantern down, unable to take his lips away from hers. She'd become as necessary to him as oxygen—if she left him now, he'd die.

Wrapping his arms around her lithe body, he held her close, making love to her with his mouth while she returned each caress of his tongue. Her soft, passionate whimpers made him hold her tighter and wish he could crawl inside her and stay forever.

Touching Kara, loving Kara, gave him an overwhelming peace he'd never known, just as the blood lust when she'd been threatened had been a type of rage that flared brighter than any he'd experienced. This woman was truly his mate for there for no other way to explain what he felt for her and how he reacted to her nearness.

Aiodhan wrenched his mouth away to press kisses along her slender throat. Then he eased her legs from around his body to set her on her feet. His fingers worked on the fastenings of her shirt as the need to be skin to skin with her overrode everything else. She seemed just as frantic, tugging at his shirt to pull it out of his waistband before a delicate growl rose from her, echoing his deeper growl at the tedious task of removing clothes.

"Here," Kara said softly, brushing away his hands. "Get your belt off, and I'll undo my buttons."

He flipped the clasp on his utility belt, grabbing it as it began to slip from his hips and setting it next to the mattress so his weapons would be within reach. He whipped his shirt over his head and dropped it by the belt. Her gasp drew his attention.

Her shirt was now open in the front, but her hands trembled as she reached for him. "God, you're handsome."

She smoothed her palms up his chest, fanning them out to his shoulders before she pressed herself against him and lifted her head.

His lips found hers as he eased her shirt from her shoulders, brushing her hands aside until the garment fell to the floor. A tight piece of lace bound her breasts, and he needed that garment gone so he could feel her nipples tighten against his palms. Yet he saw no fastener.

Kara smiled and reached one hand behind her to pop some kind of clasp, making the lace drop forward and the straps ease down her shoulders. "Ready?"

Since he was too lost in desire to find a single word, he simply nodded and reached for her. She smiled again and took a step back to evade his grasp. "Patience, Aiodhan."

So his mate liked to tease.

He dredged up a smile and plopped on the mattress to tug off his boots. Then he crooked his finger at her. Still holding the lacey garment against her breasts, she stepped forward and put her small foot on his thigh. He took that as an order to unlace her boots and awkwardly pulled them and her socks from her feet. After he tossed them all aside, he reached for her, stroking her waist and closing his eyes as her warmth seemed to seep inside him.

The sound of a zipper made his eyes fly open. Not only had Kara dropped the breast binder, but she was unfastening her pants. She eased them over her hips until they puddled at her ankles. After she kicked them aside, she faced him in nothing but more white lace. Her legs were long. Thin, yes, but nicely shaped. His eyes moved to the juncture of her thighs, and it took all his self-control not to grab for her when he saw the shadow of dark hair beneath the taunting fabric.

Aiodhan wanted to tell her how beautiful she was, how she filled him with desire. Instead, he took her hands and tugged her down onto his lap, catching her as she fell onto her knees, straddling his thighs. Holding her under her arms, he eased her back up enough that he could kiss each of her pink-tipped breasts. She threaded her fingers through his hair while he splayed his hand between her shoulder blades, then she arched her back so he could pull one of those delectable nipples deep into his mouth.

Kara closed her eyes, feeling as if she was lost in some erotic dream. Every touch, every kiss zinged through her body. Although she'd only known Aiodhan a few days, she ached as if she'd wanted him forever. As he laved and suckled her breasts, she held him close, letting her fingers slide through his long hair.

He drew her back down to rest on his lap, her core nestling his erection. She opened her eyes and stared into his. Passion had turned them nearly black. Leaning in, she pressed her lips to his, moaning in pleasure when he slid his tongue into her mouth to duel with hers. As she eased away to draw a breath, she scooted back enough to gain her feet.

Aiodhan helped steady her shaky legs by holding tight to her hips. "These off," he said, tugging at her panties.

"I was thinking the same thing about your pants."

With a smug grin, he stood up. He popped the silver clasp and dragged down a zipper—at least something a lot like a zipper. She didn't want to take the time to look at it, focusing instead on him. Sliding her hands into the sides of his pants, she pushed them over his hips, sucking in a hard breath when she realized he wore no type of underwear.

"Know what?" she asked.

"No. What?"

"I *love* a guy who goes commando."

"Commando?"

She was about to explain when the pants fell to his ankles and his hard shaft sprang forward to brush against her belly. All she could do was stare at the erection rising from a nest of ebony hair and swallow hard.

The guy was huge—big enough she nibbled on her bottom lip and wondered if he'd hurt her.

He must have seen where she stared, because he framed her face in his hands and tilted it up. "Kara? You do not like me?"

The rather smug expression on his face stole away any of her apprehension. He knew he was well-endowed, and Kara wasn't about to feed his masculine ego. Instead, she seized control, putting her palms against his broad chest and kissing the base of his throat. She slid her hands down his body, savoring each of the catches in his breath and the low moans.

Never had she considered herself sexy or enticing, but knowing his powerful body was responding to her—to skinny, plain her—made her as heady as a strong shot of tequila. After tangling her fingers through the crisp hair, she took his cock into her grasp. Her thumb and fingers couldn't span his girth.

She swallowed hard again.

Aiodhan had to bite back a teasing comment. His size intimidated Kara. She had to realize that he would never hurt her, that it was his duty to make sure she was properly prepared. He'd make her want him every bit as much as he wanted her, and before he claimed her body, he would have her hot, wet, and ready.

And he knew the best way to accomplish that. Hooking his thumbs in her lace garment, he tugged it down her body, helping her step out of it before tossing it aside. Her hands dropped to cover the juncture of her thighs, but he grabbed her wrists and gently forced them back. "Beautiful."

In one swift move, he was on his feet and had scooped Kara into his arms.

Kneeling on the mattress, he set her on her back. Before she could react, he nudged her knees apart with one of his own, then settled the length of his body over hers.

Skin to skin made it impossible to breathe for a moment. Bracing himself on his elbows so his weight wouldn't crush her fragile frame, he had to fight the strong urge to simply part her thighs and thrust inside her. Knowing that she was already afraid of his size helped him maintain control. A couple of slow inhales and exhales helped, too.

"What about a condom?" she asked. "I grabbed one from the supplies I put away. It's in my pants pocket."

"Condom?"

"You know, birth control."

This, he understood.

He was also more pleased than she could know that she'd wanted him enough to grab one before he took her to bed. He shifted to reach for her pants and dragged them over to where they lay. She fished around in the pocket and drew out a small packet. She ripped it open with her teeth and pulled out a small covering a lot like sheathes used in many cultures to prevent conception.

Since now wasn't the time for him to give his mate a child, he moved his hips enough to let Kara roll the "condom" on his *kull*. Her touch made his heart pound harder. As soon as she was done, he settled himself between her slim thighs again.

Starting with her chin, he kissed his way down her body. Nips against her flesh that he soothed with long licks. Her throat. Her breasts. Her flat stomach. When he reached the dark curls that hid her secrets, he breathed in deeply, loving her feminine scent.

"Aiodhan...don't." Kara's voice was a hoarse whisper as she tried to squeeze her knees together.

"Yes, Kara." Nudging her legs farther apart, he put his mouth on her, gently opening her up to his probing tongue. Her taste was sweet and intoxicating, making heat surge to his *kull* and a groan rise from his throat.

Kara almost arched off the bed when he found the sensitive bud of flesh and gave it suction. Her fingers splayed against his head, tangling in his hair as she drew her knees up. "Oh, God..."

When the first tremors of her release made her hips buck, he moved up her body, grasped her hips, and drove inside her.

She was so hot, so very wet. He groaned as she rocked her body up to meet his, drawing him all the way into her tight heat. "Kara..."

"Aiodhan..."

There were no more words, only the rhythm of his body withdrawing and pushing roughly into hers. He kissed her, long and deep, the thrust of his tongue matching the way his body pressed into hers. Each of her whimpers and sweet moans sent him higher, and though he wanted this to last and last, his body refused to let him temper the pace. Faster and faster he moved, savoring how her body clenched around his and her legs squeezed him tight.

He held himself up to look into her beautiful eyes. When she gasped for breath and raked her nails over his back, he knew she was close to climax. Her face was flushed, her lips swollen from his kisses. When Kara's inner muscles tightened around him as if trying to milk his seed, she called out his name and squeezed her eyes shut. A tear leaked from the corner of one.

Aiodhan was lost. Two strong thrusts sent him hurtling over the edge, and with a lusty shout, he shot his essence inside her, feeling as if part of his soul was pouring into her as well.

After the last spasm racked his body, he had to catch himself not to collapse in sated exhaustion. He eased away from her to dispose of the protection. When he again rested next to her, she cuddled against his side as he pulled her close. She sighed and stroked his chest while she rested her cheek against his shoulder.

Soon, Kara's breaths slowed, and she fell asleep.

Aiodhan kissed the top of her head, closed his eyes, and realized this was as close to perfect as his life would ever get.

Chapter Ten

Kara blinked a few times and stared at the canvas ceiling. The lantern had burned out, but shafts of sunlight pierced the tied corners of the tent, giving a dappled look to her new bedroom.

She was in Aiodhan's arms, snuggled up against his side with one leg resting over his muscular thigh. A sigh of contentment slipped out as she rubbed her cheek against the shoulder she'd used as a pillow. His deep, even breathing made her close her eyes again, yearning for this peaceful moment never to end.

The future weighed heavily on her mind. She'd given it no thought last night, not wanting reality to intrude on the most wonderful experience of her life. Now, all she could think about was how this would change everything.

Her life.

Aiodhan's life.

Good God. I'm really in love with an alien.

Had someone told her that a week ago, she would have laughed in his face before giving him a black eye. As things were now, she hardly believed it herself.

From the moment the bug-eye dressed like a cop had cornered her in the woods and hit her with that damn pulse-gun, her life had become an odyssey, the conclusion of which could be days, weeks, even months away.

Aiodhan couldn't stay. He had his mission. Not that he'd shared his goal with her. This relationship was doomed. Despite the feelings she'd developed he was going to walk away, because his feelings couldn't be involved. Not this quickly.

Why that made her feel like someone had reached into her chest and squeezed her heart too tightly remained a mystery. No logical explanation could be found for why she loved her alien so completely after such a short—embarrassingly short—time.

The noises coming from him weren't quite snores. She nestled her hand between his pecs to feel the steady beat of his heart. His heart rate was exceeding slow. Had he been human, she might have been concerned. Then she admitted to herself she *was* concerned.

Damn. She really didn't know anything about this alien, this species. Sure, he looked like a man. His body was amazing—no other word fit that sculpted physique. 20Her fingertips glided over his smooth skin, fanning out to brush a masculine nipple when she remembered the bliss he'd given her in the night.

He might be an alien, but he was a hell of a lover.

"Kara." His husky whisper made her lift her head. Those unusual eyes of his no longer startled her, especially when they were the swirling silver that showed his arousal.

Leaning up on an elbow, she stared down at him. "Good morning."

Instead of giving her a reply, Aiodhan cupped her neck and dragged her down. Firm lips brushed over hers. Once. Twice. Recognizing the invitation, she accepted by rolling to cover his body with her own.

Skin to skin was nothing short of heaven. When his tongue slipped between her lips to stroke hers, she closed her eyes and surrendered.

"Hey, Kara! Wanna get some breakfast?"

Kevin's voice reached her just before the tent flap between her room and the clinic flipped open. Her brother strolled in, and the smile that had lit his face dropped to a frown so fierce, she was amazed he didn't snarl at her. His gaze settled on Aiodhan, who had jerked the blanket up to cover them as she flopped to his side.

A few moments passed, suspended in slow motion before Kevin finally spoke. "You've got to be fucking kiddin' me."

Great. Just great.

What was she supposed to say to her brother when he found her naked in bed with her lover? She might as well have been back in high school and getting caught necking with her boyfriend.

"Kevin, let me explain."

His eyes narrowed to angry slits. "You know, I always thought you were smarter than me. I always looked up to you. But… Jesus Christ, Kara. He's an alien." A few more seconds passed as her brother huffed some breaths. Then he snatched the tattered baseball cap from his head and slapped it against his thigh. "He's an alien. A fucking *alien.*"

Sitting up and clutching the blanket to her breasts, Kara leveled a hard stare. "Stop it. He's not one of them, and you damn well know it."

"But—"

"No! No, *but.* This is my life, not yours."

Aiodhan sat up at her side, quietly watching the exchange. Grateful that he didn't jump into the fray, she focused on Kevin. His face had turned ruddy as if he was holding his breath too long.

When he spoke again, her brother's voice was surprisingly soft. "Have you forgotten about what they did to me and Dad?"

"Aiodhan didn't do anything to you and Dad. The bug-eyes did."

"So what? An alien's an alien." He scoffed at her. "He's using you, you know. And I'm ashamed you're letting him."

That comment hurt more than she'd ever let her brother know. "It's none of your damned business. This is between Aiodhan and me."

"Aiodhan and… Oh, I see. He was serious when he called you his stupid mate. Do you honestly think you're just gonna live happily ever after with some...some...*thing* from another planet? You think he cares about you?" Kevin snorted.

As if she'd admit to him that she hadn't thought that far. From the moment Earth had found itself under attack, the future had been something Kara refused to consider, let alone form hopes about. Her life had become nothing more than trying to survive from day to day. To find something to eat. To sleep someplace where she was warm and dry and wasn't afraid. To stay as far away from the Vymalns as she could.

A future with Aiodhan? Not even a remote possibility.

At least her brain understood; her heart didn't want to think about it.

"Look," she said. "I'm starving, and this isn't getting us anywhere. Why don't I meet you in a few minutes for breakfast?"

Kevin continued to glare at her, causing a small, threatening rumble to rise from Aiodhan's chest.

"Fine," Kevin snapped.

"Are there showers here?"

Not that she had any idea how many amenities a camp in the middle of the woods and full of nothing but guys would have. Since none of them smelled like a homeless person, there had to be some way to keep clean. After breakfast, she could enjoy a shower again. Such a luxury after bathing in streams for months.

"Yeah. Back by the head...um...the latrine. I'll show you later. Do you know where the mess hall is?"

"Since it's right outside my tent, yeah. I think I might be able to find it."

At least the flip reply brought a hesitant smile to her brother's lips, probably because their bantering was so familiar, so much like how they'd been before the invasion. Just a couple of siblings who liked to tease.

"Ten minutes or I'm coming back here." On that order, Kevin left before Kara could tell him to stop bossing her around.

Aiodhan threw the blanket aside and stood.

Kara couldn't stop staring. His butt was perfect. Absolutely perfect. He even had dimples where the cheeks met the small of his back. She sighed in appreciation before she could catch herself.

He turned to smile at her.

One eyeful of his body had her squirming in need and wondering if she'd ever get enough of him. He was so magnificent he might have been sculpted in marble and put in a museum for women to admire as the prototype for what males should look like. Michelangelo would have been the only artist who could do her alien justice.

"You wish to mate again." His words, given with authority and a twinkle in his gray eyes, made her straighten her spine.

"Know what?"

"No. What?"

"You really need to get a grip on that ego."

Kara didn't even bother trying to hold the blanket over her bare breasts since the three times they'd made love during the night let her know that her body pleased him. At this rate, they'd run out of condoms pretty damned fast. The soreness between her thighs reminded her just how enthusiastic a lover he was. A small groan slipped out when she stepped over to her pile of clothes.

"You are in pain." He said as he jerked his shirt over his head.

Since he didn't miss much, she didn't try to hide her grimace when she dragged her panties up her legs. "I'm fine."

Aiodhan stepped over to her as he buckled on his utility belt. "Where is pain?"

"I'm fine," she insisted, embarrassed to even be having this conversation.

Having him put his huge body directly in front of her made it difficult to finish dressing. He loomed over her like some avenging angel. "Not fine."

The stare-down commenced, lasting far too long, but she wasn't about to be the first to back down. For several long moments, he glared at her, the only movement coming as he set his hands against his hips.

The tension built until he suddenly grabbed her, tugged her into his arms, and covered her lips with his. He kissed the stubbornness right out of her.

As he eased back to look into her eyes, a grin twitched on his mouth when she conceded and admitted, "I'm a little…sore. You're just so…big. And we did it three times."

"It? What is *it?*" His grin grew.

She slapped him on the chest and pulled on her shirt. "Quit acting like you don't know what I'm talking about. You understand a lot more than what you let on, and don't think I don't know it." Plopping down, she pulled on her socks and boots as he did the same.

"Now we eat." Aiodhan grabbed her hand, jerked her to her feet, and led her out of the tent.

* * *

Aiodhan ate another scoop of breakfast. The food the men offered

85

wasn't bad. Protein. Carbohydrates. Enough to fuel his body without having to use one of his nutrition packs.

Kara liked it, judging from how she shoveled things into her mouth. She treated the hot, brown drink as if it was something precious, holding the cup between her palms and gingerly sipping. He'd found it bitter and offered his to her, pleased that she gave him a heart-stopping smile in response.

Aiodhan liked the texture of the human food. The yellow protein was airy and warm. Kara added a pinch of some ground white spice for him, and the flavor improved. After he swallowed the last bite of the protein, he pointed to the same yellow fluff left on Kara's tray. "What is this?"

"Scrambled eggs. Not sure from what kind of bird since I haven't seen any—"

"They're chicken eggs." Bill set his tray down next to hers and took a seat on the bench to her right. "We've got quite a few hiding in different places in the woods. The lizards don't do sweeps now, so we rounded up as much livestock as we could. Need a sustained food source. Chickens are cheap and easy to care for, and our hens lay like crazy." His eyes swept Kara in a way that made Aiodhan's temper rise. "Eat up, sweetheart. You need to put some meat back on those bones."

Bill grabbed a piece of fruit from his tray and set it on Kara's.

Aiodhan reached over, snatched the fruit, and tossed it back to Bill. Then he took his own fruit and held it out to Kara.

"Thanks, guys, but I have my own apple." She picked up her green fruit and took a bite.

The crunchy sound and the way she sucked in the juices she'd released had Aiodhan's body tightening in response, ready to claim her yet again. She chewed as she spoke, holding her hand in front of her mouth in some sort of social gesture, perhaps to keep people from watching the food as it was consumed. "I love Granny Smith apples."

"Enjoy 'em now," Bill said. "Come winter, there won't be much fruit."

"Try it, Aiodhan." Kara nodded at the apple he still held.

Since everything she'd had him taste had been pleasing, Aiodhan took a big bite out of the apple. His cheeks puckered as the sour juices bathed his mouth, and his first instinct was to spit it out. Only fear of offending the men who'd supplied the life-sustaining food forced him to chew and then swallow the crisp and decidedly tart fruit.

Kara's eyes glistened with amusement. Instead of giving her more satisfaction at having surprised him, he held his own apple out to her. "You take now. Put meat on bones."

She burst out laughing, a sound Aiodhan knew he'd never tire of hearing, especially knowing how much the Vymalns had made her suffer.

Her happiness had become his.

The smile on his face fell to a frown, and he turned back to his food, spooning whatever was left on his tray into his mouth, hardly tasting it. Taking a mate had become much more complicated than it should have been. The fact that he found delight in pleasing her hinted of deeper feelings, something other than the simple need to protect and honor her. Kara could become a weakness if he allowed himself to develop true affection for her.

Seekers couldn't be weak. He had a job to do, and it was time to focus on that and stop trying to please his mate or earn her love.

Her stare felt like hot rays from the Earth's sun, making his face flush warm. After a few uncomfortable moments, she thankfully returned to her meal and to talking to Bill.

"Is the clinic ready?" Bill asked.

Kara nodded as she ate.

"I'm gonna have to tell the men they can't dream up a bunch of aches and pains just to get to spend time with you."

"What do you mean?"

Bill snorted a laugh. "Most these guys haven't seen a woman, and a pretty one at that, in quite a while. They're gonna be wanting to get close to you. I imagine you'll see quite a few fake ailments 'til they get used to having you around."

Aiodhan growled as her face reddened. Sick and tired of the men in this group ignoring his claim, he stated it again. "My mate. Kara is *my* mate."

"Really?" Bill leaned in to look around her. "Well, you might have slept in her tent last night, but I haven't heard Kara say anything about being your *mate*." He turned to her. "So do you belong to him?"

After what had passed between them in the night, Aiodhan waited for Kara's affirmation. Her passionate response to his touch and the way her body had welcomed him gave the only answer he needed.

He quickly recognized that thought for the lie it was. He needed to hear Kara say it. He wanted to know she had claimed him the same way he'd claimed her. What tumbled out of her mouth came as a shock that left him speechless.

"I don't *belong* to anybody."

As Bill grinned, Aiodhan tamped down his blood lust, torn between grabbing Kara and shaking some sense into her and pounding Bill's face until that cocky smile vanished.

How could he have been so wrong?

Yes, he and Kara were from different worlds, but they had experienced a connection—a mating—of such intensity and tenderness that he couldn't accept her response.

Staring into her dark eyes, he found his voice. "You are *my mate*." The words were uttered through clenched teeth.

Kara's heart pounded so hard, she feared it would leap right out of her chest. The voraciousness behind Aiodhan's angry declaration hit her like a punch, hard enough she almost wrapped her arms around her belly to ward off the pain.

Why couldn't he understand? She had to let him go. He wasn't of this world. He was a fighter, a lone wolf. She wouldn't allow his desire to protect her become a trap that ensnared him, because he'd soon come to resent her for it.

She had Kevin now. Her brother would help her. Soon, she prayed, she'd have her father at her side again.

So why did it hurt so much to think about Aiodhan leaving her behind?

Just as his eyes had changed when they'd made love, they shifted shade again, becoming such a dark, angry gray that they reminded her of an approaching storm—a dangerous one. Of course he was mad. She would've been, too, had their roles been reversed. As it stood, he had to think she'd used him for his strength and his protection, perhaps even for that gorgeous and virile body.

Everything inside her wanted to sing out a *yes!* Yes, she was his mate. Yes, she loved him. Yes, she wanted to hold him at her side for the rest of their lives. It didn't matter a hill of beans that he was an alien—but it *did* matter that he wasn't the kind of man a woman could tie down.

She might have been stupid enough to let herself fall head over heels for him, but Kara wasn't selfish enough to try force him stay. "N-no, Aiodhan. I'm not your mate. I'm your friend."

Bill put a hand on her shoulder. "So maybe you'd like to go out on patrol with me. I can show you the booby traps and—"

Aiodhan's tray went flying, swiped from the table with a flick of his wrist as he jumped to his feet. Bill scrambled up as well, putting himself between her and an enraged Aiodhan. Before Kara could move, Aiodhan fisted his hands in Bill's vest and hauled him up until the poor guy's feet dangled in the air.

"Let him go!" She grabbed Aiodhan's arm and yanked, hoping he'd release Bill. She might as well have been trying to move a mountain.

"Kara is *my mate*." Aiodhan's words were as raw as an open wound. He gave Bill a hard shake that made the poor man's head flop like a rag doll.

Feeling both delight that Aiodhan had a strong devotion to his role as her protector and anger that he thought he needed to pound anyone who came near her, Kara adopted a tone she'd used time and time again as a nurse when she needed to get a patient stronger than her to comply. "Put him down. Now."

Bill was tossed aside with an ease that sent a shiver down her spine. If Aiodhan ever directed his anger at her, he could snap her like a twig. Yet somehow, she knew he'd never raise a hand to her.

As Bill slid across the table, he sent trays of precious food flipping and sliding.

Kara hurried to check him for injuries. "You okay?"

He turned his gaze to her, and the amusement there took her by surprise. "I'm guessing your alien doesn't think you have much choice in the matter."

Aiodhan clenched his hands at his side. "Kara. Come here."

He had no right to snap orders at her. Perhaps some kind of serious talk was in order about this "mate" nonsense.

She threw him a glare as she helped Bill from the table. "You don't get to boss me around, Tarzan."

"Boss around? I dislike your language. You learn Tirian. Soon."

"It means that you don't get to tell me what I can and can't do. And I like my language just fine."

"My mate! Must do as I say."

"Fuck that."

The situation went from bad to worse when Pashmar strolled over with her plastic tray, a smirk lighting her face. She'd clearly heard and probably seen all that had passed between him and Kara.

"A fight? So soon?" Her voice was full of mischief. "Your mate searches for another, Aiodhan?"

Chapter Eleven

When Kara hadn't moved to immediately obey, Aiodhan found himself at a loss. He thought about throwing her over his shoulder and carrying her back to the tent where he'd give her a good, long lecture. Unfortunately, it would have to be in Tirian since he was too angry to find the right English words.

Hauling her around could make her feel he was forcing his will upon her. He wanted her to come with him willingly. Why did she have to be so-so-frustrating? While Pashmar might be every bit as strong willed and stubborn, she would have done anything he asked if she was his mate.

Perhaps that was one of the things that drew him to Kara—she wasn't like Pashmar. She wasn't like anyone he'd ever known.

They stood toe-to-toe now, him with hands on hips glaring down at her, a position he found himself in far too often as he tried to intimidate her into accepting his wishes. Her intense stare told him she would never back down. Never.

When she'd said she belonged to no one, his heart felt as if something had squeezed it too tightly—an absurd reaction. His feelings weren't involved. No, this wasn't about his *feelings*. Not in the least. This was a matter of teaching his lifemate her proper place and being sure she obeyed his authority, especially when it was important to her safety. And by the stars, he'd have her acceptance if he had to stand there for eternity.

The irony made him smile. He'd never be able bully Kara into being the perfect mate, which was exactly what made her the perfect mate.

"What?" Her gaze searched his. He took comfort in the fact he'd thrown her off balance. It was a small victory, but a victory nonetheless. "Why are you smiling?"

His smile grew when she frowned.

Her species had gorgeous eyes, Kara's more beautiful than any other's. Dark and expressive. They sparkled with passion when he'd been deep inside her, when she'd been climaxing in his arms. That was a sight he needed to view more often.

Aiodhan wanted to mate with her again, and not simply because he remembered the sweet release he'd found. It was the only time she did exactly what he wished her to do.

Someone cleared his throat loudly, breaking the tension as Aiodhan and Kara both turned to Bill, the source of the interruption. "Excuse me for intruding, but... Since this is a bone of contention between you two, how 'bout we change the subject?"

"Bone?" Why was Bill speaking of skeletal structures? "From what does this bone come?"

With a smirk, Bill left that riddle behind. "What I mean is that you two can't seem to agree, so we should talk about something else."

Kara blinked a few more times as she turned back to search Aiodhan's face. Then she looked to Bill and nodded. "What do you want to talk about?"

"The raid I'm planning on the IC."

"Raid? You will go to the camp?" Aiodhan gave the leader of these fighters his full attention, grateful to be relieved from thinking about things that made him so uncomfortable—like the realization he had a long way to go to get Kara to accept her new role in his life. His mission would require him to leave her soon.

Khymer Cantu, his target, was supposed to be found in the city of Seattle. Aiodhan wouldn't rest until he was dead. His Seeker vows meant he'd have to go alone while Kara remained here, among all these men. It was vital to know she would be waiting when he returned and that she'd be faithful to him while he was away. He'd tolerate nothing less.

"Yeah, we're heading back to the IC, but we're not going in yet," Bill replied. "Thought we'd see if we could snatch a few more people out of the lizards' hands. Grab 'em while they're working in the fields."

The man had confidence. *A true leader.*

"When?" Aiodhan asked.

"Today."

"We can look for my dad," Kara said, jumping in.

Bill shook his head at the same time Aiodhan did.

"Why the hell not?" she asked, her tone belligerent. Quick as anything, she moved to Bill, giving the man the same censuring frown she'd thrown at Aiodhan several times. "If we're going into the IC—"

Bill set his hands on her shoulders, making Aiodhan swallow hard to hold back the urge to smack them away. "Relax, sweetheart. This isn't a break-into-the-main-part-of-the-IC mission. It's a grab-a-couple-of-field-workers mission."

She put her hands on her hips and shouted in his face. "Why in the hell can't we get my father?"

"If he's there, we'll try. Okay?"

"I should go with you on the raid."

"Not this time." Dismissing her, Bill turned to Aiodhan. "I'm taking a small squad to one of the fields where they have people harvesting. We're gonna see if we can sneak a couple out the way I did my sister. Pashmar's coming. Wanna come along too?"

* * *

The IC was exactly what Aiodhan expected, having seen many times the way Vymaln swooped in and claimed a planet as their own.

Nomads for millennia, their disgusting race moved from star system to star system, searching for new worlds to rape for natural resources, including enslaving the inhabitants of wherever they landed. Their economy thrived on using other species as free labor to harness all a planet had to offer, often stripping it bare before moving on. Sometimes, they set up renewable sources of food and fuel driven by those they'd enslaved.

Vymalns were the scum of the galaxy.

The field was half-harvested of its golden grain. From where he lay in the tall grass on the hill above, Aiodhan counted only four guards watching thirty humans laboring to cut and stack the stalks.

So typical of the Vymalns.

They grew complacent once a population was conquered, a habit he wondered if they'd ever break. The sentries hardly gave attention to their captives. Bill and his men would be able to spirit away a few people without the Vymalns even knowing.

Snatching people away wouldn't change things. All they'd achieve was a moral victory that would be stripped away if the Vymalns retaliated by organizing sweeping squads. Only liberating the detention camps and killing all the Vymalns would end this occupation, and the humans hadn't shown any kind of ability to accomplish either of those feats. The Tirians might be able to help, but Aiodhan knew any expectation of that happening was false hope.

Even a handful of elite Seekers might be enough to turn the tide of this war, but that wasn't within the scope of their mission—of *any* Seeker mission. His target had been pre-selected, as had Pashmar's. Taking out those targets wouldn't change the destruction of this world. There was nothing either could do to end this occupation. Once the Seekers accomplished their tasks, they'd have to leave.

The humans would never understand.

Glancing over at Bill, regret ate at Aiodhan's conscience for the first time since he'd become a Seeker. These humans weren't at all what he'd expected, and the idea of fulfilling his mission and returning to home base wasn't as cut-and-dried as his other assignments.

Normally, he'd swoop in, stalk his target, remove that future threat, then return to the Seeker ship. He'd never interacted with the natives before. All he'd ever cared about was his important job—to preserve the future of the Tirian race and end the Vymaln threat to their future world.

He wasn't supposed to offer aid to those under their tyranny.

His attack of guilt was all Kara's fault. Damn it all if she hadn't made him care about her.

That admission alone was enough to turn his mood sour. And it wasn't just Kara anymore, either. It was *all* of the people in that camp. Jayce and his tenacity to find help. Bill and his dedication in protecting the people under his care. Kevin and his genuine excitement at finding his sister after so long.

Pashmar jarred Aiodhan from his thoughts. "You should have left by now."

Although she whispered to him in English, this discussion really needed to be kept from the humans. He replied in Tirian. "I'll go. Soon."

She matched his lead. "Now. You should go *now,* and you damn well know it. The Praemons told you that Khymer Cantu—"

"Would one day rule the Vymaln. I know my mission well, Pashmar. I'll find him, and I'll kill him."

"Then stop dragging your feet. Go."

He grunted.

"What's holding you here?" Not even giving him time to form a response, she pressed on. "Her. That-that-human. You're staying for her."

"She's my mate."

"There's no place for her on my ship. She'd never make a life on Tirios. She can't go with you when you leave here, and you damn well know it."

"She *can* and she *will.*"

There was no other solution. Kara couldn't remain on Earth after he left. She'd still be in danger, and that wasn't acceptable. Not for his mate.

What if she refused him?

Pashmar shook her head.

He waved her off. "Enough. Just stop it."

"I won't *stop it.*" When Bill turned to glare at her, she lowered her volume. "We shouldn't be here. We shouldn't be helping these people. That's not our job."

"Don't tell me my job. I know my mission."

"Then do it." Pushing back, she crawled out of the overgrowth and left him to his troubled thoughts and Bill's intense frown.

"Let me guess," Bill said. "Trouble with the ladies, Aidan?"

Aiodhan had given up correcting the man because he knew he was mispronouncing his name on purpose.

"Where does Pashmar think you're supposed to be?"

"I have a job to do. In different city."

"Where?"

Figuring this close to the Vymalns wasn't the most opportune place to have this discussion, Aiodhan dismissed the question, moved out of the overgrowth and marched back to where the rest of the men were assembled.

Bill followed. "Where are you supposed to go?"

The strange word was hard to pronounce. "See-at-all."

"Seattle? You're supposed to be in Seattle?"

Sparing a nod, Aiodhan veered through the trees, picking up his pace. He didn't want to discuss his mission with Bill of all people. Should the man figure out the whole truth of his presence here on Earth, he'd run to Kara and try to poison her mind against him.

"How in the hell did you end up in Montana?" Bill asked as he hurried to keep up.

"Crashed."

"Crashed? You mean a spaceship?"

Aiodhan stopped so abruptly, Bill ran into his back. As Bill took a step back, Aiodhan whirled to confront him. "Why questions?"

"Why not? You're an alien. You're involved with people I lead, people I care about, people I'm trying to help survive. I have to watch out for them, so I need to know your motives."

Why did everything these people say cultivate more respect? They weren't the selfish, stupid creatures he'd been told about. They were caring and courageous, and he wasn't sure how he felt about that. He also wasn't up to facing any questions about his mission or the role he would—actually *wouldn't*—play in the future of this world.

"I must go to Kara." Aiodhan had to talk to her first of all.

The tight frown on Pashmar's face told him that the whole story was going to come out. Soon. She wasn't any more comfortable keeping secrets from these humans than he was. For some reason, that gave him another newfound respect. For her. She'd formed a bond with these people as well. Her feelings were involved now.

There was that word again.

Feelings.

His whole life had been about discipline. Dedication. Demands. From the time he'd hit *ungala*—the time of great physical change—he'd pushed himself to develop his body and strengthen his mind, all with one goal. To become a Seeker.

The Seeker Corps was revered on Tirios. They were given access to the temple of the Praemons. They were entrusted with the sacred task of finding the future threats predicted by the Praemons and destroying them as a way to change the future and protect Tirios from the Vymalns.

Feelings had no place in a Seeker's life. There was no room in his world for affection. Not for another species, sometimes not even for a mate.

No wonder Pashmar had been appalled at what she'd witnessed. Aiodhan could only remember two other Seekers who took mates; one was his commanding officer, the other was a Seeker who chose his mate after his time of service to the Praemons ended. Of course few in the corps lived long enough to find leisure in their elder years.

To take Kara as his mate at this time of his journey was foolhardy. Even Jaman, his commander, would tell Aiodhan so, seeing as he often joked about the shackles his mate kept on him.

Aiodhan smiled. Bucking tradition was his specialty. Hadn't he been the youngest Tirian ever accepted into service by the Praemons?

His mind was made up. He'd bring Kara back to the Seeker ship, then back to his home near the temple. He'd let all of Tirios know she was his spouse. Damn the gossips and the disapprovers. He'd always trusted his intuition, knowing it had served him well. From the moment he'd seen her, touched her, Aiodhan had known Kara Michaels was his mate. If a few tender feelings now intertwined with that intuition, so be it.

"I must see Kara now."

On that, he marched back toward camp. He needed to see her and to explain before Pashmar had the chance.

Chapter Twelve

Kara wasn't in camp.

Aiodhan had checked the clinic first. She'd been busy while he was gone. The shelves were now packed with supplies. A new glass and metal cabinet, one with a lock, held a variety of bottles—probably precious medications that she'd want to protect.

He opened the flap to the back room. The bedding was neatly arranged, and the few things she owned had been unpacked and placed in order on a small crate. Having always prized tidy surroundings, he loved that she had the same desire.

Desire.

Somehow that word was always linked with Kara.

Desire now had him gripped tightly in its talons. The whole hike back to camp, he'd fantasized about finding her and making love to her again. No woman had ever made him lose his discipline so thoroughly. At that moment, nothing mattered except Kara. Not the mission. Not the Vymalns. Not these humans.

Just her.

As Aiodhan checked the rest of the camp, his panic rose. She wasn't anywhere to be found, nor had anyone seen her in a while. Her dog seemed quite happy to curl up on a blanket and sleep next to Jayce as the boy labored over a multitude of computers, trying to reach other humans. Aiodhan hadn't even paused to give Chance an affectionate stroke because of his growing concern for Kara. When he located her brother and Kevin didn't know where she'd gone, Aiodhan yanked his locator out of his pocket and switched it on.

"What's that?" Kevin asked.

These humans asked far too many questions. "Locator."

"Locator? Like a tracking device?"

Aiodhan grunted as he waited until the icons popped up. Seeing that Kara was only a short distance away almost made him sigh in relief.

"You put some kind of tracker on Kara?"

He pointed to the pink icon. "Kara." Then he pointed to his own icon. "Me."

"Bet she had a fit over that."

Aiodhan didn't even bother to shrug.

Kevin took in the map for a few moments. "Looks like she's watching the camp—the IC." His fingers pushed into the light to tweak the pink marker. "If I'm reading this map right, I'd say she's on the hill we use to keep an eye on the lizards."

Aiodhan's heart slammed a rough tempo at the thought of her drawing close to danger. All of his rationalizations about his feelings for her being nothing more than honor and loyalty to his mate taunted him.

"I go to her."

* * *

"Fuckin' bug-eyes." Kara tossed another pebble in the air, watching it fly in an arc to land further down the hill. The sentry tower was too far away for anyone to see her let alone react to a tiny rocks tumbling down a hillside. Heaving them released some of the growing tension inside her.

The razor wire stretched in twisted loops around the top of the high chain-link fence. Although it looked like any ordinary prison, it wasn't. The place was more akin to a Nazi concentration camp than a penitentiary.

People housed there were nothing more than slaves, and her heart hurt as she thought about her father living to help the Vymalns—harvesting grain that wasn't theirs or digging minerals out of ground that didn't belong to them. She doubted the inmates were treated much better than the people who'd suffered in Auschwitz or Dachau.

"I'll help you, Daddy. I swear."

No tears came as she thought about her father. The time for crying had ended long ago. All that remained was a fury that burned inside her until she feared it would consume her soul and leave her a hollow shell.

She'd find a way to free her father. Somehow. Someday. Kevin had escaped. Bill had snatched Julie right from under their green noses. Both of those miracles happened before Aiodhan arrived.

Aiodhan.

The mere thought of him changed the heat of her rage to a different kind of fire, one that made her breath catch as she remembered making love with him. She'd never forget the way he made her burn, and she was brave enough to recognize it for what it was.

She loved him. Desperately. Ardently. Probably irrevocably.

Her nature had always been to approach every experience with arms wide open, and she faced this relationship in the same fashion. He might be an alien, but he wasn't a bug-eye. Aiodhan was a hero, a champion. He was exactly what she needed—her knight in shining armor.

She had no doubt that he'd be at her side in the fight to free her father. Yes, he had some other mission. But as soon as he completed that task, he'd come back to her, and together they'd find a way to smuggle her father out of the IC. As strong and smart as Aiodhan was, he'd probably be able to liberate the entire damned camp, maybe even help Bill's group launch some kind of attack that could lead to the Vymalns' ultimate destruction.

Closing her eyes, she sighed.

One step at a time, Kara. Dad first. The world later.

Aiodhan's pledge to take care of her meant a great deal, but what had finally convinced her of his sincerity was the way he'd made love to her. No man had ever been so honest in his reactions, and although he probably wouldn't admit it, he cared for her. Not that men were ever good at recognizing feelings for what they truly were. He had to believe he was simply protecting her.

So be it.

Lots of men stumbled through life without confessing what they felt deep in their hearts.

But Aiodhan wasn't a man.

Kara smiled over her predicament. In the middle of the conquest of Earth, she'd fallen in love with an alien.

How fucking absurd.

"Kara..."

She whirled to Aiodhan's voice to find him leaning a shoulder against a sturdy pine tree, strong arms folded over his broad chest as he watched her. Although he appeared downright bored, his unwavering stare said otherwise. Didn't he ever blink?

Suddenly self-conscious, she combed her fingers through her bangs before tightening her ponytail. His intense stare only made her more anxious. "How long have you been there?"

He shrugged but didn't make a move toward her. His relaxed body language belied the stormy passion in his eyes.

"It's getting late." The sky was turning a kaleidoscope of pink, yellow, and orange. "Wanna head back to grab some supper? Who knows what the reivers found for us to eat?"

"I do not know. Do you?"

"Don't start that again, Tarzan."

"What are ree-vers?" His eyes raked her from head to toe as if the question didn't really matter.

Kara's whole body flushed hot. Why wasn't he moving? Should she go to him? She took a hesitant step forward as she finally answered. "A nickname for the guys who, um., find our food and supplies. They call themselves that as a sort of joke. Reivers hunt for things." Not sure what else to do, she took another stride toward him.

"*Revoms.*" Aiodhan pushed away from the tree, his body unfolding until his size nearly overwhelmed her as he drew closer.

"I beg your pardon?"

"*Revoms*. Word for thieves in my language." In one swift motion, Aiodhan grabbed her wrist, kissed her palm, and tugged Kara into his arms.

Right where she wanted to be.

She melted into his embrace, opening her mouth to him the moment his lips touched hers. His responding growl when her tongue swept into his mouth sent the warmth already racing through her flaring into an inferno of desire. As he lifted her off her feet, she wrapped her legs around his hips, squeezing him tight.

All thoughts of her family and his mission floated away like dandelion seeds drifting on a strong breeze. The only thing that mattered was her alien. The feel of his arms around her. The taste of him on her lips. The masculine groans as his mouth slanted over hers again and again.

Aiodhan carried her to the shelter of the trees before he let her slide down his body. Once on her feet, she shrugged out of her down vest, hoping he realized she didn't want to wait to get back to camp. This place was plenty private, and at that moment, she needed him.

To hell with my soreness.

He yanked her shirt over her head and dropped it on top of her vest. With a naughty smile that revealed a delectable dimple on his right cheek, he fell to his knees. After he removed her boots, he fumbled with the button and zipper on her jeans before he peeled them down her body.

Kara didn't mind the cool autumn breeze rushing over her bare skin. She was warm enough to bear it, especially when Aiodhan rained kisses under her breasts. After he popped off her bra, he laved first one nipple and then the other until they both hardened into tight pebbles.

Holding his head right where she wanted him, she moaned. Each gentle tug with his teeth was followed by a soothing lick of his tongue. Tingles zinged down her limbs, centering in her core, making her throb with want.

Aiodhan pressed kisses to her ribs and down her stomach, leaving a trail of gooseflesh in his wake. His tongue circled her navel, and she wished she still had the little gold hoop she used to wear there.

What would Tarzan think of a pierced belly button?

She never had time to ask, because he pulled off her panties and cast them aside.

He stared at her body, his eyes swirling with shimmering gray. "So beautiful. My mate is so beautiful."

If there was beauty here, it was in his big, strong body. Kara wanted to tell him just how handsome he was, how much looking at him, touching him, pleased her and sent her passion soaring. She craved his hot skin beneath her fingertips.

Before she could start tugging his shirt off, wanting to be skin to skin with him, his hands settled on her hips, holding her steady. Then he nudged her thighs open by pressing his face between them.

She gasped as he stroked her with his tongue, widening her stance when he slipped a hand up the inside of her thigh to heighten the torture. His fingers stroked and teased until he was able to slide a finger deep inside her. With a whimper, she let her head fall back and gave herself over to him fully.

He made her feel so uninhibited and free that she didn't even try to slow the onslaught of the approaching orgasm. It galloped through her body, forcing her closer and closer to release. Tugging on his hair, she whispered that she wanted him to make love to her so she could climax with him inside her.

With an arrogant male chuckle, he ignored her pleas and increased his torment. Then his tongue found the most sensitive part of her.

Kara gave in to all he inspired, knowing she was safe as long as Aiodhan was there. Her knees buckled when the orgasm hit, but he caught her, holding her tight against him as he laid his cheek against her stomach. Waves of bliss washed over her, and she called his name, letting her love for him spill out in an avalanche of words that probably didn't make sense to him.

Aiodhan had never heard anything as beautiful as Kara's declarations of her feelings for him. She'd revealed her love. Loudly.

Knowing he'd brought her pleasure and that her words meant she'd accepted him as her mate, he wanted to possess her body the way he possessed her heart.

Leaving her wouldn't be as difficult now. Once he explained his duty as Seeker, she would understand and wait for him to fulfill that duty. Then he would come back to collect her. He'd take her to the base and eventually to Tirios. They could start their lives together.

He no longer felt the need to somehow mark her, to force the men of the camp to keep their distance. Her love for him would serve just as strongly, because Kara would never take another now.

She belongs to me.

Dropping to his back, he helped her as she unbuckled his belt and unfastened his pants. When his naked buttocks rested on the cold ground, he didn't give a damn. She straddled his knees and leaned down to run her tongue up the hard length of his *kull*.

He drew in a ragged breath, trying to hold off the need to simply drag her up his body so he could take her right then and there. If his mate wanted to explore his body, who was he to deny her? Somehow he'd find the strength to endure her delicious torment.

Kara's tongue was hot as she licked and teased him. Her fingernails raked up the skin of his inner thigh before she cradled his sac in her hand and gave it a gentle squeeze. While he wanted to bear her attentions, his body demanded release.

Aiodhan hauled her up the length of his body so that his *kull* pressed against her feminine core. "Now, Kara. Now."

Rising on her knees, she wrapped her fingers around his erection and guided him to her tight channel. Then she impaled herself on him as she moaned and he growled in triumph.

The pleasure she gave him was instant and consuming. Her sheath surrounded him, enfolded him, and the wet, warm feel of her was nearly enough to make him spill his seed right then and there. Holding on to what few strands of control he could, he rocked his hips up, pushing himself deeply inside her, as deep as he could go.

"So good," she purred. She leaned back, bracing her hands on his thighs and closing her eyes. Her breasts swayed with each of his thrusts, and her head fell back. "So damn good."

Tightly grasping her hips, Aiodhan lifted her and then plunged back into her as he let her drop. Over and over he savored the sensuous feel of her snug heat squeezing every last thought from his mind. When he was with her, when he loved her, the universe was nothing more than the two of them locked in ecstasy.

While he wanted to make this mating last and last, his body acted of its own volition, tightening and screaming for release. He snaked his hand between them to find her sensitive nub, and he stroked, hoping to bring her to orgasm before he claimed his own.

Kara gasped. Twice. Then she called out his name as she arched her back and came for him.

Aiodhan joined her in paradise, his climax forcing a shout of surrender from his lips.

In the aftermath, she collapsed against his chest. Her shivers made him wrap his arms around her to ward off the chill. Very little sunlight remained, and when Earth's sun disappeared, it took the warmth along. Soon, the cold would force them both to dress and leave this wonderful place.

"We should go back." She'd whispered the words as she rubbed her cheek against his chest.

Since his body was still joined with hers, he didn't think she meant for them to move too quickly, or else she would have pulled away from him. He was content to hold her as long as she would allow.

The feel of her body pressed against his and the scent of their lovemaking permeating the air made his *kull* start to harden again. No female had ever affected him so dramatically, and he doubted another ever would again.

Kara pushed up to stare into his eyes. "Again? Already?"

With a grin, he raised his hips. "Already. You do this to me."

Her smile was sensual as she pulled the tie from her headtail and let her gorgeous brown hair spill about her shoulders. "Well, then…Let me show you what *you* do to *me*."

When she leaned forward and framed his face in her palms, he lifted his head so his mouth could meet hers. Then he lost himself in her kiss.

Supper would have to wait.

Chapter Thirteen

Kara tried not to wince as she sat on the bench. Surrounded by men, they'd all tease the hell out of her if they knew why she was so tender.

Sweet heavens, she and Aiodhan had been reckless, not even thinking about using a condom. Of course she hadn't considered Aiodhan would ravage her in the woods, either. She gave a passing thought to searching for morning after pills in her stash of meds but quickly abandoned it. What would be would be, and she refused to stress over something that would probably never happen. She had more than enough worries and didn't need to borrow trouble.

The food smelled good, even if it didn't look like anything more than typical school cafeteria fare. After going so long without much, even eating lumpy instant potatoes off a plastic tray couldn't diminish her appetite.

Aiodhan sat down next to her, swallowing up enough space on the bench that his thigh rested hard against hers. He winked, a gesture Tirians evidently used the same way as humans, as he picked up the salt shaker and sprinkled it over his chicken and noodles.

Heat spread over her cheeks. It wasn't like her alien to be playful, especially in front of all the men.

Kevin gave her a brotherly frown from across the table. "You almost missed supper."

"Sorry," she replied. "I lost track of time."

Aiodhan snorted before shoveling a forkful of potatoes into his mouth.

She decided to change the subject. Quickly. "How did things go on the raid?"

"Didn't snatch anyone," Kevin replied. "But the sentries are getting lazy. Bill says we might try to grab a couple tomorrow to see just how observant the lizards are." He shifted his attention to Aiodhan. "You wanna go out with us again?" As he picked up his tin cup and sipped, he grumbled, "Maybe you'll stay a little longer next time."

Aiodhan shook his head. "I must leave before the sun returns."

"Leave?" Her eyes met his. "You're leaving tomorrow?"

He nodded before scooping some more food into his mouth.

Figuring that was a dismissal of discussing his mission in front of everyone, she dropped her gaze back to her food. Her appetite had fled as fast as a startled robin, so she just moved the food around with her fork and waited for Aiodhan to finish eating so they could go back to the tent and talk.

To complete Kara's fall from ecstasy to despair, Pashmar strolled over, chomping on a red apple. She sat down on Aiodhan's other side.

"A pleasant evening to all," she said as she stared at him.

Kevin smiled, a flirty sort of smile that took Kara by surprise. "It is now. Did you know Aiodhan's leaving?"

"You go on your mission?" Pashmar asked.

He nodded as he finished the last of his food.

As he tried to rise, she settled her hand on his shoulder. "I wish you success. I go tomorrow as well."

"You're leaving, too?" Kevin asked. "I figured you might want to help us snatch a couple of people away from the fields."

"It is a tempting offer," Pashmar replied, "but I must complete my mission. Then perhaps I shall return."

"You cannot," Aiodhan said as he threw a frown at her. "I must have use of your ship to get to See-at-all."

"Ah, yes. Your target is of higher importance than mine." She smiled at Kevin. "I shall stay and be of assistance to you. Then I shall complete my mission.

Aiodhan's mouth pulled into a grim line. "We must talk, Kara."

"You're leaving me?" Kara asked.

"You are my mate. I will not leave you."

"Then you'll be back." She wasn't sure her heart would ever settle into a normal rhythm again. While she hadn't wanted to think he'd simply abandon her, Pashmar's little bomb had frightened her.

"He will not return," Pashmar said.

Kevin looked as confused as Kara felt. "What the hell does that mean?"

"Once a Seeker completes the mission, he must receive a new mission." Pashmar's voice was calm considering the confusion that now swirled around her. Everyone was staring. "We shall not return to this place."

Laying a hand on Aiodhan's arm, Kara said, "I don't understand. You just said you'd be back."

Men who'd been carrying their trays to the wash area set them aside and surrounded the table. Jayce and Bill came striding up as well with Chance following close behind. Seeing how her dog clung to Jayce's side, she figured Chance had moved on to someone else who needed him. Her heart ached, but the dog would be better off staying in camp. This was his home now.

"Hey, Bill," Kevin called. "Did'ya know Aiodhan's leaving tomorrow? For good. Then Pashmar's outta here too."

Aiodhan frowned at Kevin. "I must talk to Kara now." His gaze flitted across the gathering crowd. "Alone."

"You two are leaving?" Bill stood behind Kevin, glaring at Aiodhan. "What's he mean 'for good'?"

Pashmar dove right in as if she'd been asked the question. "We must complete our missions as Seekers, then we shall return to be given new missions. We thank you for sharing your food and lodging with us."

The few trays left on the table bounced when Aiodhan's fist slammed down. "Do not speak for me." He rose from the bench and grabbed Kara's hand. "We must talk. Now."

As he dragged her away from the tent, she cast a glance back to see everyone staring at them.

Hell, after that little show, she'd be staring, too.

* * *

"I must go," Aiodhan said as he stroked Kara's cheek. "I have a mission."

She leaned into his touch, glad they had a few moments of privacy. They stood in the clinic area, the tips of her boots brushing his. Should they go back to the bedroom, they'd no doubt find themselves naked again in short order. First, there was a lot they needed to discuss.

No doubt, Kevin, Bill, and Pashmar would soon come to the tent, looking to continue the confusing discussion from supper. She wouldn't welcome their intrusion until she straightened out things in her own mind.

"I know," she said. "I also know you'll do what you have to do quickly. Then you can come back to me." She gave him a hesitant smile, hating that she sounded like a lovesick girlfriend, even if that was exactly what she was. "I just don't understand what Pashmar meant, that you won't come back."

"Kara, we will leave when I return."

A cold shiver ran the length of her spine. "Leave?" The word had echoed in her head like the beating of a bass drum ever since Pashmar had made her announcement. "You mean go back to the cabin? Why would we—"

"No. We will leave this place."

"I don't understand."

"Return to my ship."

"Your ship's a mess. You said you were using Pashmar's. Why would I go on her ship with you?"

Aiodhan shook his head, causing her stomach to tie itself into nervous knots. His exaggerated sigh didn't help. "Kara, we must leave. We must return to Seeker ship."

105

"Why?"

"I must report."

She expelled a relieved breath. "Oh, okay. I finally get it now. You've gotta let your boss know you did your job. But then you won't take a new one so you can help with my Dad, right? You can go back to being a Seeker later, when Daddy's free."

"Kara, please listen." His tone was downright condescending

She pressed on with her train of thought. "I don't have to go with you, though. I can just—" Her hands fisted against her hips. "Stop shaking your head at me."

"We go to Tirios."

"You're joking." Kara's thoughts spun violently, crashing into each other in a flurry of panic. As Aiodhan reached for her, she sidestepped him. "Seriously. You're fucking kidding, right?" She snapped her fingers. "I know. Pashmar put you up to this, didn't she? It's just a joke. A stupid joke. You've gotta remember, she doesn't like me, and—"

"Not a joke, *damana*."

"*Damana*?" Her temper was rising faster than a thermometer in Death Valley.

"A nickname. An in-deer-men."

"Endearment?"

"Yes. Endearment." His voice was as soft as a caress, but she was having none of it. At that moment, she didn't give a rat's ass what it even meant or that he was trying to be affectionate.

The guy was ruining her life, and he had the balls to try to sweet talk her into going along with it. "I'm not going anywhere, Tarzan. You can put that idea out of your head right stinkin' now."

"You are my mate."

"Maybe. Maybe not."

The fierce frown he threw set her legs to trembling. This was a side of him she'd never seen. At least until she remembered the same glare on his face, back in the cabin when the Vymaln had barged in. He'd been a warrior then, a creature capable of killing with the flick of his wrist.

"You are my mate," Aiodhan roared. "You go where I go."

Kara wanted to shout right back at him. A part of her wanted to weep. Yet not a single bit of her was frightened of him. Her alien would never hurt her. Never.

At least not physically...

Her mind was in turmoil. This wasn't happening. No, he wouldn't make her leave. Not Aiodhan. He was supposed to understand how awful the Vymalns were. He was supposed to care for her and help rescue her father.

An idea sprang into her head, probably a ridiculous notion, but denial was the easiest way to deal. "I get it now. You go to this...this...Seeker ship. You report to some boss. Then you go to your planet and get more Seekers to help you. There are more Seekers, right? It's not just you and Pashmar. More Seekers can help us get rid of these stupid bug-eyes."

Aiodhan narrowed his eyes. "Kara, you must listen."

"There's no reason for me to go. I don't even like the idea of going into space." She shuddered more for effect than real revulsion, although the notion of being in the vacuum of outer space seemed a bit daunting. "I can stay here while you gather the cavalry."

"Cavalry?"

"Reinforcements. More guns. More guys. Get it?"

He growled low in his throat. "You go where I go. I leave, you leave." The clipped words were spoken as if they were a lesson for some child to learn.

"I'm not going to Seattle."

"I must complete my mission alone. Then I will collect you."

"Collect me? I'm not some stupid kid who you have to *collect*." Even if she accepted that she was his mate—his wife, for want of a better word—she wasn't about to let him believe he could order her around. Evidently, his planet was stuck in some kind of 1950s sexist dynamic of male dominance.

Fuck that.

"Look, Aiodhan... We better get things straight right now. I might love you, but that doesn't give you—"

His smile was as bright as any found in a toothpaste commercial. "You love me."

She heaved a sigh at her own stupidity. One of these days, she'd learn to guard her thoughts more closely. She'd complicated an already challenging situation by spilling what was in her heart in an instant of anger and frustration when it should have come out in a tender moment.

Since he'd made a statement rather than asked a question, she didn't even try to be coy. "Yes, you big, dumb gorilla. I love you. Happy now? I. Love. You. God only knows why."

This time, Aiodhan seized her before she could move away. Although they had so much to talk about—to decide about what happened next— she let him kiss her. She even kissed him back, sliding her tongue over his and loving his taste and the way he hugged her so tightly. After all, how many times had she said those scary and vulnerable words to a lover?

Once.

Just this once.

His embrace was as ferocious as his frown had been, as though he wanted to meld their bodies. The erection pressing against her lower belly meant he probably wanted to make love again. While she wished she could let her concerns go for now, she needed him to understand she wasn't leaving—especially to head to another planet.

One day, maybe.

Going to Tirios might be an adventure, but not while her father was still the Vymalns' slave. Not while people were prisoners of the bug-eyes. Not while her world was upside down.

Kara eased away, putting her hands against his chest and pushing gently. "Wait."

His swirling gray eyes searched hers. "Wait?"

She nodded, trying to ignore the fact he didn't return her words of love.

One problem at a time...

Aiodhan sighed with enough force to part her hair. After another quick kiss, he set her at arm's length. "We will go when my mission is done."

Great. Just great. They were back to square one. "I told you, I'm not going anywhere."

"You are my mate." Each time he'd said those same words, he'd used an angry tone, not one of affection. This time, he'd clenched his jaw. "You will go where I say."

"No. I won't." Love him or not, she wasn't about to have spent all that time escaping being one kind of slave just to fall into another.

Turning on her heel, Kara marched away with a plan in mind. She would find her brother. Maybe another guy might be able to talk some sense into—

Aiodhan grabbed Kara's arm and spun her to face him, wondering exactly what human men were thinking to allow their mates such freedom. While women on Tirios could become anything they wished—even Seekers—once a family was formed, the patriarch always decided important issues. His own father had allowed his mother great input into important decisions, but Bromel Riel had always given the final word. Always.

Kara was mocking the Tirian way of life, and it was time she learned the rules. While he wished he could explain in his own language, she'd never understand his words. That flaw would be the first thing he'd fix once they were away from this dreadful planet. She was intelligent, had a quick mind. No doubt she'd swiftly master Tirian the way he'd mastered English. Besides, her language was much more difficult, one rule constantly contradicting another rule. Once he got her to Tirios and found herself immersed in his language, he had no doubt she'd grasp the vocabulary and grammar with little difficulty.

"You must go with me, Kara. I am male. I make decisions for us."

There. He'd said it, and he'd kept his tone mild instead of using the authoritarian voice of his father. She would surely see that he was giving her a big concession by letting her express her displeasure. It was more than most Tirian men would have offered.

Her eyes narrowed as she set her hands against her hips. "That's what you think? That you get to make all the decisions on what we do?"

"You *do* understand. Good. Good. Will make it easy now."

Kara laughed, a haunting sound that made him furrow his brow. "You know what?"

"No. What?"

"You've got another think coming."

"I do not understand."

Kara glared at him, but the turmoil of her thoughts was written all over her face.

He didn't comprehend her reticence. "It is the way it is done, *damana*."

"Don't *damana* me, you big bully." Her deep breath was ragged and filled with emotion. "I love you, Aiodhan. I do. But I can't be what you want me to be. I can't go where you go."

"You are my mate."

"I'm my own woman, and I'm a human being. You can't expect me to just...just...fly off into outer space with you, to forget my father. To forget what these bastards have done to my people and my planet."

"I do." By the stars, he wished he could find the words. She had to know he'd never leave her behind. She had to know that having her in danger was untenable. She had to know that he was a Seeker, how that vow was as important as the one he'd made to her.

There was only one solution. Aiodhan would have to let her know she had no choice. "When I return from my mission, you will go with me. We will discuss this no further."

"We will discuss this no—" She expelled a shuddering breath. "You really think that's the end of this, don't you?"

"Of course."

He watched her closely, wondering why she stared at him so intently. Before he could ask about her thoughts, she stepped closer, rose on tiptoe, and laid her palms against his cheeks.

"I love you, Aiodhan. You're the only man I ever truly loved. You're the only man I'll probably ever love."

Finally! She understood. He grunted his approval.

A single tear spilled over her lashes. "But where you're going, I can't follow."

She brushed a tender kiss on his lips, turned, and jogged away.

Chapter Fourteen

"Kara! Wait!"

Aiodhan's enraged bellow made Kara skid to a stop. It had taken every ounce of her strength to walk away from him, but he wasn't going to let her escape without creating an embarrassing scene. Part of her was thrilled he would fight for her. Part of her groaned at the impossibility of convincing a man who'd clearly been raised to believe women were supposed to obey men that she meant what she'd said.

If he was leaving Earth, she couldn't follow.

It hardly seemed fair. First, the Vymalns came and fucked up her planet. Then, her knight in shining armor arrived. Even though he acted like Ward Cleaver, she'd fallen in love with him anyway. Now, she was going to lose him. Probably forever.

Not one to feel sorry for herself, Kara heaved a sigh and turned to face Aiodhan, meeting the confrontation head-on. One way or another, he needed to understand why she made the painful choice to let him go. If she couldn't explain it in a way that would sink in and get him to change his mind and stay at her side, she'd have to face walking away again, something she feared she might not have the strength to do a second time.

Most of the men in camp had spilled out of their tents, probably because of Aiodhan's shouts, and they now watched the confrontation from a distance. She glanced over at them and groaned again at seeing Kevin and Pashmar bearing witness to the humiliating scene as well.

Squaring her shoulders, she ignored everyone but Aiodhan. "Don't tell me what to do."

"You are my mate." His voice echoed through the camp.

God, she was sick of that phrase. "I never said I wasn't."

"You will do as I say."

"*That*, Tarzan, is where you're mistaken."

He'd fisted his hands against his waist and stood with legs braced apart. A battle stance, to be sure, but she wouldn't let him intimidate her. She did, however, take a few steps closer, hoping to get him agree to go back to her tent.

"Look, I don't want to do this out here." She dropped her volume. "Everyone's watching."

"You made them watch, Kara." Aiodhan inclined his head back to the clinic. "You left our home. I followed. I must take care of you."

A familiar low whistle drew her attention. Her brother had a shit-eating grin on his face. "The alien's in for it now," Kevin said to Jayce, just loud enough for all to hear.

She threw him a censuring glare before focusing on Aiodhan. "Let's go back to the tent."

"No." With a hard frown, he made an exaggerated gesture of pointing at the ground. "You chose to bring disgrace *here*. We finish it *here*. You are my mate. You go where I go."

"God, you sound like a broken record!"

He clearly had no idea what she was talking about. All he did was fold his arms over his chest and glare what little curl she had right out of her hair.

Fine. He wanted to do this here. *Fine!*

"I can't go with you." Kara tried to keep her tone in control despite her tumultuous emotions. "I shouldn't have to. You've got a mission. I get that. And you'll get another mission. I get that, too. Maybe in between missions, you can give us a hand with getting people out of the IC. But my place is here, especially until I get my father out. I can't visit your home planet until I know Dad's safe."

"Our next missions may be across the galaxy." Pashmar's voice came from Kara's left.

She whirled to face the other Seeker. "What are you talking about? You came to Earth to help us. Jayce called out for help, and you and Aiodhan answered by coming here." She shifted her gaze to Aiodhan. "You're here to kill Vymalns. That's what you told me. You're here to kill bug-eyes, right?"

"He is here to kill *a* Vymaln," Pashmar replied. "Khymer Cantu is in See-at-all. Aiodhan must kill him. Then he will be given a new mission, but it may not be on this planet."

"You will not speak for me!" Aiodhan shouted.

Everything inside Kara wanted to scream. Had she eaten more, she might have vomited right there in front of the entire group, adding to her utter humiliation. Her mind searched everything Aiodhan had ever said to her, every damned word. With a sickening dread, she realized he'd never said he was here to help.

Not once.

"Kara…" He took several steps closer and reached out for her.

She retreated, trying not to snatch at her hair like some crazy woman. "Is she telling me the truth? You're not here to help us? You'll just kill this Khmer guy, and then you'll leave us to the bug-eyes?"

He stopped moving but didn't reply. His eyes never left hers, and the gray had darkened to nearly black. "Come with me. We will talk."

All she could do was blink and wonder at the numbness spreading over her body. This wasn't happening. It just wasn't happening.

"Fuck that," Bill said, striding up to Kara's right side. "We're all in this now, numb nuts."

Kevin moved forward as well, standing on her left. "If you're not here because of Jayce's calls, then why *are* you here?"

The same question Kara needed answered, even though she wasn't sure she was ready to hear the truth. With barely a thought, she fumbled for her brother's hand. Thankfully, it was there, and he gave her a bolstering squeeze.

"Well?" Bill barked. "Answer the question! Why are you here?"

Pashmar opened her mouth, but Aiodhan stopped her with a slash of his hand. "I am a Seeker. My job is to kill Khymer Cantu."

"Why him?" Kevin asked. "I've never even heard of the guy. He's not in the Vymaln Occupational Government. He's not commandant of this camp. Why do you want to kill that particular Vymaln? Why not just try to kill all of them?"

"*He* is my mission." Aiodhan's lips drew into a stiff line that made Kara even more afraid.

If it was that hard to explain, she wasn't sure she even wanted to hear anything about his mission now.

"*Zot!*" Pashmar said with a stomp of her booted foot. "You must tell them about the Praemons." Then she rattled off a string of Tirian words that made Aiodhan frown.

He shook his head and kept staring at Kara.

"Tell me," Kara said, her voice rough. "Tell me about the Praemons."

"If you do not," Pashmar warned in English, "*I* shall. They need to know why we must leave and why we cannot help in their fight."

The pain in Pashmar's voice took Kara by surprise. She'd obviously judged the woman too harshly. The feeling behind her words revealed an attachment to the people in this camp, and she wondered whether Aiodhan had formed any affection for these people. Because at that moment, she was not only convinced he didn't care for humanity, she doubted that he held an ounce of love inside his heart for her.

She'd been a fool. Nothing but a stupid, love-struck fool.

Jerking her hand away from Kevin, she strode to stand close to Aiodhan. She had to tilt her head back to look him in the eye, but she met his hard gaze and straightened her spine. "What's a Praemon?"

He unfolded his arms and let them drop to his side. His expression was unreadable, as were his obsidian eyes. "The Praemons are twins. A male and a female. They are the... I do not know the word."

"Prophets," Pashmar interjected. "They are those who see what will come."

Aiodhan gave her a curt nod, grateful for the assistance. Whenever he

112

was flustered—and facing an enraged Kara had him near crazed—he couldn't seem to find the proper English words.

He focused on his mate again. "They tell the Seekers of the future enemies of Tirios so that we seek the enemy and destroy him."

A simple explanation, the same that had been given to Tirians for generation upon generation. Those words would no doubt condemn him in Kara's eyes.

She held his gaze. "You didn't come because of Jayce's message. You came because this Khymer guy might one day be a threat to your planet."

In all the time he'd known her, he'd never considered explaining his mission. In his defense, he hadn't planned on feeling anything for her, nor could he ever have anticipated making Kara his mate. Now that he cared for her and had promised to honor and protect her, he realized how his quiet might be viewed as nothing more than a lie by omission.

He'd listened to her talk about saving her father many times, but he'd never revealed the futility of that mission. The fact that Bill had freed his sister defied all odds. To Kara, that rescue gave her false hope that would soon be crushed. By taking her to Tirios, Aiodhan would have spared her the pain of knowing her father would be killed at the hands of the Vymalns.

Her courage in wanting to launch a fight against the invaders was admirable but naïve. These humans had no future on this planet. The Praemons had spoken of the genocide that would eventually sweep away humanity. By taking Kara away from here, he would spare her that fate.

Staring at the confused faces around him, he felt a pinch in his heart. He knew their fate, and knowing these brave people would one day be no more weighed heavily on him.

Kara swallowed hard. "You were going to leave here and never come back? You were going to leave us to fight these bastards on our own, weren't you?"

"I will take you with me." Why couldn't she understand that he had her best interests in mind when he'd made the decision to be her mate, her protector?

Her culture was different, allowing women to consider themselves equal. While that might be admirable, someone had to make the ultimate decisions for a family. Women were far too emotional to make difficult choices, so he'd decided on a course of action. It was the Tirian way.

"I'm not going with you." Kara's soft voice belied the turmoil on her face.

"You are my mate."

"No," she said, stepping back. "I'm not. You're not who I thought you were. You don't care about me at all. You don't care about any of these people."

"Kara..."

"You've done nothing but lie to me from the moment we met. You weren't here to help me. You weren't here to help *anyone*. You came to commit a murder because some prophet said some lowlife Vymaln might one day be a danger to your planet."

"He will rule the Vymaln and launch an attack on my world."

"Then kill him. I can understand why you want him dead. But why not stay and help us when you're done?"

"I cannot. I have a duty, a vow. I must do as the Praemons ask."

She stared at him for several interminable moments. Her breathing sped, growing shallow, much like a pot of water bubbling before it boiled.

"You never planned on helping us, and you lied to me. You never wanted to help me release my father. Say it!"

"I am sorry."

"You're not sorry. You're not sorry at all. You *used* me. You let me believe—" She choked back a sob.

Aiodhan took a step toward her, but she held up her hand.

"Don't! Don't come near me. I'm not your mate, or your girlfriend, or *anything* to you. Understand?"

"Kara, we must talk."

"I have nothing to say to you." On that, she spun on her heel and marched toward the woods.

He couldn't take a step before Pashmar was at his side, her hand wrapping around his bicep. "Let her go. It is for the best."

"Not best for me."

She switched to Tirian. "You're a Seeker. It's time to do your job."

"You're jealous of her. Admit it. That's why you want me to go, why you won't let me explain everything to her."

"Fine. I admit it. I'm jealous. But that's not why I think you should go. Remember who you are." She squeezed his upper arm. "Remember *what* you are."

"I know what I am," he snapped as he jerked his arm away.

Pashmar's eyes were black with her anger. "Then prove it. You must kill Khymer Cantu. Do your job. Then you can return here. Then you can worry about this silly...distraction. Remember your vows."

Tirios above all, the future is in my hands.

He'd said those words, pledged his life to ensuring the future of his race.

My life belongs to the Praemons from this day forward. I will obey their wishes.

114

Never once had Aiodhan considered those vows would keep him from claiming the one woman he'd ever loved.

Loved?

Oh, yes, he loved Kara Michaels. But she'd just let everyone know she no longer loved him.

Could her love be that shallow? He didn't want to believe it. Her words had been born of her anger. Once he had a chance to explain, perhaps he could convince her of the rightness in his choices. Once he completed his mission, once Khymer Cantu was dead and his people's future was secured, then he could come back to Kara and explain all. Then he could make her understand.

"Go," Pashmar said again. "Give her time. Give yourself time. Do your duty."

Kevin stepped forward, bravely facing Aiodhan as his sister had. "I don't know what you two are talking about, but let me give you a word of advice, *friend.*"

Aiodhan clenched his jaw. "What advice, *friend?*"

"Leave. Do whatever it is you came to do, and leave us the hell alone."

"Kara is my mate."

"No, she's not. She just said so. You've hurt her enough. Just go."

"Kara is my—"

Kevin swung his fist at Aiodhan's face.

Aiodhan's hand shot out to block the blow. Catching Kevin's fist in his palm, he squeezed tightly, trying not to let the fury flowing through him find a target in Kara's brother. He could break the smaller man with little effort. Surely Kevin knew he was no match for a Seeker.

Instead of giving up, Kevin tried to throw a punch with his other hand. Aiodhan dropped Kevin's fist and shoved him away so forcefully, he landed on his backside, raising a cloud of dust.

Angry voices rose from the men in the clearing. Aiodhan couldn't make out all the words, but he understood nonetheless.

They wanted him gone.

He glanced back to the clinic as memories of Kara washed over him. Regret made him feel as if his head was being held underwater. He'd never felt panic before, always approaching each mission with stealth and patience. At that moment, fear held him tightly in its grip.

What if Kara didn't understand? What if she'd really rejected him?

"Go," Pashmar said again in Tirian. "I'll stay here and try to explain. I'll talk to Kara for you and see if I can make her see what we're all about and why we can't help these people." She grabbed something off her belt and held it out to him—the computer chip to give him control of her ship.

She held it out to him. He let her press it into him palm.

"It's south of here about three uni-merits. You can find it with the locator."

To leave like this might forever doom whatever future he had with Kara, yet he had no choice.

With a brusque nod, he left the camp.

But he made a vow to return.

For Kara.

Chapter Fifteen

Night had fallen, and the city of Seattle was deserted. All the buildings and landmarks stood in the inky darkness, silhouetted by the moon. One majestic structure—a tall spire—drew his attention. Humans called it the Space Needle. An apt name.

Aiodhan hadn't expected to see many people, knowing most would have been enslaved or murdered by now. While Vymalns normally rounded up all their conquered, they sometimes surrounded areas of cities and contained some prisoners there with fences and patrols. Then they'd force a few of their captives to survive in those cordoned areas and leave only to complete their jobs in service of the new Vymaln government. Not that they'd provide food or medicines. There were two such areas in Seattle according to Seeker intelligence.

He kept to the alleys and shadows. Finding Khymer Cantu wouldn't be easy, but since he was supposed to be the head of the sentries controlling this area of the city, staying close was Aiodhan's best hope for success. The Vymaln had risen quickly through the military ranks, and the Praemons predicted he'd soon rescue a visiting Vymaln prince from a human assassination attempt. That event would start a timeline that could see Cantu eventually usurp the throne. His becoming *konsig* could lead to another war between the Vymalns and the Tirians—a war the Praemons believed Tirios would lose.

Aiodhan was there to see that none of those predictions came to pass.

As he slipped around the corner of a business development, he caught sounds of a struggle. Approaching as silently as possible, he took in the sight.

Two Vymaln female soldiers were taunting a young human girl. Both Vymalns prodded the girl with stun-sticks that were clearly at their lowest setting. That level of voltage inflicted pain without debilitating the victim. The smiles on the tormenters' green faces were testament to the joy they found in torturing the child.

Her jaw was clenched, her dirty cheeks smeared with tears, but she refused cry out despite the fact she had to be in pain. Aiodhan couldn't have been prouder of the child if she'd been Tirian.

He knew this game, one Vymalns loved to play with their captives. They would continue to increase the strength of the shock until the girl collapsed. Since she was so young—probably ten or so human years—her heart wouldn't cease to beat the same way an elder's might. No, these Vymaln scum would torment her until they grew bored with their game. Then they'd slit her throat simply to watch the girl's life bleed out right in front of them.

Aiodhan's training kicked in, telling him to move on. Quickly. This child wasn't his problem or his responsibility. He had a job to do, a Vymaln to kill. He should just get out of there and continue to search out his target. Once that target was dead, he could go back and get Kara. Then he could leave this wretched place.

Wretched place.

That's what he'd been told. Earth was full of heathens with no brains and no strength. Humans were nothing but savages who welcomed their conquerors, naïvely embraced them and invited them to share their planet even though the Vymaln vocabulary had no word that meant "share."

But it wasn't a wretched place. These humans weren't savages with archaic technology and no hearts. They were full of life and spirit. They didn't deserve the horrors the Vymalns had inflicted upon them any more than this child deserved this torture.

He closed his eyes for a moment, his mind lost in a swirling mass of confusion. He was a Seeker, a Tirian. He had a duty and a vow to fulfill.

Then he opened his eyes as the girl's frightened gaze settled on his hiding place. Although she couldn't possibly know he was there, he felt the piercing sting of those haunted brown eyes—eyes so much like Kara's—all the way to his soul.

He sprang at the first Vymaln, grabbing her from behind and slipping his blade between her ribs, finding one of her hearts. A vicious kick disarmed the second Vymaln of her stun-stick and snapped the bone in her arm. As she fell to her knees, he tackled the first to the ground and leaned down to complete the kill, thrusting his knife into her second heart.

"Run," he told the girl. "Now!"

With wide eyes, she scrambled to her feet and scurried up the alley before disappearing into the darkness.

Watching her wasted valuable time when he should have been fishing a protective mask out of his pack. Now, he had to fight the second Vymaln just as he caught a whiff of his first victim's death gas. He gulped in a big breath and held it.

She'd found her own knife and lashed out at him. With a quick sidestep, he dodged the weapon before landing a kick to her forearm that sent the blade clattering along the concrete. With the last of his air, he wrapped his arm around her, under her armpits, and lifted before neatly stabbing each of her hearts.

His lungs burning for want of oxygen, he ran in long strides, frantic to get far enough away from the deadly fumes. Black spots flashed in his vision, and his eyes watered. He would lose consciousness soon—too soon to escape death.

"Here!" a muffled voice called from an opened glass door. The girl he'd rescued held a mask over her face and gestured with her other hand. "Here!"

Aiodhan dove through the door, landing on his back and expelling the rest of his breath.

She slammed the door shut, took the mask from her face, and held it to his mouth.

He took a few deep breaths then motioned for her to take it back as he got to his feet and retrieved his own mask.

Her small hand wrapped around a couple of his fingers, and she tugged to get him to follow. Curiosity forced him to nod and give her what she wanted.

After descending a set of marble steps, she took off her mask and shoved it into a small pink pack fastened around her thin waist. "It's okay now." She led him down a long corridor of the deserted building.

He stowed his own mask and took in his surroundings. The floors were smooth and polished, the walls lined with framed portraits and photos of men he would never recognize. About to ask where she was leading him, she stopped in front of a set of doors.

Authorized Personnel Only was emblazoned in white letters. The girl opened the unlocked door and stepped inside.

The Seeker in him kept whispering in his ear, telling him to leave. He'd saved the child, nearly costing himself his own life. He'd done more than enough. Much more.

He followed her through the door. Her smile disappeared into the darkness.

"Here. It's over here," she called.

Aiodhan's eyes quickly adjusted to see some kind of access hole in the concrete with a metal ladder rising from it.

The girl was climbing down, still smiling sweetly. Her hair was pulled into a headtail—*ponytail*, Kara had called it—and it bobbed as she nodded at him. "C'mon. I want you to meet my mom." Then she went down the ladder, dropping out of his sight.

Lying to himself that he needed to be sure she was truly safe, he peered over the side. In the darkness, he could make out a tunnel and wondered if she'd discovered a way to move beneath the city through passages to service water or electricity.

"C'mon!"

With a sigh, he stepped onto the ladder and worked his way down.

* * *

"It's a little farther," the girl said.

The child had led Aiodhan through several different access tunnels, deeper and deeper into the bowels of the city. She seemed to view their trip as some kind of adventure. He wasn't so sure. He not only flipped on his tracker to record where he was going, but he made strong mental note of the twists and turns they'd taken.

When they reached the end of one of the tunnels, she stopped and felt along the concrete wall before pushing one of the cinderblocks as if she could move it.

About to ask if the child had suffered some brain injury, Aiodhan stopped himself when the block moved, scraping back until it revealed a touchpad. The girl punched in a series of numbers, causing the wall next to her to open on a hinge.

"We're home!" Her voice echoed into the open space behind the door as she stepped through and hurried down a small staircase.

"Wait!" He tried to grab for her, but she was already skipping into the cavern. The moment he followed her down the stairs, an alarm was raised by the people close enough to see them.

Shouts of anger and fear blended together with the sound of firearms being hefted and cocked. He held his hands out—palms up—to show he meant no harm. While Vymaln skin was impenetrable to human guns, his most definitely was not.

"Don't twitch a goddamn muscle, or you're a dead man." The irate feminine voice came from above while several people, mostly women, surrounded him and pointed guns of all shapes and sizes his direction.

"I mean no harm." Aiodhan let his gaze sweep the cavern as he tried to count the number of people who now held his life in their hands.

The place was enormous. Two stories high, much of it lit by torches that lined the walls. Few signs of technology, probably because there was no power source. Along one wall was a stockpile of canned goods and large bottles of water. The woman who'd threatened him stood on a platform on the second floor, a place where she could see all that was happening around her. Her hands gripped a silver rail that ran the length of the platform. Behind her was a set of double doors.

"Mama!" The girl ran to a set of metal stairs and hurried up them.

"Claire? Oh my God, Claire! I've been so worried!"

When she reached her mother, Claire threw herself into her arms. "Don't hurt him, Mama. I made him follow me home."

The woman stared down at Aiodhan before she crouched down and grabbed her daughter's upper arms. "Where were you? We looked everywhere."

Instead of answering, the girl nibbled on her bottom lip.

She gave Claire a gentle shake. "Answer me. Where were you? You know you're not supposed to leave the shelter."

"I had to go up above."

"You went up to the streets? By *yourself?* Good God, Claire. They could have— You could have—" She hugged her daughter to her again. "Don't ever scare me like that again. And don't you ever go up to the surface alone." A glance out to Aiodhan. "Who is this, Claire?"

"I *had* to go. I was s'posed to bring him here. I went up to find him, 'cause I knew he was s'posed to come."

"You don't know who he is."

"The dream told me where he'd be, Mama. He's gonna help us. I know I shouldn't have left. But I *had* to." Claire took a deep breath and let it out. "I got caught. Two of *them* caught me."

The woman's eyes flew wide. *"What?"*

Claire pointed at Aiodhan. "He killed them. Both of them. I knew he would."

When the woman whipped her head around to stare at Aiodhan again, this time her eyes were full of curiosity rather than hatred. At least it was a start. "You killed two Vymalns? By yourself?" Her brows knit as she rose back to full height. "It's not possible."

He grunted. "I kill many Vymalns."

The people holding guns on him were murmuring, the comments ranging from disbelief to anger.

"Who *are* you?" The woman took Claire's hand and led her down the metal steps.

Since he had no idea where he was, let alone who he was now with, he saw no need to answer her question. Instead, he tossed out one of his own. "What is this place?"

"Answer me!"

He dropped his hands, causing several of the people who had been slowly lowering their weapons to re-aim. "I am Aiodhan."

Moving between her people, shoving rifle barrels aside, and frowning at the men and women holding them, she stopped when she was close enough he could see her face clearly in the torchlight.

Claire resembled her mother. Brown hair, brown eyes. Her face wasn't nearly as pretty as Kara's, but she was also a bit older, judging from the gray streaks fanning her temples. "I'm Hannah. Hannah Ford." She wrapped her arm around her daughter's shoulder. "This is my daughter Claire." She eyed him warily. "Did you really kill two of those bastards?"

He grunted again but nodded.

"He got 'em both," Claire added. "Never seen anyone move so fast."

"What about the gas?" Hannah asked.

Claire fished her mask from her pack. "He can hold his breath lots and lots, but he has a mask, too."

"Claire, you know those masks don't work well. You didn't breathe any—"

"No, Mama. I ran away. Just like you taught me." She nodded at Aiodhan. "Just like he told me when he fought them."

Hannah took a step closer, gazing into his face. Her eyes suddenly widened as she took a step back. "You're not human."

"He's not s'posed to be," Claire added. "My dream—"

Hannah put her fingers gently against Claire's lips. "We'll talk about the dream later, honey. Okay?"

Claire nodded as he mother withdrew her hand. "Like always, Mama. We'll talk about it when we're alone."

Taking in what the girl and her mother were saying so quietly was difficult, but his hearing was acute. While Hannah might not want to discuss this dream of Claire's in front of the others, he was determined to find out if this child had truly foretold his coming.

Could Earth have Praemons too?

A notion he'd have to not only consider but investigate more thoroughly.

Not wanting to get off on the wrong foot as he had with Kara, Aiodhan decided to try a different tack—to state the obvious. "I am Tirian. Vymalns are my enemy."

Claire obviously didn't fear him, drawing closer until she smiled up at him. "You're like Superman."

"Who is Superman?"

"I've read all his comic books. He's from Krypton and came here to protect people from bad guys and stuff. You're from a place like Krypton, 'cause you got super powers and stuff. Just like Superman."

"Some Superman," Hannah said with a snort. "No red cape, and he doesn't even have a coat when it's supposed to snow tonight."

"I am not this Superman." It was hard not to smile at Claire's enthusiasm and Hannah's cynicism, even if he had absolutely no idea what they were talking about.

"Claire, stop it." Hannah folded her arms under her breasts and leveled a hard stare at him. "What am I supposed to do with you?"

He had a suggestion. "Put guns down so we may talk."

"How do I know I can even trust you? For God's sake, you're an alien. Another damned alien!"

"He saved me, Mama," Claire said, tugging on her mother's arm.

"And…" She crooked her finger at her mother, who obliged by dropping her head close enough for Claire to whisper, "Remember the dream."

Hannah's eyes never left Aiodhan's. "How do I know this isn't some ruse to ferret us out? How do I know he's not going to kill all of us the way he killed the Vymalns?"

Aiodhan held his hands out again. "I have no gun. I mean you no harm." A nod to Claire. "I could not leave her out there alone."

"He made sure I got home safe," Claire added.

One of the women lowered her firearm. "How did you kill them?"

"I have blades. I stab their hearts."

She raised her rifle again. "Not possible. Their chests are like Kevlar. All we've been able to do is slow them down by putting a bullet in one of their eyes, but then they just grow another damn eye."

Although he had no idea what Kevlar was, he tried to explain. "Your guns will not work well, but they have a place beneath arms. Vulnerable to blades. Also other vulnerable targets I can teach you."

"I saw him kill the first one," Claire said. "Stabbed her, right here." She lifted her arm and pointed to her ribs.

"Put guns down," Aiodhan said again. "We can talk. I can teach you other things about Vymalns to help you."

Hannah gave him a brusque nod. "Looks like we have a visitor, everyone."

"Are you sure, Hannah?" a man asked. "You don't know anything about him."

"He kills Vymalns. That's all I need to know."

Chapter Sixteen

"Bill's gonna chew my ass from here to Wyoming and back for letting you come along." Jayce nudged Kara with his elbow. "Aiodhan wouldn't want you—"

"Aiodhan left. Remember?" Not that Kara could forget. "Besides. Bill's gonna chew your ass already for even trying this without telling him."

"Never should have told *you*," he grumbled.

"Nope. You shouldn't have. But I'm here, so let's get this done. I want to see what those bastards are up to."

If Jayce could get his bug into the IC system, maybe she could finally get some solid news about her father. Every passing day raised her anxiety at what he was suffering at the hands of the bug-eyes. When Jayce could use his device to monitor the Vymalns, she could keep her mind occupied watching for him—and off her alien.

For a solid week, she'd been on auto-pilot, going about her duties taking care of the men and treating their aches and pains. She worked her fingers to the bone to keep her mind too occupied to think. At night, she'd fall exhausted onto her mattress, sleep like the dead, and wake again to another busy day.

This morning, the denial had ended with a vengeance. No one needed her today. No stitches or scrapes or even a hangnail. The silence gave her time to finally think.

Aiodhan was gone.

Oh sure, he'd be back. From what she'd learned about him in the time they'd shared, he couldn't walk away. No, he'd be back to check on her at the very least. He'd probably try to convince her to go with him, and she'd have to face telling him *no* again. His personality was set in stone, and no matter how much she wished or hoped or dreamed he was never going to change. Since neither was she, they were doomed. Had been from the start.

Kara still loved him. With all her heart. Convincing him that she meant to stay might be difficult, but she'd find the starch her spine needed to follow through and deny him, even if her heart broke in the process. Not only did she need to stay with her own kind, but she wouldn't be an anchor around his neck. When she watched him and Pashmar leave, she'd be sending a piece of her soul along for the ride.

"He's coming back, you know," Jayce insisted. "He said so."

The boy's faith in the Seekers hadn't faded, even after everything he'd heard Aiodhan say the day he'd left about how they didn't give a damn about humanity and what they were suffering in this invasion.

Her own faith was battered and bruised. Her knight's shining armor was now pitted and tarnished. She wished she knew more about the Tirians and about the Seekers. Pashmar had given her wide berth the first few days, but after that, she'd stopped by, asking to speak to Kara. Sunk deep in her state of numbness, Kara hadn't wanted to hear anything she had to say.

Now, she did. She'd even been ready to go looking for Pashmar until Jayce had waylaid her. He'd brought Chance by for a visit and complained that Bill and Kevin were missing a great chance at getting some information about the Vymalns.

He'd been tinkering with his technology and borrowed some from Pashmar to come up with an electronic bug, a way to latch onto the communications systems in and around the IC. He'd sounded so excited, and she knew Bill and her brother saw Jayce as a child rather than a young man with much to offer the fight. When he'd taken off for some recon to try to find the perfect place to latch on his gizmo, she'd followed. His protest had been half-hearted at best.

Besides, no one was even supposed to leave the camp alone. Bill's number one rule.

Grounding herself in this mission—*her* mission—Kara vowed to show Aiodhan exactly how resilient the human race could be. If a teenager and a woman could get into the IC, tap into their computer system, and get right back out, maybe she could convince him to stay at her side and fight for her race.

A long shot, to be sure.

Who was she trying to kid? She was grasping at straws.

"I think that's the place." Jayce nodded at the small utility building on the far north side of the IC.

"There are only a few lines going in there," Kara couldn't help but point out. "I mean, if they're using the same phone lines and stuff the prison used to use—"

"They're not."

"How can you be sure?"

He pointed to the three snakes of thick, silver cable leading to the building. "They laid those when they started funneling people into the IC. They might be using all the rest of the stuff from the prison, but they're using their own communications."

"He is right."

Kara was so startled, a frightened squeal slipped from her lips.

Pashmar covered Kara's mouth with her palm. "Quiet. You must be *quiet*."

With a nod, Kara tried to relax as Pashmar pulled her hand back.

"What in the hell are you doing here?" Kara tried to keep her voice low. There weren't any bug-eyes near, and from what Jayce said, they seldom came to the service building. But she'd learned early to take every possible precaution.

"I followed."

"Why?"

"Keeping a promise."

"A promise? You mean to Aiodhan?"

Pashmar grunted, a sound Kara had learned was Seeker-speak for *yes*.

"He told you to watch me, didn't he?"

"Perhaps."

Jayce pushed up on an elbow to look over Kara. "Hey, Pashmar... you won't tell Bill about this, will ya?"

"I do not know why you are here," she replied.

Jayce dropped back down to his belly. "Yeah, well... We're on a mission."

"Mission? What mission?"

Kara glanced over to Jayce. "You should tell her. She might be able to help."

"Fine." He fished around in his pocket and pulled out something about the size of a cell phone. "I made this."

Pashmar reached across Kara to take the bug from Jayce. "What does it do?"

"What I hope it does is to patch me into the video feeds the lizards have of the IC."

The Seeker popped the back off the bug and stared at it for several long moments. "Have you entered their computer language? It is not the same as—"

"I know that!" Jayce snapped before lowering his tone. "I've been following the lizards' transmissions since they first arrived. I never trusted them. *Never.* Several of my tech friends and I deciphered their system pretty damn quick. It's not that difficult."

"Could work." Pashmar handed the bug back to him. "How will you send the images to your equipment?"

"They never powered down the wireless networks."

"You know this to be fact?"

"Yeah. I can pull up six different links."

"Aren't they password protected?" Kara asked.

Jayce snorted a laugh. "*Were* password protected. I can hack into anything."

"Doesn't surprise me they haven't shut down any of our technology.

Why bother? It's like walking out of a room and leaving the lights on."

Pashmar grunted again. "Perhaps you should tell Bill about this invention."

"I tried. He's too busy with his snatch-someone-from-the-fields plans," Jayce complained.

Pashmar mulled it all over. "How do you plan to get inside?"

"You're not telling Bill?" Jayce asked.

"No. *You* will tell Bill. When we return." She held up the bug. "Now we put this in place."

* * *

"Where in the hell have you been?" Kevin called from his perch in the tree.

Kara shielded her eyes from the sun to look up at him. "I was with Jayce."

"Jesus Christ, Kara! I went to see if you wanted to have lunch, and you weren't anywhere to be found. I've been watching for you ever since."

"Sorry," she offered with a shrug. "Couldn't find a Post-It to leave you note."

He slung his rifle over his shoulder and climbed down the rope ladder, jumping down without bothering to use the last few rungs. He stomped over to her. "You don't leave camp without telling anyone."

"Another of Bill's rules?" she asked. "I thought we just weren't supposed to leave alone."

"Answer me! Where were you?"

"Jayce and I had a little…mission." She walked right past him to keep following Jayce, even bumping him with her shoulder. A smile curved her lips when Kevin trailed her to Jayce's tent.

Jayce swept the flap open and tied it to keep it that way. Kara and Kevin followed him inside.

She'd never seen his technology set up before. Considering he had nothing but some solar-powered generators, it seemed as though he got a hell of lot out of them. A table held a line of computer monitors—*seven*, she quickly counted—showing various scenes from around the camp. Most were directed at watching anyone who could be approaching. A second table had more monitors, all dark but with cables leading to a CPU and keyboard at a small desk standing alongside.

Jayce pointed to the blank monitors. "Those should bring us pictures from the bug."

He sat down at the desk and tapped away at the keyboard. Then he jumped up and flicked on each monitor, one by one. Their screens flared to life, showing nothing but static.

Jayce sat back down in his beat-up desk chair and let his fingers fly over the keyboard again. Kara had never seen anyone type so quickly, and his movements reminded her of a pianist mastering his instrument.

"There." Kevin nodded at the third monitor.

A fuzzy image appeared. Jayce scrutinized it and frowned. "Hang on. Let me see what I can do." His fingers went right back to work.

The image cleared, and Kara gasped. Standing on the right of the image was a Vymaln sentry, stun-stick in hand as he watched a line of humans trudge past him. Before she could comment, another image popped up on another screen. And then another. Soon, all eight monitors were full of the inner workings of the IC.

"Oh, my God. You did it, Jayce. You really did it." Kara leaned over and hugged his shoulders. "You're a genius."

"Did what?" Bill's voice called from the entrance to the tent. He stepped inside, followed by Julie.

"We're in, Bill," Jayce said, his voice full of pride. "I told you I could do it."

"In where?"

"The IC. I got the bug planted and—"

"You mean you went out and put that bug on the lizards' system?" Bill cursed under his breath as he shook his head. "Are you insane? I told you not to go out and—"

"Just look!" Kara pointed at the screens.

Stomping over to the monitors, Bill narrowed his eyes at the screens. His jaw slowly dropped. "Son of a bitch. That thing really worked?"

Jayce's smile made his whole face beam. "Yeah. It really worked."

Kevin stood at Bill's side. "Look at that, will ya?"

"Yeah, I'm looking."

When Julie stepped forward, she showed no emotion whatsoever. Kara had tried to talk to her a few times since Aiodhan left, but the younger woman refused to open up about what she'd experienced in the IC. Only Bill seemed to be able to get close to her.

Kara stepped back to stand at her brother's side, reaching for his hand. "Maybe we can find Dad now."

"Kare-bear..." He returned her affectionate squeeze. "Don't get your hopes up. It's still a long shot."

Tears welled in her eyes. She hadn't heard that nickname in so long, she'd almost forgotten that Kevin and her father called her that. She sniffled for a second, squeezed his hand again, and then let hers drop to her side. "I'm gonna find him. Just you wait."

They all watched the monitors in silence for several long minutes. Kara couldn't have dragged her eyes away if she'd had to as she searched every haunted and gaunt face for Brady Michaels.

On one screen, a Vymaln sentry watched a line of prisoners accept bowls of food. How often were the inmates fed? From the size of the bowls, they weren't getting much to eat. Their hollow cheeks and sunken eyes screamed of their starvation.

On another screen, several armed Vymalns watched men sorting through a stack of technology—old computers, cell phones and gaming systems—but she had no idea what they were looking for. Every now and then, a guard would reach out with a stun-stick and jab a human. Then the horrible creature would laugh. She was grateful the bug was only visual and not auditory. Hearing the sound Vymalns made when they "laughed" would be about as welcome as the noise of a dentist's drill.

Each image felt like a stab to the heart, and she hadn't realized she was crying until Kevin reached over and wiped away one of the tears sliding down her cheek. "We'll try and find him, Kare-bear. Okay? We'll try."

Chapter Seventeen

"I used to work for the governor as his personal assistant." Hannah led the way into a room with a desk and a table with four chairs. "That's how I knew about this bunker."

"What is this place?" Aiodhan sat in the chair she indicated while she took one on the opposite side of the table.

The room was illuminated with candles, casting a golden glow over Hannah's face. Maps of areas of the Earth and black-and-white pictures of people he didn't recognize covered the walls.

"Not many people even know this exists, although Claire said she'd seen it in a dream. It was built in the 1960s right after the Cuban Missile Crisis to protect the state government during nuclear war. There's food, water, and there should have been communications with Washington. DC, that is. They put it here instead of Olympia to confuse people." She laughed. "Considering few people learn their state capitals anymore, they probably think Seattle *is* Washington's capital."

Most of what she said was confusing, but he did know about humanity's nuclear weapons. They were now in the hands of the Vymalns. Not that any of them were needed to subdue the people of this planet. Besides, both the Tirians and Vymalns—many other species, for that matter—had technology that far surpassed the weapons of this world. "I know not of this...Cube Crisis."

"Not Cube. *Cuban*," Hannah corrected. "But I doubt you want a lesson in Earth's history or geography."

"Who are the people here?"

"Secretaries. Aides. When things started getting crazy, I grabbed Claire and asked the people I work with if they wanted to join us. We hauled ass from Olympia to get here. There's only about twenty of us. Wish I could have had time to get to my sister and her kids, too, but..." She flattened her palm against the table. "Nothing I could've done at the time. So what happened with my daughter?"

"Two Vymalns were hurting her."

"And you stepped in? Why? She's human. You're not here to help humans."

He tossed her an incredulous glare. "How you know why I am here?"

She shook her head and gave a rueful laugh. "Take a look around Earth, buddy. No one's here to help us. *No one.* We're the equivalent of the Jews in Nazi Germany right now."

"I know not of these—"

Hannah waved off the rest of his words. "We're conquered. We're nothing but slaves to these creatures. Not only can we not help ourselves, there's obviously no other race that can take these guys—or one who gives a shit about humans, for that matter."

"Tirians can defeat Vymalns."

"Tirians? That's what you are? A Tirian?"

He nodded.

"So you're saying you're here to help us?" Her frown was skeptical, and she drummed her fingers against the tabletop in a steady rhythm.

Not wanting her to make the same wrong assumptions Kara and the men in the camp had made, he shook his head. "I am here to kill *a* Vymaln."

"Yeah? Well, I want to kill a whole shitload of 'em. Which one do you hate?"

His mission had already been compromised, so he saw no harm in naming his prey. Perhaps the ease in which this woman and her followers moved about their city might yield some information on where he could find the Vymaln. "Khymer Cantu. He is—"

"The son of a bitch who runs this ghetto."

"Ghetto?"

"Like I said, we're nothing more than Jews in Nazi Germany." She tilted her head in thought before adding, "I suppose it's more like Jews in Poland…"

"What is *ghetto*?"

"It's like this area of the city where people are being held prisoner." Her frown changed to a smirk. "Although those assholes probably don't even know we're hiding out here."

He returned to her original reaction to when he'd named Khymer. After days of searching, this new contact was bringing him as close as he'd been to finding his target. "You know Khymer Cantu?"

"Oh, yeah, I know the bastard. If you want to kill him, then I'll lead you right to him. And while we're there, I'm gonna kill Prince Sheemto, 'cause they're gonna be together real soon. In fact, that's been my plan since we heard Sheemto's coming here. Now that you can show me how to off a Vymaln, he's not walking away from Seattle."

The crown prince of Vymala was coming here? To Earth? To *this* city? Surely he'd heard Hannah wrong. "Explain."

"You didn't know? The people in this ghetto are being forced to help set things up for those bastards. There's a big ceremony next week, honoring their war heroes or something. Not that it was much of a *war*. Evidently, Seattle gave them a lot more trouble than most places, and they're here to rub our noses in the defeat. Even sent their prince to pin on some damned medals. If I have anything to say about it, while he's here, he's gonna die."

An admirable goal, one he hadn't expected of a human. He'd definitely judged the species incorrectly.

Now that he'd explained his mission and she'd revealed hers, his curiosity about the girl he'd rescued filled his mind. "How did Claire know me?"

"Claire is…special. She can—"

The door to the room creaked open, and Claire stuck her head inside. "Mama?"

"Hi, honey. I was just going to tell Aiodhan about your gift." Hannah pulled out the chair to her right. "C'mon in and join us."

Claire hurried inside, shutting the door behind her. She settled herself in the chair and focused her brown eyes on Aiodhan. "You don't have much time."

He tilted his head. "Much time?"

"You have to kill the prince. That's what you're here to do."

Looking to her mother, he knit his brows. "That is not my mission. I am here for another."

Hannah tossed him a lopsided smile. "Not if Claire says you're not."

Claire smiled at him. "You'll kill the prince."

He was struck by the sincerity in the child's voice. She seemed so confident, as though she'd already seen him commit the assassination. "Is she a Praemon?"

"A what?"

Damn English. "A seer. One who knows the future."

"Yeah."

When Hannah didn't expand, he pushed a little harder. "She sees what will be?"

Leaning back in her chair, she folded her arms over her chest. When she opened her mouth to speak, Claire beat her to the punch. "I dream about things that'll happen."

Since he had no idea how or when the Praemons were given their visions, he couldn't tell if that meant Claire equaled them in her abilities.

"Aiodhan," Hannah said, "Claire thinks she's supposed to go with you."

"Go with me?"

Hannah squeezed Claire's hand. "Honey, you don't know—"

"I dreamed it, Mama. I told you I dreamed it." A tear spilled over Claire's dark lashes. "You know I'm never wrong. I wanna be wrong this time, but I'm not. You know I'm not."

"Why go with me?" Aiodhan asked. "Where will we go?"

Sadness filled Hannah's eyes as she squeezed Claire's hand again before pulling her own back. "Claire believes she's supposed to belong to you when I die."

"Die?" This whole conversation was beyond confusing.

Claire swiped away her tear with the back of her hand. "Mama's gonna die when you kill the prince."

* * *

"Kara?"

Busy putting away some more medical supplies the reivers had purloined, Kara glanced over her shoulder at Jayce. "Hey. Here for some clinic help, or is this a social visit?" Since Chance wasn't at his side, she had her answer. Some days she missed the dog almost more than she could stand, but Chance belonged to Jayce now, and it was clear they needed each other.

"Um...I'm having some problems."

Used to having guys from the camp stopping by at all hours, asking questions ranging from what to do about their hemorrhoids to whether masturbating too much could cause damage to their penises, she tried to show him a comforting smile. God, she hoped Jayce wasn't here to ask about jerking off.

"Problems with what?"

"The bug."

A chuckle slipped out as she closed the cabinet and turned to face him. "Definitely not what I expected you to say."

He scrunched up his forehead. "What?"

She waved it off. "Never mind. What's wrong with the bug?"

"Some of the pictures it's sending are getting...effed up. I think the connection might be loose."

"Why aren't you talking to Bill about this instead of me? I don't know anything about technology. If you've got a gaping wound or a broken bone, then I'm your girl."

Jayce's gaze dropped to the dirt floor. "Bill already chewed my ass for putting the thing out there to begin with."

Kara frowned and folded her arms over her breasts. "You'd think he'd be grateful. Haven't we gotten some great stuff from that bug?"

The teen shrugged.

"Oh, c'mon, Jayce. We know so much more about how the bug-eyes run the IC now than we ever did before."

The rebels now knew when guards changed shifts, how they moved prisoners, and even how they processed new slaves. The only important thing they hadn't learned was whether her father was still in the camp—

still alive—but she hadn't given up. Not by a long shot.

"He always says it wasn't worth the risk," Jayce said. "Then he smacks me upside the head. Hard."

"What risk? We didn't see a single bug-eye near that building."

"Maybe we got lucky."

"Maybe you were just right. Ever think of it that way?"

He smiled. "Well, then—how'd you like to go with me again? I've watched the tech building for two days. Not a single sign of lizard life."

"You think you should go back in?"

"Yeah. I want to see what's wrong with the bug."

She wouldn't make him ask twice. "Let's rock and roll."

* * *

It was so familiar to be lying in the tall grass on the small hill overlooking the utility building. The clouds had darkened to a stormy gray, which meant snow would fall sometime today. Not a surprise since Montana had significant snowfall in late autumn.

Late autumn.

Time was getting away from her. How long had it been since Aiodhan left? Days? No, more like weeks. At least it seemed like weeks.

Damn, she missed him.

A shiver caught her unaware, and she pulled her down vest closer around her neck. The reivers had a tent set up with clothing of all shapes and sizes, and Kara made a mental note to grab herself a parka, some mittens and a nice hat next time she passed it. The place always made her smile because the guys had set a sign up outside as a joke—a Macy's sign.

She glanced over at Jayce. "Still deserted. I'd say you're right. Again." She nudged him with her shoulder.

He nudged back. "You want to come with me this time?"

"I can't help much with the bug. Shit, I'd probably make the problem worse."

"Not with the bug, but there are two more rooms in there. The second looked like a kitchen. Might have some good stuff if you search it."

"After all this time?" She sighed at the thought of what they might have missed out on by waiting so long to raid the place. She'd commit a mortal sin for a Snickers bar, even a stale one. "I guess there might be some stuff we could use. Maybe some non-perishables. Can't believe the reivers haven't been here already."

"They're good, but they're also really careful. Not worth tweaking the lizards to get some canned goods."

She snorted. "Yet here *we* are, getting ready to go down there just to make sure we get decent pictures from inside the IC. Is it worth it?" The instant the question was out of her mouth, she answered it. "Of course it is. I still haven't—"

"Found your dad."

"How'd you know—"

"You're in my tent all the time, Kara. You're always watching the monitors."

"Yeah, well…maybe I just want to see my dog."

Jayce laughed as he rose to his knees. "Let's get this done. Waiting and worrying is worse than just doing it."

Kara followed him as they worked their way down the hill. Although she could move silently, having been taught by her father and Kevin in their years of hunting, she was amazed at Jayce possessing the same skill. After a few minutes of watching, they sprinted across the tract to the door. Jayce fumbled with the entry pad for a moment before the electronic lock clicked open. He opened the door, peered inside, then inclined his head. Kara hurried inside as he followed.

The room wasn't entirely dark, but with only one small window allowing sunlight inside, it took a moment for her eyes to adjust. The inside reminded her a lot of Jayce's tent. Monitors galore. Cables everywhere.

"Where's the bug?" she whispered.

He pointed to a stack of cables.

"Get to work. I'm gonna check the break room." She left him to his job while she crept into the adjoining room.

She found a typical room where guys had to have spent a lot of time. It was a pig sty, and the smell of rotting garbage almost made her gag. Forcing herself to swallow hard, Kara went about checking the cabinets for anything that might still be useful. By the time she got to the doors under the sink, she surrendered. With the exception of some screwdrivers, dishwashing liquid, and an aerosol can full of Raid bug spray, the place had been stripped. Perhaps the reivers had been there after all.

About to go back to see if Jayce was done with his tweak, Kara froze when the door to what she'd assumed was a bathroom eased open with a creak that seemed as loud as thunder. Her heart slammed into a frantic frenzy when the Vymaln walked out. Its yellow eyes widened. Problem was it now stood between her and the door back to the tech room.

"Fuck. Jayce! Bug-eye! Get the hell out! Now!"

The alien gave her one of those grating laughs. She wanted to kick it in the face but figured getting out alive might be a better plan.

The thing stalked her, moving around the table in the center of the room to get her backed into the corner with her butt to the sink. It had her good and trapped and damn well knew it.

Her knife was still sheathed against her thigh, a precaution she took whenever she left the camp. But as Aiodhan had taught her, it wouldn't be of use unless she could slip it between the ribs under the Vymaln's armpit. At the rate it was advancing on her, she'd have her chance soon.

It dove for her, grabbing her around the waist and tackling her to the ground as she fumbled for the knife. Although she got the hilt of the blade in her grasp, the bug-eye grabbed her wrist and banged it against the floor until the knife slid out of her fingers.

Then the damn thing chuckled again. Kara rolled to her side, frantically scrambling to get into the cabinets to try to get one of the screwdrivers. One door opened, and the only thing she could grab was the bug spray. Figuring a blast in the face would at least be a satisfying insult before the thing got a hold of its stun-stick or pulse-gun and debilitated her, she wrapped her fingers tightly around the can.

The Vymaln kept trying to get a hold of her arms again, but she popped off the red cap, fumbled to get her fingers on the nozzle, and pushed. A long blast of white spray coated the bug-eyes face. It let out a scream and released her.

Kara kept spraying as she turned to sit on her ass and backpedal away from the alien. By the time she got her back pressed to the wall, the Vymaln clawed at its eyes and let out a high-pitched wail that made her fear her eardrums would burst.

She dropped the can as the alien yanked the stun-stick off its belt and flipped the switch, making it flare to life.

"Holy shit." Kara ran for the door, but it was too late.

The jolt as it hit the sole of her foot was devastating, traveling up her body and making every muscle contract into a painful knot.

The world went black.

* * *

"Are you sure, Claire?" Hannah asked. Her hand rested on the keypad to open the door from the shelter to the access hallways.

"Yeah, Mama. I'm sure."

Aiodhan had been eating one of his nutrition bars when Claire had burst from her room, shouting as if being chased by an enemy. He'd hurried to the child, reaching her only a moment before her mother. Hannah took the chore of comforting the child, who'd awakened from a frightening dream.

When Claire insisted over and over that she, Hannah, and Aiodhan needed to go into the city, she refused to be consoled until they'd agreed. While he was wary of putting them all at risk because a child had a dream, his heart needed to know if Claire truly possessed abilities to foretell in the same way as the Praemons.

He'd never felt conflicted in his mission as a Seeker. Never. Yet as he'd listened to Claire's emphatic assurances that her dream told her she had to go into Seattle, he was struck with the genuine agony she showed—as if she'd bared her soul to him. He'd agreed to the mission, feeling no qualms about seeing it through.

Hannah punched in a code, and the door swished open. "Well, then. Let's follow your dream, Claire."

Darkness had fallen on the city. The quiet was both peaceful and a bit disturbing. So many buildings surrounded him, so many places where humans had lived and worked. Seeing them all empty and dark was disconcerting.

"We're close." Claire's voice rang far too loudly.

"Shh," Hannah said. She gave her daughter's shoulder a squeeze. "We have to be quiet, honey."

"They won't find me this time, Mama." Claire pointed to a building. "We need to go in there."

Hannah eyed the place. "You're sure?"

"What is this?" Aiodhan inclined his head to the stone building.

"A church." She squinted to read the stone sign that stood on the small, overgrown lawn. "St. Joseph's."

Without a glance back, Claire skipped up the concrete walkway.

"Claire! Wait!" Hannah hurried after her, grabbing her hand and dragging her to a stop.

"But he's here, Mama. He's waiting for me."

Although Claire had insisted that her dream was leading them to something that could help in the human fight against the Vymalns, Aiodhan was still skeptical. Only his faith in the Praemons kept him moving forward. Having been raised believing that the prophecies of the Praemons were always meant to help Tirians, he wanted to believe Claire's abilities were meant to do the same for her people.

Aiodhan stared down at Claire. "Who is here?"

"I don't know his name, but he's alone now. No one's taking care of him, and he's waiting for us. He'll know what to do."

"What to do about what?" Hannah asked. "I still don't understand."

"When we need him, he'll know what to do." She flipped her wrist insistently. "C'mon. He's waiting."

The doors to the church were thick wood and stained as dark as a *demauba* tree—the same shade as Kara's eyes. Claire didn't hesitate as she wrapped her hand around the tarnished brass handle and tugged. With a groan, the door swung open.

As Aiodhan followed Claire and Hannah through the foyer and into the sanctuary, he tried to grab them to push them behind him until he had a chance to check for the enemy. Before he could grasp Claire's shoulder, she let out a happy squeal and ran down the long aisle, passing wooden bench after wooden bench.

"I knew you'd be here!" Her high-pitched greeting seemed to echo off the towering ceiling and tall walls.

On the front bench sat a boy. His curly hair was so blond it was almost white. He turned to smile at them.

"What the…" Hannah hurried after Claire but glanced over her shoulder at Aiodhan. "It's a kid. I'd pictured some—I don't know—ninja or something." Her cheeks reddened. "You'd think by now, I'd have some way of understanding my own daughter. But…"

He nodded as he followed, a bit in awe at what he was seeing.

The legend of the Praemons swirled in his head, the story he'd been told by his father until it was burned into his brain.

The Praemons had come to Tirios in a time of war more than two hundred years ago. No one knew their origins, but they appeared Tirian, down to their gray eyes. The female had revealed herself first and had thankfully been taken in by one of the planet's greatest military leaders. He'd listened to her predictions, and she had guided the general to the boy who would become the second Praemon. Through their predictions and their wisdom, they'd helped the general rid the planet of the first Vymaln invasion.

After the war ended, the Praemons were slowly accepted by the Tirian people until they became worshipped as the saviors of their civilization. They were older than anyone could remember, yet they kept their childlike appearance, stuck in their youth for all eternity.

Aiodhan found himself speechless at being witness to the same type of miracle happening on Earth. A girl with the ability to see the future had led him to a boy, one who seemed to have known they were coming.

Aiodhan's heart was pounding and his mouth went dry.

The boy's eyes were the color of Earth's sky. He smiled at Claire when she plopped down next to him on the bench, then he glanced at Hannah. "I knew you were coming."

"What's your name?" Hannah asked.

"Christopher." His gaze shifted to Aiodhan. "I knew you were coming, too."

"You dreamed it too, didn't you?" Claire asked.

138

Christopher nodded.

Hannah sat down on Christopher's other side. "Where have you been staying?"

"With my Dad." His eyes dropped to his lap. "They took him away today."

"The Vymalns?" Aiodhan asked.

The boy nodded again. "I'm s'posed to go with *you* now. You're s'posed to take care of me."

Chapter Eighteen

Kara fought coming back into consciousness with all she had. The pain in her head was overwhelming, and she wanted to slip back into the darkness and stay there until the torture ended. Her skull was too small, judging from the way her brain was trying to throb its way out.

"Kara?" Kevin's voice was filled with such concern, she stopped fighting and opened her eyes to mere slits.

The light pierced her brain like sharp knives, and she groaned as she threw one arm over her eyes to stop the invasion.

"Kara? Thank God."

"Kevin. Please... Shh..."

"What?"

She put a finger to her lips. "Shh... Headache. *Bad* headache." She groaned again, not just for effect but because she hurt like hell.

"After what happened, you're lucky that's all that's wrong with you." This time it was Bill's turn to torture her.

Bill?

What was Bill doing in her house?

Having no idea what she'd drunk to toss her into such a god-awful hangover, she tried to open her eyes again. The only other time she'd been in this kind of pickle had been Homecoming week her senior year of college. Jell-O shot after Jell-O shot until she'd puked. Why in the hell did she think she could still indulge like that?

Her thoughts were so tightly entwined with the pain in her head, separating them took great effort. She didn't want to think right now. "Go on back downstairs, guys, and let me die in peace."

"Downstairs?" Bill's voice held the same concerned tone as Kevin's. "What the hell is she talking about? Did that shock give her some kind of brain damage?"

Shock?

What shock?

Everything came flooding back to her so fast, she got dizzy. Jayce's bug. The building. The Vymaln. She tried to sit up. The movement made her nauseated. She leaned over the table and heaved.

Thankfully, Pashmar caught what little Kara threw up in an emesis basin. By the time her stomach was done rebelling, she wondered if death might have been a better outcome.

She pointed a trembling hand to the medicine cabinet. "Zofran. Advil. Get me some. Now."

Jayce was in the clinic too. He hurried to the cabinet and rifled through the pill bottles. He snatched a couple up and popped open one of the lids. "How many?"

"One Zofran. Four Advil."

He laid the pills in her shaking palm as Kevin offered her an uncapped bottle of water. She took the meds, too sick to even mutter her gratitude. The pills went down with some exaggerated swallowing, although they left a path of fire down her throat as if she'd drunk whiskey.

"What in the hell were you thinking, Kara?" Her brother's voice was thankfully soft, but the anguish was clear.

"I was helping Jayce and looking for food." Her own voice sounded as rough as sandpaper.

"Those were worth almost getting yourself killed?"

"I didn't know the bug-eye was in there." She tried to keep from screaming at him that she was doing everything she could to find their father, knowing her words wouldn't change his anger or help her migraine.

Bill snorted at her like an enraged bull. "You and Jayce are grounded. Got it? Neither of you leaves this camp without my permission."

She would have rolled her eyes if she wasn't afraid of how much it would hurt. "You can't ground me. You're not my dad."

"But I'm your brother," Kevin countered. "And I say you're grounded."

"You're my baby brother. But whatever. Not like I've got a lot of places to go."

Braving a look around the clinic, Kara grumbled at her audience. How many of the guys in camp could possibly fit in there? Since the image blurred periodically, she didn't bother counting the faces surrounding her. "Can you all just go now? I feel like shit."

"The Vymaln could have killed you," Pashmar chimed in. "You are lucky." She held up Kara's left boot. The thick sole and sides had been scorched black. "This spared you."

"I'll send Timberland a thank you note." Kara's head was still pounding. She growled and threw her arm back over her eyes. "I need some sleep. You can all go away now."

Thankfully, the sound of people shuffling out of her tent came right after her command. She braved another look when the room grew quiet. Only Pashmar remained. She watched Kara with a severe frown.

Quiet reigned for several more minutes. Then Pashmar broke the silence. "Aiodhan will not be pleased."

This time, Kara gave in and rolled her eyes. Every time she did something a person in the camp thought was out of line, she'd heard the same kind of admonition.

Aiodhan wouldn't like you doing that.
Aiodhan's gonna be pissed at you.
Aiodhan would not be pleased.

She answered in her typical response. "Yeah, well...Aiodhan's not here."

"He will return."

"Your point?"

Pashmar leaned back to rest her butt on Kara's desk. "I made a promise."

"Ah, yes... You promised to keep watch over me."

The Seeker nodded.

"Well, then—I absolve you of that responsibility." She flippantly waved her hand. "I don't need a nursemaid."

The confused look on Pashmar's face was so much like the ones Aiodhan always gave her, it made Kara's heart ache.

"What is nursemaid?" Pashmar asked. "You are a nurse, not a maid."

"It's an old term for someone who takes care of someone else who's too helpless to help herself. I'm not helpless. You don't have to take care of me. I don't need your help."

"You needed it today."

Kara sighed. Much as she hated to admit it, Pashmar was right. *"Touché."*

"I do not—"

"Means you're right, okay? You win."

Not that she wanted to owe Pashmar anything. It was crystal clear the Seeker thought Kara had intruded on her territory when she'd become Aiodhan's lover. She'd never worked up the nerve to ask again if the two had been intimate, but she'd guessed they probably had.

She planned on giving Aiodhan a good lecture on proper conduct for forcing Pashmar to make a ridiculous pledge to watch over her. It seemed cruel. Had he asked Kara to watch over an old girlfriend of his, she would have helped her right over the closest cliff. At least Pashmar's obvious jealousy hadn't prevented her from coming to Kara's aid.

Kara swallowed her pride and said what needed to be said. "Thank you."

Pashmar arched a blond eyebrow.

"For helping me. Did you kill the bug-eye who zapped me?"

"Yes."

Evidently, Pashmar was every bit as abrupt when she spoke as Aiodhan, because she never explained how she'd killed it. Kara wanted to move past that and get Pashmar to open up so that she could learn a little more about not only Aiodhan, but about Tirians in general. "Was he your target?"

"No."

"Then why aren't you out looking for the Vymaln you were sent to kill?" Since Aiodhan had always been focused on completing his mission, it seemed odd that Pashmar never talked about why she'd been sent to Earth.

"My mission must wait for Aiodhan to return."

"Oh...so you're working on that mission together?"

Instead of replying, Pashmar moved toward the tent flap as if she was ready to go. She turned back to face Kara. "Are you his mate?"

That very question haunted her night and day. When Aiodhan returned, Kara would finally have to answer. The problem was that her heart said *yes* while her brain kept asserting there was no way they could ever make a relationship work. She couldn't tie down someone like Aiodhan. Someone who desperately needed his freedom. Someone who treated her like a 1950s housewife.

In all the time she'd been running from the Vymalns, she'd dealt with being alone. Chance had eased some of the solitude, but even without him, she would have soldiered on. Yet ever since Aiodhan had left, she'd been lonely enough she ached.

Every night, she crawled under the blankets, wishing his big, warm body was there. She dreamed of him every night—sometimes pleasant dreams about the good things they'd shared, sometimes nightmares of him leaving her or dying at the hands of a bug-eye.

But he was *always* there.

Her heart had claimed him almost from the moment they met. Yet how could two people from literally different worlds ever make a life together? As the saying went, a fish could love a bird, but where would they live?

Pashmar still stared at Kara, her eyes a swirling gray. "Are you his mate?"

"I-I just don't know."

"You will destroy him."

"What did you say?"

"If you claim him as your mate, you will destroy him."

On that horrible pronouncement, Pashmar left the clinic.

* * *

Aiodhan had settled into a corner, his back to the wall, so he could find some rest.

He wasn't sure why, but he trusted these people. Once Hannah had let them know that he was there to help them not only by killing Khymer Cantu but by aiding in their strike against the prince, they'd welcomed him into their midst.

Bending one leg so he could rest his arm on his knee, he looked out over the cavern. Most of the torches had been extinguished by a young woman who they called "the lamplighter." He had no idea why they all smiled at that term. Then Hannah had explained that it was a term that went back far in Earth's history and that they found it funny because they never expected someone to again have to light torches every night.

Most of the people he'd met were women. The three *men* he'd encountered had all been nothing more than boys. Inexperienced but eager. Quite bloodthirsty as well, judging from their enthusiastic questions about what a Seeker's job was and their enraptured attention as he'd explained.

Just like the people in the camp—Bill and Kevin and Jayce—these people had shared their food and their shelter with him. Aiodhan was humbled by their generosity. Were all species as accommodating as humans?

Of course, that willingness to not only interact but help others was one of the reasons the Vymalns had infiltrated their world with such ease. Their kindness was also their greatest weakness.

His thoughts shifted to Kara, as they often did when he found a quiet moment. What was she doing? Who was she with? Did she miss him with the same intensity he missed her?

Taking a mate was much more complicated than he'd anticipated. Everything about this mission was complicated, too. He'd expected to drop in, kill his target and get out in a matter of days. His stay here had already stretched to weeks, and while he was closer to meeting his goal, his whole outlook on the universe had changed.

For the first time in his life, Aiodhan felt as if his eyes were wide open. So much of his upbringing had been focused on making him a Seeker— something his father had wanted for himself until he was filtered out of the ranks of potential Seekers. He simply wasn't good enough.

He'd laid his desires on Aiodhan's shoulders, letting his first-born son know from his earliest memories that he'd be a failure if he didn't become the Seeker his father had wished to be. The day Aiodhan gave his oath to the Praemons, Bromel had beamed with pride. When Aiodhan's younger brother Tajon also became a Seeker, Bromel had said he could die a happy man.

Aiodhan had never questioned his future. He was born to be a Seeker. He'd lived and breathed the worship of the Praemons and the safety of Tirios. Now, as he sat there thinking, for the first time in his life he wanted something more, something…*different*. Something that didn't send him on a quest to find yet another Vymaln or to hunt down a member of a species he'd never known existed.

Some of that uncertainty was Kara's fault. She'd confused him, kept him spinning in circles from the moment he'd rescued her. With nothing but a smile, she could tie him into knots of lust. With nothing but a frown, she could have him jumping to please her. She'd taken all his assumptions about other species and torn them to shreds, leaving behind an appreciation of humans he never thought he'd possess.

He missed her so much he burned. After glancing around to be sure no one was watching him, he reached inside his pocket to pull out the scarf he'd spirited from her things the day he'd left. Holding the purple fabric to his nose, he closed his eyes and breathed in her sweet scent. Not surprisingly, his body reacted, hardening with desire that he couldn't possibly appease until he returned to her.

Shoving the scarf away, he plucked his locator from his belt and set it on his palm. A quick flick of the finger, and it came to life. He expanded the range until Kara's pink icon came into view. Just seeing that she was safe in the camp made him relax. He touched the icon, wishing it were her soft skin against his fingertip.

What haunted him was more than simple lust. The feelings he held for her went beyond anything he'd ever felt for another being. The human word Kara had used was *love*. She'd bravely confessed that she loved him. He'd been not only arrogantly pleased, but something in his chest had squeezed tight when she'd said the words.

"*Ah mila, damana*. I love you, Kara," he whispered. Then he glanced around to see if anyone heard him.

Another complication, although one that surprisingly gave him strength instead of making him feel weak and weighed down. He wanted to tell her with the same courage she'd bared her feelings to him. He wanted to take her into his arms and kiss her senseless. He wanted to hold her for the rest of his life.

Movement on the balcony caught his attention. Hannah was shutting the door to the room where Claire and Christopher were sleeping. Had the children had another prophetic dream?

Hannah stopped at the railing and glanced around the shelter. Her gaze settled on Aiodhan as if she'd been seeking him. She turned, came down the stairs, and walked over to where he sat. Without a word, she dropped down next to him and leaned her back against the wall before she closed her eyes.

"The children are well?" he asked.

She nodded. "They're both asleep." Opening her eyes, she looked over at him. "God's truth, I'm having a hard time with all this."

He smiled. "Me as well."

"After raising Claire, you'd think I'd be able to, I don't know,accept his gift?"

All he did was grunt because he was having the same dilemma—trying to decide exactly what to do about Christopher and Claire.

"She says I'm gonna die tomorrow." Hannah gave a rueful chuckle. "I should be worried or something. But I'm not."

"Is she always correct?"

"Yep. Every damned time. You'd think I'd be upset about tomorrow, wouldn't you?"

"You have accepted your fate." Much as he had always accepted the fate the Praemons laid in his path.

"If I'm going, I'm taking Sheemto with me. By God, if there's only one important thing I do in my life, it's killing that bastard."

"Already have done something important."

She tilted her head.

"You are a mother to a prophet."

Her smile was genuine. "Yeah, I am, aren't I?" She patted his arm. "Get some rest. We've got a big day tomorrow." She stood up and brushed the dust off the seat of her pants. "I'd ask if you wanna get laid, but..."

"Laid?"

"Have sex."

"I have a mate."

"Figured. A guy like you wouldn't want for female company." Her smile disappeared as she drew her lips into a thin line. "You'll take care of them? If-if Claire's right and I... You'll take care of them, right?"

"Should they not stay with hu—"

"No!" Looking around for a quick moment, Hannah lowered her voice. "People here don't understand Claire. You do, and you accept her. She and Christopher need you. Besides, Claire says that's why she found you. She's supposed to go with you. Promise me. Right now, promise me you'll treat her like your own."

Aiodhan didn't hesitate. "I promise."

With a nod, she strode away, climbed the stairs, and went into her room.

The silence surrounded him again, letting his thoughts take the lead.

After all he'd seen, he accepted Claire's skills with the same blind faith he'd accepted the stories of the Praemons' abilities and the stories he'd been raised hearing. If Tirios could have guardians of their future, why couldn't Earth? If Tirios was meant to protect itself, why wasn't Earth?

Claire and Christopher were another complication—another change in his view of the universe. If he'd sworn an oath to the Tirian prophets, did he owe the same loyalty to Earth's new Praemons?

The Tirian Praemons told him this mission would bring an end to life as he knew it and forever change his destiny, but at the time, he hadn't understood the meaning of their prophecy. That wasn't unusual, for often they would make predictions that made more sense *after* the event than *before*.

Now, Aiodhan finally understood. This mission was more than just the death of Khymer Cantu and the assurance of Tirios's future. This journey was for him to find his mate and to discover the Praemons for humans. Together, he and Kara would ensure the future of her race and help these humans purge this world of the Vymaln scum.

His new destiny began to unfold before him so clearly, he could see each and every step. He would be the one to find Seekers for Earth and help the planet learn to protect itself the same way as Tirios while Kara nurtured and raised Claire and Christopher to fulfill their destinies.

His parting with his mate hadn't been good. He'd have to convince Kara that he'd discovered a new path for himself—and for her. Once she met the children and learned of their gifts, surely Kara would understand why their lives would now have to change. Claire and Christopher would need her guidance, and he could think of no other human as strong and brave as Kara. She would help the children achieve all they were meant to.

He'd have to make amends to her brother and the men of the camp. Once they knew about their new prophets and could see that they represented their future, their opinions would change. The biggest positive in his favor was that he wouldn't have to leave them now. He could fight at their sides, and he could keep Kara as his mate and still do his duty.

Accepting that Claire and Christopher were going to have to be in his life now, he wondered if Kara would as easily receive the children. While his heart felt heavy that Hannah was destined to surrender her life tomorrow, he could think of no greater honor than to die for her world. She would be a hero in the hearts of all humans. Songs would be sung in her honor as they were crooned for Seekers who gave their lives for Tirios.

Kara will accept the children.

His mate's heart was pure and larger than this planet. Together, they'd help Claire and Christopher take their places as Earth's first Praemons, for he had no doubt that was their fate. Earth was evolving, perhaps to become something as formidable as Tirios one day. They simply needed

Praemons to lead them, and they needed Aiodhan to show them the way.

Chapter Nineteen

Aiodhan had never worked with anyone on a mission before, and he was still leery of bringing Hannah and her "team," as she'd called them, along.

They'd scouted the location several times and were ready to put their plan in motion. The humans of the ghetto had set up the assembly stage and prepared for the medal ceremony. Hannah's people had blended in as much as possible to get everything they needed in place before slipping back each evening to their bomb shelter base.

Because Vymaln custom was for a prince to stand above all others, the officers who'd helped subdue the human resistance would come to the dais, one by one, and have their medals pinned on their chests. The only person who would be permitted to stand on the platform was Khymer Cantu, and even he would have to remain on the first step so his head was below the level of Sheemto's.

The strategy was simple. Hannah's team would detonate the explosive charges they'd planted throughout the park to set off chaos in the crowd. One bomb was set specifically to break the stairs away from the stage to isolate the two targets. They had to be careful not to kill the Vymalns in the crowd or among the medal recipients to prevent the release of death gas, so the charges had to be placed precisely. Aiodhan would jump through a trapdoor in the platform to eliminate Khymer, while Hannah and two of her team would get to the stage to take down the prince.

Since Claire had predicted that Aiodhan would be the one to strike the fatal blows to Sheemto, he'd move in to complete the task as soon as he killed Khymer. He'd trained Hannah in methods of holding a Vymaln so his hearts were easier to reach, and the woman had been a fast learner. He had no doubt she could get the job done, but Claire's prophecy stood between Hannah and her goal. Hannah still insisted she be the one to go after the prince.

Peeking from where he was concealed beneath the platform, Aiodhan watched Sheemto's arrival.

The prince walked among the Vymalns assembled on a grassy area, all on their knees in his presence. Stopping to press his fist to the foreheads of his followers—a Vymaln blessing given from a royal family member they believed to be a living deity—he slowly made his way to the honorees. They, too, were on their knees and far enough away from the platform they wouldn't be able to stop the assassinations. More explosions timed for after Khymer and Sheemto were dead would ensure enough confusion that they *might* all get out safely, but their lives were at definite risk.

Khymer appeared at Sheemto's side, his head bowed to keep it low. Aiodhan clenched his jaw, trying to calm the slamming of his heart. A few deep breaths, and his body was back in his control. The Praemons had predicted this Vymaln could mean the end of Tirios. Two quick stabs to the bastard's hearts would prevent that bleak future.

Taking one last look, Aiodhan ducked back down and skirted across the darkness, counting steps as he'd practiced to place himself directly below the staircase. If the Praemons were merciful, when the explosions began, all he'd have to do was get Khymer in a proper hold and end his life. At the same time, Hannah and the women would ambush the prince. Then Aiodhan would hurry over and deliver the fatal blows as Claire predicted.

He pulled his gas mask from his pack, threw the cord holding it around his neck and let the mask loll against his chest. His mask was superior to the ones the humans had, just another reason for him to finish the kill. Once he'd pierced one of his prey's hearts, the fight would be easier, and Hannah and her team could flee before Khymer's death gas could harm them. What bothered Aiodan was not knowing how Hannah's life would be threatened, let alone how it would end this day. The unknown variable made the mission less likely to succeed. He vowed both Vymalns would be dead before he left the platform.

In working with her, he'd gained respect for Hannah. Since bringing the people into the bunker—something she'd been able to do in time thanks to one of Claire's prophecies—Hannah had accepted full responsibility for their well-being, acting as their leader to keep them safe. As he'd trained the humans for this assassination, he'd grown to admire her work ethic, one that rivaled his own. She'd attacked the task with the tenacity of a Seeker. No doubt her courage and strength had been rewarded by the universe in allowing her to be the mother of one of Earth's future Praemons.

The first explosion sounded right on cue, and Aiodhan shoved his way from under the platform. Jumping up to confront Khymer on the steps, he found himself face to face with his enemy. Sheemto had skittered across the dais and was now trying to evade Hannah and her team.

Khymer's green lips pulled back into a sneer, and he grabbed the stunstick from his belt.

Aiodhan disarmed him with a well-placed kick, sending the weapon flying from Kymer's grasp.

Khymer clenched his hands into fists, threw his head back, and screeched out a battle cry. Then he attacked.

The Vymaln had been trained well in hand-to-hand combat, not a surprise considering the rank to which he'd risen. Aiodhan matched his every attempt to land a blow, needing his full concentration to keep up with Khymer. He'd finally met an adversary who was his equal.

When a human scream sounded to his left, Aiodhan glanced over and see if Hannah had been hurt. Khymer used that opportunity to sweep his feet out from under him.

Finding himself on his back, Aiodhan had to time his roll perfectly to avoid the death blow Khymer tried to deliver with the blade he now brandished. The knife ended up imbedded in the wood of the platform. While the Vymaln tried to wrestle it free, Aiodhan turned to see Hannah knocked to the stage by Sheemto's fist. Blood seeped from a gash across her face.

While he wanted to go to her, he had to focus as Khymer attacked again. Aiodhan dodged the knife. A whirling kick to Khymer's midsection sent him flying off the stage, giving Aiodhan a chance to check on the team's progress.

The two women had Sheemto's arms and were trying to stab him with the knives they wielded. Their attempts were failing, and Sheemto managed to pull one arm away and slam his fist into one of the women's cheeks. She went down, unconscious. When Sheemto turned on the second woman, Aiodhan couldn't stop himself from hurrying to her aid.

The prince's eyes widened when he looked up. Aiodhan didn't hesitate, charging forward as he made the decision to kill him first. Only then would he return to the task of ending Khymer's life.

Claire had been right, Aiodhan realized, as he stood eye-to-eye with the prince. This was his job—to end the line of succession to the Vymaln throne. With practiced ease, he had one of Sheemto's arms behind his back and slid his blade neatly into one heart. As the prince gasped and lashed out with his other arm, Aiodhan twisted it behind him and aimed his blade at the second heart.

"Stop!"

Looking up at the sharp Vymaln voice, Aiodhan had to fight hard to keep from showing a visible reaction to the sight before him. Khymer was using Hannah as a shield, his arm wrapped around her shoulders as he pressed a knife to her neck. A small stream of blood trickled from where the tip had already pierced her skin, adding to the blood steadily trickling down her forehead.

"Stop or I will kill her," Khymer said in English.

Aiodhan answered in kind. "You know I cannot."

Khymer narrowed his eyes before they suddenly flew wide. "A Seeker."

Hannah squirmed in his grasp. "Kill him!"

Khymer pressed the knife harder against her neck, making the rivulet of blood larger. "Release the prince or this human dies."

Until Kara, Aiodhan had never been concerned about the life of another species. Never. He'd always done his job with deadly efficiency, not once concerned that his job in this universe was to rob it of lives. He also knew Claire had prophesied her mother's death, but even then, he couldn't bring himself to be the one who caused Hannah's demise. The triumph in Khymer's eyes said he'd guessed as much.

"I care not," Aiodhan said, hoping his feelings weren't betrayed in his voice.

"You do care. Release Sheemto to save her life."

"Don't do it, Aiodhan," Hannah rasped out.

"Be quiet!" Khymer jerked her back hard.

Before Aiodhan even had time to consider his dilemma, Hannah's eyes caught his. "Do *my* job," she rasped out. "I'll do *yours*."

Aiodhan's gaze dropped to where her hand rested against one of the grenades still attached to her belt. Her finger was looped through the pin.

With a victorious smile, she yanked it free. "Take care of Claire."

Aiodhan slid his knife between Sheemto's ribs and ended his life. He grabbed the two women by their collars and jumped from the platform at the same moment Hannah's grenade detonated, sending a shower of debris raining over his head.

* * *

"If that doesn't clear up in two days, you come back." Kara made a few notes on her clinic log.

Not that she had a way to keep proper medical records, but she was trying. Jayce needed all the power he could generate to keep his surveillance of the IC running, so she'd never bothered to ask if he had a computer she could use.

"Thanks, Kara." The young man she'd been treating for dizziness hopped off the table.

His ear had fluid inside, but she found no infection. She wasn't about to waste precious antibiotics if he didn't truly need them. "You're welcome."

As he tried to leave, he took a step back when Bill's sister Julie appeared in the entrance. Since Kara had seldom seen her since Bill had rescued her from the IC, Kara was a bit shocked Julie would come to the clinic.

"Hi, Julie," the young man said, a blush covering his face. Then he stepped around her to leave and tripped over his own feet.

Kara tried to hide a smile. The poor guy seemed as flustered as if he was getting ready to ask Julie to the junior prom. Her desire to grin faded. She felt as old as Methuselah in comparison. She might only be twenty-five, but in "occupation years," she might as well be sixty.

She turned her attention to Julie, who stood awkwardly in the clinic entrance. "Come on in. Tell me what's bothering you. I'll see if I can fix you up."

"I...um..." Julie dragged the toe of her tennis shoe across the packed dirty floor. "I...um..."

Putting her clipboard down on the exam table, Kara took a few steps over to her. "Are you okay?"

"Um...yeah."

"Is there something I can do?"

Her eyes finally met Kara's. They were a true blue, much like Bill's. "I came to apologize."

That seemed an odd statement. "Apologize? What do think you have to apologize for?"

"Look, Kara—we're the only two women in this camp. I shouldn't have been shunning you the way I've been."

Since Kara had made the assumption that she was *persona non grata* with a lot of the people in camp because of her relationship with Aiodhan, it didn't surprise her that Julie was admitting she'd avoided her. The poor girl had been terrified of Aiodhan the day Bill had brought her back to the camp from the IC.

"It's okay, Julie."

"No, it's not. Bill told me I should apologize."

"Bill? What's Bill got to do with this?"

"He's mad at me. He said I'm being ridiculous."

Striding over to grab her otoscope, Kara took the instrument to her work table and proceeded to sterilize it, letting the familiarity of her job soothe her. She'd always loved being a nurse, and since she'd had designs on going back to school to become a nurse-practitioner, this clinic gave her a chance to hone her skills. She often felt like a doctor of old—one who was limited by what medical science had to offer and who often had to improvise. The challenge appealed to her and kept her from obsessing over what Aiodhan was doing and whether he was safe.

The weeks he'd been gone had passed at an agonizingly slow pace, and she found herself searching for him in every face that crossed her path or came into the clinic.

"Kara? You okay?" Julie asked.

"Sorry. Just thinking." She glanced over her shoulder and tried to focus on the subject at hand. "Why does Bill think you're being ridiculous?"

"Because I didn't want to talk to you. He's right. It's just… Your boyfriend. He...bothered me."

Kara turned to face Julie. "It's okay. I get it. He's an alien. Would it help to know that sometimes that makes me feel kinda weird too?"

A hesitant smile formed on Julie's face. "Yeah, it actually does."

"And I wasn't even in some damned IC."

The smile dropped to a frown.

"I'm sorry. I shouldn't have brought that up."

"No. It's okay. I kinda want to…talk about it. That's only part of the reason I'm here. I think I might be sick."

Kara patted the exam table. "Why don't you hop up here and tell me what's bugging you?"

After thinking it over for a few long moments, Julie finally nodded. She walked over to the table and sat down.

"Now, tell me what's wrong."

Julie nibbled on her bottom lip. "I haven't had a period in a long time."

"How long?"

She shrugged. "Hard to remember when there weren't any calendars in the stupid IC. Maybe three months?" She knit her brows. "At least I think it's three months."

Although her mind was flying in a thousand different directions, coming up with horrible scenarios that might have led to this teenager getting pregnant, Kara kept her expression calm. "I need to ask you some questions. Some *personal* questions."

"I'm not pregnant."

A relief, but Kara had to ask, "You're sure? I have some pregnancy tests and—"

"I haven't had sex. Ever," Julie said.

"No one in the IC tried to—"

Julie shook her head. "I'm a virgin."

Her incredulous tone and the fierce frown fixed on her pretty face made Kara believe her. "There are lots of reasons to skip a period. Top of the list is stress, and I'd say your life lately would definitely rank up there on *any* stress scale." She tried to show Julie a reassuring smile. "Let's just take a look and see what's going on, okay?"

* * *

By the time Julie left the clinic, Kara's own anxiety was running roughshod over her heart and mind. While she was sure Julie was going to be fine after checking her from head to toe, Kara wasn't so awfully sure about herself.

Instead of cleaning up her supplies, she picked up the small calendar she and Julie had used to try to figure out when her last period had been. Now, Kara did the same for herself.

How long had it been?

Too long.

Too fucking long.

She counted again, just to be sure. Damn, but she'd always been like clockwork.

At least two weeks late.

That was nothing. Really nothing. She and Aiodhan had only made love... More times than she could count.

Good God.

They'd been acting like a couple of horny teenagers, falling into bed every chance they got. Of course they'd had the sense to use condoms.

Except those two times...

Getting pregnant to hold onto her boyfriend hadn't been her intention, damn it! She'd simply been too swept away with passion to think about the consequences.

Was he coming back for her?

Of course.

Would she go with him? Would she leave her own planet and follow him across the galaxy?

No. Not now.

Not while her father was still a slave. Not while her planet was still in chains.

But what if she and Aiodhan were going to have a baby together?

Denial was an easier way to deal. Using all the same arguments she'd used to try to convince Julie there was nothing wrong with her for being late, Kara tried to reason her fears away.

For months, she'd eaten next to nothing, so her lack of body fat might be altering her menstrual cycles. She'd been under an inordinate amount of stress, and her body was simply reacting to that hormonally. For heaven's sake, a bug-eye had nearly shocked her to death. If that wouldn't screw up a girl's period, what in the hell would?

She had to know for sure.

Kara hurried to the cabinet and started shuffling around until she found one of the boxes she was looking for. Then she tucked it in her jacket pocket and headed for the latrine.

Chapter Twenty

The camp was quiet.

Kara pulled the blanket up around her neck, shivering against the cold as she wondered if she should put her parka on even though she was already sleeping in her sweatpants, thermal shirt, and a pair of cotton socks.

If the nights turned any chillier, she'd have to give up sleeping alone in the clinic altogether. Most of the men in the camp were already bunking in the mess hall where they'd put the heater. Only Kara and Julie maintained their isolation. As cold as Montana winters could get, they'd both have to head there soon too. If only Aiodhan would return, Kara could snuggle up against his warm body and keep her privacy at least for a little while longer.

Tears sprang into her eyes. What the hell was wrong with her? Self-pity had never crept into her personality before. She wasn't about to let herself wallow in it now. She immediately felt selfish for fretting about something as petty as having a place to herself to sleep when her whole planet was under the control of ruthless aliens. When had she turned so shallow?

Maybe it's hormones.

After tossing and turning for far too long, she cast aside the blankets, grabbed her parka and decided to rummage around for something to eat. After shoving her feet into her unlaced boots, she stomped through the opening from her bedroom into the clinic.

Comfort food was a necessity at this point, and she had her sights set on some of the chocolate one of the reivers had brought back for her on their last raid. Sure, the caffeine would probably make her insomnia worse, but she didn't give a shit. She needed chocolate, and she needed it now.

A shout went up from the watch before she could even stoop down to rifle through the cabinet. Hurrying to the entrance, she fumbled with the cord holding the flap down against the wind. The sounds of boots running through the newly fallen snow were muffled but still obvious, and she muttered curses until she was able to open the tent flap so she could see what was happening.

Jayce jogged by, so she grabbed his arm to drag him to a stop. "What's going on?"

"Someone's coming to the camp."

Her heart started pounding like a drum. "Bug-eyes?"

"Don't know. Go find Julie and get outta sight."

He hurried away, following the other soldiers as they ran through the snow, preparing their weapons and calling out warnings.

"The hell with that." Kara went back inside the clinic to find her knife.

Not even taking the time to strap it against her thigh or lace up her boots, she ran back outside to follow the men as they hurried to the west sentry post where the alarm had been raised.

The snow was still falling, though not as heavily as it had been earlier in the evening. Enough of it coated the ground and trees that she could see everything as clearly as if the sun still shone in the sky. The crunch of the snow beneath her boots blended with the sound of her rapid breaths.

The men had formed a double line facing the woods. Every time she tried to elbow her way forward, one of them shoved her behind his back. She glanced up to where Bill stood in the platform they'd build high in the trees. He held night vision binoculars and stared into the distance.

His fist went into the air, and quiet fell over the group. Then Bill lowered the binoculars. "False alarm, guys. No lizards. Aiodhan's back."

Kara gasped loud enough several of the guys turned and grinned at her. She tried to stand on tiptoe to look over their shoulders, needing to see him for herself. The only things in her line of vision were pines and the snowflakes that kept falling in a steady rhythm. Even those were blurry from the tears forming in her eyes.

Then she saw him marching toward the camp. Someone had helped him find winter clothes, because he wore a down jacket with a fur-lined hood. He glanced down and spoke to a child who walked at his side before he turned his head and said a few words to another child who was riding piggyback.

Although her curiosity about the children was immense, she shoved it aside, focusing on checking Aiodhan from head to toe as she searched for injury. His gait was cocky, and he even smiled at the children.

She wasn't sure when she started running to him, but she ran right out of her boots. Didn't matter. She kept on going.

Aiodhan wasn't disturbed when the alarm went up at his arrival. He was quite pleased to know Kara was being cared for by people who took her safety seriously. As he grew closer to the camp, he'd dropped his hood and had Claire and Christopher do the same so anyone on sentry duty could see their faces and recognize they weren't a threat.

Claire clung to his neck, so he eased her hands away before teasing her by flipping her over his shoulder to put her on her feet. She squealed, but not in fright, her giggles following right behind. Her trust in him—and Christopher's as well—had been instant and absolute. They treated him like a long lost relative, and the trip back to the camp had been uneventful. Neither had seemed at all impressed with Pashmar's ship, either.

He took off his gloves and jammed them in his pockets before he saw Kara push her way through the men. Her eyes flew wide before she broke away and sprinted toward him.

Starved for the sight of her, Aiodhan watched her run, her long hair flying behind her. First one boot was left behind in the snow, then the other. And still she came, striding through the layer of white, throwing tufts of it behind her. When she drew close, he opened his arms wide. Kara launched herself at him. He wrapped his arms around her waist while she wrapped her legs around his hips.

His mind was so full of her—her scent, her warmth—he couldn't find the words of greeting he knew he should say. She rained kisses across his cheeks, whispering how much she'd missed him and how glad she was he was safe. As the English finally formed in his mind, he was stopped from uttering a single word when Kara pressed her cool palms against his cheeks and settled her mouth against his.

She kissed him with such abandon Aiodhan couldn't help but respond in kind. Drinking her in and relearning her taste, he growled as he forced his tongue past her lips to reclaim what was his.

Her tongue was every bit as wild as his, and when he realized he wouldn't be satisfied until he was buried deep inside her, he tried to pull back. She must have found some sanity at the same moment, ending the kiss as they both panted for breath.

Content to have his mate back in his arms, he rested his forehead against hers. "I missed you."

"I missed you too." She looped her arms around his neck and squeezed.

Arms still wrapped around her, he started for the camp, glancing over his shoulder to be sure Claire and Christopher followed. He should have introduced them to Kara, but having told them stories about her the whole trip back, they had to know who had run out to greet him. Both children fell into step behind him.

Kara rested her chin on his shoulder, no doubt looking at his companions. "Did you save them?" she said, her voice whisper quiet.

Since he wasn't sure how to answer her question without opening up a huge discussion over who Claire and Christopher were, he grunted. At that moment, all he could think about was getting Kara back to her tent and making love to her until neither of them could move. Her core was pressing against his hard *kull*, and with each stride, he had to grit his teeth against the pleasure of the contact to maintain any kind of self-control.

As they passed her boots, first Claire and then Christopher picked one up. When they reached her, each handed the boots back to Kara. Aiodhan didn't even put her down to let her put them back on. Her socks were soaked, and he was concerned she would take ill if he didn't get her warm soon.

Bill swung down on the rope from the sentry post in the tree, landing close to Aiodhan's side. He slapped him hard on the back. "Glad to have you back." He nodded at the children. "Looks like you brought us some company."

"Claire and Christopher. They are hungry and in need of rest."

"I'll take them to Julie. She'll love having some kids around. Used to be an elementary school teacher. That'll give you and Kara some...privacy." Bill winked before he put a hand on each of the children's shoulder. "Let's get you two something to eat."

Both Claire and Christopher looked to Aiodhan, the question of trust clear in their eyes.

He nodded. "These people will treat you well."

The children smiled, and he was humbled at their acceptance of his guidance. After explaining to them about the people at the camp on their trip to Montana, they had to know they'd be in good hands.

Kara tried to wiggle out of his arms, but he held her tight. "Shouldn't I help?"

Aiodhan gave her a squeeze. "We will go to your tent. Must get you warm."

She laughed, a sound he'd missed far more than he'd realized. Her happiness wrapped around his heart, making him close his eyes for a moment, simply content to know she was safe and back in his embrace.

The men nodded greetings or pounded his back and shoulders as he passed them on the way to the clinic. If they were surprised to see him, they sure didn't show it. He was humbled by their quick acceptance of his return back to their ranks, especially when his parting had been unpleasant. He hoped they'd be as accepting of their new Praemons when he had the chance to reveal Christopher and Claire's gifts to them.

None of that mattered at the moment.

Only Kara did.

She helped open the flap to her tent so he could duck inside. He set her on the table and went back to lace together the entrance. Not only would it help keep the cold out, it would ensure some privacy.

Turning back to her, he smiled.

She smiled back and tried to jump off the table.

Aiodhan caught her before her feet touched the dirt floor. "Feet are wet."

"I don't care."

"I do." He ducked into the back room, carrying her along for the ride.

A look around told him she had no heat source. He frowned. "You are cold."

She pressed her lips to his neck. "No, I'm not. I'm hot. *Very* hot." Her tongue circled the shell of his ear.

He shivered, but not from the chill. "You have no heat."

"Don't care," she replied before she kissed him again.

While all he wanted to do was rip off her clothes and thrust inside her so he could feel her wet heat surround him again, he didn't want her taking ill from the cold. Crouching to set her on the bed, he unzipped his jacket, fumbling around on his belt for his lava crystal. His fingers closed around it and he brought it out. After removing it from the waterproof covering, he showed it to her.

"This will help." He nodded at the gray crystal he now cradled on his palm.

"What is it?"

Aiodhan reached for the bottle of water Kara had resting on the small table next to her bed. He splashed water over the stone.

"I don't—"

"Watch."

The stone grew until it was getting too large for him to hold. He set it down between the bed and the side of the tent. It continued to grow as its color changed from gray to orange. The heat radiated from the stone.

"What is it?"

"Lava stone. From Pashmar's ship."

"Will it keep getting bigger?"

Since the stone had now reached full growth, he shook his head.

"It won't cause a fire?"

Kneeling next to her, he shook his head again. He took one of her feet and pulled off the wet and dirty sock. Her toes felt like icicles. Holding her foot between his palms, he returned the circulation by gently rubbing.

Kara tried to pull her foot away.

He wouldn't let her.

"You don't have to—"

He gave her a hard kiss to stop her protests and kept up his comforting. Once her toes grew pink, he dropped to sit next to her on the mattress, turning her to face him. He set her warm foot down and grabbed the other, repeating the warming process.

Kara took off her jacket and tossed it aside. "I'm fine now, Aiodhan."

The interior of the tent had warmed, so he let her pull her foot away. He unlaced his own boots and jerked them off before unbuckling his utility belt and setting it aside.

Rising on her knees, she crawled to him as he turned to face her again. She pushed her hands inside his jacket and shoved it off his shoulders. After he shrugged out of it, he pulled his arms free and threw the coat on top of hers. Her fingers tangled in his hair and she tugged him forward.

Right before her lips captured his, she whispered, "I love you."

Kara's declaration set his passion soaring. He put his hands on her waist and dragged her forward. Falling back against the mattress, he pulled her with him until she was sprawled on top of him. Their tongues mated, the kisses savage and fierce. He combed his fingers through her soft hair as he swallowed each of her sweet moans.

Aiodhan's hands cupped her backside and pressed her hard against him so she could feel his erection. She sat up and straddled his hips. With a smile full of promise, she whipped her sweater over her head and popped off her bra.

He rose to take one of her pink nipples deep in his mouth, suckling as she arched into him with a mewl of pleasure. Her fingers roamed his back, tugging his shirt up. He released her nipple long enough to allow her to drag his shirt over his head, then he lavished her other breast with attention as she raked her fingernails across his shoulders.

Hands under Kara's knees to support her, Aiodhan flipped her to press her back to the mattress. He palmed her breasts before sliding his hands down her ribcage to her pants, which he peeled down her body. Her lacy panties joined their rest of her clothes on the floor.

Standing long enough to step out of his own pants and yank off his socks, he blanketed her with his body. The warmth of her skin seeped into his blood, and he buried his face where her shoulder met her neck, inhaling her womanly scent and sighing. "I missed this."

Her fingers glided down his back until they rested on his backside. She gave him a playful pinch. "I missed *you*."

Aiodhan smiled against her skin. Then he kissed his way down her body, tracing her collarbone with his tongue and licking the valley between her beautiful breasts. His tongue tickled her navel as he slipped a hand between her slim thighs and separated them so he could kiss the very heat of her.

Kara cried out. He stabbed his tongue in and out of her tight channel, trying to drive her higher and higher. He found her sensitive nub and swirled his tongue around it until she writhed beneath him, begging for him to be inside her. "Please. I need you now."

He stopped long enough to look up at her and grin. "You beg me?"

"Aiodhan. Now!"

Instead of answering her plea, he brought her to climax with his mouth.

Lost in pleasure, she whispered her love for him again.

Then he was there, covering her with his strong, warm body. He pushed her thighs farther apart and rubbed his erection against her core.

"Now," she said, her voice raspy.

Aiodhan plunged inside her in one dominant thrust. He groaned against her neck. "*Ah mila vo, damana.*"

She would never understand his words, but he needed her to.

Her eyes were pressed tightly closed.

"Look at me."

Eyelashes fluttering, she opened her eyes to stare deeply into his.

He kissed her—one hard kiss. "I love you, *damana.*"

"You love me?"

He nodded.

"Then make love to me. Now."

Aiodhan moved, drawing out and then plunging back inside her, gritting his teeth against the pleasure he felt as her tight heat surrounded his *kull.*

Telling her what was in his heart seemed so easy now. The way she'd responded to his touch and his kiss with such abandon told him she truly was his mate, and he felt more for her than simple loyalty or the need to protect her. He loved her. With all his heart. He used his body to show her, pouring all his passion into his lovemaking.

She lifted her legs to wrap them around his hips, squeezing to draw him deeper inside. He responded by giving in and surrendering all his control. Again and again he slammed into her, savoring each of her growls and moans until he felt the beginning of her climax as her muscles contracted around him. She called his name and dug her fingernails into his backside, forcing his own orgasm.

His release seemed limitless yet over too soon. Bracing himself on his elbows to protect her from his weight, he smoothed her tangled hair away from her face. *Zot*, but she was more beautiful than he'd remembered. Her cheeks were flushed, her brown eyes dark with passion. When she looked so tenderly up at him, he felt a contentment he'd never known existed.

"That was wonderful." Her voice was a purr. "But you're heavy."

Rolling to his side, he dragged Kara with him. She tucked herself up against his side and threw her leg over his thighs. He held her close as he pulled the blanket over them. The lava stone had created enough heat that they'd be warm throughout the night.

When she yawned, Aiodhan kissed her forehead. "I missed this."

"Me, too." She heaved a sigh. "We need to talk about the kid now."

"Kid?"

"Child."

"Not one. Two. They are Claire and Christopher."

She shook her head, her nose brushing against his shoulder before she pushed up on one elbow to stare down at him. "Not them. I mean *our* kid."

Her smile was so mysterious, and a faint blush colored her cheeks.

He couldn't help but point out the obvious. "We have no kid."

"We will in about seven months."

Chapter Twenty-One

Kara took another bite of eggs as she stared at the children.

They were precious and a bit precocious as well. She and Aiodhan had spent so much time in the night talking about the baby they were expecting—and making love—she hadn't asked him much about Claire and Christopher. Now, her curiosity blanketed her, and she had plans to get Aiodhan alone and find out exactly what made him bring them to the camp.

From what he'd told her about his missions, he'd never interacted with other species, let alone taken any of them under his wing. She wanted to believe his affection for her had made him change his rules.

What forced him take charge of these children? Hell, he'd been talking about dragging her ass to Tirios before he left. Had he changed his mind? Had he finally decided to help humans in their fights against Vymalns?

Considering she was also a Seeker, Pashmar seemed to have settled in the camp and among humans well. She spent a great deal of time with Bill, watching the IC and the comings and goings of the bug-eyes on Jayce's monitors. They'd managed to get a good idea of the work schedules so they knew when the guards changed, and they'd also located places in the IC that were poorly guarded and could be possible access points.

If Kara had to guess, she'd say Pashmar was staying on Earth for the long haul. Plus, Pashmar still had a mission to complete, unless she'd abandoned it. Although she wanted to try to understand Pashmar, Kara found herself frustrated. The Tirian's moods changed like the wind, and figuring her out was like trying to solve a Rubik's Cube blindfolded.

Claire and Christopher laughed at something Julie said, the sound of their happiness reminding Kara that there was still some good in the world—a notion she wanted to cling to with her whole heart. The children ate everything they were given without a complaint. They were such pleasant kids. Downright adorable.

Claire reminded Kara a lot of herself as a child, a bit skinny with hair and eyes of the same brown. Although Claire was probably ten, she talked like an adult. She smiled often, as if she had not a care in the world.

Christopher was every bit as unguarded. His eyes were an enchanting shade of blue, and Kara had to resist the urge to tousle his curly blond hair. He accepted the attention of the men in the militia, and he clung to Julie.

She sat between the children as they ate, and she smiled just as often as they did. Caring for Claire and Christopher would help her finally heal after her ordeal in the IC.

When they finished their breakfast, Julie had the children get up and bus their trays. Then she led them back toward Bill's tent, saying she was going to set up a school schedule for them. Julie insisted that just because the Vymalns were being cruel didn't mean that the children shouldn't receive a proper education.

"One day, we'll need to build a new government," she promised as they walked away. "You need an education to do it properly."

"What happened to their parents?" Kara asked Aiodhan once they were gone.

"Claire's mother died," he replied. "I do not know about Christopher."

"Why did you bring them here?" Bill asked.

Aiodhan shrugged. "They needed me."

"You mean there weren't any humans who could take care of them?"

Kara resented the implication. "Why would they be better off with humans than Aiodhan?"

Bill's ferocious frown should have warned her off, but it didn't. "You know what I mean. He's...different."

"Aiodhan would be a great father," she insisted.

Aiodhan set his hand against her thigh and rubbed her gently.

"Yeah, but..." Bill sighed. "I just thought they'd be better with their own kind."

"Tirians are much like humans." Aiodhan tossed Kara a wink. "We are combative."

A laugh bubbled out when she realized what he meant. "Compatible, not combative."

"Coom-pat-babble?"

She bit her bottom lip so he wouldn't think she was laughing at him instead of with him. "Com. Pat. Able. *Compatible*. Means we go together well." She leaned into him, smiling in contentment. "We obviously go *very* well together."

Kevin had been sitting next to Claire, and now he scooted his tray further down the table so he sat opposite Kara. "Except for the eyes, looks pretty human to me." He shrugged before shoveling some more food into his mouth.

Watching her brother, she wondered if the time had come to share her news. He seemed to be a good mood and much more accommodating to Aiodhan since he'd returned than when he'd left. Kevin had practically put his boot to Aiodhan's ass to get him to go.

With Kevin's change of heart, perhaps now was the best time. She struggled with finding the right way to tell him.

Aiodhan beat her to the punch. The arrogant smile on his face didn't surprise her one bit. He leaned back and grinned like he'd just won the lottery. "Kara will have my child soon."

Kevin choked on his eggs. "*What?*"

"I'm pregnant," she announced.

"Jesus Christ." Bits of chewed scrambled egg flew with Kevin's shouted words. "What in the hell were you thinking?"

Aiodhan's fist came down on the table, his grin vanishing like a mirage in the desert. "She is my mate. She will bear my child. Do not yell at her."

She laid a hand on his arm. "It's okay."

"He may not yell at you!"

She figured it wasn't the time to point out he was the one yelling at her now.

"For God's sake, Kara." Kevin closed his eyes, pinched the bridge of his nose, and took a couple of deep breaths before he leveled an accusing glare at her. "Why wouldn't you use birth control? I mean…how could you be so-so irresponsible? You really want to bring a baby into all—this—this—*bullshit?* What about the lizards?"

Bill nodded but said nothing.

"This isn't any of your business," she scolded.

Problem was, she agreed with Kevin more than she wanted to admit, even to herself. His words made her face the stark truth.

Raising a child in their terrifying situation turned her stomach. If she allowed it, her fear for her baby would tie her into anxious knots she'd never be able to unravel. While she'd counted on her brother's support, she also knew it was naïve to think that everyone would welcome her news.

What kind of life did her child face? Hiding in camps like this or becoming a slave to the bastard Vymalns?

No. No.

No!

That wasn't what the future held. Humans were more resourceful and courageous than the bug-eyes could ever anticipate. The Vymalns might have won the battle.

But the war was just beginning.

"I think it's great." Jayce smiled at Kara and then at Aiodhan.

An incredulous frown fixed on Kevin's face. "Great? How is it *great?*"

"Yeah, Jayce," Bill added. "How is having a baby in the middle of our world being destroyed a *great* thing?"

Jayce's smile felt like a hug to Kara. "Think about what we're fighting for. Our way of life, right?"

Kevin kept frowning. "Yeah, but-but—"

"Listen. In World War II, did everyone stop living just 'cause the Nazis were trying to take over the world?" Jayce didn't wait more than a beat. "Hell, no. They went right on getting married and having babies."

Several of the men nodded, raising her spirits and easing her angst.

"Seriously," Jayce went on, "what better way to tell the lizards to go fuck themselves than by living our lives the way we want to live 'em? Even if we're the last people left free on this planet, I'm not letting them ruin my future."

"There are more like you," Aiodhan added.

"What do you mean?" Bill asked.

"Claire lived in a place with people not ruled by Vymalns."

Jayce nodded. "I'm trying to contact other groups. So far, I've got people in Indiana and California, but I can't seem to raise too many other places. Damn well going to stay at it, though. The more of us that can connect, the better chance we have of kicking some Vymaln ass."

"Looks like the Montana Militia isn't alone anymore," Kara added.

Pashmar came over with her breakfast tray and sat down next to Aiodhan. She reached for the shakers Jayce had on his tray and sprinkled a generous amount of salt over her eggs before doing the same with the pepper. Since Aiodhan also enjoyed Earth's spices, Pashmar drowning her eggs in salt and pepper didn't come as a surprise.

Unsure as to how Pashmar would handle the news of the baby, Kara hesitated. Aiodhan might want to break the news to his friend in private.

Aiodhan obviously didn't care. "I am to be a father." His chest puffed out.

It took all Kara's self-control not to roll her eyes at his masculine arrogance.

Pashmar sat as still as a statue and stared at her food.

Kara held her breath, waiting for an explosion. It never came. Instead, Pashmar stood up and simply walked away. No shouting. No tears. No scolding.

Nothing.

"Did you not hear me?" Aiodhan called after her. "Kara will have my child."

Pashmar didn't even break stride.

"She's upset," Kara said. "Let her be."

He gave her a confused frown. "Let her be what?"

"I mean you should leave her alone. She needs some time to process the news."

* * *

Aiodhan didn't catch up to Pashmar until the sun was setting, which it seemed to do earlier and earlier every day. The extra darkness made it difficult for the sentries who watched the camp, but his own eyes easily made the adjustment.

The snow, however, took some getting used to. Although he liked the crunching sound it made when he walked over it and the barren landscape was now a bit easier to look at, he hated how so many people in the camp liked to pack it into balls and hurl the missiles at each other. He'd been hit several times—by Jayce, by Bill, even by Kevin—and had assumed it was an insult. Then Kara explained it was one of Earth's customs, right after she hit him in the face with one of the snowballs when she'd been playing with Claire and Christopher.

Her laughter had been as refreshing as any drink could be to a thirsty man. Now that he was back, he knew he'd never have to leave her again. Her quick acceptance of the children boded well, and he was sure once he explained the important role she'd play in the new Praemons' lives, Kara would rise to the challenge.

After tossing a few of the snowballs at the children and allowing them to throw a few at him, he'd caught a glimpse of Pashmar entering the weapons tent. Even though she made eye contact, she ducked through the flap without giving him any kind of greeting. He left Claire and Christopher with Kara and followed Pashmar.

When he entered, she whirled around, wide-eyed. Then she all but dismissed him by turning her back.

"You're mad at me," he said in Tirian, leaning against one of the crates.

She didn't reply as she grabbed a box of bullets. In the time he'd been gone, she'd begun carrying a human sidearm, so he assumed she was getting ammunition for it.

He nodded at the gun. "Did one of the men show you how to use that properly? According to Bill, humans poorly trained with them end up shooting themselves. It won't do much good against a Vymaln."

Her eyes shot fire. "You think I don't know my job?"

"Your job—ah, yes. Now that I've killed Khymer Cantu, I imagine you'll want to finish your mission."

"The time isn't right yet." She counted out some bullets before shoving them in her pocket.

"What did the Praemons tell you?"

"They told me what I needed to know." Closing the box, she shoved it back into a crate. Turning to face him, she frowned. "Why, Aiodhan?"

"Why what?"

"Why her? Why a child? Why not—" With a shake of her head she tried to push past him.

Aiodhan grabbed her arm. "I didn't make her my mate to hurt you. I wasn't thinking about you. I thought all we'd ever be was friends."

"You knew I wanted more."

He sighed in resignation. "Perhaps. But I'd also made it clear—several times—I didn't."

"And the child?"

"The child was unintended. Created in the heat of the moment. An accident."

A lie.

Yes, he'd been swept away by passion and hadn't given any thought to birth control, but from the moment he'd taken Kara as his mate, he'd wondered what it would be like to make a family with her. He might not have planned on having a baby with her so soon, but he wasn't one to question a blessing. He'd simply attributed Kara's pregnancy to the fact that they were clearly a fertile—and *compatible*—couple.

"Then get rid of it. Even humans have to know how to—"

"Stop it! You know I consider that an abomination."

"This child wasn't meant to be."

"I love Kara. We're having a baby together. It's time to get past this. My job's done; now get your mission over with." He smiled, hoping to help her see how much she still meant to him. "We have a new job to do."

Her eyes widened. "How could you know about a new mission? You haven't been back to the Seeker ship, have you?"

"No. I found this mission without our Praemons. I've discovered that Earth has created its own Praemons."

Pashmar gasped. "You speak blasphemy. The Praemons are sacred. They're—"

"It's not blasphemy. The children I brought here, they're destined to be Praemons."

"How do you know that? By the stars, Aiodhan, if any Tirian hears you speak such-such... nonsense..." She grabbed his upper arms, her grip fierce. "We won't speak of this again. You'll put it out of your head. You'll forget it. Then no one will know that you've—" She swallowed hard. "We won't speak of this again. No one will know. Understand?" Her voice trembled with some emotion he couldn't read, but tears spilled over her lashes.

In all the years they'd known each other, he'd never seen her lose control. They'd faced some terrifying situations, and each time, Pashmar had maintained a cool head. Now, she was weeping, something he'd been convinced she wasn't even capable of doing, and her fingers dug into his muscles.

"What's wrong with you?"

"Leave her here. Leave her behind. That child she's carrying is half human. Tirians would never accept it. Let it stay with her, with those-those...*humans*." Her eyes had changed, clouded now in a chorus of stormy gray. "Come with me. We'll go back to the way we were. We'll go back to being who we are—*what* we are."

Aiodhan broke her tenacious grip. "You think I'd abandon my mate? My child? For what?"

"For me."

He growled low in his throat. "I love her."

"You don't even know her!"

"I love her, Pashmar. I won't leave her. I won't leave my child. I've seen my new path, the one the Praemons told me would come. The children I brought back have a destiny, and I'm the one to help them achieve it."

Pashmar turned her back and wrapped her arms around her waist. "You choose her, then? You choose her instead of—" Her sigh was a long, drawn-out affair that made her shoulders shake. "You'll let her take you away from your Seeker vow to the Praemons?"

"I've done everything the Praemons asked of me. *Everything*. What I choose now is simply fulfilling my final duty to them and following the path they put before me."

With a choked sob, she turned and tried to hurry past him.

He grabbed her shoulder, refusing to let go when she tried to roll it out of his grasp. "We could share this new destiny. These humans need us—just like they need Claire and Christopher. After your mission, we'll talk. Maybe if you spend some time with them, you'll see what I see. These children will be Earth's Praemons, and I'll do everything in my power to see it happen."

"She'll destroy you."

The certainty in her voice sent a chill racing down his spine. Seekers who spoke about things with such authority usually knew something that only the Praemons could have shared, something they were usually forbidden to reveal to others. "What do you mean?"

With a shake of her head, Pashmar shrugged his hand away and ducked out of the tent.

Chapter Twenty-Two

Kara couldn't help but smile up at Aiodhan when he stood next to the mattress, hands on his hips while he frowned down at her.

"You will wear all *that* to sleep?" he asked.

Sitting up and hugging her knees, she nodded. Since she'd bundled herself in a thick thermal shirt and flannel pants, he must have thought she was wearing them like some kind of chastity wear. He was wrong. She'd be glad to prove it to him when she got warmer, but she couldn't resist the urge to tease him. "It's winter, Aiodhan. I'm freezing my ass off. I doubt I'll ever be naked again."

He narrowed his eyes at her. "My mate should come to bed naked."

"Not in the winter, she shouldn't."

Crouching down, he picked up the shrunken, gray lava stone, poured some water over it and set it aside as it rapidly changed to orange. "Will be warm soon." Whipping his shirt over his head, he dropped it next to the boots he'd removed. Then he pulled off his socks. "I will warm you."

As he unzipped his pants, she watched him, thinking that the man could make a fortune as a Chippendale's dancer. The play of his muscles rolling under his bronze skin was enough to make her pant in desire.

Shoving his pants over his hips, his erection sprang forward. If the tent hadn't felt like an icebox, she would have thrown her own clothes aside and jumped him right then and there.

Aiodhan lifted the quilt, flopped on the mattress and pulled the blanket up to his waist. Turning to his side, he ran his palm over her arm. He tugged the material of her shirt. "Take this off."

"When the tent's warmer."

He stretched out on his back and held his arm wide as he patted his shoulder in invitation. Kara crawled under the quilt and snuggled up to him, trying to absorb his heat. The lava stone was warming the room, but nothing felt as wonderful as being pressed up against her alien.

"What do you think he'll look like?" she asked.

"Who?"

"Our baby." She playfully pinched his waist, marveling again at his incredible body. Honest to God, there wasn't an ounce of fat on him.

"I wish him to have your eyes."

"Really?"

"Your eyes are like the *demauba* tree."

"Since I don't have a clue what a *demauba* tree is, I'm not sure if that's a compliment or an insult."

He grunted. "I would not wish my son to have your eyes if I did not like them."

"What's a *demauba* tree?"

"A beautiful brown tree."

Kara lifted her head from his shoulder and kissed his cheek. "That was sweet. What are we gonna do about Christopher and Claire?"

His exaggerated shrug almost tossed her off the mattress.

Pushing herself up on an elbow, she frowned. They should have had this conversation when he first returned, but she'd been so damned happy to see him, all she'd wanted to do was drown in him. Then she'd wanted to share the news of their baby. Now, she'd had time to think, and she'd realized that Aiodhan had accepted responsibility for the children who'd made the trek back to Montana with him.

"You don't know?" she asked. "But you brought them all the way back here?"

"They belong to us now."

"They don't have any relatives?"

"I did not ask."

"What if they have aunts or uncles—or grandparents—searching for them?"

Aiodhan reached up to cup her neck and tugged her down so he could settle his mouth on hers. His way of shutting her up. Kara let herself fall into the kiss, giving him a moan of delight when his tongue pushed past her lips.

The kiss could have easily led to more, but they'd been discussing an important topic. This time, she wouldn't let him distract her. Pulling back, she brushed her braid over her shoulder.

"We need to talk about this, Tarzan. Why these kids? You said there were lots of people in Seattle who probably knew them better than you. Shouldn't they have stayed there?"

Aiodhan had thought long and hard about what to say when Kara questioned him about Claire and Christopher. He'd also considered the best way to explain to the other humans the significance of what these children meant for their future.

While he wanted to announce that he'd found Earth's new Praemons, he'd discovered in dealing with humans they resisted being told what to do. Diplomacy wasn't one of his skills, and he didn't know how to coax Kara's cooperation. Whenever something needed done, he just went ahead and did it. No cajoling. No encouraging. No explaining.

Kara was his mate, and she handled sticky situations well—better than he could where humans were concerned. If he was as open and honest with her as he could be about what he saw as the path humans were now destined to follow, maybe she could help ease the news to her kind.

Perhaps *she* could be the diplomat.

"Aiodhan? What's wrong?" Leaning over him, her eyes searched his.

"The children are...*special*."

"Special? What do you mean special?"

His thoughts were always too far ahead of his ability to express them in her language. "You must learn Tirian," he snapped.

"What does my learning your language have to do with the kids?" she snapped right back at him.

Since he didn't have the ability to tell her what he needed with any finesse, he took his typical blunt tack. "They see the future."

Kara sat up and folded her legs under her. "I don't understand."

"They can see the future."

"Saying it again and slower doesn't help."

"They are Praemons."

Her brown eyes flew wide. "What?"

"They are—"

She slapped his shoulder. "I heard you. I just didn't... I mean... Aren't the Praemons your gods or something?"

"Not gods. They know the future. These children, they see the future as well."

She pulled her braid against her cheeks, and her fingers tripped over it. "How do you know?"

As Aiodhan told the story of how Claire found him and how she led him to Christopher, he watched Kara's expression. For the first time since he'd met her, she revealed nothing. He ended the tale by explaining about Hannah's noble sacrifice—the one Claire predicted—and waited for his mate's reaction.

Kara sat facing him, stroking her braid—a telling gesture that revealed her concern.

"What is in your thoughts?" he finally asked, unable to bear the silence.

He needed her help, something he was loathe to admit. His whole life, he'd been alone. Each goal, each achievement as a Seeker, had been accomplished through his own hard work and perseverance. To acknowledge her importance in his helping him achieve this goal—and in this, his most important mission—came as a surprise. The vulnerable feeling didn't sit well.

Aiodhan sat up and glared at her.

"What is in your thoughts?" he repeated in a near roar.

"I-I just don't know," she replied, her voice a whisper.

A growl rumbled his chest.

"I'm sorry, Aiodhan. I really don't know what to tell you." Her hand dropped from her hair to her stomach.

He wondered if she knew she was stroking their unborn child. That thought drove away his scowl. Leaning in, he brushed her hand away. Then he lifted the hem of her shirt and settled his hand on her belly.

Kara's hand returned to rest over his.

"Do you plan to take them back to Tirios when you leave?" she asked.

No wonder she was so hesitant. "You do not understand."

"I understand perfectly. You think you're taking Claire and Christopher back with you to the Seeker ship when you and Pashmar—"

He shut her up with a quick, hard kiss. "I will not leave."

"But-but I thought... Aren't the kids supposed to be your new Praemons?"

"They shall be Praemons to Earth."

"You mean you're not leaving? You're not going back to Tirios?"

One of these days, he would have to remember that he needed to tell his mate his plans. She couldn't read his mind, so she had no way to know he'd made the decision to remain. His only excuse was that he was used to doing things on his own and not sharing his thoughts.

"*We* will stay here," he announced. "Our child will be raised on Earth."

Her smile was so full of joy, it stole his breath away.

"We will tell the others tomorrow," he continued. Deciding they'd talked long enough, Aiodhan tried to kiss Kara.

She dodged him.

He tried again. "Kara?"

Her smile had fallen to a stern frown. "You really think it'll be that easy?"

Clearly, this discussion wasn't over.

"I'm not sure that's a good idea," she said.

Earth had just been given a miracle by the powers of the universe. How could she possibly think that telling the humans they now stood a chance against the Vymalns be bad? "Why?"

"What if you're wrong? What if they're not really...Praemons?"

His frustration took the lead. "You will trust me!"

Kara shoved his hand aside and folded her arms over her breasts. "This has nothing to do with trust. Claire predicted a couple of things. That doesn't make her a Praemon. Or a prophet. Or whatever the hell you want to call her and Christopher. You can't march out to Kevin and the men and tell them those kids are going to start telling them what to do. 'Cause that's what you planned to do, right? Tell them they have to do what Claire and Christopher say? Just like you do what the Praemons tell you?"

"They are Praemons. We must obey."

174

His voice was filled with anger, and the gray of his eyes twisted and turned as they darkened with his emotions. While their language difficulties had often been amusing, now Kara felt as if she was trying to fight with one hand tied behind her back. This discussion required more than she could express with his limited English, despite some help from Pashmar, she wasn't even at a level she could speak pidgin Tirian.

She chose her words carefully. "These people wouldn't understand what you think Claire and Christopher are supposed to be."

"The children will show them. The humans will follow once they see."

She shook her head. "I don't think we should tell anyone. Not yet."

While she wanted to believe Aiodhan wasn't exaggerating what had happened, she'd always been someone who needed to see things with her own eyes. Until she was entirely convinced these children did indeed have special abilities, she needed to protect them. Hell, they'd probably need more protection if they really could see into the future.

"We should keep their gifts a secret for now," she insisted.

"Explain."

Having expected him to erupt like a volcano, Kara breathed a little easier. "If we tell everyone that they can, you know, see the future, people could exploit them."

"Exploit?"

"Use them. Abuse them."

"How?"

"Humans have a bad habit of treating people who are special badly. Following them around. Using them to get things they want for themselves."

The gray in his eyes had calmed and now reminded her less of an approaching storm. "We should protect them. Keep them secret."

She almost sighed in relief. "For now. We should wait until the right moment."

"What if they have a mission for us?"

"We'll play it by ear."

His fingers touched his ear, and she knew that he was taking her too literally again.

"I meant we'll decide when that time comes," she said.

Since they seemed to finally be agreeing, Kara figured distraction was the best course of action. The tent was plenty warm now, and from that moment she'd gotten a glimpse of Aiodhan in all his glory she'd wanted him. With a naughty smile, she rose on her knees and whipped her thermal shirt over her head.

"You are not cold?" Aiodhan's question came out choked, as though he hated asking it.

175

For a caveman, he was considerate. "You'll keep me warm."

When she tried to wiggle out of her flannel pants, he helped. Then he yanked off her socks. Pressing her back to the sheets, he gave her a thorough look from head to toe and back again. His hands settled on her hips, and he frowned.

"You are small."

"I'm just skinny. Wait a few months. I'll look like a water buffalo."

"Your hips. Too small for our baby."

The worry in his voice touched her heart. "I'm not too small. Kevin was almost ten pounds, and I was nine. Mom was the same size as me— maybe even a little bit smaller—and she gave birth to both of us with no problems at all."

His lips touched her stomach. "You will be well." He smiled at her. "You will both be well."

"We'll both be well. Now kiss me."

Instead of obeying, Aiodhan kissed her belly again. With no warning at all, his hands spread her thighs as his mouth dipped to caress her core.

Kara nearly came off the mattress. With a groan of delight, she threaded her fingers through his long, dark hair and tugged. "I thought you were gonna kiss me."

He stopped long enough to say, "I *am* kissing you." Then he proceeded to chase away all her control with his mouth and his tongue. The harder she pulled his hair, the more it seemed to drive him on.

"Aiodhan, now. I want you *now*." Her voice was so husky with need she barely recognized it.

Her pleas went unheeded, and the tension inside her built to a crescendo before the splendor of her orgasm burst through her. As she called out to him again, he was there, grasping her hips and thrusting deep inside her. Kara drew up her knees and trailed her hands down his broad back.

The rhythm was fast and rough. His groans blended with her whimpers. When his lips covered hers, she pushed her tongue into his mouth in sync with him driving into her body.

A second climax grabbed her, making her cry out and sending stars shooting across her vision. Aiodhan thrust into her once more and growled her name in her ear.

* * *

Kara's breathing became slow, deep, and even when sleep claimed her.

Aiodhan rested on his side, watching her as she lay sprawled on her back. Her cheeks were still bright with color, probably because the lava stone had made the tent a little warmer than he'd anticipated. It was a fairly large stone, and the tent was small.

She was beautiful, nothing short of perfect in his eyes. She was not only a worthy mate, but that she'd be the kind of mother Christopher and Claire needed.

Keeping their status a secret chafed him, but her words had convinced him she was correct. Humans were such an odd species, and he'd deferred to her knowledge of their strange tendencies. Everything about these people contradicted the values he held dear.

Abilities that should be celebrated needed to be hidden. Instead of letting these children take their place as Earth's Praemons, he and Kara would have to shelter and protect them from their own kind. How could the humans benefit from Praemons they didn't even know existed?

His job would be to listen to Claire and Christopher and use what they told him to teach the humans how to drive back the Vymaln invasion. In time, he could help the humans learn to trust their Praemons the same way the Tirians trusted the twins who protected their future. Once they did, Aiodhan could help train Earth's Seekers.

He rested his hand on Kara's abdomen, thinking about his child. He vowed he would allow his son to choose his own destiny. While Aiodhan never once regretted becoming a Seeker, he'd often wondered what he would have been if his father hadn't pushed him with his own expectations.

A teacher? A healer? A politician?

None of those would have led him here, and he'd figured out exactly what the Praemons had meant about his life changing. This planet was where he was meant to be, and this woman was his mate.

He fell asleep, convinced this new life in this strange place was his destiny.

Chapter Twenty-Three

"I will not be gone long." Aiodhan buckled on his tool belt.

Kara laughed, a sound he'd never tire of hearing. "Sure you will. I was with you the last time you tried to hunt, remember? The only thing that got caught was us." She winked.

"This time, you will not scare animals with constant talk." He tossed a wink back at her.

After she finished tying the laces on her boots, she went to him. He wrapped his arms around her and kissed the top of her head. Each time he held her, contentment made him hesitant to ever let her go. The child she nurtured in her womb was growing rapidly. He loved how the small bump in her belly rubbed against him when they hugged. At night, he often fell asleep with his palm resting over his unborn child, waiting to capture those first movements.

Knowing her enjoyment of humor, he couldn't resist a tease. "I will be unable to reach you soon. Your stomach will be too large."

"Yeah, I'm getting kinda fat."

"Not fat, Kara. Beautiful as you grow with my child."

She gave him a tight squeeze. "I need to get to the clinic."

"I must hunt. I shall bring back food for us all."

"You do that, Tarzan. Go out and bag us a nice stag so we have venison on the menu for a few days."

A few days.

Supplying food for the group was getting more and more difficult. In the weeks since he'd brought Claire and Christopher to the camp, a few of the people from Seattle had made their way to Montana. They claimed to want to follow Aiodhan since he'd been successful in killing the Vymaln prince.

Now that winter had come on with a vengeance, blanketing the ground in snow and dropping temperatures to frigid levels, feeding the group became a priority. Thankfully, the area was ripe with game, and the Seattle escapees had brought along quite a few canned provisions.

Bill set up a hunting schedule to be sure there was always enough meat. So far, Aiodhan had tasted deer, elk, and moose. Today was his turn to venture into the woods. After hearing Jayce talking about bears, he hoped to find one. They sounded like fascinating creatures and a good test of his strength.

"I not look for stag. I want a bear," he said.

She looked up at him with concern in her brown eyes. "Stay away from bears. They're dangerous."

"I am more dangerous."

"You're probably right, but I still want you to stay away from bears." Her confident smile and her concern for his safety pleased him.

Rising on tiptoes, she brushed a kiss over his lips before leaving his embrace. Then she grabbed her coat and a pair of thick mittens. "I'm going to the clinic."

"I will see you soon, *damana*."

Kara ducked out of the tent.

Aiodhan took a look around and frowned. The tent was cozy and more than enough to meet his needs, but he worried about Kara. According to her, the winter would get worse before it got better. She talked of cold that could freeze skin in a matter of moments and snow deep enough the tent might be buried it in. He was consumed with worry.

She was with child. She deserved to stay in a warm home with comforts this camp didn't provide. Not that she'd ever complained—her nature wouldn't allow it. But he knew life wasn't easy for her.

With the child pressing on her bladder, she needed to relieve herself often. She would don her boots and coat and head to the latrine. When she returned, he always had to hold her close to share his body heat until she stopped shivering. Since the child would only continue to grow, her visits would increase. Although he offered to carry her each time she left, she refused.

Back at the cabin, Kara wouldn't have that problem. She'd have running water and a warm bed. Aiodhan could bring her food and still help at the camp.

He made up his mind to take her back to the cabin soon, no matter how much she argued against it. Claire and Christopher could go as well. Perhaps even Julie since she had become their teacher. Then he'd see what he could do to prepare for Kara's delivery, hoping Jayce might be able to contact someone with experience delivering human babies.

Pleased with his plans, he strode out of the tent and headed for the armory. Human guns did a great job in bringing down game, so he'd use one of their weapons on his hunt.

Pashmar was inside the tent. She glanced up from the gun she was loading with bullets. "You go to hunt today?"

Aiodhan nodded. He grabbed one of the rifles and some bullets and loaded the weapon.

"I shall go too." She set the loaded gun down on a crate.

He drew his mouth into a grim line. Things between them hadn't been good since Kara's pregnancy was announced. For weeks, Pashmar had gone out of her way to avoid Kara. Whenever he was with Pashmar, she acted distant and moody.

"I can hunt alone," he insisted.

"Going together, we can seek larger targets."

A grunt slipped out.

"Let me go with you. I can help."

"When will you go on your mission?" he asked.

Pashmar shrugged. "Soon."

How odd. Seekers normally weren't given to linger. Missions were short. Get in, eliminate the threat, and get right back out. He'd asked Pashmar several times about her target, but she'd never given him a clear answer. She'd been even more evasive about when she was supposed to return to the Seeker ship. He had composed a message to his commander to tell of completing his mission, and he'd recorded another message for his family to explain his choice to stay with his mate. Those messages wouldn't be delivered until Pashmar's mission was over.

Aiodhan blamed himself for Pashmar's black mood. She was surely still hanging around the camp because of him. Whenever she opened up and talked to him, she'd begged him to return to the Seeker ship with her. Each time, he would explain—yet again—that he wasn't leaving Earth, and she'd stomp away.

One of these days, he needed to pin her down and find out what she was supposed to be doing, help her get that task done, and then get her back to the Seeker ship. Pashmar's future was on Tirios, not here among people she considered beneath her.

"Let me hunt with you today," Pashmar said, the plea clear in her tone.

About to turn down her offer, Aiodhan stopped when Claire came into the armory. "You may not be in here," he scolded.

Claire gave him an innocent smile. "I know, but I needed to see you before you left for the woods."

Aiodhan arched an eyebrow.

"I had a dream."

His heart skipped a beat. In all the time the children had been in camp, they'd had no prophetic dreams. Would this prophecy be good news or bad?

Pashmar loomed over Claire. "Dream? You mean a prophecy?" Her voice quivered in a way he'd never heard before, not even when they'd faced danger of epic proportions.

"I dreamed about you." Claire raised her chin, locking gazes with Pashmar. "You're going on your mission today."

Pashmar's eyes widened. "What do *you* know of my mission?"

"Choose wisely what you want, because your life will belong to that world from that moment on. The other world faces a horrible future." Claire's voice was mature, authoritarian, and surprisingly calm.

"She's torn between two worlds?" Aiodhan asked, hoping Claire's prophecies weren't the typical enigmas that came from the Tirian Praemons.

Claire ignored him, still staring at Pashmar. "The world you choose will one day steal your heart." With a sweet smile that belied the austerity of her prophecy, the girl skipped out of the tent.

"You're seeking your target today?" Aiodhan asked in Tirian.

Pashmar stayed frozen to the spot, gaping at the entrance to the armory.

"Answer me! Is your mission today?"

She gave him a curt nod.

"Do you need my help?"

Turning her back to him, she heaved a sigh and grabbed her gun. She shoved it into her waistband so it rested against the small of her back. "We hunt first. Then I'll do my job."

"You want to hunt first?"

"I need to leave this place and think about my mission. Can I go with you? We-we can talk."

"Fine." Aiodhan slung the shotgun strap over his shoulder and led the way out of the tent.

* * *

"I'm getting sick of this heartburn." Kara rifled through one of the two boxes of new supplies the reivers brought her. "Any Tums in that box?"

Julie searched through it and frowned. "Nope. But—lookie here!" She held up a large white bottle. "Prenatal vitamins. Those should come in handy."

"I'd rather have the Tums."

"You know...big as you're getting, you might be having twins."

Kara's hands dropped to her baby bump. "I'm not *that* big." Ready to dismiss the vanity, she stopped and pulled her shirt tight against her. "Am I?"

Julie's laughter filled the tent. "No, silly. I'm teasing. The only reason you're even showing is 'cause you're so skinny. You've got lots of months of growing to do."

The women worked in quiet companionship putting away the new supplies until Bill came into the tent. Following close on his heels were Christopher and Claire.

"Brought you some company," Bill said.

Julie snorted at him. "They were driving you crazy with questions again, weren't they?"

"Absolutely." He smiled at his sister. "They're as bad as you were as a kid. Why, why, why, why—"

Holding up her hands in surrender, Julie said, "Fine. I get it. I was precocious. Hey, kiddos. Wanna learn more about medicine today?"

Normally, they would dive into a litany of questions about whatever topic they were given. When Bill bid them farewell and quiet returned, Kara glanced up from her task.

The children were staring at her with an intensity that made the hair on the back of her neck stand on end. Then they spoke to each other in whispers so low Kara couldn't make out their words.

Part of her wanted to find out what they were thinking and why their eyes were drilling holes right through her. Another part wanted to cover her ears and avoid whatever they were talking about.

Aiodhan believed, with all his heart, that Claire and Christopher could predict the future. He considered it the greatest gift a creature could be given—knowledge of what was to come.

Kara didn't agree. Knowing one's future seemed more of a curse. Part of the joy of living was never knowing what the next day would bring, and a human's personality was based on how she approached that unknown. As a pessimist, always assuming the worst? Or as an optimist who believed the future could mean great things?

When they again stared at her, she swallowed hard. "You had a dream, didn't you?"

Both children nodded.

"About me?"

"About Aiodhan," Christopher answered.

"And Pashmar," Claire added.

"You *both* had dreams?" Julie moved to crouch in front of the children. She searched their faces, but their gazes remained focused on Kara.

"We had the same dream," Claire replied.

Kara crossed her arms over her waist to hug herself against the chill that now encased her. "You had the same dream about Aiodhan?"

"And Pashmar," Christopher said.

"Tell us about it," Julie ordered.

It took every ounce of strength Kara had to force herself to stay and listen.

"Today is Pashmar's mission." Claire's lips dropped to a frown.

"Today?" Kara asked. "She's going after her target today? Is it one of the IC guards?"

Since Aiodhan had returned from Seattle, she'd assumed Pashmar would be on her way. Yet instead of following through on whatever quest the Tirian Praemons had given her, she'd stayed with the humans.

She hunted for fresh meat with the men, and she trained the guys who didn't know how to use firearms. Most of the people in the camp assumed she'd decided to stay and help fight the Vymalns.

Kara knew better. Seekers didn't abandon their missions. Pashmar had been waiting.

But for what?

Claire went to stand in front of Kara. "She has to choose today."

"Choose? What does Pashmar have to choose?" Kara asked.

"Whether to finish her mission. She doesn't *want* to kill him, but she *has* to if she wants to go home again."

The words took a moment for the words to register in Kara's mind. When they did, her heart started slamming in her chest and bile rose in the back of her throat. "Oh God, you're talking about Aiodhan? She's supposed to kill Aiodhan?"

Claire nodded.

So did Christopher.

"Kill Aiodhan?" Julie wrung her hands together. "Why in the devil would Pashmar want to kill Aiodhan? They're friends."

"Her mission," Kara replied as the pieces fell into place. "*He's* her fucking mission!"

Everything suddenly made sense. Pashmar had never named her target. Not once. She hadn't left as Aiodhan had to go to her target. All Pashmar had done was hang around camp and try to talk Aiodhan into going back to Tirios, telling him over and over that he'd destroy himself by staying on Earth.

Kara had always attributed it to simple jealousy.

She'd been wrong.

Pashmar had dragged her feet and kept arguing with Aiodhan because she didn't want to have to kill him—a hit only the Praemons could have ordered. They must have foreseen what would happen to him when he came here.

What threat could Aiodhan possibly pose to Tirios if he stayed on Earth? Would they want to destroy a Seeker who abandoned them? Would they fear Aiodhan's defection would make other Tirians lose faith and stop seeing them as living gods?

Her hand dropped to her belly again. Even her baby could be a threat in the eyes of the Praemons. So could Claire and Christopher since Aiodhan had declared their abilities equal to that of the Praemons. What god would allow his power to be challenged so openly?

Kara ran out of the tent. Searching frantically for help, she screamed out, "Bill! Kevin!"

Bill ran from the armory, gun in hand, his eyes wide. "Kara? What the hell?"

"Where's Aiodhan?"

"Hunting. What's the matter?"

"I need to find him! Now!"

Kevin followed Bill out of the tent, holding his rifle at ready. He hurried to her and settled a hand on her shoulders. "Jesus, Kara…you scared the shit outta me. What's wrong?"

"It's Aiodhan! Pashmar's going to kill Aiodhan! Where is he?"

The men exchanged a worried look before Bill spoke. "Where did you hear something like that?"

"The kids. They dreamed it. Pashmar's going to murder Aiodhan." Why weren't they moving? "Aiodhan's in danger, damn it! Where did he go hunting?"

"Pashmar wouldn't hurt him," Bill insisted. "They're both Seekers. Besides, she told me this morning she was leaving on whatever mission she needs to do. She was gone at sunup."

"Don't you see—killing Aiodhan *is* her mission!"

"You're being silly," Kevin insisted. "Probably pregnancy hormones."

She was done trying to convince them. Aiodhan needed her. Striding into the armory, she grabbed a gun and a box of bullets.

Bill holstered his weapon and swiped the gun right out of her hand. "You're not going off anywhere half-cocked. We need to figure this out."

"Where *is* he?" She was screaming, near hysteria.

Kevin's hand gripped hers. "Calm down for a second, sis. Getting worked up like this can't be good for the baby."

"Neither is growing up without a father," she shot back.

"Keep cool. We just need to figure all this out."

"What is there to figure out? Pashmar is going to kill Aiodhan."

"First off," Bill said, pushing her to sit on a crate, "Aiodhan can handle himself. Pashmar's good, but he's better. Second, you can't just start running around the woods looking for him. You're a pregnant woman. Hell, you don't even have a coat on. Let us handle this."

"But—"

Bill shook his head. "Kevin, go get Darby. He's the best tracker we've got. Tell him to bring his weapon."

Kevin slung the rifle strap over his shoulder and ran out of the tent.

Kara jumped to her feet, but Bill's hands on her shoulders pushed her right back down. "When Darby figures out where Aiodhan went, I'll take Kevin and a few other guys, and we'll see if we can find him."

"I need to go too!"

"Not happening. Stay in the clinic. We'll find out what's going on and bring Aiodhan and Pashmar back here. Okay?"

She wanted to argue, but from the stubborn set of Bill's jaw, quarrelling would be a waste of breath. The leader of this group was the epitome of stubborn. "Fine."

He eyed her skeptically. "You'll stay here until we get back?"

She nodded.

"Let's get you back to your tent."

"I can get there by myself. I'm pregnant, not an invalid."

Kevin stuck his head through the flap. "Darby's already got Aiodhan's trail. You coming?"

Bill gave her a hard stare. "You'll stay here?"

She glared right back at him and folded her arms over her baby bump.

"C'mon, Bill," Kevin said with an insistent flip of his wrist. "Darby's chomping the bit." He ducked back outside.

"Promise me, Kara," Bill demanded. "Promise me you'll stay here until we get back."

With a disgusted grunt, she said, "I'll go to my tent. Okay? Just go find him! Now!"

She followed Bill outside and marched toward the clinic, taking careful note of what way the search party was heading.

Fulfilling her promise, she went inside the clinic. Julie and the children were gone.

In her bedroom, Kara plopped on the mattress and tried not to crawl out of her own skin with worry. Bill said Pashmar left at sunup—a long time before Aiodhan went hunting. She'd have to be a psychopath to plan ahead like that and then stalk him all day, knowing she was planning to murder him. While Kara might be a bit jealous of the Seekers' history, she would never think of Pashmar as being that coldblooded.

Perhaps Claire and Christopher had been wrong in thinking Pashmar was a danger to Aiodhan. Maybe he was wrong as well in believing the children were prophets. In all their time in Montana, they'd never once talked about their dreams, let alone predicted anything important happening.

Why can't I calm down?

Kara's gaze drifted to the things Aiodhan left on the milk crate that served as their nightstand. He'd left his tracker. If she could use it to see for herself that Pashmar and Aiodhan were nowhere near each other, maybe her heart rate could finally return to a normal level.

She picked up the small disk and fumbled to see if she could turn it on. The frustrating gadget wouldn't open. She pushed the blue button again and again, about ready to give up when her thumb brushed across it. The disk sprang open, projecting a map of light exactly as it had back at the cabin.

Her pink symbol was the first to pop up. What confused her was that there were no blue or red symbols so she could find Aiodhan and Pashmar. Instead, a purple icon floated not far from Kara's pink.

Purple.

"Fuck. They're together."

Chapter Twenty-Four

Kara stopped again to check Aiodhan's gadget, wanting to be sure she was still heading in the right direction.

The nearer she drew to Aiodhan and Pashmar, the more she worried. Their symbols had separated to one blue and one red, and they remained side by side. She wasn't sure if the continued presence of the blue icon meant Aiodhan was still safe. Would it disappear if he died?

Don't think that way!

Aiodhan was all right. He just had to be. They were having a baby together. He'd promised to stay here on Earth. She couldn't survive without him at her side.

Trying hard to hold onto some calm, Kara closed the tracker and hiked in the direction of the icons. The Seekers were close—not only could she see her icon moving nearer each time she'd checked the projected map, she could feel it in her heart.

The forest was quiet, which meant Bill, Kevin, and Darby had guessed wrong about where Aiodhan and Pashmar were heading.

So much for Darby being the master tracker.

The snap of a twig made her gasp. She whirled to see a doe standing about ten yards away.

Big brown eyes stared at Kara for several heartbeats before the doe startled. Ears and tail twitching, she ran, gracefully jumping falling logs before she disappeared into the trees.

Then Kara heard the voices, the deep baritone from her alien making her heart skip a beat.

"Aiodhan," she whispered. She bit her tongue to keep from shouting out when she had no idea if she would put him in further danger.

Hurrying toward his voice, Kara dodged branches that hit her like lashes from a whip. Thankfully, most landed against her thick parka. Only a few left stinging cuts on her face.

"Aiodhan, *sein!*" Pashmar's voice echoed through the air. "*Sein nal mei fir!*"

A gunshot forced a scream from Kara's throat.

I'm too late!

* * *

Pashmar kept scaring away his prey. Aiodhan had never known her to be so talkative.

His temper grew, but he held it in check—until she scared away yet another deer.

"Enough!" he shouted in Tirian.

"Don't you dare shout at me, Aiodhan Riel!"

"Then be quiet or go back to camp. You're frightening all the game. People are counting on me so they don't starve."

"People. You mean *humans*," she sneered. "So they die. Who cares? We should be returning to the ship. Let's go. Now. Let's go to my ship and get off this disgusting planet."

The woman was more stubborn than should be allowed, and he'd grown weary of explaining his plans to her. One more time, then he would haul her back to her ship and launch the damn thing himself.

"I already told you—more times than I can remember—I'm not going back to Tirios. You have my messages to give to Jaman and my family. If you're so anxious to go, *then go*."

"I can't go back. Not until my mission is—"

"I'm starting to think you don't even *have* a mission. How many weeks have we been here, Pashmar? Too many for any mission the Praemons have ever given before. Did you claim to have a job here on Earth just to follow me?"

While the thought was flattering, it also boded ill. Pashmar's jealousy was already a poison inside her. She constantly stared at Kara with hatred in her eyes as though she were looking at a Vymaln. It was time for her to give up the ridiculous notion that he'd ever have taken her as a mate. Kara was, and would always be, the only woman in his life.

He wouldn't allow Pashmar's hatred to infect Kara any longer. "What exactly is your mission? I'll help you get your target, then you can go home."

Pashmar turned her back, her fists clenched against her sides. "I'm giving you one more chance, Aiodhan. Come back with me. Today. This very minute. Come to my ship. We'll go back to Tirios. It'll be like none of this ever happened. I'll make you happy. I swear I will."

He heaved a weary sigh and slung the rifle over his shoulder. "That's it. I'm done fighting with you. The minute I get you back to camp, you're gathering your things and you're leaving this planet."

A sob slipped out and her shoulders shook. "My-my mission—"

"Your *mission*—whatever it is—is over. You failed. I'm sorry, but you failed."

"I didn't fail." Whirling to face him, Pashmar plucked her gun from her waistband and held it in her trembling hands. "Not yet." She raised the weapon, aiming at his heart. "I have to take out my target."

"What are you talking about?"

"The Praemons sent me to kill you."

"You're not making any sense. Seekers eliminate threats to Tirios. Why would the Praemons think I'd be a danger to my home world?"

"They knew you'd defect." She swallowed hard. "They knew! They said if you stayed on Earth that you would start a chain of events that could lead to the destruction of our planet. If you chose to remain here, I'm supposed to eliminate you."

"That's your jealousy talking. This isn't about the Praemons—it's about you being angry that I chose Kara over you."

"You're wrong."

He snorted. "And here I thought you were different because you were a Seeker. You're not. You're nothing but another ridiculous female who feels sorry for herself because she was spurned." Turning on his heel, he stomped away.

"Aiodhan, *stop!*" Pashmar's voice echoed through the air. "*Stop or I'll shoot!*"

He kept walking.

With an angry snarl, she fired a shot.

He whirled back to face her. At least she'd shot into the air instead of at him. "Have you lost your mind?

She leveled the gun at him again. "I will *not* fail at my mission. The Praemons told me if I couldn't convince you to come home, I was to leave your body to rot on this cursed planet."

An eerie calm settled over him when he should have been seething with rage. He'd pledge his whole life in service to the Praemons. He'd revered them as gods. He'd given them his loyalty and his heart. And how had they repaid him?

By ordering his murder.

"You're lying," Aiodhan insisted. "They'd never eliminate one of their Seekers."

She gave him an unnerving laugh. "No one would be sick enough to make up a story like this. You have no idea how long I had to beg them to let me try to reason with you instead of just ending your life. The only thing that would spare you was taking out your target and then returning with me. But you had to have that-that...*human*. You couldn't leave her be. She destroyed you, don't you see?"

"Kara is my mate. She makes me strong."

"She'll make you *dead*." Pashmar pulled back the hammer on the revolver. "Please don't make me do this. *Please*. Come back with me. Leave her behind."

"The Praemons are wrong. I'd never threaten Tirios. I love my home."

"They're never wrong. Remember? You taught me that."

"So that's it? You're just going to murder me out here in the woods, hop in your ship, and go back to Tirios? After all we've been through together? I thought you were my friend."

"It's not *murder*. It's fulfilling my mission."

A large rock came flying from the trees, landing between him and Pashmar at the same time Kara darted from the woods to jump on Pashmar's back. Wrapping an arm around Pashmar's throat, Kara tried to choke her.

In one swift motion, Pashmar flipped Kara over her head.

Kara landed hard on her back, her breath coming out in a loud "oof." Then she lay still.

Aiodhan rushed to her, but Pashmar stopped him by switching her target.

To Kara.

"I'll kill her." Pashmar's eyes were wild. "Then you'll come back with me. That's the solution." She let out a crazed laugh. "Why didn't I think of that sooner? That's what I should have done before. I should have let that Vymaln kill her back at the IC. She should already be dead. Then I wouldn't have to kill her now."

Several clicks of weapons being readied to fire echoed through the clearing.

"Drop the gun, Pashmar," Bill ordered. "Drop it now or you're gonna have three bullets in your brain."

Her head whipped around toward the voices. "I have a mission!"

"I don't give a shit," Bill replied. "Drop the damn gun!"

Kara let out a groan, so Aiodhan—keeping his gaze on Pashmar—crouched at his mate's side, blocking Pashmar's shot. "Stay down."

"One more chance," Bill warned. "Put the gun down. Don't make us kill you!"

Tears rolled down Pashmar's cheeks. "I've failed. Kill me," she replied in English. "Just kill me now."

Bill emerged from the trees, his rifle still at ready. "I don't want to hurt you."

Pashmar raised the gun to her own temple.

Aiodhan sprang at her, jerking the gun from her hand and tossing it aside as he tackled her to the ground. She didn't fight him as he plucked her stun-pistol from her belt and got back to his feet.

Kevin and Darby hurried from their hiding places while Bill picked up Pashmar's discarded weapon.

Hurrying back to Kara, Aiodhan ran his hands over her head and neck. "Injuries?"

He helped her sit up as she groaned. "I'm fine."

His hand dropped to her rounded belly. "Our baby?"

She scrunched up her brow as if in deep thought. Then she smiled. "He just moved, so I'd say he's fine, too."

Helping her to her feet, he didn't give her a chance to protest as he swept her into his arms. "You were foolish to come out here."

"Yeah...like I'd let her kill you."

"You knew her mission?"

Kara nodded. "Once I put all the pieces of the puzzle together, I knew."

He cradled her close against his chest, feeling blessed to have a mate who was full of courage and intelligence. Seeing her lying on the ground and fearing for her safety and the safety of his child had shaved a good five years off his life. "You must rest now."

Her fingertips stroked his cheek. "I'm fine. Really."

"You rest. I demand it."

Kevin laughed. "Now you're in trouble, big guy. No one *orders* Kara to do anything."

Kara laid her head against his shoulder. "This one time, I'll choose to obey. But only because I hurt like hell."

"I'm taking Pashmar back," Bill called. He held her wrists together behind her back. "I need to figure out what to do with her now."

"You?" Kara asked. "Seems to me we all should have a say."

"Send her back," Aiodhan suggested. "Just put her on ship and send her on her way."

Bill shook his head. "After what she did? It's not that simple. She's a threat."

"I care not—"

"I'm not talking about just you, Aiden," Bill snapped. "She knows everything about our operation. We can't let her leave."

"It's Aiodhan," Kara corrected. "And you fucking well know it."

"Pashmar needs to answer for her crimes, Kara," Kevin said. "She tried to kill Aiodhan and she hurt you."

"We'll talk about it back at camp," Bill said. He nudged the subdued Pashmar between the shoulder blades.

The more Kara heard, the more she thought the men were being ridiculous.

Pashmar reacted to Bill's prodding by taking a few steps before she planted her feet. Her gaze caught Kara's. The defeat and sadness there struck her hard.

"What will happen if she goes back to the Seeker ship?" she whispered to Aiodhan.

"She failed, *damana*. She will be put to death."

An outraged gasp escaped Kara's lips. "They'll kill her?"

"She failed at her mission. It is our way."

She fought against his hold, wanting to get to her feet. "Put me down."

He squeezed her tighter against him. "You are in pain? Why do you squirm so?"

"Put me down."

"No."

She fought harder. "I'm not letting anyone send her back, not if they're going to execute her."

Aiodhan let Kara slide down his body. "You will have no say."

"The hell I won't! Bill, wait!"

On shaky legs, she moved to block Pashmar's path.

"Kara, get out of the way," Bill ordered.

"You're not sending her back."

"I don't know what the hell I'm doing with her yet."

"If you send her back they'll kill her."

"And that's my problem because?"

Pashmar's eyes searched Kara's. "Why would you care?"

Kara shrugged. "I just do. You saved my life, remember? I owe you."

Bill sighed, a reaction she'd heard far too often when people were exasperated with her. "What do you suggest, Kara? Remember, she was going to kill you and Aiodhan."

She didn't have a clue, but she wasn't about to let anyone in on that little tidbit of information. "Look, we're trying to save our way of life, right?"

He arched an eyebrow at her.

"Then shouldn't we follow our own justice system? I mean…if we let Bill decide her fate, aren't we making him our monarch?"

"Kara…" Aiodhan's warning tone didn't make her back down an inch.

"I mean it. We should let her defend herself, and then we should decide together what is fair as punishment."

"She's right," Kevin chimed in. "We should tell everyone what happened, then we can talk about what to do."

Pashmar's gaze shifted to Aiodhan. "*Hadalla. Mein riga hadalla.*"

Aiodhan vehemently shook his head, letting a string of angry Tirian fall from his lips.

Pashmar narrowed her eyes at him. "*Hadalla!*"

He badgered her some more.

"What in the hell are you two talking about?" Kara asked.

Aiodhan lips all but disappeared into a thin line. "She demands *hadalla.*"

"What's that?"

"A rite of honorable death of a Seeker who is captured by Vymalns or close to capture. Vymalns would kill her or she would kill herself."

Kara shifted her gaze from Aiodhan to Pashmar and back again. "She wants you to kill her?"

He nodded.

"Not happening."

"We'll take her back," Bill announced. "Then we'll figure all this out."

Aiodhan scooped Kara into his arms again. "You will rest now."

"I will?"

"You will."

Since she seemed to be winning her argument, she gave in to this request. "Fine, Tarzan. Take me home."

Chapter Twenty-Five

The argument over Pashmar's fate raged into the wee hours of the morning, and Kara was having a hard time staying awake. She leaned against Aiodhan's shoulder, absorbing his warmth as the debate went on and on.

A few in the camp wanted to execute her for threatening to kill Aiodhan and Kara, but many considered her a hero for all she'd done in saving Kara's life and helping them prepare for the raid on the internment camp. The group had gathered around the large fire, sitting on logs, and floating ideas.

The only person who didn't voice an opinion was Bill, which didn't come as a surprise. The man kept his own counsel on most issues until he'd weighed all the facts. In a lot of ways, he reminded Kara of Aiodhan. Smart. Strong. Bill made a great leader, and she wondered if the people in this ragtag collection of refugees knew just how lucky they were to have him to lean on.

Kara finally grew disgusted with the machismo surrounding her and decided to check in on Claire and Christopher and then see what Jayce had found with his bug today. She kissed Aiodhan's cheek. "I'm leaving."

"You should sleep."

She didn't reply, happy to let him assume she was going back to the clinic. She would. But only after she learned if Jayce had seen her father.

Not surprisingly, Claire and Christopher were sleeping. They'd blended into the group as though they'd always been a part of the Montana Militia. Thankfully, no one treated them as odd because of their gifts, but then again, they seldom made predictions to anyone but Aiodhan, Kara, Bill, or Julie.

The glow outlining the seams of Jayce's tent told her he was still up— probably watching his monitors and sending messages to search for more people to join their fight against the bug-eyes. She ducked inside quickly, pulling the tent flap closed behind her to try to keep some of the heat from escaping. Damn, but when winter came on with a vengeance, they'd all have to find ways to keep warm.

Bill had suggested everyone sleeping in the mess hall so they only needed one heat source. So long as Aiodhan's heat stone worked, Kara would keep her privacy and stay in the clinic with her alien.

"Hey, Kara," Jayce called over his shoulder as his fingers flew over one of his keyboards. "I might have something for you."

She hurried to him, placing her hands on his shoulders to look at the screen. "You do? What?"

"A group of inmates I hadn't seen before was moved into the IC today. There were a few guys that match the description you gave me of your dad." He tapped out a few more commands and a grid of six pictures popped up. "Take a look at these and see if any are your dad."

After the first three, Kara's hopes started to slip away. Then she saw the fourth face.

"Oh, my God..."

Her father was alive. She'd always believed it in her heart, but to see him looking back at her from the screen—thin and tired, but *alive*—brought tears to her eyes.

"I knew it!" Jayce pumped his fist in the air. "I knew I'd find him for you!"

Everything inside her screamed to run all the way to the IC now, to march right out of there with her father and kill any Vymaln who got in her path.

Pure insanity, but tempting nonetheless.

She wanted to run to Aiodhan, to beg him to rescue her father. Now. He'd help her. He'd make sure her father got away from the IC. He knew how to kill fucking bug-eyes.

So did someone else...someone close.

"I've gotta go," she said, hurrying out of Jayce's tent.

* * *

The guard didn't try to stop her when Kara entered the tent where Pashmar was being held. Not that she'd expected him to interfere when he was sound asleep at his post.

Pashmar was lying on a cot, hands stacked behind her head. She didn't even glance in Kara's direction. "What do you want?"

"I came to see how you were doing."

"Go away."

"Nope. I came to talk, and I intend to have my say."

"I shall not listen."

Kara laughed. "Ignoring me doesn't work for anyone else. What makes you think it'll work for you?"

"Say what you want, then go."

"Fine. I have one question for you. Would you have killed him?"

The Seeker sat up, threw her legs over the side of the bed, and leveled a hard stare at her.

"Well?" Kara grabbed the folding chair, dragged it close to the cot, and sat herself down. "Would you? Could you really have killed Aiodhan?"

Propping her elbows against her knees, Pashmar dropped her head to her hands. "I do not know."

The anguish in her words told Kara everything she wanted to know. "You wouldn't." She gave Pashmar a decisive nod. "I knew you wouldn't. You care for him. A lot. There's no way you could kill him."

"I-I would not."

"That's why you stuck around for so long. You knew this was a mission you couldn't complete. So my next question is...now what? You can't go back."

Pashmar raised her head enough to catch Kara's gaze. "I should die. Will your people see to that?"

"Pardon?"

"Execute, yes? They shall execute me?"

Kara snorted. "Not if *I* have any say so. If we're going into the IC, we need you. *I* need you."

"You would trust me? After what I did, you would trust me?"

"Any enemy of my enemy is my friend."

Pashmar let out a rueful chuckle. "You say strange things."

"So I've been told." Kara got to her feet, the movement setting the baby to kicking. Her hand stroked her stomach. "Damn. I'm barely showing, and this kid's already a whirling dervish."

"It is wearing what?"

"Not *wearing. Whirling.* Spinning. And a dervish is a-a...um... Shit, I don't know *what* a dervish is." She laughed. "Let's just say this baby's gonna be a gymnast."

Pashmar extended her hand before quickly withdrawing it.

Kara was getting used to everyone wanting to touch her belly, as though this baby offered them some kind of hope for the future. By the time she was as a big as a water buffalo, she'd feel like a Buddha statue always getting its stomach rubbed for good luck. "You want to feel the baby move, don't you?"

"I-I should not."

Grabbing Pashmar's hand, Kara spread it over her baby bump. "Sure you should."

The baby wasn't cooperating, having grown still.

When Pashmar shook her head and tried to pull away, Kara flattened her hand over Pashmar's. "Wait. Be patient."

Long moments passed before the baby gave them what they wanted, a hard kick.

Pashmar's eyes flew wide. "It moves."

"Sure does. All the time. Mostly when I'm trying to sleep."

"I shall protect your child."

"What?"

Pashmar withdrew her hand. "I shall be guardian of your child."

"Why would you do that?"

"To make a menses."

"Menses? Why are you talking about having periods?"

"What is periods?"

"Never mind. What were you trying to say?"

Pashmar thought about it for a few long seconds. "I wish to make what I did more right."

Kara smiled. "You mean *amends*. And if you want to keep an eye out for this little guy, go right ahead. I imagine Aiodhan and I could use all the help we can get. But right now, let's talk about the raid on the IC. We'll need you, so first thing is to get you outta here and back into the group. We've got some major plans to be making."

Leaning back, Pashmar folded her arms under her breasts. "Why do you help me?"

"You saved my life."

"It is more, I think."

Kara sat back down. "Look…We need to put the past behind us and start making plans."

"Do the others agree?"

"They will or else I'll just have to convince them."

Pashmar tilted her head, staring hard. "What do you know I do not?"

There was no use keeping anything secret, not in a camp this close and with someone as talkative as Jayce already knowing. "Jayce found my father. He's in the camp."

"You wish me to save your father."

As though she could deny it. "Damn right I do. He's alive, and I want him to stay that way. Best chance we have of defeating those bastards and getting Dad out is having you and Aiodhan train and lead us. You know how to kill bug-eyes. So teach me—teach *all* of us."

"Aiodhan will not let you join the fight."

"He won't have a say."

Pashmar chuckled. "You underestimal him."

"Underesti*mate*. And maybe he's the one who underestimates me." Kara returned Pashmar's hard stare. "Will you help us? If I can get everyone to let you out of here, will you help us?"

"Yes. I will help."

* * *

Taking a deep breath, Kara marched right into the middle of the circle of men.

"I thought you slept," Aiodhan said. "You need rest."

She rolled her eyes. "I'm pregnant, I'm not an invalid."

"Kara…" He started to stand up.

"Wait. Let me say my piece, then I'll go."

After a short stare down, he gave her a curt nod and dropped back down on the log.

She let her gaze wander the faces of the men, wishing for a minute Julie and the new women were there to even the odds a little. Men were by nature stubborn, and she needed them to listen. "I want to tell you all what I think we should do."

Several of them grunted, a sound she took as meaning her feminine opinion wasn't welcome.

She didn't give a shit. "Listen to me. Pashmar made a mistake, but we need her."

"A mistake?" Kevin shot back at her. "God, Kara. It was a helluva lot more than a *mistake*. She tried to kill you and Aiodhan."

She narrowed her eyes at her brother. "Okay, a *big* mistake. She thought she was doing her job. That's all there is to it. She had a mission—given to her by people she considers god. You all know about the Seekers now, so you understand why she had no choice."

"Of course she had a choice," Darby chimed in.

Kara shook her head. "Look, we can sit here and argue all night about what she truly intended, but we'll come right back to the same place. She fucked up. We all have. Every single one of us has done things we're ashamed of since the bug-eyes came. Pashmar is no different."

A murmur moved through the crowd, giving her hope that at least they considered her words food for thought—as least as much thought as the male sex could muster.

"Not only do we need her, but she needs us. If we're going after the IC, her help will be invaluable."

"What do you mean she needs us?" Bill's temperate voice was barely loud enough to be heard above the continued buzz of talk and the crackling of the fire.

At least he's listening…

"She's a woman without a country right now," she said, pressing the point.

"You mean without a planet." Kevin's wisecrack almost earned him a smack upside the head.

Instead, she blistered him with a stern frown that made him choke on his own laughter. "If she tries to go back to Tirios, she faces execution. She's got nowhere else to go."

"So we just forgive and forget?" Kevin asked. "Just like that? It never happened?"

Kara nodded. "She was fighting for a cause she believed in and found out she'd put her trust in something that wasn't real. She was a soldier in a war she thought was right. It just...wasn't."

"Like Vietnam," Bill added.

She tossed him a grateful smile. "Exactly! They thought they were fighting for the American way of life, but our government lied to them. The Praemons did the same thing to Pashmar—they wanted her to do their dirty work."

"Why would they want her to kill Aiodhan?" one of the men asked.

"Haven't quite figured that out yet," she replied. "They're obviously afraid of what he's capable of doing. Maybe they're afraid the other Seekers will follow him. Who knows? Boils down to this, Pashmar's on our side now."

When Bill nodded, she hoped she'd won the day.

"She needs us," Kara insisted. "We've never turned anyone away. Hell, look at all of us! We're exactly like her—we're here together because we needed each other. Pashmar is one of us. Just another refugee."

Bill stood up, adjusting his gun belt. "It's late. I think we should all get some shut eye. We can meet again after breakfast." He checked his watch. "We'll talk again in the mess hall at oh-nine-hundred."

On that pronouncement, he walked away.

Kevin slung his rifle over his shoulder, holding tight to the strap. "Looks like sentry duty for me."

"Right behind you," Darby replied.

While she watched her brother and Darby heading toward the tower, Aiodhan came up behind her, wrapped his arms around her waist, and pulled her back against him. "You should sleep, *damana*."

"Yeah." A yawn slipped out. "Let's go to bed." She turned in his embrace and kissed his chin.

He swept her into his arms and gave her a rumbling growl. "I take you to bed, we shall not sleep."

Kara was suddenly wide awake. She pressed a kiss to his neck, loving how he shivered in response. "Sounds like a plan." Her teeth tugged his earlobe.

Aiodhan marched through the snow, anxious to get back to their tent so he could mate with her. He promised himself he'd be a gentle lover. She was, after all, carrying his child. He needed to treat her with great care despite the passion running roughshod over his body.

When he and Kara entered the tent, their clothes were shed and carelessly discarded. They fumbled their way through the dark into the back room. The heat stone had cooled to a dull orange that barely cast light in the room, but instead of rewetting it, he finished undressing and helped her remove the rest of her clothing.

Falling back onto the mattress, he pulled her on top of him and then tossed the blanket over them. He held her close as he waited for her shivering to end, wrapping his body around hers to warm her. She nuzzled his neck, giving him stinging bites that she soothed with soft licks. As she worked her way down his chest, she drew the blanket over her head.

Aiodhan lifted the edge to peek, but there wasn't enough light for him to see her. Her lips brushed his nipple before she grasped it between her teeth and gently tugged. He released the blanket and closed his eyes, letting himself get lost in simply feeling her touch. Her cool fingers closed around his *kull* at the same time her mouth covered the crown.

Having not expected her to be so direct in her assault, he almost bucked right off the mattress. Hissing out a breath, he fought for control, wanting the gift of pleasure she was giving him to last and last. The heat of her mouth and the caress of her tongue pushed him farther and farther toward release. "*Damana*...come to me."

She refused him by continuing her blissful torture, sucking and licking his erection as her soft hand slipped between his thighs to cradle his sac.

If she didn't stop soon, he'd explode in her mouth. "Now, Kara! Please!"

With a chuckle, Kara kissed her way back up his body until she straddled his hips. "This time, *you* begged." She guided him to her core and then inside her body.

Cupping her neck, he dragged her closer so he could cover her lips with his. He thrust his tongue into her mouth the same way he thrust into her tight, wet heat. She whimpered, chasing his tongue back into his mouth so he could suck her tongue.

The tension built with each push of his hips and each beautiful moan that slipped from her. Close to release, he sped the tempo, wanting her to reach the pinnacle with him.

And she did, putting her palms against his chest, rearing back, and calling his name as her body clenched around his.

With a harsh groan, Aiodhan held tight to her hips and thrust up one last time, pouring his essence into her.

Kara collapsed against him, combing her fingers through the patch of hair on his chest. Before long, his *kull* softened and slipped from her body, but he wouldn't let her leave his arms.

He fell asleep to the heat of her breath brushing his skin.

Chapter Twenty-Six

Kara couldn't find an ounce of patience.

One look at her breakfast tray sent her stomach rebelling, tossing around the stale Ding Dong she'd wolfed down when she got up to pee in the middle of the night. Up until now, she hadn't been bothered much by morning sickness. Perhaps her nausea was born of her fear that group would decide something stupid—like exiling Pashmar. Without her help, Kara's father might stay in the bug-eyes' hands. But *two* Seekers could get him out and maybe cull the herd of Vymalns. If her fantasies took flight, they'd liberate the entire camp and leave the bug-eyes' bodies to rot in that hellhole.

Pushing her tray away, she watched the men as they ate and talked. There were too many conversations for her to pick out any single exchange, which left her even more concerned. Had any of them listened to her last night? Had her words in support of Pashmar made a difference?

Aiodhan's hand covered hers. "All will be well."

"How do you know that?"

"I went to Pashmar to talk. She was not there."

"She escaped?" Kara's heart jumped into a faster rhythm as her brain filled with visions of the Montana Militia forming a lynch mob to chase Pashmar and string her up from one of the tall pines. "How could she escape?"

"Probably because her guard was asleep again." Bill set his tray down, pushing Kara's back toward her to make room. "She didn't escape, Kara. I let her out. She and Jayce are working on some secret project."

"So she won't be punished?"

"Nope," he replied. "You were right. We need her as much as she needs us. After your eloquent little speech, everyone decided to let the whole thing drop and chalk it up as a stupid mistake."

"Thank God." Now, she could make some solid plans. "My dad's definitely in the IC."

Aiodhan knit his brows. "How do you know this?"

"Because I found him," Jayce announced as he and Pashmar strode to the table. Both held a small fire extinguisher and smiled as if they'd grabbed the big, brass ring on the carousel.

Bill gestured to one of the red canisters. "I know the chow's bad, but it's definitely not on fire."

Jayce looked down at the extinguisher in his hand and chuckled. "It's not for fires. Pashmar and I just finished making these. They're our secret weapon."

"Our what?" Kara asked.

"Our secret weapon. It's bug spray."

"Bug spray?" Bill shook his head. "No bugs in the winter."

"Sure there are. Big bugs—bug-*eyes* as Kara calls 'em." Jayce inclined his head her direction. "You can thank her for helping us come up with the idea."

"What are you talking about?" she asked.

"You discovered it back in the tech building," he replied. "You sprayed that Raid in the face of the lizard...um...*bug-eye* that zapped you."

"So? It's not like he died."

Jayce's enigmatic smile frustrated the hell out of Kara. "You're right. He didn't die—but he was sure down for the count."

"Jayce..." Bill growled in warning. "Quit farting around and tell us what this stuff is."

Pashmar took up the story, her gaze on Kara. "While Jayce tended to you, I went to kill the Vymaln. The chemicals you put on his face blinded him."

"A bullet will do that," Kara couldn't help but point out. "But they just grow another eye."

"Not this time," Jayce replied. "You blinded the guy, and the Raid melted his skin like some kind of acid. I think he was actually grateful when Pashmar put him out of his misery, 'cause he looked like shit and screamed something fierce until she finished him off."

"Let me see one of those." Bill held out his hand.

Pashmar handed him the canister.

He turned it this way and that. "How does it work?"

"Just like a fire extinguisher," Jayce replied. "Only it sprays ESAD instead of white stuff."

"ESAD?" Kara asked. "Is that what you're calling it?"

Jayce's cheeks reddened. "It's an acronym."

"For?"

"Eat shit and die."

The men laughed while Kara rolled her eyes.

"You got a better idea?" Jayce asked.

"Nah," she replied. "It fits. Good job, Jayce."

"Pashmar helped," he insisted.

Kara gave Pashmar a nod. "Good job, Pashmar."

The Seeker's mouth twitched, the closest thing to a smile Kara had seen from her.

"How fast can you make a shitload of these?" Bill asked.

"Pretty damned quick." Jayce grinned, his pride beaming from his face.

"Send the reivers on a run for some chemicals and more canisters, and we're in business."

"Well, then…get me a list and get your asses to work," Bill ordered. "We're going into the IC in three days, and we're spraying this stuff on every lizard we see."

"And I'm getting my dad out of there," Kara said.

Both Aiodhan and Bill frowned at her, but she brushed their reactions aside. If they were going into the IC, she would be right beside them.

* * *

"What do you mean I'm not going?" Kara set her fists against her hips and glared at Aiodhan and Bill.

"Just what I said," Bill replied. "I'm not letting a pregnant woman go near the IC."

Aiodhan nodded as he crossed his arms sternly over his chest.

The two of them were ganging up on her, and she wasn't about to let them run her life. It was her father who was captive, and she was damn well going to help get him out.

"Male chauvinist pigs," she muttered.

Bill's reaction was a cocky grin. "Stick and stones, Kara. Call me all the names you want, but you're still not going."

"You don't get a say!" She picked up another box the reivers had brought back when they'd hunted down every can of bug spray in the area. She started stacking the bandages in the cabinet.

"You are my mate," Aiodhan scolded. "You will do as I say."

She slammed the box down hard. "Get this through your thick skull, Tarzan—I might be your *mate*, but I'm not your *property*. Just 'cause I've got a bun in the oven—"

Aiodhan tilted his head. "Bun? Oven?"

Not in the mood to translate, Kara let her temper take control. "My father's in the IC. Pregnant or not, I'm going after him. If you guys don't want to help, then fuck off."

She stomped out of the tent without even grabbing her parka, wishing there was a nice, heavy door to slam so she could make her point. Her boot had barely hit snow when a hand gripped her arm and dragged her to a stop.

Whirling to confront whoever thought he'd stop her, she gaped at Pashmar. "What do you want?"

"You must show me your father's picture."

"Why?"

"I must know his face so I can find him. You may not go into the IC, but I shall. *I* will find your father."

"I can find him just fine," Kara insisted. "I don't need any help."

Pashmar gave her head a stubborn shake. "I made a promise. Do you not remember?" She hesitantly reached out to brush her fingers across Kara's belly. "I will protect this child."

"What's my baby got to do with me getting my dad out of the IC?"

"You put the child in danger." Pashmar pulled her hand back. "Stay here and keep him safe. Let me do this mission. Please."

Common sense warred with Kara's fears and desires. Her father was alive—for now. The longer he stayed in the IC, the greater her risk of losing him. She wanted to march right into the camp, take him by the hand, and march right back out, dousing every bug-eye she saw with Jayce's new ESAD just so she could hear them scream as she walked away.

Then the baby moved.

She closed her eyes and took a steadying breath. Everyone was right, loathe though she was to admit it. This child—this new life inside her—needed her to make a wise choice. Her heart ached that she wouldn't be the one to right the wrong that had happened months ago when her father had allowed himself to be captured to protect her.

But she had to protect her unborn child.

"Fine," Kara finally said as Aiodhan and Bill exited the clinic.

"Fine?" Pashmar smiled. "You will not go?"

"I won't go. Happy now?" She frowned at the men. "Well? Are you happy?"

"Ecstatic," Bill replied.

Aiodhan just grunted.

"I may find your father?" Pashmar asked.

"*I* shall find her father," Aiodhan insisted.

"We'll all be there," Bill added. "One way or another, we'll get him out, Kara."

She had no choice but to trust them.

Chapter Twenty-Seven

Aiodhan held up his hand for the men to stop training when Pashmar approached.

Her hesitation took him by surprise. The faltering step, the bowed head? Not the traits of the self-assured downright cocky Seeker he knew. The men stopped and gaped at her, some even dropping the sandbag effigies of Vymalns they were using so he could teach them ways to quickly subdue the enemy.

Bill had asked him to prepare the men for the liberation of the internment camp, and Aiodhan had discovered he enjoyed teaching as much as he'd loved his Seeker missions. Perhaps he could settle into an important role here on Earth—much like Seekers were prized on Tirios.

Tirios. His home world. Would he ever see it again?

Not likely.

Not only did his heart ache at not being able to inform his family about his fate, he was still dealing with the sting of betrayal. After devoting his whole life to the Praemons, they'd tossed him aside like trash.

Part of him ached for revenge, but a saner part told him to remember that Kara and his child needed him. Any attempt to pay back the duplicity would be a suicide mission. From now on, Aiodhan would be a wanted man.

Pashmar would have a price on her head as well. Would she be able to find a new life for herself here too?

"May I participate?" she asked, her voice hushed.

He knew what she was asking. Would the men accept her?

Feelings had run hot and angry for a few days after she'd tried to complete her Seeker mission by killing him. He, of course, had already forgiven her. A duty was a duty, and she'd been honor bound to follow the Praemons' orders—just as he'd always blindly followed them.

Now, he knew better. The Praemons were selfish and capricious. They were not the gods the people of Tirios believed them to be. He'd never again dance to their song. Earth was his home. His heart belonged to this planet the same way his heart belonged to Kara.

A murmur rose from the men. Some of the people in the camp shunned Pashmar—at least they had until Kara let them know she held no grudges. The first evening after Bill turned Pashmar loose, Kara had motioned for her to come sit by them at the evening meal. Since Aiodhan and his mate could forgive Pashmar, the rest of the Montana Militia followed her example.

"I would be glad of your help," Aiodhan replied. Then he turned to the men. "Divide into two groups. Pashmar and I have much to show you."

* * *

"We're ready," Kara said with a firm nod. Her gaze wandered the mess hall, taking in the hard work she, Julie and the new women from Seattle put into getting things ready for the liberation of the internment camp.

"Are you sure?" Julie's voice quavered.

"Plenty of bandages. Plenty of meds. Plenty of beds. Yep, we're ready."

"I mean...am *I* ready?"

"Just don't faint if you see blood."

Julie's face blanched.

"Don't worry. I'm sure someone will catch you if you do." Kara shot her a wink.

All her years of nursing had desensitized her to things like blood or bones sticking through skin. Other people simply didn't handle a little puke or a gaping wound with such aplomb. When things got going tomorrow, she might find herself with her hands full and no one to pick up the slack.

She refused to be maudlin. Aiodhan was getting the men ready. Thanks to Jayce, they had "eyes" on the inside by watching the monitors, and Bill would be in touch through the whole raid. If only Aiodhan could talk to them too, she wouldn't worry so much. Her stubborn alien had refused to have a mic, saying he acted alone in every mission he'd ever been on and saw no need to change now. He gave her some Tirian adage that boiled down to "if it ain't broke, don't fix it." Thanks to his stubborn stance to go solo, he'd been given the most dangerous task—one only a brave, strong person could accomplish.

Aiodhan was going to get inside the guard tower.

There was only one entrance, and it was in the center of the IC. Getting men into the old prison was going to be difficult. Making it to the tower, let alone getting *inside* it, was next to impossible.

Swallowing her concern, she thought about Aiodhan's skills, remembering the way he'd handled the bug-eye who'd zapped her the day they met. While she'd lay there like a mannequin, he'd killed the damn thing and gotten it far enough away its death gas wasn't a danger. He could handle slipping into the IC, working his way into the tower, and killing any Vymalns.

At least that was what she kept telling herself to keep from screaming.

When Bill had set the date for the incursion, she'd immediately volunteered to set up the triage. The task kept her hands and mind busy, which held her worries at bay. Now—on the eve of battle—all those concerns came flooding back.

Claire and Christopher carried in a few more folded blankets.

Kara spared them a hesitant smile, still not comfortable with the idea that the two of them were some kind of prophets.

Remembering their warning to Pashmar sent a shiver down her spine. They'd known what she was supposed to do. But had they also known how that dark day would end?

"Creepy," she muttered to herself.

Claire set the blankets on one of the cots and strode over to Kara. She didn't say a thing, just stared up at her with big brown eyes.

"Did you and Chris have supper?"

Claire nodded.

"Thanks for bringing the blankets over. I think we're all set here now."

"I wish I could tell you, but I can't," Claire said.

"Tell me what?"

"If Aiodhan will find your dad."

Before Kara could respond, Christopher marched over and set his pile of blankets next to Claire's. He came to Kara's side and tugged on her shirt tail. "Can we help tomorrow?"

Kara tousled his hair. "Of course you can. You and Claire can be my go-getters."

"Your what?"

"My go-getters. When I need something, I'll have you two go get it for me. Besides, you helped put most of the stuff away. You'll know exactly where things are."

They both yawned.

"Go put your pajamas on and brush your teeth. I'll be there to tuck you in soon."

The children nodded and left.

Taking one last look around, Kara tried to calm herself.

Everything depended on what happened tomorrow. Once they went on the offensive, they'd be exposed. No more hiding in the forest. The Vymalns would know where to find them. Because of that, Bill had decided if the mission was successful, the Montana Militia was going to relocate inside the prison walls.

Winter hadn't hit hard yet, but it would. Surviving in tents was going to be more and more difficult. By holing up inside the prison, there would be shelter from the deep snow and bitter cold. From what the cameras showed, the place was still in pretty good order. Some of the men thought they would be able to get the wind turbines that powered the place repaired since only a few were still being used by the bug-eyes.

So much hope was wrapped up in this raid. Their very survival might depend on its success.

Her hand brushed her belly. If she counted correctly, the baby wouldn't arrive until spring.

Exactly where she'd be by then might be decided tomorrow.

Chapter Twenty-Eight

"You might as well sit down," Jayce said. "Pacing won't make this go down any faster and Chance is going nuts watching you." He inclined his head at the bed he'd made for Chance. The dog wagged his tail as though nothing unusual was happening.

Kara ignored him, wearing a path in the dirt as she walked the length of Jayce's tent and back again. "I can't stay still."

"Sure you can. Sit your pretty little ass down here—" He patted the desk chair next to his. "—and help me watch the IC. We need to feed info to Bill."

"You found some remote communications?"

His smile was cheeky. "Not found. *Made* from some of the stuff the reivers brought me, although we didn't have much time to test it properly."

"What about Aiodhan? With all his gadgets, I'd have figured he'd have something you could use."

Jayce shook his head. "I asked, but no go. Seekers work alone. They don't ever talk to anyone during a mission."

"Doesn't he have one of the ones you made?"

"I'm sorry, Kara. I only had one. If it works, I'll make more."

She almost scolded him but bit her lip instead. Bill led this group. Of course he'd have to have a way to reach home base. "It's fine, Jayce." Even if it wasn't. What if she saw something on one of those video screens that she needed to warn Aiodhan about? He'd be helpless.

Bowing her head, she sighed. There wasn't one damn thing helpless about her lover. Aiodhan was the alien equivalent of a Navy SEAL. He wasn't helpless, and her calling out any warning might only distract him. His burden was to liberate the camp and rescue her father. Her burden was to have to watch.

She was the one who was truly helpless.

"Jayce?" Bill's voice crackled over the speakers. "You getting this?"

"Yep."

"Everyone in place at the IC?"

Jayce scanned the monitors again. "Roger that."

"And Kara's ass is sitting next to you?"

"Roger that, too."

"She moves a muscle, duct tape her to the chair."

"Hear that?" Jayce grinned. "You can't pace anymore."

A low growl rumbled from her throat, which made Chance bark and wag his tail. "Don't fuck me with right now. I'm full of hormones and have absolutely no sense of humor."

"Noted."

She tried to take in all that was happening, impressed that Jayce seemed to have a handle on the ten screens facing him. Dusk was just setting in, which meant they'd be catching the guards rounding up the people in the fields. It also meant they'd have the cover of darkness soon, allowing the invaders a better chance to hide since the bug-eyes never used the flood lights in the compound, just like they didn't bother with the cameras littered throughout the old prison.

Thank God the bug-eyes abhorred human technology. Her heart was lodged in her throat simply thinking about what would happen if those bastards could see everything she was seeing.

"Where's Aiodhan?" she asked.

"He won't be on camera for a while. Neither will Kevin or Pashmar. Sucks that all the guys heading to the fields won't *ever* be on camera. Bill will hafta keep us updated."

The plan was simple. Overwhelm the Vymalns who ran the IC and make the captors the captives. They'd become complacent and lazy. In their view, they'd captured a large number of humans as slaves and killed most of the rest. They figured Earthlings had been thoroughly conquered and posed them no threat.

They'd figured wrong.

Several teams would hit the fields, spraying the Vymalns with ESAD and freeing the workers. Since those raids held the least risk, part of her wished Kevin and Aiodhan were in one of those squads. But they had more important tasks.

There were two ways in and out of the IC. Her brother would take one; her lover, the other. The thought of losing either of them made tears well up.

"Stupid hormones," she whispered as she wiped her forearm across her eyes.

"They're gonna be okay," Jayce consoled with a weak smile. "A couple of hours from now, we'll be the ones controlling that IC. Biggest problems we'll have are keeping the wind turbines up and running so we can have power and figuring out what to do with a few dozen pissed of lizards. I figure we'll have to execute them. Somehow. Might be a problem, but I'm sure we'll find a way."

Jayce was only trying to help, but she didn't want to hear another prediction as long as she lived. Between the stories Aiodhan and Pashmar had shared about the Praemons and the hints Claire and Christopher dropped as if they were Hansel and Gretel leaving a trail of breadcrumbs, Kara was up to her sore boobs in premonitions.

"Look." He pointed to a monitor. "Pashmar must have done her job."

"How can you tell?"

"The bug-eyes are all checking their earpieces. That means they don't hear each other anymore."

* * *

Aiodhan stood with his back to the wall, waiting patiently for his prey.

If Pashmar had completed her task and brought down the Vymaln transmitter, which he was sure she had, the Vymalns would send someone out to check the communication grid.

Aiodhan positioned himself right outside the entrance to the command center at the top of the tower. His plan was simple: he would spray the formula into the guard's face, then he'd slip inside and subdue the Vymalns keeping watch over the IC.

He'd watched their movements and knew their habits—how many would be in the tower and what kind of weapons they would wield. The odds against him would be three to one.

A smile crossed his lips. Three to one would at least be a challenge to his skills.

The door opened. A Vymaln took a step outside.

Grabbing the alien by the throat, Aiodhan jerked it the rest of the way out of the room and slammed the door shut with his foot. The Vymaln struggled, raking its claw-like nails over Aiodhan's arm and opening its mouth.

Aiodhan pulled the pin from the canister of ESAD with his teeth and sprayed it down the Vymaln's throat.

Instead of being able to raise a warning, the creature gurgled and writhed as the formula did its work. The fight went out of the Vymaln as a seizure racked its body.

While Aiodhan wanted nothing more than to slide his blade through both of its hearts, he was content to let it suffer. He used the plastic zip-ties Bill had given him to binds the Vymaln's hands and pulled a long strip of tape from the silver roll on his belt to seal its mouth.

Searching the Vymaln's uniform, he found a stun-stick and attached it to his belt. Then he plucked the key card from the lanyard around his enemy's neck. With a deep breath to steady himself and prepare for the fight ahead, he swiped the card through the reader. The lock clicked and the door opened a crack.

Aiodhan flung it the rest of the way open and strode inside. The Vymalns' screeches of surprise grated on his ears, but he savored them as he faced the three aliens by taking a fighting stance. He chose to speak in their language so he could see their reaction to his words.

"Now, you will die."

They all rushed him at the same time, a mistake that caused them to block each other in their haste to get to him.

The first fell to its knees when Aiodhan sprayed it, clawing at its face. He brought the second down by grabbing the stun-stick and zapping the Vymaln's chest directly over one of its hearts. As it lay in a heap, he dropped the stick and pulled out his knife, catching the third Vymaln's arm when it tried to land a blow and neatly slipping his blade between the alien's ribs. The fight ended when he sprayed it and it collapsed to the floor.

Hurrying to the console, Aiodhan set aside the spray and got down to business. He flipped the switches that opened the doors to the cellblocks. Then he went about the tedious task of triggering the release of each cell.

As Jayce had anticipated, not all of the switches worked. Popping open as many doors as he could, Aiodhan hurried through the rest of the checklist of tasks that needed to be completed before the Vymalns could send enough reinforcements to stop him.

Electrified fence. Off.

Flood lights in courtyard. On.

Weapons storage doors. Open.

He picked up his weapons and was preparing to tie up the three injured Vymalns when flashes to his right caught his eye. Striding over to the observation window, he scanned the courtyard.

The battle was on in earnest, Kevin leading the charge from the door Aiodhan had opened on the west wall. The flashes were bottle-bombs full of the formula exploding as they were tossed at the Vymalns shooting pulse-guns at their invaders.

With a grunt of satisfaction at how quickly the aliens were falling victim to the debilitating spray, he checked the main cell block entrance, hoping to see humans streaming out now that they were free. They weren't. Instead, a couple of guards were forcing them back with stun-sticks while two more tried to close the door.

Then a fifth Vymaln appeared. He carried a lit torch and a large can.

"Zot!"

* * *

"No!" Kara said, jumping from her chair and pointing at the monitor fixed on the cell block exit. "That's a gas can! Those bastard bug-eyes are going to try to kill their prisoners by burning them alive! I have to stop this!" She reached for her coat.

Jayce grabbed her arm. "I see what's happening too, but what exactly do you think *you* can do about it?"

"Stop them!"

"How? The camp's over a mile away."

"What if my dad's in there?"

"Just hang on…" He leaned in to the mic. "Bill, we've got a major problem. Are you reading me?"

The only reply was static.

"He'll never get there in time," Kara insisted. She shoved her arms into the sleeves of her parka and then zipped it closed.

"I promised Bill and Aiodhan you wouldn't go."

"Fuck that." She lifted the tent flap only to come face to face with Christopher.

The boy had obviously been hurrying because each of his panted breaths raised a white cloud in front of his lips. "You have to be here."

Claire skidded to a stop, slamming into his back. Neither wore a coat.

"You're both supposed to be with Julie."

"We needed to warn you," Claire insisted, wrapping her arms around.

"Get inside," Kara ordered. "It's freezing out here." She opened the tent flap wider and motioned them in.

Neither moved, just stared up at her with their wide eyes as both of them shivered in the frigid air.

"C'mon, kiddos. Get inside."

Claire had stepped to the side, throwing Kara a fierce frown. "You have to be here."

Kara held a check on her escalating temper even though her heart was racing and panic sizzled through her. "I have to help my father."

"You *have* to stay *here*," Claire insisted as tears formed in her eyes.

Christopher stomped his foot, sending the mud at the tent's entrance splattering over the piles of shoveled snow. "You can't leave, Kara."

A hard swallow kept Kara from screaming in frustration. She had to get to the IC. Her father needed her, and here she stood having to deal with two kids throwing temper tantrums because they weren't getting their way.

"I'd listen to 'em." Jayce called over his shoulder. "They're Praemons and—"

"They're *not* Praemons!" She almost stomped her foot the same way Christopher had.

"That's not what Aiodhan says," he retorted.

Her heart skipped a beat at his name. They hadn't seen him since he got inside the tower because the Vymalns had disabled all the cameras in the control room. If she got to the IC, she could help him after she

213

stopped the bug-eyes.

But she'd promised him she'd stay put—for their baby's sake. Added to the weight of Claire and Christopher demanding she stay in camp, circumstances became too heavy for her to bear.

Tears sprang into her eyes. "They'll die. If I don't help, They'll—"

"Kevin's stopping them!" Jayce exclaimed.

Kara ran back inside, the children hot on her heels. "Show me!"

Pointing at the top left monitor, Jayce said, "Look. Kevin's spraying the lizard with the torch."

She had to hold her breath as she watched her brother attack the Vymaln—who weighed a good fifty pounds more than Kevin—trying to get the torch away from the creature. It was stumbling around, blindly swinging the torch like a sword. When Kevin kicked it in the groin, it bent forward, dropping the torch in the snow. Her brother quickly smothered the fire by kicking more snow over it.

"You can breathe, Kara." Jayce grabbed her hand and giving it a squeeze. "He's fine."

Shrugging out of her coat, she collapsed back into her chair. "Aiodhan?"

"Not yet."

"Jayce?" Bill's voice crackled over the speaker.

"'Bout fucking time," Jayce replied.

"Sorry, but I was a little busy. Report?"

"The lizards were trying to incinerate the people on the main cell block. Kevin stopped them. How are things on your end?"

"All of us are heading to the IC. Left a bunch of wounded lizards behind. Most of the people are following us to the IC. A few are watching our prisoners, probably enjoying jabbing them with stun-sticks."

"The doors are wide open for you."

"Good. We'll be…and…I'll…" Bill's voice disappeared into the growing static.

"There's Aiodhan!" Claire pointed at the screen.

Two men had emerged from the guards' area, both holding shotguns.

"Shit." Jayce's fingers flew across the keyboard. "Who the hell are *they?* If they kill any of the Vymalns—"

"They'll release death gas," Kara said. "But they can't kill them with those guns, right? Surely they know that. Why would they—"

Everything inside her froze when the men marched forward, pointed their shotguns at her brother and his team, and started shooting.

Chapter Twenty-Nine

Aiodhan had the Vymaln sympathizers in his sights as he used the shadows to cloak himself.

He'd expected to have to deal with at least a few humans who'd decided to cooperate with their captors. It happened in every culture—the conquered tried to curry favor with their conquerors to receive special privileges. Jayce might not have seen them on his monitors before, but Aiodhan had known there would be at least a few. Only Bill had wanted to hear of the possibility while the rest of the Montana Militia insisted—repeatedly—no human would ever conspire with Vymalns.

The two men with the shotguns were well-fed. That alone spoke volumes. Now that the Vymaln were defeated, these desperate men had nothing left to lose. The instant they lowered the weapons to aim at Kevin's group, Aiodhan reacted. He sprang from the shadows and threw his knife, rushing toward them as he wondered how many more humans he'd have to kill.

The first man took Aiodhan's blade in the neck. He dropped the shotgun as a gurgle spilled from his lips. He jerked the knife out and tossed it aside. Blood spurted between his fingers as he clutched at the wound.

Without missing a step, Aiodhan forced the barrel of the second man's shotgun to the side, the shot finishing off the first man with a direct hit to the chest. Then Aiodhan brought the second man's arm down hard against his knee. The bone made a loud crack as it fractured, sending the shotgun tumbling to the concrete walkway. One solid punch to the man's face knocked him unconscious. Now all Aiodhan had to worry about was how many more of these traitors would pop up.

Bill and the teams who'd returned from the fields swarmed into the courtyard. Since they didn't take precious time to assess the situation, they had to know what had been happening—which meant Bill was still in touch with Jayce. Within a matter of moments, they'd begun evacuating the main cell block and approaching the entrances to the walkways. Prisoners stumbled into the courtyard, taking in the waning battle around them with wide eyes.

Pain ripped through Aiodhan's shoulder a second before a shot echoed through the air. Gritting his teeth to hold back any reaction, he looked to the other guards' walk along the fence row. Two humans—no doubt more men who'd cooperated with the Vymalns—were making their last stand.

Several of the liberators were already aiming for them, but their targets had ducked low enough, any shot meant to bring them down missed. Bill held up a fist, calling a halt to his men.

Quiet reigned for a few moments before another shot ripped through the air. One of the prisoners in the courtyard fell forward, planting his face in the mud. As things were now, everyone in the courtyard was an easy target for desperate men. Someone had to act.

Aiodhan strode over to the prisoners cowering in the entrance, shielding them best he could as Bill and Kevin barked out orders.

"Get your asses down!" A thin man stepped to the front of the pack and shouted at the prisoners as though he were their leader. He had brown hair that had grayed at the temples and needed to put some muscle back on his tall frame. His brown eyes were sunken from starvation but held the spark of intelligence.

Aiodhan knew those eyes well. Before he could ask whether the man was indeed Kara's father, a gunshot brought down another human. Aiodhan pushed the brown-eyed man behind him. "Move!"

Bill gave the signal to scatter, and several of the militia worked on gaining entrance to the second walkway. Aiodhan forced the humans back toward the cell block, understanding why they didn't want to return but knowing it was the best shelter at that moment.

Running footsteps approached, and he whirled to face whatever was charging him.

Kevin was heading his way. "Dad! Dad, is that you?"

"Kevin?" the old man called. "Kevin! It's me!"

"Get inside," Aiodhan insisted, grabbing Kevin's arm and shoving him toward the men at the cell block's opening. He was happy they were reunited, but in their haste, they'd forgotten the danger that still stalked them.

The men embraced, both talking at the same time and so quickly that Aiodhan couldn't understand most of what they said. One thing was certain, Kara would be pleased. He could almost see the happiness radiating from her beautiful face when she saw her father after so long.

"No!" Pashmar came running his direction at full sprint. Throwing herself against his chest before he could even brace for the impact. A single shot from above was followed by a volley of gunfire in retaliation.

Pashmar went still. He held her in his arms. Her eyes were closed, her mouth twisted in pain.

Kevin ordered his men to move out onto the now quiet walkways. After a few moments, someone called the all clear.

The IC was theirs.

Bill ran to Aiodhan. His hand trembled as he smoothed it over

Pashmar's forehead. "What in the hell happened?"

Aiodhan could hardly speak. Pashmar had saved his life, but in doing so might have given her own. "She was shot."

"Get her to Kara. Quickly."

* * *

Jayce let out a loud whoop. "We did it! We beat those bastards!"

"For now…" Kara was too afraid to celebrate. Just because the fighting had ended didn't mean they were all in the clear. She got up and put on her parka. "I'm heading to triage. They'll all be coming back soon. You two stay with Jayce," she said to the children. "Julie and I will have our hands full."

At least Aiodhan and Kevin were safe, although she'd lost track of Aiodhan on camera when he moved out of range.

"Shit!" Jayce shouted.

Hurrying to Jayce, she leaned over his shoulder, trying to figure out which monitor he was shouting about. "Is it Aiodhan? He was fine when he—"

"It's not Aiodhan. It's Pashmar…"

Then she saw Aiodhan holding Pashmar in his arms and striding away, Bill right behind. "What happened?"

"I-I don't know. I was watching them tear down the Vymaln flag from the guard tower. Think she got hit by one of the snipers?"

"I have no idea, but she's not moving. I better get to triage."

The frigid air burned Kara's lungs as she ran from Jayce's tent across the camp to where she'd prepared the mess hall for injuries. She lifted the heavy flap and strode inside, discarding her coat and grabbing one of the stethoscopes lying on one of the supply tables. Draping it over her neck, she picked up an otoscope and shoved it in her pocket.

Damn, I miss my scrubs.

The people who waited to help with the injured looked up from where they sat on one of the cots, drinking something warm enough to have tendrils of steam rising from the cups.

"Company's coming," Kara said. "Are we ready?"

Julie got to her feet, setting her cup aside as the rest of the workers followed suit. "After everything you've done to set up this place? Um…*yeah.*"

"Remember…worst injuries first. The people who were prisoners in the IC aren't given anything to eat that's too heavy on their systems. Broth or—"

Julie interrupted. "We know, Kara. You did a super job getting us ready."

No sooner did she stop speaking when the tent flap opened again and men spilled into the tent—some under their own power, some carried by their comrades.

Kara lost herself to the job, treating their mostly minor injuries while she waited for Aiodhan to bring her Pashmar. Instead, Kevin came running into the tent.

"Kevin! Are you hurt?"

"You've got to come with me."

"But the wounded."

"Kara, we need you there. Now."

She sprang to her feet.

"Pashmar's bad. There's a clinic at the IC. There are better supplies there, and we've got the lights running. Come with me. Now."

* * *

By the time she made it to the IC, things were well in hand. The Vymaln prisoners had all been removed, and the men were moving freely in and around the buildings. Her gaze took in every face, searching for her father. But he was nowhere to be seen.

Kevin led her to one of the smaller structures and held the door open while she hurried inside. Aiodhan was waiting. His eyes found Kara's. The anguish there raced through her.

"Where's Pashmar?" she asked as she tossed her mittens and then her parka on one of the benches in the corridor.

He hadn't worn a coat, claiming his own clothing was made for extremes in temperatures. The damn thing might adjust to the cold, but it obviously wasn't bulletproof. "You've been shot!"

"Yes. Help Pashmar first," he insisted when she tried to touch him.

While she knew the wound in his shoulder wasn't mortal, yet she couldn't stop her heart slamming against her ribcage. "I should look at that before—"

"Pashmar first."

He was right. Not that she'd admit it. "Where is she?"

Aiodhan took her hand and led her into the prison's clinic.

The nurse inside Kara flared to life. She lifted Pashmar's shirt to look at her wound. "She was shot?"

"Yes."

After removing the utility belt, Kara set it aside. Then she grabbed a pair of scissors and tried to cut the shirt open. The material was thick and nearly impossible to get through. "No wonder this stuff keeps you warm."

"Let me." Aiodhan reached down and ripped the shirt wide open with a loud grunt. His hand again flew to his shoulder.

"Kevin!" Kara called.

Kevin said a few words to one of his men before hurrying to help Kara. "What do you want?"

"Get Aiodhan to sit down and take his shirt off. You need to assess his gunshot wound for me."

"I must help you with Pashmar," Aiodhan said. "She saved my life."

"You're not helping me by staring over my shoulder. Let Kevin look at you. Please."

Once she could concentrate solely on her patient, Kara had to resist the urge to scream in frustration. Pashmar's pulse was slow, her breathing shallow. While she registered a blood pressure and her heart sounded strong, she still hadn't gained consciousness. Rolling her, Kara checked her back for an exit wound. There was none, so she set Pashmar gently on her back again.

The injuries were more than Kara could possibly handle alone. Pashmar needed surgery—probably blood transfusions as well. Not only were the supplies she would require limited, Kara in no way had the expertise to run a bowel or take out a spleen. Best she could do in surgery was fetch and hold instruments for a surgeon and tie off bleeders. She knew next to nothing about Tirian anatomy. Did they have all the same organs and systems as humans? Would human blood even be compatible?

She simply couldn't do this.

But there was no one else.

"I'm going to have to go in," she said in a whisper.

"You're *what?*" Bill's voice exploded behind her, making her jump since Kara hadn't heard him come in. He stood with hands against his hips, glaring down at her as if she was the one who'd caused the wound instead of the one who was going to try and fix it.

"She's bleeding somewhere inside. I've got to find out where and get it stopped. I just wish I had better supplies." *And a medical school degree...*

"You're going to do surgery? Here?" Bill's voice was nothing short of frantic. The cool, controlled leader had disappeared.

"I've got no choice."

"Can you truly do this, *damana?*" Aiodhan asked.

He deserved the same reply. "I've got no choice."

"Maybe I can help."

Kara froze at the familiar voice. Turning slowly and praying silently,

219

she was afraid to hope. "Daddy?"

Her father looked like he'd been through hell, but she'd never seen a more beautiful sight than him opening his arms to her.

Kara was on her feet in a heartbeat, in her father's embrace a moment later. "Daddy...Oh, God, Daddy. I was so worried."

He held her in a hug so tight she could barely draw a breath. "Kare-bear. Oh, sweetheart, stop crying. It's okay now. I'm here. Daddy's here."

"I was afraid I'd never see you again."

The baby did a flip-flop in her womb. Her father held her back and gaped at her rounded belly. "From the looks of it, you've got something important to tell me."

A laugh bubbled out. Her father was okay. He was really okay.

Bill tapped her on the shoulder none too gently. "I'm glad you two are enjoying the family reunion, but Pashmar needs you. *Now.*"

Wiping away her tears, Kara tried to give her father a smile. "You're gonna have to help me with her, Daddy."

"There are surgical supplies here," her father said. "We can help her. Together."

"You're a doctor?" Bill asked.

"Yes...and no," Kara replied. Back in nurse mode, she started a mental list of the things they'd have to have to help Pashmar.

"What the hell does that mean?"

"It means I'm a veterinarian, son," Peter Michaels said in his normal matter of fact tone. He leaned in, lifted each of Pashmar's eyelids, and looked into her eyes. "But I figure I'm the best chance she's got right now."

Chapter Thirty

"How's she doing?" Bill asked the moment Kara walked out of the room they were using as a recovery suite.

She put her hand over his, knowing that although he might not admit it, Bill had become very fond of Pashmar. "Doing well, I'm pleased to report."

She'd been worried about keeping Pashmar at the IC, but her father insisted he had the supplies they needed there. From the snatches of conversation they'd had, she learned that the Vymalns kept him virtually chained to the prison's medical area. Not to help any of the humans. To help *them*.

His veterinary education made him the best candidate to minister to the lizard-like creatures. While he might have healed their wounds and nursed their ills, he'd also been searching for their weaknesses. Everything he learned, he shared with his staff, who in turn spread the information through the IC. If the Montana Militia hadn't come to liberate them, the inmates had been planning their own insurrection come spring.

For a veterinarian instead of a surgeon, he'd handled Pashmar's operation like a pro. With Kevin's working as anesthesiologist and Kara performing scrub nurse duties, the Michaels family had pulled together to save the Seeker's life.

Her father stepped out of the room. "Thanks for all the help, Kare-bear. You're a damn fine nurse."

"How long will she be out?" Bill demanded.

Kara had never seen him so agitated. "Easy, Bill. She's gonna be okay."

"She's already coming around," Peter added. "You can go in and see her soon."

Several of the men waited with Bill, but Aiodhan wasn't among them. "Where's Aiodhan?"

"I am here," he called as he strode down the corridor. His left arm was in a sling, and from the way he tugged at the strap around his neck, she could tell she'd have a hard time keeping him in it until the injury healed.

"Who patched you up?" she asked.

"Julie."

"I'll want to look at the wound to make sure she cleaned it well. Might have to give you stitches again. I should also get you some antibiotics to fight any—"

He grabbed her hand and pulled her close. Then he ended her words with a quick, no-nonsense kiss. "I am fine. You must not worry."

Her face heated to what had to be a vivid blush. She hadn't had a chance to explain much to her father about her relationship with Aiodhan. Kevin had let Peter know that Aiodhan was an alien, but they'd been focused on helping Pashmar. Now that the surgery was over, all Kara wanted was some sleep. Then she could figure out what to tell her father.

Aiodhan hauled her up against his side and threw his good arm over her shoulder, anchoring her.

"I guess that answers my question," her father said. His eyes narrowed and he frowned at her the same way he had when she was a child and had been naughty.

Her face flushed warmer. "What question, Daddy?"

He laid his hand on her belly. "I was going to ask who the father of your child is." His gaze drilled through Aiodhan. "So when's the wedding?"

"Wedding?" Aiodhan's tone was familiar—he'd used it often when there was an English word he didn't understand.

"Not now, Daddy. Please. We've got too much to do to get set up here. We've got to drag all the stuff from the camp inside the walls and figure out what to do with the bug-eyes." When she tried to pull away, Aiodhan tightened his hold.

"What is wedding?" he asked.

Bill stuck his nose where it didn't belong. "He wants to know if you're going to marry Kara since you knocked her up."

"Gee, Bill," she grumbled. "That was eloquent."

"What is notched up?" Aiodhan asked, although his smile told her he was teasing.

"It's *knocked* up. It means I'm having your baby," Kara replied. "Can we drop this now?" She yawned, hoping they'd all take the hint.

"And what is this marry?" Aiodhan asked.

"You'll take her as your wife," Peter replied, his stern frown implying there would be no argument. "You say your vows that you'll love, honor, and cherish her until the day you die."

"Oh for God's sake... Can we stop the Montana Inquisition?" She heaved a sigh. "We're in the middle of a prison, surrounded by alien invaders, and trying not to get killed. Who really gives a shit whether we're married or not?"

"You are my mate," Aiodhan insisted.

"Mate?" Her father quirked an eyebrow. "So you *are* married?"

Aiodhan nodded. "I have already taken Kara as my mate."

"Which means?"

"I shall stay with her always."

"Can we *please* drop this now?" Kara had already put her faith in Aiodhan's pledge to remain on Earth. She didn't need anyone to twist his arm to get him to marry her too. "Things are fine just the way they are."

"Kara Marie Michaels, you're *pregnant*. I haven't even started to address *that* idiocy in the middle of this whole ridiculous situation. But what's done is done. Your baby deserves a father."

"He has a father," she insisted.

"Don't mince words with me, young lady. You know exactly what I mean. You need a husband."

"What I need is for us to get stuff moved inside the walls, to find a place to rest that isn't inside a damn tent, and to sleep for the next two days. I'm gonna go check Pashmar, then I'm finding someplace private to get some shut-eye." She shrugged Aiodhan's arm away and stomped back into the clinic.

Zot but Kara was beautiful when someone got her riled.

Aiodhan had been teasing. He knew exactly what a wedding was.

His own culture marked the taking of a mate with a private family ceremony, but many of Earth's cultures required a more public proclamation of a mating. There simply hadn't been time to plan anything except the liberation of the IC.

Kara was right—there was a lot of work that needed to be done. Everything from the camp had to be hauled back to the IC. Sleeping quarters had to be assigned. Supplies would have to be inventoried and plans made for feeding everyone throughout the winter. There were twenty Vymalns being held captive that needed to be dealt with. Schedules for guarding the walls had to be created and followed.

More Vymalns would return. Tomorrow. A week from now. A month from now. No one knew for sure. But one thing was certain—they wouldn't let this defeat go unaddressed.

For now, he would do the right thing and abide by her father's wishes. "Kara does not wish this weeding."

"*Wedding*," Peter corrected. "My Kara's not one for frills. But you need to understand—I'm her father. I want what's best for her. What you need to convince me is that the best for her is *you*."

* * *

"How's she doing?" Kara asked as she pulled up a chair next to Pashmar's bed.

"She is awake." Pashmar opened her eyes. Although they were still a little glazed and her skin pale, she appeared to be recovering well.

"How do you feel?"

"Sore."

"You're lucky to be alive. I owe you one. You saved Aiodhan's life."

"We are even now." Pashmar closed her eyes and her lips bowed into a satisfied smile.

Kara patted her shoulder. "Sleep. It's the best thing to help you heal. I'm going to do the same. I'll check on you soon."

Kevin came to her side. "I'll take first shift. From the looks of you, you could use some sleep."

"Gee, thanks."

"You're welcome," he said with a wink. "Dad did good, didn't he?"

"He did *great*. So did you. Who knew two vets could handle taking out a spleen?"

"We had a fantastic nurse helping." He sat in the chair she'd just left. "Go get some sleep, sis. You've earned it."

She started to walk away but hesitated when she reached for the door. "Daddy's gonna be okay, isn't he? I mean...after all his time in here..."

"He's fine, Kara. He was lucky. They needed his help."

"Won't the other guys we saved think he's a bug-eye sympathizer?"

Kevin shook his head. "When he wasn't tending a Vymaln, he was smuggling out medicines and information to the prisoners. No one's gonna think anything but good about him."

"That's a relief."

When she left the clinic, she found Aiodhan still waiting and breathed a relieved sigh. While she was thankful her father was safe and well, she didn't want him pressuring Aiodhan into doing something he didn't want to do.

"Pashmar?" he asked.

"She's fine." A yawn slipped out. "Is there someplace I can catch some sleep?"

"We have a place to stay now." He took her hand in his and led her a few doors down.

The room he guided her into was small but comfortable. At least it wasn't a cell, and there wasn't any snow blowing in through the seams like there had been in her tent. The bed was a double, which might be a bit cozy between Aiodhan's height and her ever-expanding tummy. But it was a real bed with a mattress and sheets, and she couldn't wait to collapse on it.

Kara kicked off her shoes and jerked off her socks. Wiggling her toes, she smiled. "It's warm in here."

Aiodhan nodded. "We have restored many systems."

Flopping onto her back on the bed, she stared at the ceiling. "I'm sorry about my dad."

"Why are you sorry?" The bedframe groaned when he sat down next to her.

"I hate all his wedding talk. He's an old guy—thinks everyone should get married before having kids."

"We are mated."

She sat up on her elbows and grinned. "No, we *mated*—the act. We aren't *mated* as in recognized as a legal couple."

"I declared you my mate. We are mated."

"That might be the way it works on Tirios, but not on Earth." She scooted around to put her head on the pillow and closed her eyes. "I'm getting some sleep."

He rolled on top of her, bracing his weight on his forearms. "You are *my mate*."

She opened her eyes to see the stormy gray of his anger. His eyes still fascinated her, and she reached up to run her fingertips over his cheek. She loved how forcefully he continued to declare her as his own. "Yeah, Tarzan. I'm your mate. And I love you."

"Then I wish us to marry."

"Why? Because of my dad?"

"Because it is what your people do when they love."

She gave him a sleepy smile. "Then I guess that's what we'll do."

* * *

"I say we just kill them all!"

The shout could have come from anyone because most of the people gathered in the dining hall were of one mind.

Kill the Vymalns.

Aiodhan had waited until Kara was asleep. He'd covered her with a blanket and then joined the rest of the people in the courtyard to make some decisions about the future. Since he wasn't a human, he tried to keep from enforcing his choices on them. He wasn't of this world, even if he would claim it as his own from now on. Still, he was an outsider.

Hearing their cries to kill the Vymaln prisoners made him change his mind about interfering. While he would enjoy nothing more than relieving the universe of some Vymaln scum, that solution would be far too difficult.

Bill held up his hand, forcing most of the crowd to fall silent. The vast majority of the people who'd been prisoners of the Vymalns had already left the prison—despite the threat of recapture and the perils of traveling in the winter. The handful who remained were those calling loudest for execution, and they were hesitant to recognize Bill's authority.

"Enough!" Bill shouted, finally achieving control. "We have to make a decision. Now. While it might make you all feel better, I really don't think a mass execution is the right way to go. Do we really want to put aside our own morality for a little revenge."

"I have a suggestion," Aiodhan offered.

Bill waved him forward. "Then by all means...suggest away."

"I must send word to Tirios of my mission. My ship cannot be repaired."

"Which means?"

"Pashmar must send word as well. Her ship can do this."

"Still not seeing what you mean, Aiodhan."

Aiodhan. He couldn't help but cuff Bill on the shoulder. "I think we should use her ship to do more than send word."

A slow smile grew on Bill's face. "We can send a few lizards along with the word."

"We can send *all.*"

Bill chuckled. "I like the way you think. But how big is her ship?"

"Big enough if we pack it full."

Sending the Vymalns to the Seeker main ship wouldn't just address their immediate problem, it would also deliver a strong message to the Praemons. They'd betrayed him. He wanted them to understand the consequences of that betrayal. They'd lost not one but two strong Seekers. Once the rest of his kind learned of the Praemons tyranny, they would better be able to protect themselves.

"Perhaps," Aiodhan added, "we can also ask for other Seekers to join us."

"Damn good idea. Let's make it work."

Chapter Thirty-One

Kara and Aiodhan stated their vows in the prison chapel one week later.

Julie stood as her bridesmaid, and Kevin acted as best man. No one dressed up, because there simply weren't any fancy clothes available. Since Bill was the leader, Kara asked him to perform the ceremony. He'd agreed, although he made it quite clear that he'd rather be having a root canal.

The reception was in the dining hall. Aiodhan led her to the table that had been decorated with a pinecone wreath. A small cake sat beside the wreath—at least she thought it was a cake. It leaned precariously to the left, and she smiled at the thought of it tumbling over onto the pinecones.

This might not be the wedding day she'd imagined, but it was still perfect in her eyes.

Most of the people were dancing to old CDs that Bill had found in the guard's locker room. The prison held a wealth of unusual things for them to use—personal items the guards left behind, equipment used as part of running a large prison, and enough technological gadgets to keep Jayce happy for years to come. He'd already started trying to reach other resistance forces with grand hopes of uniting to drive the Vymalns from Earth for good.

Their new home was christened the Alamo. Although Kara thought it was a little too morbid, most of the people living there were determined that they wouldn't be forced out again. The Vymalns were sure to come back, but they'd have a few surprises ready when they did. This Alamo was going to be as hard—if not *harder*—to take than its predecessor.

The people she'd watched fight the good fight could finally let the weight off their shoulders, if only for a short respite. Since the bug-eyes hadn't used the human food, the prison was well-stocked. Adding a stag that Jayce had shot on his first hunting trip made for hell of a wedding feast.

Julie hurried over and set down a ledger book before sitting at Kara's side. "I need to enter you and Aiodhan's wedding in the register."

"The what?"

"The ledger."

Aiodhan came up behind Kara and put his hands on her shoulders. "What is ledger?"

Julie put her palm on the book. "I decided someone needs to keep track of everything that happens. I'm doing a census to have the names of everyone who lives here, and I'm going to add new things—like marriages and births."

Bill came over and gaped down at his sister. "Exactly how long do you think we're gonna hole up in this place?"

She shrugged. "I'm just trying to keep some...*normal* while we're here."

Kara put her hand over Julie's. "I think it's a great idea. Despite what those bug-eyes have done to hurt us, life goes on. One day, someone will thank you for doing all this work."

Julie's smile was radiant. "So what's your married name going to be?"

"I-I don't really know." Kara glanced over her shoulder at her new husband, feeling a bit guilty for not having asked. "Do you have a last name?"

He nodded. "Riel."

"How do you spell that?" Julie asked. He rattled off some Tirian before Julie raised her hand in surrender. "I'll just do my best and guess. You know, your baby will be the first birth we enter."

"My son should be named for my father," he said, giving Kara's shoulders a squeeze.

"My *daughter* should be named for my mother," Kara retorted. Then she smiled, thinking back to the day she'd met her tall, dark and handsome alien. "Know what, Tarzan?"

His smile was as warm as sunshine on a summer day. "No. What?"

"I don't really care if we have a boy or a girl."

"I do not care, either—for it will be your child. That is what matters to me."

For a man of few words, he always seemed to choose the right ones. Tears welled in her eyes and spilled over onto her cheeks.

Aiodhan straddled the bench so he faced her, then he cupped her face in his hands, wiping away her tears with his thumbs. "You must be happy today."

"Oh, I am." She put her hands over his. "I'm *very* happy.

Aiodhan kissed her forehead. "You are my wife."

"Yeah, I'm your wife now. God help you."

"We shall make a family. You. Me. Our child. And the Praemons."

Although she was well aware he was talking about Claire and Christopher and not the Tirian Praemons, her anger swelled. "Don't call them that."

"But—"

"The Praemons are on Tirios. They wanted you dead. Please don't call the kids Praemons."

He opened his mouth, probably to argue, before he closed it again and gave her a curt nod.

Julie had been shifting her nervous gaze between them. "You know, the kids are doing great with their studies."

"Nice segue," Kara said with a wink. "They think you're a great teacher."

Jayce came over, looking a bit sheepish. He dragged the toe of his shoe across the concrete floor as Chance trotted over to nudge Kara's hand for an affectionate pat. Where Jayce had found a black bow tie for the dog was beyond her.

"Um...hi, Julie," Jayce said. "Um...would you want to, I don't know, dance?"

Closing the ledger, Julie got to her feet. "I'd love to."

Chance followed the couple to the dance floor, wagging his tail.

Aiodhan nudged Kara to turn her face back to him. "I have heard that after wedding is honeymoan."

Kara burst out laughing. Sweet Lord, she loved this man—this *alien*—with every piece of her heart. "It's *honeymoon*."

"I did not say it wrong," he countered. "I shall make you moan."

Before she could react, he stood and lifted her into his arms.

"You shouldn't be using that shoulder. Doesn't it still hurt?"

He shook his head. "I used some Tirian herbs. Is healed."

"If that work that well, I'm definitely going to use some after I give birth."

As he carried her down the long corridor, she combed her fingers through his long, dark hair. "You know something?"

"I know many things. What *something* do you wish me to know?"

She chuckled, and she knew she'd never tire of their bantering. "When you found me that day in the forest, I thought my life was over, that my future was nothing but bleak."

"And now?"

"Now, the future's looking pretty damn sweet."

The End

Author Biography:

Sandy James lives in a quiet suburb of Indianapolis with her husband. She's a high school social studies teacher who especially loves psychology and United States history. Since she and her husband own a small stable of harness racehorses, they often spend time together at the two Indiana racetracks.

Sandy is published through Forever Yours, Carina Press, and BookStrand, as well as self-published. She has been an Amazon Bestseller and has won numerous awards, including a HOLT Medallion. Find her as "sandyjamesbooks" on Twitter, Facebook, and Pinterest. Email her at sandy@sandyjames.com

Other Sandy James Books:

Turning Thirty-Twelve
Rules of the Game
Murphy's Law (Damaged Heroes 1)
Free Falling (Damaged Heroes 2)
All the Right Reasons (Damaged Heroes 3)
Faith of the Heart (Damaged Heroes 4)
Twist of Fate (Damaged Heroes 5)
The Bottom Line (Ladies Who Lunch 1)
Signed, Sealed, Delivered (Ladies Who Lunch 2)
Sealing the Deal (Ladies Who Lunch 3)
Fringe Benefits (Ladies Who Lunch 4)
Saving Grace (Safe Havens 1)
Runaway (Safe Havens 2)
Redeemed (Safe Havens 3)
The Reluctant Amazon (Alliance of the Amazons 1)
The Impetuous Amazon (Alliance of the Amazons 2)
The Brazen Amazon (Alliance of the Amazons 3)
The Volatile Amazon (Alliance of the Amazons 4)